A FALL IN DENVER

AN EM HANSEN MYSTERY

Sarah Andrews

A SIGNET BOOK

SIGNET
Published by the Penguin Group
Penguin Books USA Inc., 375 Hudson Street,
New York, New York 10014, U.S.A.
Penguin Books Ltd, 27 Wrights Lane,
London W8 5TZ, England
Penguin Books Australia Ltd, Ringwood,
Victoria, Australia
Penguin Books Canada Ltd, 10 Alcorn Avenue,
Toronto, Ontario, Canada M4V 3B2
Penguin Books (N.Z.) Ltd, 182–190 Wairau Road,
Auckland 10, New Zealand

Penguin Books Ltd, Registered Offices:
Harmondsworth, Middlesex, England

Published by Signet, an imprint of Dutton Signet, a division of Penguin Books USA
Inc. This is an authorized reprint of a hardcover edition published by Scribner. For
information address: Scribner, A Division of Simon & Schuster, Inc., 1230 Avenue
of the Americas, New York, NY 10020.

First Signet Printing, December 1996
10 9 8 7 6 5 4 3 2 1

PUBLISHER'S NOTE
This is a work of fiction. Names, characters, places, and incidents either are the
product of the author's imagination or are used fictitiously, and any resemblance to
actual persons, living or dead, events, or locales is entirely coincidental.

PRAISE FOR SARAH ANDREWS AND
TENSLEEP

"Oil drilling operations and the rough-mouthed, rough-living characters who do the work get robust treatment here, but with the same sweet edge that enriches Em's spiky character and gives subtle meaning to geologist Andrews's unhackneyed, accomplished first novel."   —*Kirkus Reviews*

"First-novelist Andrews is a geologist who has worked the oil patch, and it shows: her colorful description of the literal nuts and bolts of the business bring the rough work and its rougher workers to life. *Tensleep* offers a new voice and new amateur sleuth, Wyoming's answer to Sherlock Holmes."   —*Booklist*

"This is a tough world Andrews paints, raw and basic, where women will always be outsiders, in a way. Em is an interesting character, edgy, difficult. . . . It is fun to watch Em trying to find herself."   —*Roanoke Times-World News*

"It's common talent among writers to tell a good story and evoke a time or a place. Andrews does it all, but she can also turn a phrase, giving her story a moment of music."
—*Knoxville News Sentinel*

"Fascinating. Sarah Andrews gives us a tour of the Wyoming oil patch she knows so well. The bonus is the lively mystery. Don't miss it!"   —Tony Hillerman, bestselling author of *Sacred Clowns*

"A triple-triumph—the Wyoming setting is bleak and beautiful, Em Hansen is vulnerable and true, and the mystery answers all these questions and leaves the reader begging for more."   —Dana Stabenow, Edgar Award–winning author of *A Cold Day for Murder*

"A fresh-voiced new heroine . . . a winner!"   —Marcia Muller

SIGNET   **ONYX** (0451)

SUPER SLEUTHS

☐ **TENSLEEP** *An Em Hansen Mystery* **by Sarah Andrews.** Stuck on an oil-drilling rig in the Wyoming Badlands with a bunch of roughnecks is a tough place for a woman. But feisty, sharp-edged Emily "Em" Hansen, working as a mudlogger, calls this patch of Tensleep Sanstone home. She is about to call it deadly. "Lively . . . don't miss it!"—Tony Hillerman (186060—$4.99)

☐ **HEIR CONDITION** *A Schuyler Ridgway Mystery* **by Tierney McClellan.** Schuyler Ridgway works as a real estate agent and watches videos at home alone on Saturday nights. She is definitely not having an illicit affair with the rich, elderly Ephraim Benjamin Cross and she certainly hasn't murdered him. So why has he left her a small fortune in his will? Now the Cross clan believes she's his mistress, and the police think she's his killer. (181441—$5.50)

☐ **FOLLOWING JANE** *A Barrett Lake Mystery* **by Shelly Singer.** Teenager Jane Wahlman had witnessed the brutal stabbing of a high school teacher in a local supermarket and then suddenly vanished. Berkeley teacher Barrett Lake will follow Jane's trail in return for a break into the private eye business—the toughest task she's ever faced. (175239—$4.50)

☐ **FINAL ATONEMENT** *A Doug Orlando Mystery* **by Steve Johnson.** Detective Doug Orlando must catch the murderer of Rabbi Avraham Rabowitz, in a case that moves from the depths of the ghetto to the highrise office of a glamor-boy real estate tycoon. (403320—$3.99)

☐ **MURDER CAN KILL YOUR SOCIAL LIFE** *A Desiree Shapiro Mystery* **by Selma Eichler.** New York P.I., Desiree Shapiro is a chubby gumshoe who has a mind as sharp as a Cuisinart and a queen-size talent for sleuthing. She takes on the case of the poor grocery boy accused of killing the old lady in apartment 15D for the money stashed in her freezer. Before anyone can say Haagen-Dazs, Desiree bets she will be able to finger the real killer. (181395—$5.50)

Prices slightly higher in Canada

Buy them at your local bookstore or use this convenient coupon for ordering.

PENGUIN USA
P.O. Box 999 — Dept. #17109
Bergenfield, New Jersey 07621

Please send me the books I have checked above.
I am enclosing $_____ (please add $2.00 to cover postage and handling). Send check or money order (no cash or C.O.D.'s) or charge by Mastercard or VISA (with a $15.00 minimum). Prices and numbers are subject to change without notice.

Card #_____ Exp. Date _____
Signature_____
Name_____
Address_____
City _____ State _____ Zip Code _____

For faster service when ordering by credit card call **1-800-253-6476**

Allow a minimum of 4-6 weeks for delivery. This offer is subject to change without notice.

For Susan,
partner in reverence, joy, and pain:
I love you bunches and oodles.

Acknowledgments

My thanks first of all to Kate Stine, in whom ruthlessness is a great virtue, and to Deborah Schneider, who's a real pro. Three cheers also to Susanne Kirk, Jen Medearis, and all the rest of you at Scribner, who treated me with such grace.

I am grateful to many others also, especially: Robert J. Bowman, Larry Yurdin, and Susan Oliver, for constructive criticisms and words of encouragement when I needed them most; J. David Love, Scientist Emeritus, U. S. Geological Survey, and Gary E. Aho, Senior Engineer, Mobil Oil Corporation, for technical review; Cruz Enciso and Robin Hayes, for help with my Spanish; Mary Hallock, Mary Bowen Hall (may she rest in peace), Patricia Williams, Joel Quigley, Cathleen McCullough, and Thea Castleman of the Golden Machete critique group, for a good howl always; Deborah Dix, Director of Public Relations at the Brown Palace Hotel, for bringing me up to date on the Queen City of the plains; that nice Denver cop who didn't want to be identified by name, for all the gruesome details; Johnny Maxwell, for notes on the railroad history of Colorado; and Clint Smith, for being a steadfast fan of *la femme que cherche*.

I save the greatest thanks for last. Damon, true to your name, you are unshakable.

1

If I had seen the body fall past the window, I wouldn't have taken the job. At least, that's what I kept telling myself, but maybe I would have rationalized my way around that, too.

In hindsight, the first day on that job was full of omens, and the body was hardly the first. If I'd been wiser, I would have tucked tail and run the instant the brown cloud that passes for air in Denver turned to acid on the moist parts of my face, burning my eyes and leaving a foul taste on my tongue. But no. When Gerald Luftweiller hit terminal velocity outside that twelfth-floor window, I was sitting with my back to it, so instead of witnessing the penultimate instant of his life, I was taking in the exquisitely tanned and shaven face of J. C. Menken, president of Blackfeet Oil Company. Menken was giving me his "welcome aboard" speech, just getting to the part where he favors the new hire with a congenially arrogant smile and compliments himself for hiring "such a keen mind—another company asset."

Old J.C. had been lounging back into the soft leather of his chair before the body fell. When he saw it, he sat up abruptly, but moved to cover his surprise by leaning onto his desk, as if that was where he'd been heading all the while. His face writhed through a bizarre bit of gymnastics, concealing shock before it arranged itself into a display of rational detachment.

"Damn," he said, his tone conversational, "looks like another suicide. That's two in a week—there was one off the Radisson Hotel last Thursday. These people, they can't seem to think up a better option than killing themselves. Now, if I found myself in tough circumstances"—he smiled at the thought that he, Josiah Carberry Menken, would ever find himself in such straits—"I'd certainly think up something better. A man can always head out for the South Seas and spawn illegitimate children with a dusky-skinned maiden. Suicide, Jesus Christ. And worse yet, it starts a trend and you get two or three together. I can't imagine having that little self-respect: not only killing myself, but being unoriginal in the way I went about it."

"Someone's committed suicide?" I said, rising from my chair. I pressed my face to the glass, but couldn't see the part of the sidewalk straight down, only the adjacent curb and street. Traffic below had stopped in a weirdly skewed pattern. There were people running around like ants do when you rip the top off their nest.

Menken said, "Sit down, Emily."

I kept standing. "Are you telling me someone just *fell* past this window?"

"Oh, forget it, forget it," he answered, his tone becoming somewhat paternal, a touch irritated. "Come, sit down."

In my confusion, I did as he said.

"You must forgive me," he continued. "I forget that you're not a city girl. I might have forgotten, what with this elegant outfit you're wearing. I must say, it becomes you." He smiled, perhaps a shade more broadly than was quite decent.

Tensing, I thought: *Is this why he hired me?* I forced a self-assured smile.

"In fact," he went on, "I hardly recognized you. You look so different from the way you did in Wyoming. I had in my mind's eye the picture of a young woman dressed like she was on her way to a rodeo. I could see, of course, how intelligent you were. I said to myself right away, 'J.C., you must hire this girl; she's going to waste working as a mere mudlogger. Make a geologist out of her. Bring her to Denver, where you can keep an eye on her.' "

I exhaled quietly. Regardless of whether I was doing *Pygmalion* or *Lolita*, I wasn't used to being noticed, any more than I was used to wearing a skirt. I glanced down furtively at my new suit and my pantyhose-encased shins, in fear that my mother's long-discarded Bostonian heritage was erupting through my Wyoming upbringing like a demon seed. Confused, I focused back on the room. And that window.

Drawing a deep breath, I tried another tack: "Um, excuse me, sir, but what exactly did you see outside the window just now?"

"Yes," he said, "I told myself, 'J.C., wits like hers are hard to come by; it doesn't matter how they come packaged, it's the raw intelligence that counts.' Although, I'm most pleasantly surprised at the way you've turned yourself out. Most professional."

"Huh? Um, ah—I'll try to live up to the challenge, sir. I sure appreciate your giving me this chance."

Menken beamed. "I'll be watching you. As a matter of fact, I'm intrigued with this intelligence of yours. A woman's intuition? Eh? If you have any more of your sharp little insights, I want you to report them directly to me, Emily." He flashed me a million-dollar smile, shining with self-satisfaction.

My own smile sagged somewhat. It appalled me that he could refer to the impromptu detective work I'd done in one of Blackfeet's oil fields in Wyoming as "having a sharp little insight." And while I could adjust to being called "girl" by the company president, especially a man almost old enough to be my father, I wasn't sure at all how I felt about becoming his pet female. And worse yet, was I doomed to being called Emily, my whole unabridged antique moniker?

"Ah, my friends call me Em," I ventured.

"Eh?"

"My friends—"

The phone rang.

"You'll excuse me, Emily," he said, waving one large, perfectly manicured hand over the phone. I rose to go, but before I was even on my feet, he had pressed the receiver to his ear and swung his mammoth chair away from me in dismissal, his universe already perfectly adjusted to the loss of one of its citizens.

2

That left me standing outside Menken's door, feeling like I had just gotten off a train in the wrong dimension.

Menken's executive secretary looked at me expectantly, fixing me with an impersonal gaze. I stood staring into her middle-aged I've-seen-it-all eyes, my mind flooding with questions. Nowhere in my fantasies had my first hour as a professional geologist included death. My hands began to tremble.

The secretary's almost-smile became politely bland. "Personnel has some papers for you to sign, Miss Hansen," she said, in a low, growly voice.

"What?" I thought, *How can she be so callous? Someone's just died!* Then I realized that in this climate-controlled office, twelve stories above street level, the news, whatever it was, had not yet reached this woman. *Her back is to the windows. She didn't see.*

In the middle of all of this, my mind registered the fact that someone years my senior had just called me "miss." Was this what it meant to be a professional? People were going to treat me with respect? Much as I liked being treated like a superior being, the experience also came with a twinge of guilt. I opened my mouth to say something sociable. What came out was, "There's been some kind of accident on the street." I gestured toward the window beyond her shoulder, immediately wishing I had chosen a more neutral topic.

Her smile began to congeal. "City living. You'll get used to it, dear." She nodded toward the hall. "Third door on the right," she added, as she swiveled her chair back toward her computer.

So give me a break; not having seen the guy fall with my own eyes, I began to figure I had dreamt it, or misunderstood Menken, or something. When in doubt, do what is expected of you, right? So I just got back on that train, hoping the next stop would make more sense.

I counted doors to the right until I found Personnel.

Personnel gave me her canned welcome and led the way farther down the hall toward my office-to-be. She moved quickly for someone leaning backward in an affected slouch, somehow maintaining her balance on needle-sharp heels while rolling her mighty buttocks beneath an emerald-green knit. I cast furtive glances left and right into the bull pens and offices we were passing, trying to catch glimpses of my new colleagues. Personnel chattered along about my retirement plan and health benefits in her high monotone, finishing with, "Fill out these forms, that's your desk in there, you share the office with Maddie McNutt, good luck."

Good luck? Maddie McNutt looked harmless enough, but perhaps I had mistaken the nonemphasis in Personnel's voice, and it was the forms that were dangerous.

My office mate sat thrashing a map with an eraser, all but tearing the paper in her vigor. She was a muscular little unit, blessed with a wild head of black curls and dressed to stop traffic. No demure East Coast tweeds for this lady; she liked stripes: big, wide, sharp-edged green and pink stripes, running all up and down a dress that fit like paint. As she scrubbed the map, the stripes worked back and forth with gusto, twisting and jumping over her body. She finished her job with a spray of eraser crumbs and a resounding thump, hollered "Take that, motherfucker!" in a lusty, West Texas drawl, leaned back, and smiled at the map cheerfully. By and by she looked up and turned that smile on me.

I felt moved to speak. "Ah, hi, I'm Em Hansen, I guess I'm your new office mate."

"Y'all sure?"

"Huh?"

"Take your time," she said, and went back to work.

This scene wasn't in my hotshot-geologist-goes-to-Denver fantasy, either. Half a minute later, I was still standing on the threshold between my fluorescently lit beige office and the fluorescently lit beige hallway, the sheaf of papers Personnel had given me growing damp in my hand. I eyed my desk, whose hard, immaculate beige surface seemed to rebuff me. Some little flywheel in my brain was spinning, whining around and around in annoying complaint. It was a little voice, surprisingly like my mother's. It said: *It's time you toughened up, Emily*.

Right. So I walked over to my assigned desk, lowered my body into my assigned beige swivel chair, and set to work on Personnel's papers.

That kept me busy all of ten minutes.

I sat fidgeting. My mind kept straying down the hallway to Menken's office, wondering what he had seen outside that window. That good old mind of mine consumed itself with the image of a body falling, growing smaller and smaller as it plummeted toward the street. I longed for a radio, so I could at least get a news broadcast, find out what had really happened.

I considered asking Maddie McNutt what to do next, or maybe broaching the subject of whether or not someone had just jumped out of one of the windows of our building, but just then she got up and left the room.

After another ten minutes I couldn't stand it any longer, I had to know. I got up and marched right out of the office, caught the elevator to the lobby, and hurried to the front door, just in time to see two police cruisers and a van pull away from the curb at Seventeenth Street. Yellow caution tape fluttered in the morning breeze, and a uniformed cop was signaling people, hustling them across the street to avoid an obstruction that was just out of sight to my left. People shuffled by slowly or stood staring, their mouths twisted in disgusted fascination. I started out the door to get a better look past the caution tape, but stopped when I saw two men in dark suits hunched down over the sidewalk, examining a great, dark stain.

On the way back to my desk I discovered, mercifully, that Blackfeet had a little kitchenette stocked with big, heavy mugs and all the strong, black coffee a person could gag down. I wished I had something stronger yet to flavor it with, to help me forget what I'd just seen.

At last news began filtering through the office. Some of the other inmates of Blackfeet Oil gravitated into the kitchenette to get the lowdown. They eyed me frankly and I introduced myself, a little thrill of excitement rising within me. *This is it, I'm a professional geologist meeting my new colleagues*.

Their eyes dimmed like shutters closing. Oh, you're the new geologist, they said. Hi.

I pulled back and eyed *them*. They were a tense bunch of

people with softening waistlines and uncomfortable-looking shoes. As the conversation got rolling, they turned out to be pretty blasé about the demise of Gerald Luftweiller, the man who had dived past J. C. Menken's window. Lots of no-shits and you-don't-says went back and forth.

I began to wonder if these city folks were just as cold and alienated from one another as I had always heard. They began retreading dead baby jokes as Gerald Luftweiller suicide jokes. Okay, the oil business has always been full of sick humor, but this was the limit.

I asked if anyone had known him. I meant it to sound right-eous, and it did. All I got for my trouble was a lot of *Huh? . . . Well of course no one knew him, did you, Scott? Me? Oh, no. No. Did you, Angie? Ah, no . . . no, people like that don't know anyone, know what I mean? I hear he was an accountant or something, worked for Love and Christiansen up on sixteen—not even thirty and a burnout already—you know, those people are always a little weird, look at numbers too much or something. Hey, did you see the sidewalk? Oh, yeah, and how about that hole he made bashing the glass out of that window? That sucker must have hit hard, man! Yeah, I hear he took three runs at it before he crashed through. No kidding? Shit, yes, the janitor told me, and like, he talked to the janitor on sixteen where it happened, and he heard from someone who was standing right there, man . . .*

Through a slight ringing in my ears, I heard details of the scene on the sidewalk. *Couldn't identify the body at first, but he had a map of Hat Rock Field in his pocket, with Love and Christiansen's logo on the title block. Hat Rock? Yeah, soaked him up like a blotter, they had trouble reading it. No shit?*

I escaped to my office.

From that moment I began to develop a thing about Gerald Luftweiller's death. A fascination, almost, a bit like my cousin Lester's interest in cats. You see, Lester was asthmatic as hell, but he'd hold my brother's cat on his lap and stroke its fur, wheezing away in defiance, just to prove to us older cousins that this weakness was not a limitation.

Now that I think of it, I was even crazier that cousin Lester. I wasn't just being tough, I was being a full-blown martyr. I was the good guy in the white hat, riding into town to call Gerald Luftweiller's enemies out of the saloon for a duel. Call it rage against the heartlessness of humanity. Call it sympathy as a subversive activity. But don't call it empathy. I wouldn't want to know that about myself.

So that's how the whole thing got started. One hour after becoming a real live geologist at Blackfeet Oil Company, I began collecting information about a dead man. I opened a mental file, and called it the Gerald Luftweiller Case.

3

The ancient dog whined softly as Elyria bent to give him his morning kiss, then he staggered across the kitchen to the food dish to await his breakfast.

"There, you sorry old thing," Elyria said, emptying a ration of kibbles into his bowl. "Just the item. Very nutritious. Yum, yum. Eat up."

The dog groaned. I kept my silence. I figured I could put up with Elyria's morning ritual, as long as she was being so generous as to put up with me until I found a place of my own.

Elyria straightened up and ran a hand through her taffy-colored hair. She looked how I would have looked if I'd had any say in the matter: hypnotic eyes and fabulous cheekbones reigning serene over a slender, impossibly graceful carriage. At ten or fifteen years my senior, it was she who drew the stares as we walked down the street, not me. So much for the American youth cult.

I spilled coffee on the Wednesday morning *Rocky Mountain News*. "Sorry," I said, mopping the spill with my place mat.

Elyria set a bowl of granola down in front of me. "Relax. Eat this. It's good for you."

"Yum, yum?"

Elyria raised a shoulder in mock haughtiness. "Be like that. Don't let me care."

I ducked my head and smiled sheepishly. Elyria was one of the few people on earth who knew how to care about me without giving me a total screaming case of claustrophobia. Way back in April, when Menken offered me the job, she had given me one of her matter-of-fact nods and said, "And you'll stay with me until you're settled."

Normally I'd have been a mite shy about accepting such a lavish invitation, but by the time I was ready to take the job, I knew she needed me, too. As busy as Elyria was with her work, her evenings had been lonely since her husband, Bill, died. That was how we'd gotten to know each other, after all: investigating his murder. It had made us fast friends.

And for my part, I needed her more than I cared to admit. Much as I'd always liked my solitude back home in Wyoming, where alone meant being out there in the wide open spaces with the rest of creation, I was damned nervous about living alone in the city. Perhaps that was why I'd cut things so close, arriving in Denver the evening before I had to report to work.

Elyria glanced pointedly at the newspaper as she took her seat at the table. "Looking for news of your falling man?"

Of course I was. And my search was rewarded: a terse paragraph at the bottom of page 1 carried the headline "SECOND MAN FALLS TO DEATH." It gave the dead man's name (Gerald Luftweiller), his place of employment (Love and Christiansen), and the surprising information that the police had yet to rule his death a suicide, continued on page 22.

I turned the damned pages so fast I tore a few, but that was the end of the juicy stuff. The rest of the article just said that he was twenty-seven—a year younger than I—and that he had hailed from Haverford, Pennsylvania. Luftweiller was a graduate of Haverford College, and was survived by his parents and two sisters, all of Haverford. I didn't get much from that, but I speculated that he was the only member of his family with enough sense of adventure to leave the old hometown. That presumption didn't fit with my preconceived notions about accountants as a personality type.

"What does it say?" Elyria asked. "Come on. Here I drag myself in from a business trip at midnight and find the strength to ask you about your first two days at work, and all you say is, 'Someone jumped out the window, things have to improve from here.'" She was exaggerating, of course: I had waited up and told her everything, lingering over details of Menken and Maddie and all the others.

"You don't really want to hear any more about this at breakfast, do you?"

Elyria gave me one of her don't-patronize-me looks. "Come now, Em, there has to be at least a paragraph on the poor man. Let's put him to his rest."

"Well, there's more here than the *Denver Post* had yesterday morning, but it doesn't say why he did it. Or if he did it, for that matter."

Elyria came and read the article over my shoulder. "Hmm, Love and Christiansen, they're not in good shape financially."

"Really? This guy was one of their accountants. Maybe he was falling on his sword."

"Or just celebrating the equinox," she said, dryly.

I glanced at the date at the top of the page. She was right, it was now September twenty-fourth, two days after the equinox. In the confusion of starting a new job, I had forgotten to celebrate it myself. "What does jumping out of a window have to do with celebrating the equinox?"

"First day of fall, dear."

"That's sick, Elyria."

"Mm-hm. I've been in the oil business too long." She lifted a spoonful of cereal to her lips with her pinky crooked in mock elegance. "I'm sure you'll figure out who or what killed this man. It didn't take you long to find out what happened to Bill."

I was Bill's replacement at Blackfeet. Working as his mud-logger—a lowly subcontractor's technician—on two of his wells in Wyoming had been my entree to Blackfeet Oil Company. For years I'd dreamed of getting a chance to really use my college degree in geology, and Bill had redoubled my longing by making the work look fascinating. Now here I was facing a third day of twiddling my thumbs at an empty desk. "I'm just bored, Elyria. If I had anything to do, Gerald Luftweiller would have been a sad but fading memory by lunchtime."

Elyria's look grew sharper. "They haven't given you anything to do yet?"

"No." It had been more glamorous to skip that detail during our debriefing of the night before.

"Who's your boss?"

"Someone named Fred Crick. But he's out of town, and he left no instructions for me. I spent Monday reading the company policy manual, stocking my desk with paper clips, and trying to look important. I spent yesterday reading the paper."

"Sounds stimulating."

"Yeah. It was a big moment when I got my first memo. Something earth-shattering like, 'Words to the Wise: President Menken's parking space in the basement parking garage is reserved for President Menken's Mercedes only. All other vehicles will be towed.'"

"Sage advice. What marvel of office acumen sent that around?"

"It was signed 'Irma Tiff, executive secretary,' or chief valkyrie, or whatever she is. I filed it in the wastebasket under 'H' for who cares."

"You have all the makings of an executive."

The dog collapsed in the corner and sighed. Elyria looked pointedly at the clock over the stove. "I'd offer to drop you at work, but I'm heading out to Golden this morning. A little business at the School of Mines."

"That's okay, the bus is pretty quick."

"And so environmentally conscious."

The truth was, I didn't own a car of my own. Or a truck, which would have been my preference. I'd always driven my father's truck, or one belonging to the mudlogging company.

I drank the last of my coffee and hurried out the door to the bus stop, trying for the first time to jog in high-heeled shoes.

As the 7:35 A.M. Number 32 local squealed to a stop and engulfed me in diesel fumes, I held my breath, then climbed aboard and took the last available seat, squeezing myself in next to Howie, a young man with Down's syndrome who was in the habit of calling out a loud, cheerful "Good morning" as each new passenger boarded the bus. He fixed me with his enormous, thick-tongued smile.

"Good morning, Howie," I replied, grateful for his enthusiasm. I wished anyone at Blackfeet seemed as glad to see me.

The bus turned onto Speer Boulevard and crossed over the North Platte River. I thought wistfully how much more I'd be enjoying myself if I was on horseback getting wet fording the stream a hundred years ago, when Denver was still a frontier town, instead of rumbling over a bridge crammed into this sardine can with a bunch of disconsolate commuters today. My father told me Denver grew up along the riverbank as tenderfeet from the East arrived with the gold and silver booms. As ranching and commerce flourished, Denver competed with the city of Golden, fifteen miles west, to become territorial capital. Denver won. In 1870, the railroad barons brought their iron horses across the plains. By the turn of the century, trains connected from coast to coast and north to south, with interchanges from standard to narrow gage for the climb into Georgetown, Idaho Springs, Central City, and Blackhawk.

Denver grew like a weed, filling the broad, shallow downwarp in the Great Plains where they meet the Front Range of the Rocky Mountains. It's a dramatic setting, skyscrapers rising against a backdrop of ragged, snowcapped peaks that scrape the sky themselves at up to fourteen thousand feet. Denver calls itself the Mile High City, the elevation of City Park being just that. It boasts a fine collection of Victorian brick buildings down by the railroad station, a handsome formal Civic Center with government buildings dominated by a gilded capitol dome, and the requisite clutch of modern skyscrapers. Bronco Stadium perches on the bluffs along the west bank of the Platte, as does McNichols Arena, a hamburger-shaped sports palace. It was named for the mayor in office at the time it was built. McNichols was later ousted after sending most of the city's snow plows to clear the arena's parking lot during the worst snowstorm of the eighties, while the rest of the city set up in a hopeless mass of frozen ruts. McNichols was replaced by Federico Peña, the bachelor mayor, who prettied the city with federal matching funds and improved highway interchanges before moving on to the loftier post of secretary of transportation for the Clinton administration.

On this, my third day at work, it was still strange going into downtown Denver without my father. He used to take me to Denver every year for the National Western Stock Show, but when the day was done, we'd always hurry back to Wyoming, hopping over the border to the safety of the open plains. He didn't cotton to cities, said they confused his sensibilities, and as the Number 32 bus neared the transit mall, I heaved a sigh of empathy. To be honest, I'm kind of afraid of cities. Taking this job had been an exercise in trying to demote that fear to a discomfort.

At the office, there was still nothing for me to do except drink more coffee and make a study of the way the steel girders that formed the floor sent shock waves clear into our office, up through my chair, and into my spine as cranky-looking people stalked by in the hallway. I didn't like being reminded that I was sitting over a hundred feet above terra firma on what resembled a stack of old 45-rpm records on a concrete skewer dressed up with fancy glass. It fascinated me that the damned building even managed to stay upright, considering its concrete tap root was only sunk in mungy old river gravels.

I dusted off my pristine desk, rechecked my supply of paper clips, and tried to look confident. As usual, Maddie had her mind firmly trained on her work, and my attempts at striking up conversations with my other new colleagues got me nowhere in a hurry. Damn it, it bothered me that they wouldn't talk to me. *I thought I was a professional now, a member of the club. Is there some secret handshake I'm supposed to know?* I caught myself staring down at my brand-new white-

collar uniform, wondering if it was too new. I flicked a piece
of lint off it to cover my awkwardness, and wondered mo-
rosely why I'd ever left Wyoming. I missed the clean air, I
missed the open sky, and I missed my boyfriend, Frank.

Toward noon, I discarded the preoccupying question of why
I'd taken the job for the greater mystery of why I'd been hired.
There were layoffs throughout the industry. Why had Menken
hired me, when there clearly was nothing for me to do?

By two o'clock I was so bored that I was ready to pack my
tweed suits in mothballs and leave town, when a skinny little
guy in tight jeans scuffled into the office and brought me my
first assignment. "Crick says, 'Look this field over, evaluate this
new drilling location.'" he said. He unloaded a thick file and a
rolled-up map onto my desk as if they were hot to the touch. I
thought, *This is it, cowgirl; saddle up and say your prayers.*

The orange label on the tab at the top of the file said "LOST
COYOTE FIELD." I had heard of it; gas and light crudes in a
Cretaceous-aged sandstone, about three thousand feet below
surface, eastern Wyoming. A strong discovery in this time of
severely limited exploration budgets.

"Ah, just what am I supposed to do with this?" I asked.

"I already said." He vanished.

"Oh. Right." *You little twink.* To Maddie, I said, "Who was
that?"

"That's Fritz, the technician who works with us geologists."

"Oh."

"Ain't it sad when cousins marry," she added.

"Sure," I said. I was learning to take Maddie in stride. I
stared at the file. How was I supposed to do this? I'd been on
plenty of drilling rigs, but I didn't have a clue what went into
deciding where to drill.

I turned the file around and flipped it open to the middle, riffled through its contents. No revelations, just a bunch of
memos with technical gibberish about casing pipe, and so forth.
The memo on the top of the stack clasped to the first division of
the file folder was signed by some dude named Peter Tutaraitis.

I sighed, wishing it had been signed by Bill Kretzmer,
Elyria's late husband, my departed mentor. If Bill had worked
this field, he would have made so many notes I'd know the field
backward and forward by lunchtime. How I wished he were
here. But then, if he were here, I wouldn't be here, and . . .

My mind began to wander again, musing on the good old
days with Bill, and my boyfriend, Frank, out among the sage-

brush. Simpler times. High plains. Endless horizon. Wyoming. Life lonely, but making sense. Two hours' drive north of Denver, life becomes real. I could be home by dinnertime. . . .

Maddie sneezed. My mind crashed back to Denver, to my new clothes, my new title, and to the job before me. *Screw it,* I thought savagely, *screw them all.* I started reading through the file.

The pages were clipped in chronologically. A glance at the earlier memos told me something about the history of the project. Blackfeet had acquired the lease and drilled the wildcat discovery well about two years earlier, and had thus far drilled ten more wells. The credit for the discovery belonged to this geologist named Peter Tutaraitis. So why wasn't *he* evaluating this goddamned location?

"Hey, Maddie," I asked, "who's this . . . Peter . . . ah, Two-tar-ray-tis? Did he leave the company or something?"

My office mate straightened up and stretched in the day's answer to fashion, which featured rather large polka dots, two of which barely missed being too well placed on her bosom. "Naw, he's still here. And you pronounce that ' Tutor-itis,' like a rash you get from teachers."

"Does he still work Wyoming? I thought the territories were pretty clearly drawn here."

"That's the story. Used to be a little looser, but the big dogs got to rearranging the kennels a couple weeks ago, and got all formal about who sniffs whose ass. Big Pete's California now."

Roughly translated, that probably meant Management had drawn a few boundaries on the map, reassigning Lost Coyote Field to me, and maybe there was some politics involved, and maybe this guy Tutaraitis had an ego. I said, "So when in doubt, I call him Pete?"

Without quite her characteristic volume, Maddie said something that sounded like, "When in doubt, don't call him."

"What?"

No answer. This was very interesting: it was the first time Maddie had been anything but screw-you and fully in charge. I flipped back to the first memo, to see if I could reconstruct the drama written between the lines.

No luck. The file seemed overly tidy, devoid of marginal notes, calculations, or work sketches. I wondered what kind of a geologist this Tutaraitis guy was, if he didn't fiddle with his data any. Either this guy was so damned sharp that he could keep it all in his head, or he was asleep at the switch.

There were some large blueprinted sheets folded up in a pocket at the back of the file. I pulled them out and unfolded them. They were a bunch of graphs, plotted to show oil and gas production over time, with annotations indicating when various wells had been brought on-line. The production rates looked pretty good. Damned good, in fact. But something had sure turned down Maddie's voltage. And Fritz the inbred technician had handled the file like he needed oven mitts. Odd. I dug through the rest of the file, trying to find a good old-fashioned cross-sectional view of the oil field, a stratigraphic correlation from well to well that would show me something about the rocks from which the oil and gas were flowing. There wasn't a single cross section in there. Odder yet.

I tried again: "Can you tell me anything about this field?"

"What field is that?"

"Lost Coyote."

"Nope. Wouldn't want to crowd your job security, sweet peach."

That stung. I was trying to think up a suitable rejoinder when I heard a voice at the doorway announce, "Committee, ten minutes." I looked up to see an engineer named Scott Dinsmoore leveling a look on me that said, *Yeah, you.* Maddie looked up and observed him dispassionately.

"Huh?" I said.

"Committee meeting, in ten minutes," Scott repeated. He looked put upon, tried to puff up his slight frame to fill a greater portion of the doorway.

"Cool your jets, Scottie," Maddie drawled, "that's just Emmy's word. 'Huh' means lots of things to her, like in this cage, 'Roger and acknowledge that, big fellah, see y'all's ass in committee.' "

"Who asked you, McNutt?" Scott shot her a look of pure disgust and departed. Maddie smiled beatifically and bowed her raven curls back over her work.

How I envied Maddie's cool. I counted to ten, hoping she'd look up and at last take pity. Finally, at great cost to my pride, I cleared my throat and said, "Ah, what's committee?"

"Do what, honey?"

"Okay, honey," I said, trying to match her tone of amiable defamation, "in this case 'Huh' means 'What the fuck is committee and what the fuck do I do when I get there?' "

Maddie straightened, reappraising me. Then she slapped down her pencil and came over to my desk. "All right, now: committee's where y'all's taking this well proposal. All the dogs get together and have a good scratch and figure out which cars to chase. Piece of cake." She pointed at one of the production curves. "See here, this last well they drilled ain't producing so good as the others, so y'all's supposed to tell 'em if the company's outta its furry little mind to drill this one here."

"But I only just got this file half an hour ago."

"So?"

"So how am I supposed to tell them anything? I haven't had time to get to know the geology worth shit."

"Honey bun," said Maddie patiently, "that ain't the point. This field spits hydrocarbons like a motherfucker. See, in this case 'good' is a relative thing, so all's you have to tell 'em is calm down and drill. And then if they don't want to drill, they don't drill. It's just a matter of form. These boys is just sitting around in the committee room all day jerkin' off anyway."

"Huh?" I said, with gusto.

"Justifying their salaries, love duck."

"Oh."

Maddie raised a polka-dotted shoulder coquettishly. "You might want to take a look at that map, so's you can practice pointing out the well location."

I gave her one of those *I knew that* looks.

"Y'all knock 'em dead, I just know it." She gave me a merry wink and went back to her desk.

Bracing myself with a deep breath, I slipped the rubber bands off the map and unrolled it. I had to move everything around on top of my desk to accommodate the size of the unrolled map, arranging my stapler and tape dispenser to keep it from rolling up again. At first the map didn't tell me much. Just a spattering of black dots signifying existing wells—eighty-acre spacing, it looked like—a big orange sticker in the shape of an oil derrick in the proposed location, and dashed lines for our minerals lease boundaries, marked "Blackfeet Oil Company." But then I shifted the stapler to unroll the map a little farther, to see how far west the lease went, and found something interesting.

The adjoining lease belonged to Love and Christiansen, Gerald Luftweiller's employer.

More interesting yet, the lease comprised Hat Rock Field, whose map Gerald had taken with him to his death. I imagined the pattern of wells before me drenched in blood.

4

I was so entranced with this new puzzle that Scott Dinsmoore's peevish "Ahem" from the doorway caught me by surprise. In my excitement, I'd clean forgotten about our committee meeting.

I rolled up the map and hurried down the hallway after him, excitement mounting in my breast. Suddenly Crick committee was no longer a trial to be endured, it was a source of answers. All I needed now were the questions that went with them. I got Scott to explain who the players were as the executives filed into the committee room and took their seats.

"That's Jon Hathaway, the financial officer; you know, head of accounting, treasurer." A chain-smoking greaseball with thinning hair shambled in and dropped into a seat as if he'd just suffered cardiac arrest.

"That's Menken, the president and CEO."

"Right."

"That's Dave Smith, the chief reservoir engineer, my boss. The chief operations engineer won't be here; he's in Tulsa."

"Gotcha. And who's that?"

Scott squinted at me in disbelief. "That's Fred Crick, the chief geologist. *Your* boss."

The committee meeting began with a clearing of throats and scuffling of chairs. Maddie was right; I needn't have worried about my part in the show. All I did was lay the map out on the big mahogany table and roll it up again. Once, Fred Crick asked me to point out the proposed well location. The rest of the time, I stood around decorating the carpet, wondering if anyone noticed the run I was getting in my stockings.

The fact is, I couldn't follow much of what was being said. I thought a good drilling location was a good drilling location, and I couldn't understand why six people had to get together and debate it. By and by, my mind started to wander. I made a study of the wood grain in the conference table, and admired the effect of the subtly offset lighting which cast a saintly corona on the wall behind Menken's head. Our president's somewhat priestly hand gestures added to the effect, giving the scene a touch of the Last Supper tableau. As the debate ground on, I studied the players.

Fred Crick was a nervous piece of fluff. The chief geologist sat in a cramped, caved-in position, fiddling with his eyeglasses and mustache. I wondered why he had sent my assignment through Fritz, instead of contacting me directly, maybe welcoming me aboard personally and giving me a clue what he wanted done. *Maybe I was supposed to go to him,* I thought. *Did I screw up? Is that why he hasn't even looked at me?* Maybe there was something taught in the master's program I never enrolled in that would have clued me in to the rules of this game. Or maybe Blackfeet was a mess, and Crick gave orders by osmosis, and everyone kind of sloshed around and got the work done as best they could.

I glanced at Scott. He sat at rigid attention next to the chief engineer, saying "Yessir" an awful lot. His slender fingers danced in tight circles on the table top and blotches of color came and went on his face and throat, bringing out the delicate angle of his jaw here and the fine, lightly freckled skin of his cheeks there. As the session wore on, I became concerned that if the pressure within him built up any higher he might explode, blowing thin, freckled flesh all over the room.

Dave Smith, the chief engineer, was as loose as Scott Dinsmoore was tight. His face was impassive, relaxed to the point of near coma. The few times he spoke, though, his voice rolled out smooth and richly assertive, cracking an invisible whip that made Scott's shoulders tighten. The same courtly, self-assured tones seemed to have the opposite effect on J. C. Menken, whose slightly overplump cheeks crimped into a smug little smile whenever Smith spoke.

I tried once more to focus on what was being said. The conversation chewed for a few minutes around the issue of whether to drill or not to drill the new well at Lost Coyote Field, bouncing off the oil and gas production data onto the cost of drilling and through a maze of acronyms like ROR and ROI. As I listened, I became vaguely aware that my stomach was cramping up with gas.

"Then it's all very straightforward," Smith was saying. "Forty percent ROR and twenty-seven ROI. Standard well.

Three thousand feet, gentlemen—in, out, and on-line in twenty-one days."

"I'm not happy," Crick muttered. "No, I really think we need to get Pete Tutaraitis in here to look at this edge of the field, make sure we're not stepping out too far. He'll be back from L.A. in a couple days. We can wait that long."

"What do you think, Emily?" Menken said, smiling generously my way.

His attention caught me by surprise. Smiling nervously, I trained my eyes studiously at the map, as if the answer lay there. I tried to speak, but my eyes skipped over to Hat Rock Field, and I forgot what I was going to say. As I started to mutter something about good production rates Dave Smith butted in, his voice warm and unctuous: "We're taking up the president's time on needless worries, here, gentlemen. I'm sure Pete will concur." His voice oozed insinuation. "I can't imagine what your problem is with this, Fred. Can you tell us what your problem is? Hmm?"

The chief geologist's mustache twitched. I contemplated offering up Maddie's *everything's relative, I'm happy drilling this well here* speech, but thought better of it as Fred's fist tightened on the table top. Instead I smiled, something a notch more puckery than the Mona Lisa's, and wondered idly if Dave Smith really thought I was a gentleman.

Smith turned toward the president. His cheeks tightened slightly, exposing his upper teeth in what I suppose was meant to look like a smile.

The president beamed back. "We'll drill it," Menken said, gave the table a loving little swat, rose, and left the room.

Fred Crick rolled his eyes at no one in particular, muttered "Shit" under his breath, and left.

Jon Hathaway assumed a look of penitence and rose ponderously from the table, his left hand working convulsively, as if he were saying a rosary.

Scott Dinsmoore looked as if he might pass out with the tension. He jerked to his feet and followed the herd.

Dave Smith hoisted himself out of his chair and strolled out of the room, his long, pale fingers hanging listless and unnaturally straight at his sides. As he receded down the wasteland of the endless beige hallway, his suit jacket hung as motionless as if it were being wheeled away on a rack.

5

Thursday morning, I read and reread the entire Lost Coyote file, hoping to find some reference to Hat Rock Field. I tried to strike up a few conversations in the coffee room about it, or Gerald Luftweiller, or even the weather, but no luck. While they'd been glad enough to gossip in front of me while the Luftweiller news was hot, now folks clammed up at the sight of me. The notion that I was some little nit they wanted to get rid of grew so strong that I finally asked Maddie about it.

"Do these people hate me, or did they just eat alum for breakfast?" I asked, trying to affect the right tone of disinterest.

Maddie leaned back and scratched her shapely abdomen. "They hate you."

"Why?"

"Y'all got hired a month after they took a bunch of the good ol' boys and girls out back and shot 'em."

"Huh?"

"Fired 'em. Budget cuts. Folks get to feeling a mite sensitive." Maddie smiled. "Then y'all shows your face. Guess they figure you're scab labor."

"How's that?"

"Well, now, I hope this ain't indelicate, but y'all don't cost the company as much, seeing as you don't have a master's or any experience."

Perfect, I thought. *I'm working in a business that has people flying out of sixteenth-story windows, and my workmates hate my guts.*

I took an anxiety break and left the office. I walked down the hallway past an original Remington and two Russell watercolors in swank gilded frames, crossed the sumptuously carpeted entrance past the expensive sweep of the receptionist's desk, and slipped into the windowless recesses of the women's room. Budget cuts, indeed: they could have sold that Remington and kept the payroll afloat for a year.

I locked the stall door, went through the formalities, and sat staring at my feet, trying to figure out whose shoes were on them. Surely not mine: they were alien things, made of exquisite, supple leather. Grandmama had bought them for me the week before as the "decent foundation for your new professional image." One pair in brown, and one in black. Thursday was a brown day, to go with a nice tick tweed jacket and brown sheath skirt with a handsome kick pleat in the back that she'd picked out. I couldn't fault the old dame's taste, but I didn't know who the hell I was, either, wearing clothes I couldn't run, drive a truck, or ride a horse in. It felt like some weird disguise. Not for the first time in the three days I'd been in Denver, I fantasized ripping them off and running down Seventeenth Street naked.

Five minutes of this ersatz meditation barely made a dent in my angst. I gave up when the receptionist came in, locked herself in the next stall and vomited (she was easy to recognize under the divider, with her itsy-bitsy open-toed shoes).

I flushed the bowl to make it seem like I'd been there for the usual reason, and came out of my stall. I dawdled for a moment, wondering whether she needed any assistance, but when the receptionist emerged, she seemed perfectly composed. She stepped briskly to the sink, primly rinsed her mouth, and left, having glanced neither left nor right. Great: I was working with a bunch of geologists who wanted to burn me in effigy, and now even the damned receptionist was treating me like I was part of the wallpaper. So much for the women's room as sanctuary.

So I left. So where to? I wasn't ready yet to go back to my desk and continue faking it, so I opted for a field trip to the sixteenth floor, to see what I could add to the Gerald Luftweiller case file.

I headed for the stairs, swinging open the heavy fire door in the twelfth-floor lobby. Irma Triff watched me over the tops of her half-glasses as I went by. I gave her a who-are-you-staring-at look and she averted her eyes in a somewhat leisurely manner. I could almost hear her sniff. I yanked the fire door shut between us.

I found myself in an eery column of rough-finished concrete with grey steps that descended into an uncertain emptiness. The only embellishments were rubber treads and black iron handrails. No windows. Deep echo. Reek of cement. Every two landings I came to another door, and imagined the corporate sumptuousness that lay beyond it. It was damned weird, having spent so much time being slightly intimidated by this posh building, to find out that its guts were made of such plain stuff.

I was expecting four flights, but reached the sixteenth floor after three. It seemed there was no thirteenth floor. Thirteen's bad luck, I guess; someone might commit suicide or something.

The door to the sixteenth floor opened onto a hallway that ran the length of the building, front to back, punctuated with massive oak doors, three of which bore corporate plaques. At the Seventeenth Street end of the hall was a row of floor-to-ceiling windows. One of them was smashed.

It was a mess. The impersonal steel-grey carpet had certainly been cleaned up, but oh, that window. The window frame held a sheet of plywood, indelicately bound to the remaining patchwork of glass shards with duct tape. It didn't look safe, but the glass turned out to be quite thick, and the whole mass held against a gentle shoving. Gerald must have been serious, all right, to make it through that thickness. Why?

"Don't push too hard, lady," a man's voice said, quite close to my ear. I spun around to find myself eye-to-eye with a man dressed in dark green work clothes. He had silently emerged from the janitorial closet carrying a carton of paper goods for the bathroom. He was a pensive-looking man, with a long face as dark and bloodless as powdered cocoa. His body seemed caved in, as if it were saying, *All these years I work on this building, no recognition, lousy pay, and now this.* He observed me patiently, waiting for me to speak.

"Um, so this is the one that, ah, the guy, ah . . ." I trailed off idiotically.

"Yeh, this is the one." The man nodded, the jaundiced whites of his great dark eyes slightly spooky under the fluorescent lights of the hallway. He sucked at his lower lip, and then the upper. "Yeh. Nasty, nasty, nasty. Hell of a way to go."

"Did you know him?"

He shifted his spine, bringing it to repose in a more dignified arrangement. "Sure. Nice fella, worked here at Love and Christiansen." He gestured over his shoulder. "Allus had a nice word." He began to deflate again, staring at the plywood sadly. "Got the glass on order. Got to come from Corning, in

New York State. Be another week." He shook his head, wiped his face down with one long hand, and left.

I pondered the row of doors, with their fancy brass plaques. The large one on the double-hung doors that commanded one whole side of the hallway read "LOVE, CHRISTIANSEN & ASSOCIATES, PETROLEUM PROPERTIES."

Gerald Luftweiller, I thought, *you were human enough to notice the janitor was alive. What got to you?*

6

Friday morning, the wind had blown the smog into Kansas, leaving the foothills a deep blue. The high peaks of the Rockies rose naked and majestic, their cool dance under the cobalt sky cheering me considerably. Elyria and I took our breakfasts out onto the deck and basked in the early-morning sunshine, admiring the view glimpsed over the roofs of Denver.

"Do you miss Frank?" Elyria asked.

I pondered that. "Not like I expected. I miss him at night, because he seems so far away. In the day, he seems a long way off in other ways. I get kind of caught up in things."

"What do you mean?"

What did I mean? I'd been trying to figure that out myself. "I get lonely."

"That's to be expected."

"No, I mean in a way I don't like."

Elyria looked a question at me.

I looked away in embarrassment. "It's a selfish kind of lonely. Not *I miss you,* but *I wish you were here so I wouldn't feel this way.*"

Elyria's face hardened with seriousness. "Pay attention to that."

My embarrassment deepened. Pay attention and do what? The feeling sneaked up on me at odd times during the day, gnawing at me like hunger. Deflecting her attention in what I quickly hoped wasn't a cruel way, I asked, "Do you miss Bill a lot?"

Elyria turned her gaze toward the far mountains and smiled, relaxing for a moment into the bittersweet well of memory. "Always."

At work, I installed myself at my desk with a fresh cup of coffee and read some professional journal articles about the oil-bearing sandstones of northeast Wyoming. One article made reference to Hat Rock Field, but none mentioned Lost Coyote. I thought this odd at first, but then I looked at the publication dates on the articles. Lost Coyote hadn't been discovered when they were written. I began to feel I might yet get a handle on the geology of the area, and as I walked down the Sixteenth Street Mall in search of lunch at noon, the loneliness dispersed for a moment and I laughed at myself a little, wondering why I'd been so upset for the past four days. My nervousness over the untimely end of Gerald Luftweiller, an oil field with no problems that was somehow a problem, and the icy welcome I was still getting from my workmates dissolved from my mind like the stray shreds of a nightmare.

I treated myself to a beer with lunch.

The beer tasted so good that I chased it with a nice, big slice of black bottom pie for dessert. This gave me such a sugar rush that by the time I walked back up Seventeenth Street I was experimenting with a certain swagger. On high-heeled shoes, no less. Imagine yours truly, Emily Bradstreet Hansen, rolling her hips in a tailored skirt. *They calls me Em, an' I tells you when . . .*

Here we are, folks, back at the Cattlemen's Exchange Building, in the heart of Denver's oil patch. All twenty-one floors of slip-formed concrete and reflective glass house the finest in oil companies, oil and gas lawyers, and oil field service companies' reps. We are awaiting Miss Em Hansen, famed hot shit geologist from Chugwater, Wyoming, as she returns from a typical hot shit geologist's lunch of liverwurst on rye at the ptomaine palace down the street. She's coming, folks! Our voices hush, lest we miss even one word of wisdom Ms. Hansen might impart. . . .

About there I stepped on a fresh wad of chewing gum, which sticks to Italian leather every bit as well as it does to cowboy boots, and I had to break stride to scrape my shoe on the curb. *She still looks cute in those tweeds, folks, but bwaaap! sorry, her dignity is down the drain. Next contestant, please. . . .*

Scott Dinsmoore was closing fast from the other direction. In an attempt to ignore my inelegance, he averted his eyes from my feet to the adjacent sidewalk, taking in the fading stain where Gerald Luftweiller had contacted the Hereafter. Blushing deeply, he dodged into the building without even his customary terse hello.

I couldn't get all the gum off my shoe, the damned soles

were so flimsy. *The rest will just have to wear off,* I thought, as I gave up and pushed past the brushed steel door into the coolly lit lobby. My shoe caught with each step on the pearl-grey carpeting, making a little Velcro ripping noise as inconspicuous as an elephant fart.

I touched the heat-sensitive button to summon the elevator. The Up light went on with a muted *ding* and the doors sighed open, revealing a sexily lit car. I hate elevators, no matter how much they try to soothe or distract me with interior design, but as always I stepped in anyway, mentally reciting a litany against falling.

The doors were already starting to close when a woman in a finely tailored suit stepped toward the car, moving briskly, all squared shoulders and spike heels, viewing me narrowly from beneath heavy-lashed eyelids. As she blocked the doors deftly with one delicate wrist, I caught a whiff of dusky perfume. The doors shuddered and cowered open again, holding their mechanical sheaves at full attention until the woman had entered the car, punched one button for the floor she wanted and another to order the doors closed at a speed to match her importance. I shuffled to one side, observing the elevator etiquette of equal ground, eyes forward.

I found myself for the first time truly thankful that my grandmother had drop-kicked me into the suit I had on. I straightened up a quarter inch and sucked in my gut, oddly proud, hoping the leather in my shoes reeked of the money they had cost the old bean. Maybe I didn't fill my clothes the way this woman filled hers, but my tailor was up to snuff. I only hoped Ms. Eyelashes would get off the elevator before I did, in case the gum had seized my shoe to the floor of the car.

Ms. Eyelashes departed five floors later, as self-absorbed and unimpressed as she had arrived. I gave the Close Door button a good poke, and was gratified at how quickly the doors said *Yes'm.*

Twelfth floor, Jeeves, I mentally commanded the elevator, but on floor ten it stopped again. This time when the doors opened, I was faced with a man.

He was looking straight into my eyes.

Now, let me preface this next by saying that I count myself a reasonably sober personality. I make it a rule, for instance, not to mix work and play, and in fact I'm usually so focused on the job that I don't even notice men as men. But this man was another breed of cat.

He had riveting dark eyes—black, not brown—under heavy brows. A full mustache that framed a sensuous mouth now widening into a smile. A beguiling dimple sprang up in one of his cheeks as his lips parted ever so slightly, suggesting a welcome. He studied me with amusement.

I smiled back, I think.

As he moved into the elevator, his shoulders rolled slightly with his stride, speaking of athletic prowess, of knowledge of things physical. He moved to punch a button for his floor, but saw that it was already lit—my floor—and instead his hand wavered for a moment, then dropped, swept back the side of his suit jacket and came to rest on his hip, revealing the firm outline of his buttock draped in warm grey flannel. My eyes moved helplessly down that grey flannel, taking in every muscular curve that led to the oxblood loafers below. In an effort to stop staring, I shifted my eyes to the files he was carrying in the other hand, trying to read the name of the oil field on the orange labels.

He hitched the files back a quarter inch, shifted his hips a touch farther my way. My eyes strayed to his near hip again. I looked up, only to find him staring quite frankly into my eyes. Again the smile. I returned his stare just as frankly, uncomfortably aware that my pulse had quickened.

Too soon, the car stopped and he stepped out. With a brief backward glance, he crossed the lobby to the smaller door, drew a key out of his pocket, and let himself in.

The elevator doors closed again before I realized that I had frozen to the spot. I had to move quickly to punch the Open Door button and pull myself together before someone called the car to another floor.

Maddie looked up as I walked into our office, making her usual split-second evaluation. She raised an eyebrow.

I tried to make it look like the task of putting my purse in my desk drawer had consumed my attention. *This is grand; the guy had a key, so he probably works right here at Blackfeet. Yes, this really gilds the lily,* I thought irrationally; *in five minutes, Maddie will have told the whole office that I've gone into heat over some dude on the elevator. Or how about the direct approach? I could send out for a dozen raw oysters, then just stretch out on his desk and howl!*

Half a minute later when I glanced up, Maddie was still staring at me.

When Scott Dinsmoore bustled into the office a few minutes

later I welcomed the distraction, even though something had
him so upset that his well-bred little face was screwed up like
he'd been sucking a lemon.

"Hi, Scottie," Maddie cooed. "Jockey shorts too tight?"

"I won't dignify that with a reply, McNutt," he spat, raking
her with a look of finely chiseled indignation. To me, he said,
"Do you have all the files for Lost Coyote in here?"

"No, just the geology file, the discovery well and a few surrounding it."

"Are you sure? What are those files on your bookcase?"

"Those are Maddie's. Why? What's up?"

"Oh, nothing." Scott tried to affect a casual manner by shifting his weight to one foot, but he still looked like he had a
poker up his ass.

"Spill it, Scottie," Maddie crooned, rolling her head back
and leaning her torso toward him until the bodice of her hot
pink dress threatened to spill her melons.

Scott wheeled around toward her again, checked, turned
back toward me. His narrow face had gone from white to pur-
ple. "May I look through what you do have?"

"Sure."

Scott pawed feverishly through my stacks of files, reading
the name on each tab. After one quick pass, he went through
them again, his hands clearly shaking. Frustrated in his search,
he cast his eyes left and right, then hurried out the door.

I looked a question at Maddie.

"Pete must be back in town," she offered.

"Huh? Pete who?"

"Tutaraitis. Gets Scott real stirred up these days, somehow."

"Why? I thought this guy Pete was in charge of California.
Scott is Wyoming's engineer. Besides, since when do engineers get excited about geologists?"

"Got me. But y'see, Pete still has a financial interest in Lost
Coyote, even if the geology's in y'all's sweaty little hands."

"A financial interest?"

"This room sprouting an echo?"

"You mean this Pete guy's got a percentage of the gross on
this field and he's not even working it?"

Maddie bent closely over her work. "Not according to the
organizational charts, he ain't working it. But I reckon y'all be
hearing from him by and by."

*Fine, now I get some senior geologist with an overriding
royalty breathing down my neck.* Few geologists commanded

royalty interests in oil field production anymore. That meant this Tutaraitis guy was really talented, either as a geologist or as a salesman. This was the guy who didn't have to make notes, right? But then, if he was that good, why wasn't he doing the geological oversight on the field anymore? The whole situation made no sense.

I imitated Maddie's pose, willing the papers on my desk to please engage and hold my interest. It had been a long week, I was discovering that I hated office work, and now I was going to be micromanaged by some jerk with a vested interest in my project.

I was just finally settling back down to work when I heard someone else walk into the office. Out of the corner of my eye, I detected warm grey flannel and oxblood loafers. Maddie's chair squeaked as she said, "Hi, Pete."

"Madeline." The voice was as good as the smile.

He turned my way. "You must be Emily Hansen, the new geologist for Wyoming." He walked toward my desk with no special hurry. "Welcome to Blackfeet." His smile was friendly, winning; but the eyes shot me that same spark that I had caught on the elevator.

I said, "Ah, hi."

"Well, I'm pleased to meet you, Emily."

I had never heard my name spoken with such warmth, such music. Always before, I had insisted on the abbreviated, more succinct nickname of Em, cringing at the sound of my full given name, railing against its archaic, squishy, nasal qualities; but Pete made it sound rich and vital. I caught myself wondering where had I been. "Yeah," I said.

"I'm Pete Tutaraitis."

"Yeah."

"I hear you're proposing a new well at Lost Coyote Field."

"Right."

"We'll have to get together for lunch sometime."

"Sure."

"Sometime soon." He observed me with amusement for several long moments before heading back out into the hall and turning toward Scott's office.

7

I spent Saturday alone, homesick for the companionable emptiness of Wyoming.

Elyria was out of town on business again. She's a consulting minerals economist, one of the best in the industry. She provides numbers and wisdom to the corporate bigwigs, so they can plan their courtships with investors and boards of directors. With the continued unpredictability in oil prices, her work had becoming increasingly hectic.

As *pro tempore* house sitter, I walked the old pooch a few times, but quickly tired of the hard sidewalks. It was all the same to the dog.

Elyria got back late Saturday afternoon, her eyes glazed from a series of missed flight connections. "It's still summer in Houston," she said. "Give me a few minutes to shower and change, and we'll run up to Idaho Springs for dinner." Half an hour later, as she accelerated past the hogbacks that flank Denver's suburbs to the west and up Interstate 70 through the foothills, she opened the sunroof and let down the windows, the better to bathe in the fresh mountain air. The sun angled low across the foothills, touching each twig of aspen and mountain mahogany with gold. We roared up Mount Vernon Canyon, into the craggy granite spine of the Rockies. As the sun set we reached Idaho Springs, a mining town resplendent in nineteenth-century gingerbread, perched on a hillside between several large, oxidized mine tipples. We ordered thick, delicious pizzas and draft beer at a place called Beau-Jo's in an old brick building with high arched windows, and for a moment, I didn't care about the mysteries locked up in the Cattlemen's Exchange Building in downtown Denver.

Elyria spent most of Sunday afternoon stretched out in the backyard, the dog at her side. I checked on her periodically, to make sure the shade from the apple tree was still on her, so her fair skin wouldn't burn in the thin mile-high Denver air.

At three, I was just about to put a blanket over her, and perhaps the dog, when the phone rang.

It was my grandmother, phoning from Boston to see if I'd done her bidding and called my old prep school contacts. *No, not yet, Grannie. Yes, of course, right away, Grannie, you old battle-axe.* I wanted to see my old classmates like I wanted to gargle mud. I hurried her off the phone, wondering what had ever possessed me to include her in my preparation for going to work at Blackfeet. Any fool knew that you could get from Wyoming to Denver without going through Boston. I was so angry at myself for letting her know Elyria's phone number (although she wouldn't have let me get back on the plane if I hadn't) that I lassoed the dog and dragged him on a long march up Sheridan Boulevard, where I could snarl at the traffic.

When I got back, Elyria said someone else had phoned.

"It was an odd name. Toppy? No, Topsy Warren. She said you went to school together. She wanted to invite you to lunch."

Score another one for Grannie: she was calling in the favors through her ancient henchwomen. The sky crackled as those crones breathed fire into the transcontinental satellite linkups, calling their granddaughters with orders to call me. How I loathed compulsory socialization.

The phone rang again.

"That will be her, I expect," Elyria said. "I told her you'd be back soon. I knew you'd tire of carrying the dog."

I dragged myself to the phone in the kitchen like a cow going down the chute to the slaughter. "Hello?"

It was my mother, calling from Wyoming.

I squeezed my eyes shut.

"Emily dear," she began, in a tone that suggested that the word *dear* was something of an epithet, "how was the first week at the new job?" Her question was punctuated with a telltale clink, as she missed and struck her vodka glass against the receiver.

"Fine," I said, all but swallowing the word as I spoke it.

"What did you say, Emily? Speak up."

"Fine, Mother," I said, louder this time. It sounded defensive even to me.

There was silence on the line, broken only by the slim sound of air hissing inward through her cigarette.

I waited, my mind wandering aimlessly as it tried to find somewhere else to be. Why had I left the protection of the oil fields, where she could not phone me?

"I hear you have a new wardrobe," she said, missing her mark: instead of sounding angry, she sounded pathetic, lost.

"Yes."

Pause. "Well, your grandmother just called me to let me know you were to call your schoolmates." Full irritation. She was back in stride. "Do it, Emily. I will not have her calling me like this."

My hand started to ache from squeezing the receiver.

The line went dead.

Elyria came into the kitchen and looked at me, patiently waiting for me to fill her in on the phone call. After a moment, she gently removed the receiver from my hand and hung it up. "Your mother?" she asked.

I couldn't answer. I was still in a phone line somewhere, arguing. *Why the hell can't you two leave me out of your fight? All right, it was my own stupidity to tell Father about the job, and he told you, but you were the one who wrote the bragging letter to Grannie. The old bat reached out and snatched me eastward like a hawk nailing a jackrabbit. Success at last: her daughter may have run off to some obscure territory with a cowboy, but look! The granddaughter, back to the fold!* I inhaled deeply, trying to still a deep trembling in my stomach.

"Em?" Elyria spoke quietly, as if trying not to be overheard by an imaginary third person in the room. When I didn't answer, she moved over to the refrigerator and opened the door. What seemed like a lifetime later, she pried my fist open and inserted a cold beer.

A few minutes later, the phone rang one more time. Elyria answered, covered the mouthpiece, and said, "Topsy Warren again. Shall I tell her you're still out?"

"It's okay," I said. *I'd rather get it over with.* I put down the beer and pressed the instrument to my ear.

Topsy's nasal honk of a voice filled my ear. "Lunch?" she said. She knew the drill as well as I did. This meal was obligatory. "Ship Tavern, Brown Palace Hotel, Thursday, eleven-thirty? You know: avoid the rush."

"Great."

"Well, won't this be fun," she said, in a tone of voice as

rousing as mildewed laundry. "I'll ask Rachel and Libby, too. It'll be like a little class reunion."

Monday, when the alarm went off, I lay still with an arm across my eyes. I longed to roll over into Frank's comforting arms, but of course he wasn't there. I'd left him behind in Wyoming.

With a stab of guilt, I realized how little I had thought of him since I'd started the job. I thought of phoning him to say good-morning, but in my muddled early-morning state, I couldn't remember what shift he was working, and told myself I didn't want to chance waking him if he had worked the evening tower.

As soon as I got to the office, I had another visit from Scott Dinsmoore. "Have you gotten the morning report?" he demanded. Here it was only eight-fifteen or Monday morning, and he looked like his blood pressure was already dangerously high. And like he hadn't slept all weekend. It was a ghastly effect, kind of like the preppie from hell.

"Morning report?"

"Yes, morning report. You should learn these things. It's the report that comes in from the fields every morning to keep you apprised of wells that are drilling. You're supposed to keep track of these things."

Well, fuck you very much. "I know that," I retorted. "I used to have to send the goddamn things." *Shit, watch your language, Em, and what are you doing letting this little sheep tick get under your skin?*

Scott straightened his narrow spine. "Oh, that's right. You were a *mudlogger*. Excuse *me*."

I was just about to come back with something despicably defensive like, *Thanks, so I was nobody. So at least I'm not some brain-dead engineer with flaming hemorrhoids,* when Maddie came to my rescue. She leaned forward onto her soft parts and stopped chewing her gum long enough to drawl, "Cool your jets, Scottie, it's too early in the day to give a shit."

Scott held his ground, his back still turned to Maddie, but closed his eyes.

Maddie grinned, snapped her gum. "So Scott, you get laid this weekend?"

This question struck Scott with the impact of a pile driver. He spun on Maddie, his narrow fingers squeezing into fists, and shrieked "Shut up!" at a surprisingly high pitch.

"Sure." She straightened up, dazed at his reaction. "You okay, Scott?"

No answer.

At this juncture Fritz sloped in with a copy of the morning report. He stepped around Scott as if he were a hazard on the sidewalk and sullenly dropped the sheet of paper on my desk. "Morn' report," he muttered on his way out.

I spun it around and read it. Scott moved on it in a motion somewhere between a lurch and a lunge.

Lost Coyote was the only field listed, being the only one Blackfeet had drilling, and the record was terse:

Sept. 27: Spud RACO #2 10:55 a.m. Drl to 200.
Sept. 28: Set sfc condr & cmt w/ 30 sx. MIRU.
Sept. 29: Drlg 400.

Translated, that was: Saturday the twenty-seventh, started drilling the eighteen-inch-diameter initial section of the second well drilled on land leased from someone or some company named Raco. Drilled to two hundred feet. Sunday the twenty-eighth, placed surface conductor (a casing pipe) in the hole to keep the groundwater from getting contaminated and cemented it in place with thirty sacks of cement. Moved in, rigged up the drilling rig (set up the derrick, drill string and bit, motors, and mud pit). As of Monday morning the twenty-ninth at 8:00 A.M. when the report was phoned in, drilling at depth of four hundred feet.

That was fast work. We had only met on Wednesday to decide on drilling the well, and now it was spud and drilling. That meant they must have graded the location on Thursday or Friday. If the drilling was going so well, why was Scott so worked up about it?

Watching him devour the morning report, it occurred to me that he might have been caught napping, that he hadn't read it yet himself, that his offense at me was the best defense he could conjure. But as engineer assigned to the field, he shouldn't have had to go to the morning report for his information. The tool pusher on the drilling site should have been reporting to him directly, all weekend.

Then it hit me: as geologist assigned to the field, I should have been getting reports, too. I had been told nothing about the scheduling for this well. I, too, had found out from the morning report that the well had been spud and drilling all

weekend. Sure, Menken had okayed the well, but who was
calling the geological shots if I wasn't? I was being ignored,
circumvented. Just how the hell was I supposed to do my job?
How was Scott supposed to do his, for that matter?

I said, "Jesus, Scott, I didn't realize."

His pale eyes met my gaze. For a moment, he forgot to
maintain his antipersonnel smoke screen of pissy behavior.
Neither of us said anything, but for the first time since I'd reported to work at Blackfeet Oil, I felt I belonged.

Okay, I knew I had a problem here, but I had no idea how to
go about solving it. I could go to Fred Crick, but what if I was
somehow supposed to have known the well was drilling? For
the same reason, I wasn't any happier with the thought of asking any of my so-called colleagues.

And Maddie? Good ol' Maddie had her eyes trained firmly
on her work. I had come to know the signs of her I'm-staying-
out-of-this-you-sucker mode.

But to do my job I had to know what was going on at that
field.

I thought about phoning Elyria and asking in code what to
do, but right then even the phone got the drop on me, ringing
before I could reach for it. I answered it.

"Hansen speaking," I said.

It was Pete Tutaraitis. "Hi, Hansen. Are you free for lunch?"

Major change of gears. I barely stopped myself in time from
making a cute reply like, *No, but I'm reasonable.*

So Pete took me to lunch. I told myself, *This is business.*

As we left the office together, he spoke to me out of the corner of his mouth in low, conspiratorial tones, eyes dancing. He
had me laughing, something I hadn't done since I left
Wyoming. We rode the elevator clear to the bottom level of
the parking garage, and as the door opened he guided me out,
one hand molding itself to the small of my back. It felt good.

We drove a scant mile west and ate Japanese food at a joint
on Twentieth Street, just north of Sakura Square. Udon and
tempura. I stared into my soup most of the time, because his
eyes were so distracting. Pete chatted about Oriental cuisines
and this and that, and as lunchtime drew to a close, finally got
down to business.

"So, Emily," he said, leaning across the table. "Let's make
this meal official, so I can put it on the old expense account.

You're working on Lost Coyote Field. I used to. You're new to our little clan. Can I help with anything?"

"Yeah, maybe you can tell me what the big mystery is," I said, more bluntly than I had intended.

"Mystery?"

"Well, you know; why everybody's so uptight about this field. And why they started drilling without calling in the daily drilling reports to me."

Pete stared at me blankly, his elbows on the edge of the table and his hands together, obscuring the lower half of his face. Finally he said, "I don't know what you mean. Didn't you leave your home number with the operations engineers?"

"No . . ."

"And what do you mean, 'uptight'?"

Tentatively, I said, "Well, like at the committee meeting last Wednesday."

"I wasn't there." He smiled angelically.

"Well," I tried again, "it just seems that people are real hyper about this field. I don't know. Maybe it's just my imagination." I shrugged my shoulders, trying to make it look like idle curiosity.

Pete reached across the table and squeezed my hand. "You'll get used to it," he whispered. He looked at his watch, smiled, and added, "You're a pleasure to dine with, Miss Emily . . . can we do this again soon?"

All the way back to the Cattlemen's Exchange Building, I could still feel the warm pressure of his hand.

The elevator stopped in the lobby on its way up from parking level two. Pete was telling me a funny story about a recent trip to L.A. and Bakersfield when the door opened.

There stood Scott. When he saw Pete his lips pulled back from his teeth in a grimace.

Unmoved, Pete sidled toward me, gesturing to Scott that he was making room for him. "Scottie," he said, "something you ate?"

Scott's complexion turned frighteningly red. He stepped into the car and turned toward the front. After a moment, he shot me a sidelong glance.

"Hi, Scott," I said. Scott didn't reply. His full attention was on Pete, even though his gaze was now riveted on the floor, and when the doors opened at the twelfth floor, he bolted from the car like he'd been goosed with a cattle prod.

Pete squeezed my shoulder in farewell and headed for the far door. I headed for my office, muttering, "I know nothing, I know nothing." Which was true.

As soon as I sat down at my desk, the phone rang. It was Scott, his voice tight with restrained fury. "Listen, ah, Em, can you come down to my office? Um, we need to talk."

The thing that went through my mind was, *I do believe I am at last going to learn something about this goddamn oil field.*

8

Scott Dinsmoore's office was remarkably tidy. No, strike that. It wasn't tidy, it was obsessively neat. Anal retentive. Rigid. The only decoration was one small, framed print of a biplane on the wall above his desk. There was a mechanical pencil out on his desk, carefully laid parallel to one lone well file, which was lined up square with the edge of the desk. Everything else was put away somewhere. Even the bookcase had every little spine lined up neatly, and not a speck of dust.

Scott sat very straight in his chair, his tie and button-down collar perfectly straight, his blue blazer perfectly free of lint. He gestured to the second chair, which, like his, stood perfectly aligned to the desk, as if the two pieces of furniture were squared off for a staring match.

I sat.

Having taken the initiative of calling me in there, Scott now seemed at a loss for words. He stared at his hands, clasped tightly on the desk top.

"You wanted to speak with me?" I asked.

Scott pursed his lips as if straining to contain some inner pressure.

I felt moved to fill in the awkward silence. "Um, Scott, I guess it's not typical that they should start drilling the well without telling us," I began, and then ran out of words myself. Maybe Pete was right, and I just didn't know the system yet. I said "Um" a few more times.

"That's not it. Or yes it is, but it's not. You see," he began, but then lost courage, deflating into his shirtfront.

"What the hell's eating you, Scott?"

"Listen, Em, this is none of my business, but—"

His false starts were beginning to wear on my general lack of patience. "What is none of your business?" I snapped.

Scott's eyes flashed anger at me. Or was it contempt? "Just be careful, damn it," he muttered.

"About what?" I snapped. "Listen, enough with the veiled threats. Are we going to talk about Lost Coyote or aren't we?"

"Okay, the damned field."

"Right, the goddamned field." I opened my mouth to say *So talk, goddamn it,* but curiosity got the better of me. Steadying the tone of my voice into neutrality, I repeated, "*What* is none of your business?"

Scott looked wretched. After several more false starts, he finally said, "Listen, Em, Pete Tutaraitis can be trouble. I don't really want to go into it, but—"

"Shit, Scottie, stay out of my personal business!"

Scott looked as if he'd been slapped. He stared at his desk top.

"I'm sorry, Scott," I mumbled, trying to put the best face on my temper. "Let's just talk about the field."

Scott fiddled with his pencil. Finally he nodded. "Listen, this doesn't have to involve you. Maybe it's really best if you stay out of this."

"Except that it does involve me. I am the geologist for this field."

"Right, you are. Nominally, anyway."

"Right." I bit back another outburst. "So tell me."

Scott looked at me rather miserably. "They're supposed to call us on the weekends with the drilling report. I spoke with the field engineers right after committee last Wednesday and gave them both our home numbers."

So I hadn't screwed up! "Then who were they reporting to, if not to us?"

"I don't know."

"Should I call the field office or something, and give them hell? You know, ask them why we weren't told what was happening."

"Maybe that would help. I don't know. But that's the least of it." He clamped his teeth together so hard that his jaw muscles bunched, and he looked all about before he spoke. He even cast a little glance back over his shoulder, although the only thing behind him was a blank wall beyond which lay the elevator shaft and other building guts. Then he hissed, "Listen, you notice anything funny about this field?" He clutched both ends of his mechanical pencil tightly, staring at me with intensity surprising even for Scott, as if he were about to initiate me into some arcane truth.

Before I could open my mouth, Scott's phone rang. He

grabbed the receiver, said, "Dinsmoore here." As he listened to the voice on the other end of the line, his lips disappeared into a thin line. He pulled open the lap drawer of his desk, extracted a red spiral-bound notebook, and began writing furiously in a tight little hand.

Well, I couldn't help but see a little of what was in that notebook; he had opened it right in front of me, after all. And for all the speed with which he was writing, his handwriting was as obsessively tidy as the rest of him, and with my eyesight I could have read it from at least another ten inches away.

It was a desk diary of some sort. The day's date was neatly inscribed at the top of the page, followed by several lines that appeared to report in some detail what he'd already done that morning; who had phoned him; that sort of stuff. He said, "Yes they are. Yes. I think so too." In the book, he wrote: "Simon ph. 9/16 13:30 ltst gas tsts wet, cyclng?"

I had only a vague notion of what that meant. As much time as I'd spent in the oil patch, the engineers were still coming up with little goodies I didn't understand, and they were always abbreviated out of recognition. I knew what a wet gas was; gas was rated as wet or dry depending on how much liquid hydrocarbon was dissolved in it. But what was "cycling"?

Scott was saying, "That tears it. Right, I am. Yes, right now." He hung up, rose abruptly from his chair, and stood at attention beside his desk, as if waiting for me to move before he could pass. He said, "Ah, I've got something I need to do. I was right in not wanting to involve you."

I felt moved to grab him by his tidy little lapels and yank him off the floor, in case that might persuade him to be a little more talkative, but I settled for, "*Please,* Scott."

An odd light of heroism, either real or imagined, shone from Scott's eyes. "No," he said, now quite calm. "It's not right that you be hurt by this, too." Smiling faintly, Scott left the room and turned toward Menken's office.

Hurt? I followed, dawdling in the hallway for a minute, pretending to look at a Bama painting, in hope of at least seeing where he was going in such a hurry. He marched down the hall past the receptionist, right up to the door of Menken's office, then caved in, stared at his feet, examined his hands.

Unless I had just witnessed the final moments of a nervous breakdown, something very important was up. Going in to see Menken was a very bold move for Scott; he was jumping his own rails, circumventing the chain of command. For a shy, fastidious and painstaking person like Scott, such a brash effort at communication was heroic.

But he was a hero with the momentum of a slug. At length, the executive valkyrie that sat outside Menken's office asked him if he wanted to see Menken, phoned ahead for permission, and bade him pass. Scott's spine stiffened resolutely as he opened the door.

I couldn't find him later that day; he had apparently left the office. Tuesday, I was told he was on leave. Meanwhile, I asked Elyria if she knew what Scott's cryptic note had meant, and she said she didn't know, either, and why? I said, oh, nothing, and she looked at me knowingly and said she'd ask around. I told her not to trouble herself. She looked at me huffily. She knew all about keeping things under her hat, she said. I was nervous anyway. I was treading very close to the First Commandment of the oil patch: Thou shalt not discuss proprietary information outside thy company.

Late Wednesday afternoon, Scott was back at work. I found him sitting in his barren office, hands folded neatly on his completely empty desk, apparently doing nothing at all. I stepped in to ask him if he was free to continue our conversation about Lost Coyote Field.

"Yes, I guess so," he answered, with all the affect of a slice of bread. He showed no signs of breaking out of his trance, save for the faintest twist to one corner of his mouth, as if I had just uttered the name of a vaguely remembered sweetheart who had worn a pleasant perfume.

"Scott?" I prompted, wondering if he were asleep with his eyes open.

"Yeah."

"What's 'cycling'?"

He looked up at me, actually smiled. Then he leaned back in his chair and put his feet up on the desk.

I wasn't ready for his pants. They were a wide, crisp red tartan, quite surprising on a little twitch like Scott. I was floored.

His phone rang. He lifted the receiver off the cradle with a light motion, held it delicately to his ear. "Scott Dinsmoore," he said, his voice serene. When he heard the party at the other end of the line speak, a smile sprung to his lips, and widened as he spun around in his swivel chair, putting his shoulder toward me. "Certainly," he said into the phone. He glanced at me, blushing. "Will you excuse me please, Emily?"

Irritated, I left the room. I stood outside in the hall for a few moments, wondering what could have caused such a change in this nervous little man.

9

I remember that it was dark. I was leaving work late, trying to make the big impression, and was shrugging my way into my coat as I crossed the lobby on my way out to Seventeenth Street.

Something flicked past my peripheral vision, outside the plate glass windows that lined the lobby. Like something dropping past the windows. As I pushed the door open to the street, I heard a sharp intake of air, and then a full-throated scream.

The scream went on and on and on.

A woman was screaming, right near me, her skin pale and greenish under the streetlight. She stood with her hands framing her contorted face, fingers stiff like claws. Cars were stopping in the middle of the street. People were converging near her, turning white, turning away, crouching down toward a strange heap of something on the sidewalk. One man moved to the curb and vomited.

My eyes saw the heap but my brain wouldn't compute what it was. It tried several times. To this day I have trouble with it.

What was on the sidewalk was, well, sort of like a person, only its parts were lying at funny angles, and it lay in a pool of darkness. It was dressed up like a person too, wearing a blue blazer, and bright red tartan pants.

10

The next thing I remember, I was sitting on a bench in the lobby.

I wasn't alone on the bench. Pete Tutaraitis was sitting next to me. I felt so dizzy that I leaned forward and put my cheek on one knee. I felt his hand touch the middle of my back and wait there, patiently.

Gradually, the buzzing noise in my ears subsided, only to be replaced by the sound of a siren, almost human in its rising and falling complaint against the atrocity that had just occurred. *Wa-wa-wa-wa*, it shrieked, as it drew up in front of the building, finishing with a perfunctory *whump*. The spinning lights of a police cruiser swept through the lobby, chasing around its nooks and recesses like crazed swallows. From my sideways view of the world, the policeman who got out seemed to spill from the driver's seat, hand by his side at the ready, head on a swivel. In three long strides he was out of my line of view, moving toward the body. Moments later, two other cruisers arrived. One quickly backed away from the curb and steered around toward the back of the building.

An officer stepped into the lobby. "Everyone please hold your positions," he barked. The words were polite, but the tone was far from it.

I sat up, and was surprised to find that there were other people in the lobby with us. The woman who had screamed sat at a nearby bench, staring into space. Someone was just stepping off an elevator, and others were milling nearby, trying to get the policeman's attention. Ignoring their inquiries, he growled: "I'll see your licenses, please." He advanced on us, collecting our documents like a ticket taker, brusque yet businesslike.

Another elevator dinged and two more people stepped out: J. C. Menken and Dave Smith, the chief engineer.

Menken took the scene in at a glance. "What's going on here, Officer?" he inquired.

The cop moved toward him slowly, concentrating on the driver's licenses in his hands, shuffling them around like fortune cards. "Your license, sir," he said.

"My what? Look here, Officer, what's going on?"

Dave Smith had already set his attaché case on the floor and was reaching for his wallet. "I think he needs to see some identification, J.C.," he said, soothingly. "Seems there's been some kind of a little problem outside the building here, and the officer just needs to keep track of everybody." He handed over his license, nodding to the cop as man to man. "I'm sure there'll just be a short delay, J.C., and as soon as this good man gets things sorted out, why then we can just get along to dinner."

Menken affected regal annoyance. Setting his attaché down, he produced his license, held it up for the cop to examine. "There. Now, we have reservations at the Broker Restaurant, and we're late as it is."

The cop plucked the license from Menken's hand with surprising delicacy for such a burly man. "You'll have to wait with the others, sir. Sorry."

I was distracted from the rest of their exchange by more arrivals outside. A Fire Department pumper pulled up to the curb, and two men with medic kits jumped out and made their way over the yellow tape barrier that now enclosed the sidewalk and the cars parked along it. When I returned my attention to the big cop, he was standing just a few feet away from us. Another officer came inside and reported to him. "Everything secured outside, Sergeant, sir," she said, producing a pad of paper from her pocket. "The building's got three routes of egress." She whipped a pen out of her breast pocket, pointed to the features on her drawing. "This one here"—she gestured to the front doors—"a loading dock, and the parking garage. Garage has two doors into it, staircase and elevator. There's a man on the vehicular exit at Welton, you know, taking parking fees. The vehicular entrance is right next to it, so like he sits between the two in his glass booth. Guy says two cars came out in the last ten minutes, both monthly pass holders, so he knows them. Here's the specs here; he had the tag numbers, so forth. There's a couple pedestrian exits, one on Welton, one on Glenarm. The guy can see the one on Welton, says no customers. Glenarm he can't see; no dice. The dock is locked with a dead bolt; no witnesses to make sure no one left by key, but we got her covered now. Janitors say no one has a key but them. You can get to it from the staircase into the garage, up a flight, or you know, down from above and all, or from I guess that door. Yeah." She pointed to a heavy steel fire door beyond the elevator bank. "Fairmont Hotel's the other building to the northeast. They got their own entrances and all; you know what it looks like. Harland's back there questioning the doorman on duty now."

An ambulance pulled up in front of the building, lights flashing. The med techs from the Fire Department shook their heads at the driver, who got out and wandered amiably toward them anyway.

The sergeant laconically observed the new arrival before turning back to the reporting officer. "Homicide been called, right?"

"Yes, sir, and the M.E."

"Deceased's name?"

"License in wallet says Harold Scott Dinsmoore, sir. Business card same name, Petroleum Engineer, Blackfeet Oil Company, this address, suite twelve hundred. So twelfth floor, but looks like he came out a few floors higher."

"Last week's jumper came out of sixteen."

"Yes, sir. Looks like the same window. Wasn't repaired yet. There's some plywood splinters caught in the back of his jacket."

"Jones, you don't have to call me 'sir' all the time. I'm only a sergeant, after all. Relax. You sound like a rookie. Just 'cause you're a rookie don't mean you have to sound like a rookie."

"Certainly, sir."

"Feeling okay, Patrolman?"

"Yes." She caught herself before she said "sir" again.

"Okay, looks like we got everything buttoned up then. Soon as Homicide gets here, they'll probably need you and a couple of the others for a search upstairs."

"Right, sir."

Another car pulled up in what now looked like a showcase for official vehicles. Two men in business suits got out. One was short and rather round, and the other tall, bony and muttfaced. As they moved toward the lump on the sidewalk, everyone stepped out of their way. The short one took a fairly quick look, spoke briefly with the uniformed officer who was standing by, and passed through the lobby to the elevators.

Menken was pacing up and back in the center of the lobby.

Smith stood characteristically still, watching him pace. Menken said, "We're wasting time here. This is just another one of these damned suicide cases."

Smith's face was impassive, but his voice was sonorous. "Ah, perhaps, sir, but it's one of your employees this time."

"What? Who?" Menken stopped pacing.

Smith peered out the window. "I believe it's Scott Dinsmoore, J.C.," he said, his voice the only animation in his motionless body.

Menken drew back. His face stiffened into a mask. "Dinsmoore?" The two men stared at each other with no discernible emotion for perhaps ten seconds before Menken reorganized his features into an expression of dismay and said, "This is most shocking. We'll have to make the proper gesture to the family."

"Of course."

Another pause. "Will we have to replace him?"

"I don't think so. No, I'm pretty sure the rest of the engineering staff can pick up the few chores he was performing."

Menken's face fell into an expression of mild brooding. Presently he looked over at me, as if he expected me to say something. I looked away, bile rising in my throat. How could they speak of the dead so casually?

I noticed then that Blackfeet Oil's receptionist was over by the elevator bank smoking a cigarette. She was a pale, pretty thing, with that rare, luminous, porcelain skin which at the moment seemed almost transparent. She stood staring toward Pete and me, pulled up against the wall as if claiming shelter from a high wind, her tiny little open-toed shoes drawn close together. She was frowning, the most emotion I'd seen her display to date. This time, her stomach seemed plenty steady.

There were other familiar faces now in the lobby: Fred Crick, my phantom boss; Irma Triff, Menken's executive secretary; and Jon Hathaway, the financial manager. I was beginning to recover enough to wonder why so many people had stayed so late.

Bursts of light came from outside. Someone was taking flash pictures of the scene on the sidewalk; the tall bony plainclothes cop. A second was crouched down, tying plastic bags over the limp, bloody hands. A third was hauling gear out of a small van that had two red spotlights and a police antenna. Tall Bony put away the camera, blew his nose, got out a pad of paper and a pencil, and started sketching a picture of the scene. The Rembrandt of the macabre.

Pete said, "I wonder how long this is going to take. Seems like a lot of fuss for a suicide."

The sergeant observed him askance. "How do you know it's a suicide, Mr. ah—" He shuffled through the licenses, looking for Pete's. "Toot-o-ray . . ."

I watched for Pete to react to the mispronunciation of his name, like Maddie had suggested. But he didn't. He looked downright sociable, like the cop was some old boy just dropped around for a beer, and how are ya? He cheerfully corrected the cop's attempt. "Tutaraitis. Well, I don't know it's a suicide, of course. It's just a trend that's been going on around here." He smiled. "You got me on that one. Here I'm a scientist, and I'm supposed to know better than to make assumptions."

"Are you acquainted with the deceased?" asked the sergeant.

"I don't know. Who is the deceased?" Pete asked.

"His name is Scott Dinsmoore. You know him, Mr. Tootaritis?"

Pete's face fell. "It's Scottie? Shit, I didn't realize. Oh, that must sound very callous of me. I'm sorry." Pete looked at his hands, fluttering them about. "Good God. Scottie's dead. You can't be serious." I wondered whether it was his turn to be getting shocky or faint.

"Then you did know him. How well?"

"Why, we worked together, right here at Blackfeet Oil. It's up on the twelfth floor; I was just coming from there. I just saw Scott a few hours ago. Good geologist, I thought he'd gone home."

"Exactly when did you last see him?"

"Oh, I don't know, about four or five. Really, that's Scott Dinsmoore out there?"

About then the little round detective returned from his visit upstairs, flagged his partner in from the sidewalk, and everything got real regimented and organized, real fast. As uniformed officers fanned out for a search of the building, the two detectives sorted out everyone in the lobby and questioned us, quickly and efficiently, sending each home in turn. Those of us from Blackfeet were questioned somewhat more extensively, each taken out of earshot of the others.

My turn came with the little round detective. He walked me away from the dwindling group.

"Hi there," he said. "I'm Sergeant Ortega. I'll just be asking you a few questions here. First, your name please."

"Em Hansen."

"Spell that please?" He smiled at me from his round face, his dark eyes alight with a small confusion, or curiosity perhaps. His voice was soft, slightly whispery, with just a trace of an Hispanic accent. It was something in the vowels, and in the way he pronounced each word very deliberately.

"Hansen. H-A-N-S-E-N."

"No, I mean the 'M.' "

Outside, the ambulance and pumper departed, and a van arrived, marked "M & M Removal Service."

"The M?"

"Miss Hansen? Miss? How do you spell that first name?"

"E-M. It's short for Emily."

"Ohhh, I get it. Okay." Sergeant Ortega smiled his warm round smile, then squinted up at me again. "I'm sorry for staring, but you look familiar somehow. I'm sorry. I don't mean to be rude."

"It's okay." I guessed it was okay, anyway. I really didn't have any room to complain, under the circumstances, and he was being awfully nice about it. But mostly I was starting to feel kind of woozy again. I stared helplessly out at the scene on the sidewalk.

"Okay. Okay. Now, Miss Hansen. I understand that you work at Blackfeet, like ah, Mr. Dinsmoore. Is that right?"

The men from M & M Removal were hauling a stretcher out of the back of their van. One was unfolding a big plastic bag.

Sergeant Ortega touched me lightly on the shoulder, turning me so that I faced him, my back to the windows that looked onto the street. "That's better. I'll repeat my question, okay?"

"Yeah. No, it's okay. Um, I just came to work here a week ago."

"Oh, okay, okay. Very sad for you, to come to work just now. Very upsetting. Where did you work before here?"

"I worked for a mudlogging contractor out of Casper, Wyoming. I was on drilling rigs, mostly in Wyoming."

"Nice. Wyoming is nice. Very big sky. Now, are you a— what, mudlogger for Blackfeet?"

"No, now I'm a geologist."

"I see. Now, where were you when the deceased ah—died?"

I felt a vein start pulsing in my forehead. "Right here, I guess. I was just coming out of the elevator when . . ."

"Right. Okay. So you were here inside the lobby."

"Yeah."

"And you saw Mr. Dinsmoore, ah—land."

"Yeah?"

"Oh, you didn't see it?"

"No, I saw something, but um, I . . ." My ears began to ring again.

"What did you see?"

"It was kind of like something just came by the windows."

"What did it look like? Can you describe it?"

"It was, well—" I made a few gestures, trying to explain the inexplicable. I was having a lot of trouble staying on the topic.

Ortega nodded. "And then what?"

"Then . . . um, I'm not sure. Then, well, I'm sitting on the bench here, and Pete—Mr. Tutaraitis—is with me, and there are other people here."

"Were they here when you came out of the elevator?"

"I don't—" The picture this questioning was painting began to dawn on me. He was asking me to report on other members of my company. I could just hear the whispering that would set off in the coffee room. I reflexively drew back, like a calf bolting from a cowboy's hands as he tries to corner it against a fence to brand it. "I don't remember."

"How long do you suppose it was between the time you saw what you saw and the time you were sitting on the bench?"

"I don't know." How long had it been? A moment? Several minutes? Even coming out of the elevator was beginning to fade.

Sergeant Ortega scribbled little notes on a pad of paper. He smiled again. "Right! So you were in here, and all that was out there. Got it!" He sounded so cheerful, and his smile was so sweet, that I found myself concentrating very hard on what he was saying, waiting for each soft word to come out of his mouth. "And, um, when was the last time you saw Mr. Dinsmoore alive?"

"Early this afternoon. He was in his office. I stopped in to speak with him."

"Okay. And, how did he seem to you? You know, mood."

"Weird."

He scribbled. "How so, weird?"

I fought the urge to start spilling the whole story. This guy was easy to talk to, and I sure needed to talk; but I wasn't going to do it here, with my boss and all my co-workers, not to mention Pete, watching. I wished we were alone, on a long walk on a country road, so I could tell him.

Sergeant Ortega smiled again, with a certain tenderness.

I had to say something. "Well, sir, I didn't know him hardly at all, just a week, you see, or nine days, to be exact, but always before he was—well, a real tense sort of guy. He got tenser and tenser until today, and then he seemed all of a sudden real relaxed, almost like he was sleepwalking. Kind of cheerful." I hurried the words out, hoping that would do.

It didn't work. Sergeant Ortega seemed very interested in this, and questioned me further about what I'd said, and what Scott had said. He was so sweet and solicitous that I felt like shit telling him I couldn't really remember anything particular that was said. I did go so far as to give him my opinion, on prompting, about whether or not I thought Scott was the suicidal type. My opinion was half-baked at best; I've never known anyone who committed suicide, at least not all at once like that, and so who was I to know? But I went ahead and said my piece anyway, stating that I thought Scott was more angry than despairing. Hurray for Em Hansen, amateur shrink. I was embarrassed when I got to thinking about it later on, but at the time, it made me feel better to talk, it really did.

About then the stairwell door whanged open and a very strange man stumbled out into the lobby, hunched over as if he were one hundred and eighty years old. It took me a moment to realize that this was not a feeble old drunk, it was a perfectly sober man being goose-walked by a cop, who came through the door behind him. I realized with a shock that the man was hardly any older than I was; the effect of age was caused by his posture, and the grizzle of a three-day growth of beard. Wildly colored layers of shirts blossomed between the lapels of his bedraggled-looking army greatcoat. He was bending forward so far that the front hem of the coat swept the floor.

"Look who I found in the parking garage, Sarge," said the cop, his sloppy face spreading into a foolish grin.

Sergeant Ortega nodded patiently. "Very nice, Stanlon. Now, you may release him."

The cop's face sagged into a dull frown as he dropped the man's arm. Shrugging, he stepped back. The man painfully straightened his arm around to his side and rubbed it. "Sergeant!" he sang, breaking into a lunatic smile.

Ortega's face brightened. "Archie Arch. My man. Long

time; I thought you must of left town. So. What were you doing in the garage this evening, my friend?"'

Archie swayed gently from the knees and brought his shoulders coyly to his earlobes.

"Okay. Okay, I'll get to you later. Go visit Floyd, okay?"

Archie smiled and shuffled away, rolling his eyes.

"Now, don't get lost," Ortega called after him. When he returned his attention to me, he said, "Nice guy. Makes nice poems."

Sergeant Ortega wrapped up the interview by asking me where I could be reached that evening. I gave him Elyria's number.

He paused after writing it down. "Where is this number located?"

"On West Thirtieth Avenue, near Oceola."

"Ohhh, okay. Now I know where I seen you before. You live with Elyria Kretzmer, right near my parents."

"The house by the corner? I thought I'd seen a police cruiser there."

"No, that's my little brother, Norberto. He's uniform. I'm the detective." Ortega smiled, merry and proud, then raised his eyebrows. "Yes, that Elyria, she's one fine lady. And very pretty."

That's an understatement, I thought haughtily. "Yeah. She's nice."

"Well, okay, Miss Em Hansen, I can reach you at Elyria's then, this evening, if I have any more questions?"

"Yeah."

And that was it. Except that Pete Tutaraitis drove me home.

11

I had thought Pete might come in, but when he pulled his Saab up in front of the house, he said, "Oh, you're staying at Elyria's?"

"Yeah. You know Elyria?"

"Sure. I used to see her at the company Christmas parties, when Bill was alive. Besides, everybody in the business knows Elyria. Bright lady." He moved to put the car in first gear.

"Can you come in?" I asked.

"No. Better get home." He looked at his watch. "I hadn't realized how late it was getting." He flashed me a very nice smile, added, "Rain check, okay?" and then, "You sure you'll be all right?"

"Yeah." I wasn't sure at all. Suddenly my head felt heavy again. I lowered it into my hands.

Pete put his arms around me and held me against his chest, and I fell into warmth and masculine smells of tweed and day-old shirt. Tears burned my eyes. Without thinking about it, I slid my arms in between his shirt and his jacket. A shirt button pressed against my nose. The warm, firm muscle that lay so close beneath the fine white pinpoint cotton was deeply comforting, but at the same time, added to my confusion. He murmured, "It's okay, Emily, it's okay."

The awkwardness of stretching across the space between the seats soon brought me back to my senses. Finding myself so cozy with a near stranger, I shot upright.

Abruptly, he leaned across me, opened my door, smiled, and said, "See you around the rodeo, Cisco."

I hopped out and stood shivering under the streetlights, even though I felt quite warm. "Sure thing, Pancho."

The next day, my workmates kept gravitating into the coffee room, where they stood around with their shoulders hunched over their cups, like so many cold, wet birds waiting for bad weather to pass. They sucked up their coffee slowly, hesitant to leave their fellows and return to their lonely offices. There were three classes of people in the place that day: Those Who Were There When It Happened; Those Who Weren't; and then me, The New One to Whom We Don't Speak.

Maddie took everything in with a straighter face than usual, and didn't comment. She hadn't heard about Scott's death until she arrived in the building that morning; otherwise, just maybe, she wouldn't have worn red.

Menken called us into the conference room in groups, and gave us the news we already knew. He informed us that we should cooperate fully with the police—who were for some reason beyond his powers of rational understanding not yet satisfied that Scott's death was a suicide, and would probably be questioning various members of the staff, just background information, don't worry—but of course, the company policy regarding proprietary information was to be honored. The company would be holding a memorial service on Monday morning, at St. Andrew's Episcopal down on Broadway, the receptionist would give details. Scott's remains would be returned to Albany, New York, for interment in the family burial plot. An expression of sympathy for the family was being made on behalf of the company. Any questions, see Dave Smith.

Sergeant Ortega poked his head in my door at about ten. "Good morning," he said. "I have a few more questions for you, okay?"

"Um—"

Maddie went on point.

Ortega nodded to her in a pleasant, mannerly way.

I wasn't sure what to do. I wanted to do my civic duty, but perhaps the Eau de Police Informant wouldn't do much to improve my already questionable welcome at Blackfeet. I defaulted to good manners. "Sergeant Ortega, this is Maddie McNutt. Maddie for Madeline." Maddie began to show some spirit, rolling her eyes at my introduction.

Ortega bowed to Maddie with grave courtesy, then gave her one of his best smiles. He turned back to me. "Well, okay now," he said, pulling the spare chair up across the desk from me. He pulled out his little pad and made a show of getting a pen from his inside jacket pocket, sweeping it out with a flourish. "Mr. Menken here says you and Mr. Dinsmoore were working on the same project. Can you tell me something about that?"

It was clear that the sergeant didn't know the first thing about the oil business, namely that special knowledge is invaluable. Work is simply not discussed with outsiders, unless there is something to be gained by leaking certain bits of information, and even then only selected details would be divulged. If I sat here and chirped away to the first outsider who came along—someone whose notes might become a matter of public record, no less—I could hang up the hope of ever becoming an insider. I glanced over at Maddie. She was staring with her usual candor.

Ortega beamed a smile at her, even went so far as to wave.

She nodded back, held her pose.

He cleared his throat, with gusto.

She smiled, beatifically.

Ortega crooned, "Perhaps we could use the conference room, Miss Hansen, so Madeline"—he sang her name and bowed deeply toward her—"can get some work done." He smiled shyly, as if he were asking me down to the soda shop for a malt.

Oh, perfect: I'll just go behind closed doors with the guy. Now everyone can speculate on what was said, get fully paranoid. I gave Ortega a smile designed to look like my mouth was full of wet plaster.

Ortega rose to his feet, I heaved a sigh and followed him down the hall, figuring I'd strike a balance between cooperation and conservatism, so that I wouldn't spill any company beans, and would not be questioned again.

As we trooped down that hard beige hallway, we passed through the scrutiny of several geologists and engineers, two secretaries, and a technician. They examined us with brooding eyes, silently marking our passage, staring darkly over their coffee mugs.

I'll admit that once we were in the conference room with that door shut, curiosity got the better of me, and I said, "This was suicide, right?"

"These are just some routine questions," Ortega said, not answering my question.

That sparked a pang of jealousy. Damn it, *I* wanted to be asking the questions.

Ortega took a seat at the big table and made a show of settling in, making it clear he could and would outwait any attempt to withhold information. So what the hell: I stated in matter-of-fact tones that yes, I was working on the same field Scott had, and was having minor problems with it, mostly because I was so new. I was rather proud of that bit of obfuscation.

"And like you told me last night, you knew the deceased for only ten days?" Ortega asked.

"Nine. I can probably name each time I laid eyes on him." I thought this would sound extremely earnest and get me off the hot seat.

"Try me." Ortega smiled and sat poised to drink up my words, like I was the Oracle herself snorting fumes at Delphi.

So I told him what I knew of Scottie, short of speculation on the significance of his tartan pants. I described how Scottie had behaved each time I met him, without quite telling him how that reflected on company business. I described his nervousness at the committee meeting, his histrionics over the morning report, his secretiveness over the phone call he'd gotten from the mysterious Simon, his march down to Menken's office on Monday, and his odd behavior around the call on Wednesday afternoon. I slipped up a little by mentioning that Scott kept a desk diary in a red notebook, but rationalized that the police either already had it or that it wouldn't mean anything to them, any more than it had to me.

When I got out of my chair at the end of the interview, I smiled confidently, relieved that this would be my last discussion with the good sergeant. And a tiny bit disappointed.

"Okay, thanks, Emily," he said. "See you around."

"Around, sir?"

"The neighborhood."

"The what?"

He laughed. "We're sort of neighbors, remember? On West Thirtieth. Welcome to the *barrio*."

At eleven, Pete phoned me at my desk: "Hi, Emily. Can your stomach handle lunch after your little chat with the Gold Dust twins?"

"Who?"

"Officers Mutt and Jeff."

"I got just the one; how do you rate?"

"Perhaps because . . . ," he paused for greater significance, "I don't have . . . *an alibi*."

I drawled, "You do shock me, sir."

"So; lunch with a wanted man?"

"Just one moment, please, I must check with Mizz Hansen's social calendar." I thought I was joking, but my desk calendar announced, "Brown Palace 11:30." The dreaded Boston Brahmin Memorial Lunch. I had so happily forgotten. "Damn. Um, sorry, not today. Got a command performance with some old acquaintances from school."

"Curse the luck. Ah, well, if the old school tie binds, I shall dine alone." Pete laughed deliciously as he hung up the phone.

The thought of consuming a meal with Topsy Warren and friends gave me gas. I had sworn, upon graduating from prep school, that I would never trouble myself to see them again. But here I was, once again doing what my grandmother expected of me. *What a wimp,* I thought, as the elevator coughed me out at the street-level lobby.

I stepped out into the midday Colorado brilliance and squinted upward at the bright slot of blue sky overhead. Deep shadows accentuated the canyonlike walls of the skyscrapers that had been tossed up along Seventeenth Street during the building boom of the early eighties, when Canadian investment money had flowed across the border in search of greener pastures. Scores of offices still lay empty, their blank windows hanging over the street like gaping maws, mute testimony to a recession in the global economy that reached far beyond commodities.

I looked up Seventeenth Street toward the Platte River, wishing I were heading that way, instead of toward lunch with people I was sure, like me, would rather skip it. I couldn't quite see Union Station, where the street begins. The street rises from the station like an architectural history lesson, passing between Victorian brick hotels, turn-of-the-century stone massifs, and fifties low-rises, to the reflective-glass-and-steel behemoths of the eighties. The Cattlemen's Exchange Building loomed over my head, its copper-tinted windows reflecting the traffic and opposite buildings at street level and the sky high above. One-way traffic churned past me like rapids at the bottom of a canyon, sluicing toward its confluence with Broadway, where a thirty-six-story steel obelisk of offices split the stream with its sharp-edged geometry.

I turned toward the Brown Palace Hotel and urged myself to move. My feet dragged as if they were made of lead, much as I love that beautiful old hotel.

It boggled my imagination that these classmates were here in Denver. This little cow town wasn't half classy enough for them, even if they were still in the beginning of the big career climb. Why hadn't their family connections bought them into Boston, or New York?

Topsy Warren. I cringed at the thought of listening to her nasal laugh while I tried to swallow lunch.

Rachel Conant. She had always been too preoccupied with the boys at Phillips Academy to give me much trouble. Not the little social-climbing shit-stirrer that Topsy was. *But very well connected, so why is she here?*

And Libby Hopkins? I was in fact glad Libby might be there. Libby was separate; not aloof exactly, but sort of detached, marking time. I remembered her as one of the few girls at school who never felt the need to put me in my place. Why would Libby Hopkins take a job as far away from the social hub of the universe as Denver? Certainly, she never *had* to take a job at all.

Just then, I caught a glimpse of myself in the glass front of another building. All I saw was one more businessperson in a pack of businesspeople that stalked the Denver pavement like so many carnivores on the veldt.

Who was this person who stared back at me?

This wasn't a geologist, it was just a scared little girl in her grannie's tweeds, the twisted result of an ill-planned breeding experiment, in which the offspring has neither the thoroughbred lines of the dam, nor the easy temperament of the sire.

As I stared into my reflection in the glass, I saw something that scared me senseless: I was starting to look like my grandmother. As this shock rang through me, I watched my eyes widen, hollowing at the realization that the ghost of my inheritance had invaded my bones. It only strengthened the resemblance.

I spun around and stared across the street, hoping I could somehow escape, but there I was again, my reflection distorted in three different panes of glass.

Mercifully, someone stepped between me and my reflections.

Pete Tutaraitis. Sauntering down the sidewalk on the opposite side of the street. I matched his progress on my side of the street, watching him, wishing I were walking with him instead of dragging myself alone to lunch with the ghosts of prep school past.

Pete turned the corner at Tremont Place. I stopped and watched, still in no hurry to reach the Brown Palace.

About a block down, a man stepped out from a doorway and athletically matched Pete's stride, moving up next to him. He was more broad-shouldered and taller than Pete, wore a similar sort of suit jacket and slacks, and had blond hair. Catching up with Pete, he grabbed him by the arm and said something to him, his lips moving in earnest conversation. Pete turned and stopped, his body English shouting of anger. I was startled; it hadn't occurred to me until that moment that anything could move Pete to rage.

The man pulled at Pete's arm, trying to drag him along. Pete held his ground. The man raised his hands and started backing away down the sidewalk, and judging by his gestures, saying something derogatory. Then he turned and stalked angrily away. Pete followed, caught up and walked close to him, as if he didn't want passersby to hear what he was saying.

12

The Brown Palace Hotel is a very special place, a Denver landmark, the grand gathering place of all the old silver kings and railroad barons. My father used to take me there for lunch, a special treat when we came south for the annual Stock Show. It was built in 1892 by Henry C. Brown, on a plot of land where he used to graze his cow. It is triangular in plan, just like the lot, because it stands at that place where Denver's streets make a forty-five-degree turn to accommodate the clash between two camps of founding developers, one of which thought Denver should align itself with the banks of the Platte River, and the other of which adhered to the north-south-east-west orthodoxy of the Great Plains. The hotel's architecture is handsome and opulent, eight floors of red sandstone and granite Italian Renaissance splendor rising majestically from the very heart of Denver. Inside, the bright Colorado sunlight filters down through a stained-glass roof onto the seven floors of balconies, ornate cast-iron grillwork, and white onyx pillars that line the atrium lobby. How I used to tip back my head and stare.

Today I was trying to look blasé.

Topsy was waiting in the lobby, her indelicate bulk cranked sideways a bit as she peered into one of the illuminated display boxes that advertised the fine shops housed around the street level of the hotel. "Emmy," she said, straightening up to give me a tiny peck on the cheek. "What fun. This is almost like being back in Boston. It's so nice having a few people from the real world show up out here. I'd lose my mind if Rachel and Libby weren't here. Really. I mean, Denver is trying to be a real city, but you know. Oh, here's Rachel; what timing. Raaaachel," she cooed, rushing up and pressing an awkward hug onto Rachel's uninterested body.

Rachel disengaged from Topsy's embrace and brushed back a lock of her perfect, chocolate-brown hair. She said, "Em.

Nice to see you. Libby won't be joining us. She's still away."
No smiles. Vintage Rachel. I felt gratified when she raised an
eyebrow ever so slightly at my new appearance.

We crossed the lobby to the Ship Tavern, and at Rachel's
command were seated at the center of the room, near the massive ship's mast that holds up the timbered ceiling. I gazed
longingly at the antique ship models; my father used to sit me
on his shoulders so I could touch the one over the door. But
today I was here on business, and trying to be an adult, whatever that was.

While we examined the menu, Topsy chatted about how
boring the Colorado autumn was, next to good old New England; how she missed the *marvelous* reds and oranges of the
sugar maples, how the locals here *did* go on about the aspen
gold, when all she could see was plain, boring yellow.

Rachel wasn't listening, apparently preoccupied with some
young buck at the bar. When the waiter materialized to take
our orders, she said, "The trout. White wine," without shifting
her gaze.

"Oh, yes, doesn't that sound marvelous," Topsy exulted.
"Good idea. I'll have that, too."

"Mmm, yes, I haven't had trout since last month, in Yellow-
stone," I said, feeling a little blasphemous for contorting my
fishing trips with decent, straightforward Frank into a competi-
tive chip. "Nice twelve-inch native cutthroat trout," I added, as
if they knew the difference. Then I glanced at the price of *this*
trout. Fifteen dollars. I considered ordering a buffalo burger
with Swiss cheese instead, but my pride couldn't wait until I
had a few paychecks under my belt.

Somewhere over the salad course Topsy's conspiratorial
lament about the horrors of cow town living broadened to the
surrounding territories, and she asked me, "Surely you understand, Emmy. You lived out west somewhere before school,
didn't you? Where was it, Minnesota? Or was it Wisconsin or
something?"

"Wyoming. The other 'W' state."

"Oh, right. That's north of here, right?"

"Yeah." *It's the next state, dipshit, and if you hate
cows* . . . Struggling to keep my temper down, I changed the
subject. "So, where are you guys working?"

Topsy answered for both. "I'm a buyer for the Denver Dry.
It's good experience. It'll ready me for Bergdorf's, or some
other New York store. Soon. When I'm ready. Rachel's work-

ing for the governor at the state capitol until her husband"—
she said the word with an odd, perhaps jealous zest, pointedly
mimicking Rachel's steady gaze toward the bar—"gets pro-
moted back out of here. Her dad got her the job. You remember, he's a senator. Connections; right, Rachel?"

Rachel didn't reply. Her quarry at the bar was answering
with a steady loaded stare. She appeared not to notice as the
waiter expertly set her entree down in front of her.

"You like your work, Rachel?" I asked.

"Yes."

"What's your husband do?"

"Merrill Lynch."

Topsy continued her dissertation: "Libby doesn't work, of
course. For money, I mean; she does charity work for the art
museum when she's here. Like Rachel, she's only here because of her husband, too." Her attention veered back to
Rachel. "So where's Libby gotten herself to this time, Rachel?
Back east with Mum and Daddy again? Getting tired of *her*
husband?" Topsy ripped off one of her nasal laughs and forked
some trout into her mouth. "So Emmy, you're doing something with the oil business? I forget what Mother said." As I
opened my mouth to reply, Topsy suddenly grabbed Rachel's
shoulder. "Oh, Rachel! The oil business! I almost forgot to tell
you! Did you hear that Scott Dinsmoore died last night?"

Rachel's brow furrowed. Slowly, her gaze shifted to the
tablecloth, and then to the end of Topsy's nose. When she finally spoke, her words came out small and wistful: "Scottie?
What happened?"

I said, "You guys knew—" but Topsy cut across my words.

"Marcie Jacobson phoned last night late from Virginia to
tell me. She heard from Scottie's sister. I couldn't sleep *all
night.*"

I set down my fork, my stomach sinking.

Rachel looked irritated, disconsolate; like she was being
awakened from sleep with a hangover. "Scottie?" she whispered.

Topsy slapped a hand across her mouth in horror. "Rachel! I
forgot! You used to *date* him, didn't you?"

A look of sulking irritation weighted Rachel's flawless face.
"I'd hardly call it that. I tired of him rather quickly." She
glanced at me. My face must have shown my horror, because
she quickly added, "The poor sap. I hadn't seen him in
months."

"You'll never believe how he did it," said Topsy.

My trout came to life again, thrashing in my stomach like it had just been hooked. I said, "Hey listen, guys—"

"He went out that sixteenth-floor window of the building that Gerry what's-his-name went out last week. Oh!" She slapped her hand over her mouth again, and then clamped back onto Rachel's already half-crushed shoulder. "They *knew* each other, didn't they? Do you suppose there's a *connection?*"

Rachel's reply was tart. "No. One fool committing suicide is happenstance, two is coincidence, *three* is perversion."

"Well. Anyway, he was dead on arrival at Denver General—"

"Topsy, I'm eating!" Rachel snapped.

Even as my stomach turned on edge, my mind whirred with questions: how did they know Scott Dinsmoore and Gerald Luftweiller, for that matter? And just what *was* the connection between them?

Topsy stared morbidly at her trout, enraptured by the drama of the situation. "We have to tell Libby, don't we." It was a statement, not a question.

Rachel signaled the waiter for the check, so forcefully that he all but slid up to the table like a runner making home plate. Rachel pulled a five and a ten out of her pocketbook, slapped it onto the check, rose, and slung her pocketbook onto her shoulder, all in one cool motion. She smoothed her skirt, staring levelly at Topsy. "I forgot. I have a meeting. Em, nice to see you. We'll have lunch again sometime." She left the restaurant, with the barest glance toward the bar. Two heartbeats later, Mr. Interesting glanced theatrically at his watch and excused himself from his companions, abandoning a full beer.

Topsy hunched her head down between her meaty shoulders. "Do you think she's upset about something?" she asked.

I chose not to dignify her question with an answer, instead concentrating on the check: forty-five dollars and change; with tip, it would be something over fifty. Rachel had pulled the old preppie stunt of ordering the most and then dividing the tab in even thirds, this time not even accounting for the tip. Glowering, I pulled out a twenty. My dear classmates always did have a way of spending my money for me.

On another channel, my mind was still racing, trying to fit Scott and Gerald Luftweiller together in the jigsaw puzzle. What Topsy had just said didn't jibe with a statement Scott had made in the coffee room chatter that first day: he had said he did not know the man who had jumped.

On the way out to the street, I tried to pump Topsy for information about Scott and Gerald Luftweiller. She didn't say much, except that they had all known each other in college, "after we knew Scottie at school." When I looked blank on that one, she screwed up her face and stared at me, appalled at my ignorance. "Come now; you remember Scottie and Rachel." She turned her gaze down Broadway, toward the Sixteenth Street Mall, where a shuttle bus was just squealing up to the stop. "Oh, damn it, there's my shuttle."

"Was he at Phillips Academy?" I asked. It was the obvious guess.

"No, Holderness."

Her tone suggested dismissal. Digging down for my last ounce of persistence, I said: "In fact, I don't remember him."

"I've got to go, Emmy; we can catch up on social things another time." Her tone was now decidedly condescending. Topsy never had been capable of sustained subtlety. As the light changed, she stepped off the curb, her square hips lurching as she lengthened her stride.

I clenched my teeth together, trying not to say what I was thinking. *Okay, so you got yourself snubbed; must you pass it on to me?* Anger rising in my throat, I called, "Speak into the mike, Topsy; when would I have met Scott?"

Topsy didn't break stride. As another bus hove into view, she accelerated into an ungainly trot I hadn't seen since our last game of field hockey senior year. Over her shoulder she hollered, "The dances. You know."

The dances I didn't know. I had managed to miss most of those insufferable dances with the boys' schools, feigning stomach flu or menstrual cramps, or simply hiding in the stables. Having my horse with me at school had been the thing that made those years bearable.

I stood in the mile-high Denver sunlight, remembering the darkness of my prep school's stables where I'd hide, cuddling Gypsy's wonderful arching neck, trying not to get my best dress smelling like horse. That had been long ago and far away. I tried to assure myself that I was a grown woman now, free to come and go as I wished. But deep inside, I was acutely aware that I was once again dressed up in pretty clothes that would bind me if I tried to run.

13

The concrete sidewalk was hard under my feet as I stalked back up Seventeenth Street. I stopped short of the entrance to the Cattlemen's Exchange Building and leaned back, tipping my head to search for the openness of the sky, but clouds slid by on an autumn wind, giving the weird impression that the building was falling forward, rather than that the clouds were moving past.

A voice within asked, *Why go back to this non-job?* I didn't have a viable answer. Traffic ground by behind me, filling the air with its din. For a moment, I teetered on the brink of aiming my feet toward the bus station and heading home, wherever that was. My left hand floated west, a precursor to turning.

One of Blackfeet's engineers came into view, closing fast from uptown. I squinted at her, trying to remember her name. Angie? A glint of recognition shot through her eyes, too, but she quickly looked away.

As Angie swept past me in her musky perfume and silk, I followed her, hurrying through the doorway in an effort to stay close. Pride had once again overwhelmed fear: at least this day I would continue as planned. If I ever did back down, disappearing back into the prairie like a wounded coyote, I would do it without witnesses.

Upstairs in the coffee room, I found a klatsch of my so-called colleagues lounging against the counter. As I stepped in, they abruptly ended their conversation and just stared at me, unsmiling. Ignoring them as best I could, I poured a mug and headed to my desk, my grip so tight my knuckles turned white.

How I'd envied the geologists and engineers who had come out to the drill rigs to "slum it" and take a break from office routine. For nearly five years, I had existed in the lowest strata of the oil business, avoiding rejection, not daring to seek work as a geologist, never admitting even to myself how dearly I

coveted the authority and self-confidence that seemed to come
with the job. Even when Menken had thrown this job in my
lap, I'd put him off for months. But in the end, Frank had
pressed me to give the job a try. "You got machinery you've
never used," he'd said. "You'll always wonder what you
missed. Maybe you'll start feeling sorry you stayed." He had
smiled sadly. "Go get it out of your system, Em, then come
back to me."

Just now "back" seemed painfully far away.

After downing that cup of coffee, I phoned the field office
at Lost Coyote to knock a few heads over the fact that I was
still having to consult the daily reports to get any information
on the drilling. No one answered.

The rest of that day crawled by. Nothing I put my eyes to
made sense. I tried to read some on the Mesozoic sandstones
of Wyoming, the better to understand the vagaries of Lost
Coyote Field, but over and again I found that I had read whole
pages without absorbing a single word. The mind of a geologist does not think in a straight line. It's a frustrating thing,
given to long periods of anxiety-ridden data-gathering followed by the rare but breathtaking leap of intuition.

If I could grasp the geometry of the sandstone—distance
and thickness and quality and repetition of pattern—and embrace them all at once, I would know where the porous sandstone would be most bountiful in its production of oil and gas.
Then I would have something. Then I could march into the
committee room and say *Pay attention, boys and girls, I have
the answer*.

But no such understanding came. I kept staring at a drawing
in one article that illustrated the sequence of rock layers in the
neighborhood of the field, from surface down to the bottom of
the Mesozoic-aged strata. It was drawn like a column, showing
alternating layers of sandstone, shale, sandstone, shale, sandstone, and shale, ad nauseam. An uneven layer cake made of
grit.

Even less enlightening was the electrical log printed next to
the rock column. As a petroleum geologist, I was supposed to
be able to glance at an E-log and "see" the rock column that
had produced it; but much as I stared, the E-log was still just a
wiggly line to me.

I tried to imagine myself in the oil field, standing by the
wellhead on the drilling rig as the boys from the logging com-

pany lowered the electrical resistivity sensor on a cable down thousands of feet of bore hole, their massive winch humming with the effort. The boys always cursed and worried and ate too many doughnuts, afraid the sensor would snag on a rough spot in the hole. They'd get the gadget on bottom and then climb into the air-conditioned electronics parlor in the back of their truck and tune their recording instruments, like so many wizards making sure their magic toad's foot was working. Then they'd reverse the winch and slowly draw the sensor back up the hole, data flowing up the cable and into their computer by the megabyte. Many a time I had hung out and mooched their coffee, watching the pen sway left and right on the CRT monitor as the enormous winch slowly wound the cable back up into daylight. Or starlight, as the case may be. A rig runs around the clock.

I knew that if I could get good at working with the E-logs, I could recognize one rock formation from another at a glance, just like a signature. I could use the log signature to correlate a single sandstone layer from one well to the next clear across a field. I could lay the logs out next to each other and say *Ah, yes, this well is good, but see here? The sand pinches out before we get to this well, over here*.

But today I threw down my pen in frustration. One wiggle still looked just like another to me. For all I knew, I would be correlating a sandstone to a limestone.

I left at four-thirty sharp, the earliest instant I could leave with dignity. The bus ride home was the usual exercise in culture shock. I tripped on a crack in the sidewalk as I approached the house. When I found a note from Elyria on the kitchen counter saying she had been called away to New Orleans, my day was complete.

Feeling supremely sorry for myself, I pulled a tortilla out of the refrigerator and tossed it onto a burner on the stove to heat while I chased into the bathroom for a good piss. Upon my return, the tortilla was in flames. I flipped it into the sink with a pair of tongs, switched off the gas, and stomped into my bedroom, where I tore off my fancy duds, heaving the tweeds onto the floor. The sleeves of the suit jacket seemed to reach menacingly for my ankles. I snarled at it.

I sprinted down the basement stairs in my underwear, in search of the blue jeans I'd dropped through the laundry chute the night before. I wrestled my way into the least filthy pair of denims and a flannel cowboy shirt, yanked an abandoned load from the washer into the dryer, thrashed the rest of my jeans into the washing machine, tossed in some soap, punched the machine onto the heavy-duty, extra-hot, no-holds-barred cycle, and whipped my hands into the air. *The crowd cheers! Once again, folks, the remarkable Em Hansen of Chugwater, Wyoming, has ridden the barrels perfectly, and at record speed! Let's give the little lady a hand, how 'bout it?*

I stood in front of the big white appliances as they whooshed and growled into life. There was something nice about being down there, in the far dark corner of Elyria's basement, dealing with known quantities like a washer and dryer. I leaned against the washer. Its warmth and gurgling reminded me of naps I used to take when I was a little girl, curled up on top of my mother's mammoth old machine. As it settled into an agitation cycle, the rhythms of memory gently carried me far away from new jobs, old enemies, falling bodies, and the surety that I was in way over my head. The dryer ticked and whocked happily as the zipper on something heavy went round and round. The machines grew warm to the touch. I crawled up and stretched out on top of them and in no time at all fell asleep.

Having had that nap on top of the washing machines, I couldn't fall asleep when I went to bed. Night city noises moaned and crashed all around me, reminding me minute by sleepless minute that I wasn't in Wyoming. I lay awake, my mind caught up in Blackfeet's unsolved puzzles and my body roused by the image of Pete Tutaraitis's smile. My mind kept gnawing at the inconsistencies in Lost Coyote Field, at the mystery of Scott's death, and at Pete's odd lack of information about the field. Pete again. Pete seemed to think there was nothing wrong with the field, it was my job to prove that, wasn't it? Either way, there was nothing I could do about it until morning, so why not sleep? What, sleep when your co-worker has thrown himself out of a sixteenth-floor window?

At eleven-thirty, I tried to phone Frank, but got no answer. It felt weird to be so out of touch with him. I tried to bring his face to mind, but was discomfited to find that his face was already beginning to fade from my memory.

Along about midnight, I gave up on the game of lying rigid with my eyes squeezed shut, and went into the living room to watch the Tonight Show and most of a very dreary movie that followed. It must have been two or three when I finally dozed off on the couch. The ensuing neck crick awoke me at five, at which time I staggered back to my bed and slept fitfully. As the sky grew light, I finally fell into a deep sleep and snoozed through the radio alarm as it croaked out all sorts of National Public Radio death, doom, intellectual analysis, and disaster.

The phone woke me at seven-twenty, minutes before I should have been hustling out the door to the bus stop. *I can't handle this job,* I thought, as I fumbled the phone off its cradle.

It was Elyria, calling from New Orleans to ask if I would please cram an antiobitic tablet down the dog's muzzle.

"Sure," I croaked into the phone. This suited me just fine: take my mood out on the aging, flatulent doggie.

"Em, is everything okay?"

"What can I say?"

"Ah. Well, I hate to ask, then, but can you take care of the dog until Sunday? I've run into some friends, and we were thinking of taking in some music and crawfish *étouffée.*"

"No problem," I said, my heart sinking at the thought of a weekend alone in Greater Metropolitan Denver. I rang off. *I can't handle this job. Why did I come here?*

Dog and I eyed each other across the kitchen with treachery in our hearts. Cornering his ancient, malodorous frame next to the refrigerator, I pinned him between my knees, pried open his fetid mouth, crammed the monster pill past his horrible yellow fangs, and jumped up with my hands in the air, signaling to the rodeo judges that the calf was tied. *The crowd roars. The smell of the steers and bucking broncos fills my nostrils. The dog spits the pill onto the linoleum.*

I can't handle this job. It became a mantra.

After wrestling pooch-o down again, banging my knee against the stove in the process, I dumped some kibbles in his dish and some star-shaped doodads in the cat's, stuffed a doughnut in my mouth, and hastily took stock of what morning rituals I could skip in hopes of making the 7:42 bus.

I can't handle this job. "I can skip everything but clothes," I muttered to the dog, as I stumbled back into my bedroom, leaving a trail of doughnut crumbs. "I don't need a shower, do I? You and your friends won't follow me down the block, will you?"

The dog sighed and crunched his kibbles. I guess nobody with any class does notice.

I gassed myself with deodorant, jumped back into yesterday's pantyhose and the least wrinkled blouse out of the dryer, kicked the dog outside, and ran for the bus.

The 7:42 was on time that morning. As I reached Thirty-second Avenue, I could just see the metal leviathan fading toward town in a haze of diesel fumes.

When I finally did get to work, half an hour late, I wondered what my hurry had been. I was depressed and angry and scared and slightly giddy, all at once. *Two weeks on the job,* I mused, *I don't know shit, my coffee's cold, and I hate these shoes. Maybe the world will end today, and make life a little simpler.*

Fritz, as sniveling and snakelike as ever, brought me the morning report at nine o'clock. This time, he didn't even grunt.

Maddie made big eyes at him and crooned, "I hear jackalopes ride by the full moon, sweetie pea." Her fashion statement for the day featured a very large scale black-and-yellow hound's-tooth check on linen with a Peter Pan collar. Somehow it reminded me of Elyria's dog. She squeezed her shoulders forward voluptuously, eclipsing two columns of teeth.

Fritz didn't react. I guess his Walkman was up so high it had pureed whatever it was he had for a brain. Ten seconds later he returned and tossed a box onto my desk. "Forgot," he said, as he sloped back out of the room.

As I watched Fritz's narrow behind retreat, I asked Maddie, "Who's in charge of drilling at Lost Coyote now?"

"Same as always."

That didn't tally. Scott was supposed to have been in charge, and he sure wasn't calling the shots now. "To whom do you refer, Mizz McNutt?" I said, trying to mix haughty grammar with a Texan drawl.

"El Smith-o, whom else?" she drawled in reply.

"But didn't Scott—"

"Smith makes his own rules."

"Of course."

"Knew y'all'd understand," Maddie said, giving me her best Shirley Temple golly-gee smile, complete with the dimples.

Dead end. I couldn't understand Lost Coyote Field from the data I had, and it would be weeks before the well was completed and logged and new information would be available. I sure wasn't going to trot into Dave Smith's office and ask him what was going on.

I clamped my teeth together and concentrated, trying to

fight back the fog of irritation that was obscuring my thought. I contemplated the drill bit, grinding away thousands of feet below the surface, and willed it to chew faster. No luck. When I opened my eyes, I was still stuck in that unnatural box called an office. I opened the box Fritz had left.

It was full of business cards. My business cards. Real, live Blackfeet Oil Company business cards, with my name on them and everything, and right under my name they said "Geologist."

I pulled one card out of the box and laid it on my desk. I ran my fingers over it. The ink was even raised, as if it were engraved, not printed. I couldn't help but grin—it was stupid, perhaps, in light of the fact that I was just sitting there doing nothing, but I felt I had finally arrived. I was downright fondling the thing when Maddie took notice, so I stuffed it into one of the pockets of my suit jacket and forced my attention on the morning report.

The morning report held no surprises. Drilling away at so many thousand feet below surface. Just for the hell of it, I pulled out the Lost Coyote file to see if the earlier wells had been drilled in about the same way. Maybe it would show me something I'd been missing.

The drilling information was not in the file.

"Hey Maddie," I said, "where do they file the dailies for the other wells?"

"In the vault."

"The what?"

"The vault. Ever since someone just walked in here one day and ripped off a whole bunch of files for Bar Diamond Field. Big room down on the tenth floor. You got to sign things out, and all."

I was about to indulge in a fit of frustration over my ignorance when I remembered: that's where Pete got onto the elevator the day I met him. And he'd been carrying a file. Probably one from some field he was working on in California. "So I just go down there and tell them what I want? What all's down there?"

Maddie held up one lovely little hand and enumerated the treasures. "Field files, well files, maps, cross sections, well logs, field reports. You name it. They's getting real particular these days what gets left lying around."

"Field reports? Like on *this* field?"

Maddie snapped her gum. "Doubt it." She went back to work.

"Why?"

"No reason."

"Maddie!"

She looked up. "Aw, loosen up, Emmy, it's a new field. You do a field study on an *old* field, to figure out how to jazz up production."

I reckoned it was time for a trip to the vault.

It wasn't hard to figure out where it was. The elevator disgorged me in a rather plain expanse of hallway, not pretentiously gussied up like the lobby that gave way to the main entrance to Blackfeet Oil, or the one where Gerald Luftweiller had sallied forth from the offices of Love and Christiansen to end whatever pain confounded him. There was only one door. When I stepped through it, I found myself confronted by another hallway leading down toward what looked like a set of bull pens, but close by was a large window with a counter over the lower half of a Dutch door that had a mean-looking dead bolt in it. On the counter was a silver bell like the ones that sit on hotel managers' desks in old movies. Beyond the counter, there was rank upon rank of metal shelving, specially sized to hold Blackfeet's files. I rang the bell.

Deep within the confines of the vault room, I heard a cough. A juicy cough, the sort of cough that comes with years of smoking and goes nowhere.

At length, I heard a chair scrape. Plodding footfalls labored toward the window.

The creature that emerged was a short, pallid woman in her fifties. Her pillowy flesh was loose and unevenly arranged, pushing her shoulders up under her ears, her belly bulging and her buttocks were almost nonexistent. *She drinks, too,* I speculated, gauging the imbalanced nutrients and lack of exercise that created that kind of effect. I forced myself to smile.

And wished I hadn't. The woman smiled back through thin lips that were painted too widely with a bad shade of lipstick. The smile gave way to an unsuccessful attempt to muffle another sodden cough.

"May I have the well files for Lost Coyote Field?" I asked, and as an afterthought added, "And the well logs?"

She coughed again, apparently kick-starting her voice,

which wheezed out with overtones of oiled gravel: "And whom might you be?"

Points for trying with the grammar, I thought. "I'm Em Hansen, the new geologist for Wyoming."

"Hansen, Hansen," she said, thumbing through a sheaf of well-worn pages on a clipboard. "Not here."

My face fell. Was I really this much of a nonperson?

Catching my expression, she said, "Hold on, let me call Personnel." She stepped to a wall phone and dialed, said, "I've got a girl here named Hansen, says she works for us. Uh-huh, uh-huh. Okay, thanks." After hanging up, she shuffled off down between the stacks and started pulling files.

I stared down the shelves full of files. Whole shelves had yellow tabs, others had green. The ones she brought me were orange. "What do the colors on the tabs mean?" I asked, leaning over the counter so she could hear me.

Her voice hacked out from behind a shelf ten feet away. "Orange is Wyoming. Green, California; yellow, Texas; and so on." She hurried the end of her sentence to make way for a cough.

Something niggled at the back of my mind. Something funny about the colored tabs. Then I remembered the file Pete had been carrying, the day I met him on the elevator. It was orange for Wyoming, not green for California. He had gotten on the elevator on ten. He had been coming from here. What had he been doing with a Wyoming file?

"You got to sign for these, honey," the woman rasped, from the depths of the vault. "Notebook on the counter."

The notebook was lying open, with a ballpoint pen attached to it by a white string. The page had a column for the date, one for my name, and one for the files I was taking. Mine was the first entry under October third. There was a heavy line drawn under the last entry for October second.

I quickly flipped backward, trying to calculate the date for the previous Friday, when I'd met Pete on the elevator. *Let's see, thirty days hath September . . . that makes last Friday the twenty-sixth.*

Pete's name was not on the list for Friday, September twenty-sixth. I looked backward three days and forward two, but no Pete Tutaraitis.

As the woman brought the first load toward the counter, she said, "Do you want me to have Fritz take these up for you?"

"No." Maybe paranoia was setting in, but it occurred to me

that if it got out that I was actually looking at real data, someone might come take it away from me. Instead, I had her load
the fan-folded well logs and the stacks of manila folders into a
cardboard box, but I wound up making two trips, anyway.

Back in my office, I stuffed the booty into an available shelf
on my bookcase (they were all available, in fact, except for the
top rack, which held my company policy manual), and started
to read the files. Sorry to say, they didn't tell me much. For
which, read: I really didn't know what I was looking at. Broken record, I know.

What I was looking at were drawings of well completion di-
agrams, showing details of casing pipe and sucker rods. Then
there were the dailies, listing details of the drilling and also
how long the field crew had to swab the well to get the flow
started when they had completed drilling and casing the well.
Like milking a cow, it's sometimes hard to get her to let down
her milk.

Now, I've been on dozens of rigs as a mudlogger, and know
a lot about what goes into drilling a well, but my job was always over when the drill bit hit TD, or total depth. I'd have my
trailer packed up and I'd be towing it out of the yard as the
semi tractors pulled in hauling the casing pipe. The tender
mysteries of well completion and stimulation I had never witnessed. I knew that there was lots of pumping and testing that
was done after the well was put on-line, to gauge production
rates and the most economical way to produce the field.

I began to sink into a mire of despair, brought on by my
own ignorance. *Yawn. They test the pressure, they test the production rates . . .*

Latest gas tests wet.

Scott's little notebook. Of course!

I jumped up from my chair and hurried down the hall toward Scott's office, to see if it was still there.

It wasn't there. The lap drawer of Scott's desk held no red
spiral-bound notebook. I leaned at an awkward angle over
Scott's desk, my heart surging with excitement, digging
through the drawer beyond the lap drawer. I was on the edge
of discovery, I knew it. I was going to figure out something
important, something that would show these people that I had
talent, if not knowledge. I'd show these jumped-up baboons in
business clothes, I'd show Topsy and Rachel, I'd show Mad-

die, I'd show . . . I leaned farther over the desk to pull out the next drawer down.

"I couldn't find it either."

I about jumped out of my skin. I had been so intent on my quarry that I hadn't heard Sergeant Ortega enter the room. When I whirled around to face him, he was smiling his little happy smile, his dark eyes warm and friendly.

"Are you sure he kept it in that drawer?" Ortega continued.

I recovered as best I could, hoping I was not about to get arrested for tampering with evidence. "Well, I only saw it the once. Do you suppose he had it with him when he fell?" Maybe it was time the nice man told *me* a few things.

"No, not much but his wallet. He left his attaché case here, by his desk." Ortega indicated the space between the end of the desk and the wall. "Not much in it but a calculator and the *Denver Post*." He shrugged his shoulders, like the joke was on him. "Any more ideas?"

"His house?"

His eyes danced appreciatively. "Okay, we checked there. His house was tidy as this place. I don't think we missed anything."

Of course, you've been through everything, haven't you. I said, "How about his car?"

"Okay, we looked through his car, too. Nothing but a little service record book and a bunch of gas credit card receipts." He smiled, rolling his eyes skyward. "And evidence that he had a dog."

"A dog? What kind, a Scottie?"

Ortega laughed. "No, an Irish setter, I think. There were stiff red hairs in his car, not like human. Funny thing, though, there was no dog at his house."

"Maybe it was just a buddy hitching a ride."

Ortega laughed again, a kind of charming little snort. As he patted his knee to magnify his appreciation of my wit, he ever so casually asked, "So what do you need the notebook for?"

I glanced reflexively at the door, to make sure no one was listening.

Ortega smiled his little smile and shrugged his shoulders, as if to say, *Well, you can't fault me for trying.*

At which juncture I realized that I was having more fun than I'd had since I'd arrived in Denver. So I smiled.

Ortega grinned. Then he bowed, a quick dip forward with

his head and shoulders. How's a dame supposed to resist such charm?

"You were saying," he said.

I sat down in Scott's chair. *To hell with the office mafia. The police have permission to be here, and I'm going to have a little fun with this guy.* "I was saying. I was saying that I was looking for the red notebook in the hope that I could figure out what Scott was about to tell me. So you were saying, maybe, why Scott went to talk to Menken instead, and what he said when he got there."

"Oh, okay. Okay, fair enough." Ortega sat down in the chair across the desk, as if now I was Scott and Ortega was me. "They talked about his promotion."

"His what?"

Ortega turned his palms toward the ceiling. "That's what the man said. He says Mr. Dinsmoore wanted to know what his future was with the company, and whether he was going to get a promotion."

"That doesn't fit."

Ortega shrugged.

I got an inspiration. "Did you go through the newspaper in his attaché? Was there anything marked up?"

Ortega rolled his eyes heavenward, emitted a faint whistle. "Smart woman. Yes, he had circled several houses to rent in the classifieds. He ever talk to you about moving?"

Ortega peered at me so intently that the seriousness of the game came back to me. "Why are you telling me this, Sergeant? Isn't it your usual procedure to keep details of the case from the public until it's solved?"

Ortega gazed at the ceiling, as if considering his answer. "Oh, I don't know. Let's just say it seems okay to tell you. Who knows? Maybe you'll help me figure things out." He made a gesture with both hands, wiggling his fingers toward each other as if they were sparring partners, and smiled.

"Then tell me why this 'case' hasn't been put to rest as a suicide yet."

Ortega nodded, and proceeded with utter seriousness: "Yes, okay—here's how it is. A person dies. No one saw this person die, or should I say, we have no known witness to tell us why or how this person died. Okay, so that is what we call an unexplained death. Okay. So the law says the police must investigate and make a case for the mode of death: is this death homicide, suicide, or accident?"

"He didn't seem suicidal."

Ortega looked at me with deep sadness. "That's not always easy to know. Miss Emily, you are a funny mixture. In some ways you are old, very old, a true *sabio*. In others, you are so, so *candida, sin afectación* . . . pardon me, please; at times *inglés* does not provide the word that has the feeling. I mean no offense. *Inglés* is my language as much as *castellaño,* but it's such a cold language sometimes."

Embarrassed at this sudden intimacy, I changed the subject: "So what you're telling me is that you haven't been able to establish which category Scott's death belongs in. Your evidence is inconclusive."

"At this time, let's say inconclusive, yes. So tell me more about this Lost Coyote Field." He pronounced *Coyote* as three syllables, with the accent on the second. It made the word sound much more vital, even romantic.

"Well, I don't know that much," I began, but stopped.

Ortega smiled encouragingly. "Perhaps you can tell me what Mr. Dinsmoore wrote in his red notebook that day."

"Oh, that the gas was testing wet." I shrugged, making it seem unimportant. I began to fiddle nervously with a button on my jacket.

"Anything else?"

I stuck my hands in my suit jacket pockets, trying to bring them and my mouth under control. Inside the pocket, my right hand closed over my brand-new business card, and I ran my fingertips over its raised letters as I considered my next move.

Ortega watched me patiently. It reminded me of a look I'd seen in my Uncle Skinny's eyes, when he was observing a new colt he was about to ride for the first time: a look of deeply centered patience, as if he was taking time to plan his approach. "I talked to Elyria yesterday afternoon," he said.

"Oh?" *Why is he bringing her up all of a sudden?*

"Yes, she was getting ready to go to New Orleans. So pretty, in a suit the color of the sky." He panned his left hand up in an arc and looked skyward, as if he could see the heavens through the stories of steel and plaster that hung over his head.

God, he was good.

He smiled his smile. "My heart always lifts at the sight of her. I say, 'Okay, Elyria, where you off to this time?' and she says New Orleans. Always running off somewhere. 'You need my baby brother Salvador to feed the dog?' I ask, but she says no, she's got Em Hansen staying there, and how happy she is to have you. She's been so alone without Bill. I say, 'Of course, I've met that Em, I questioned her about this case I'm on,' and she says stick close to that Em Hansen, she's the one who figured out who killed Bill. Yes, we had quite a little talk." He tipped his round head to one side expectantly, softening the gravity of his unspoken request.

How dearly I would have preferred that Elyria had kept her mouth shut. Now I would be hearing from this cop until the case was solved. My choice seemed clear: I could cooperate, tell the nice policeman everything I learned and risk losing my job, or I could be faithful to the hand that fed me—that big, insensate hand that gave me a cushy office and a fat salary.

I pulled the business card out of my pocket and looked at it. As I studied that card, I noticed that the hand that held it was beginning to heal from the rigors of drill rig life. The cuticles were no longer cracked, and the once-omnipresent cuts and calluses were fading. I thought of how my mother chided me each time she saw my hands. "Have some pride, Emily," she'd say, "wear gloves, or at least rub those miserable hands of yours with lotion." How I used to stare at her elegant, smooth fingers, which seldom did more work than lighting another cigarette. My hands had been like my father's, short-fingered and rough. My father's hands were working hands, like Frank's.

Frank. His calluses used to catch in my hair.

I thought of Peter Tutaraitis, with warm, smooth muscle beneath his pinpoint shirts and flannel slacks. *His* hands were not chapped or callused. His hand against my back had been a new sensation, warm and fine.

I sighed. "That was a fluke, Sergeant," I said, in tones measured to sound sincere. "I'm a geologist, not a detective."

14

I returned to my office and sat, waiting for the morning to melt away. If the job was just to sit, then fine, I'd just sit. Maybe Pete would call, asking me to lunch. I managed to sit for twenty minutes, after which I decided that Pete must be out of town, and I was ready for a nice, long anxiety break. I headed down the hallway and installed myself in a stall.

I was just realizing that if I stayed in the women's room long enough I wouldn't have to worry about whether Pete called me or not, when I heard the outer door open. Two of the engineering staff came in, in mid-conversation:

". . . this weekend? You and Gary heading up to Vail again?"

"Yeah, [sigh] you know the drill: champagne breakfast, fuck, fuck, fuck, and then he's out on the links 'til dark. I can't wait until it snows."

"God, woman; you're complaining? I haven't been laid since . . . hey, speaking of laid, maybe that's what Pete Tutaraitis's problem is. He sure was a bastard in committee this morning."

"Naw, it's like McNutt says: his Jockey shorts are too tight."

"Rumor has it he wears boxers."

"Yeah, well, all the same, I think Pete's just being an asshole about that meeting in Bakersfield because of his wife. You know how he gets."

"Yeah. Men."

"I hear that woman—"

I flushed the toilet, literally drowning the conversation. *He's married? I thought*— I hurried out of the women's room, not meeting the engineers' eyes, pretending that my cuff button completely consumed my attention. As I made an ass of myself trying to hurl shut the pneumatically controlled outer door behind me, I heard one of them say, "What do you suppose *her* problem is?"

"Dunno," came the reply, as the door hissed slowly shut. "Maybe *her* Jockey shorts are too tight."

I felt like throwing a fair-sized filing cabinet through a wall. I looked at my watch. Eleven forty-five. *He still might call,* I thought frantically. *I can't see him. What a goddamn idiot I am; he was never interested in me, it was the damned oil field!*

Maddie came into our office, plopped into her seat, and stared at me. I got up and left. I hid in the coffee room, numbly watching someone's brick of frozen lasagne undergo a phase change in the microwave oven. As its digital timer flicked slowly down past five minutes, the aroma of marinara sauce permeated the air. It turned my stomach. My hands trembled.

Someone approached from the hallway. I lurched toward the sink and hastened to justify my presence with the ritual of making a pot of coffee.

It was Menken. "Aha, Emily! Isn't that a fine coffeemaker? Makes the best coffee in town. I tell you, the way the grounds come prepackaged—just right for one pot—it's great. What American industry won't think up next. And these microwave meals; truly great. Ever had one of these?" Vague dimples sprang up in his cheeks as he grinned into my face.

"No, sir." My voice came out as a ghost. The pot shook in my hand as I poured water into the coffeemaker, sloshing it onto the countertop.

"Here, Emily, let me help." Menken smiled at his prowess as he steadied my hand. "Relax, everyone goes through this when they start a new job." He laughed, putting his other hand on my shoulder and giving it a little squeeze. "Even I did, once," he added, in an incredulous tone.

"Thank you, sir. I'll be all right."

"That's the spirit. Now, hasn't anyone given you a tour of the freezer? Here." He opened the upper compartment of the refrigerator, displaying a tightly stacked assortment of Stouffer's frozen goombah. "I have these stocked so that we don't have to go out for lunch. Saves time, my dear. Really, you should try one. The Salisbury steak's pretty good, but this lasagne is tremendous." He pulled one out and tossed it onto the counter.

I observed it with about the same interest I would afford a brick of dung, trying to imagine what would be left of my sanity if I stayed in this building all day without a midday break, and distractedly weighing this idea against my dislike of the two extra elevator rides the lunch break generated. "Looks great," I said, in a flat monotone, remembering that I could always take the stairs. Better yet, I could hide in the stairwell until Christmas or so.

The timer flicked down to zero and beeped. "Ah, now here's mine, all ready to eat." He pulled it out. "Care to join me?"

"Huh?"

"Here, I'll show you. They're stocked at cost; you just put your money in the sugar bowl here. But for for you, my dear, the first one's free." Laughing at his unparalleled wit, he ripped open the package on the counter, dumped the frozen chunk out onto a plate, and shoved it into the microwave. "Eight minutes. Couldn't be easier. Modern technology at its best. Come along." He picked up his cooked lasagne and headed for his office. "Irma, my dear," he called to his secretary, "bring Miss Hansen's lasagne in when it's done, won't you?"

I didn't open my mouth much, except to gag down the lasagne when Irma Triff brought it in, and listened with only half an ear as Menken discussed ranching practices, as if he'd ever had his round rump any closer to a real working spread than a hot-tub-and-hayride dude ranch. After a while I considered asking him some questions about Lost Coyote, if he ever paused for breath.

But the more he talked, the more it seemed Maddie was right: Menken was a lightweight, the last person to approach for an understanding of Lost Coyote Field. The ignorant way he prattled on about beef futures and sugar beet farming in southeast Wyoming. I began to wonder if someone else was making the decisions around Blackfeet. Otherwise the company wouldn't be in business. The beef and sugar beet industries have been dying slow deaths ever since Americans realized they could choose which disease of overindulgence they were going to die of.

This raised an obvious question: if Menken wasn't shrewd enough to run Blackfeet, then who *was* running it? A few hazy notions about ways Dave Smith might be driving Blackfeet Oil from the back seat flitted around in my head. If Menken was Smith's puppet, where were the strings attached?

Then all of a sudden, Menken himself steered the conversation around to Lost Coyote Field: "So, Emily, what have you learned about our little oil field?"

"It's quite a field," I replied, trying to make the observation sound like praise for his keen business acumen. "I have a few questions about it—"

"I'm sure you do. And I expect you to dig in and find the answers for me."

Something in his tone began to make me feel uncomfortable. It seemed suggestive, invasive. I crossed my legs awkwardly. "How did you acquire the acreage?" I asked. If he wasn't going to give me any technical information—whether he had any to give or not—then at least I could learn a little more about the political climate around the field.

"That's a wonderful story." Menken leaned back in his chair and admired the ceiling. "Pete Tutaraitis made the contact. Bright boy. I remember the day we laid the lease map out on the conference room table and decided where to drill. Just Pete and I. We didn't tell the engineers what we were doing. I trained in geology, you know." He laughed, as my eyes involuntarily widened. "Yes, I've put in my time in the ranks. Worked as a roughneck two summers during college. Good, honest work." My evaluation of Menken inched up a notch. "Yes, Pete and I had the explorationist's blood rushing in our veins that afternoon. I had Irma send out for beer and pastrami sandwiches, in honor of Pete's ethnic heritage."

My evaluation of the man sank again.

Menken continued. "The entire lease looked good, so we each had another beer and flipped a coin."

"Flipped a coin, sir? You mean, between two possible drilling locations?"

"No, I mean flipped one onto the map."

I was appalled. My mouth hung open.

Menken grinned. "Had you going there for a moment, didn't I? Now tell me, Emily, what have you learned about Lost Coyote? I notice that you're hard at work." He eyed me closely. "Did Scott teach you what he knew about it before he left?"

Left? "Ah, no sir. Was there something in particular he was supposed to teach me?"

Menken smiled and seemed to relax. "No, no, no. I like to leave the details to you folks. That's what I pay you for. Come now, tell me what you're discovering." This time when he watched me, I watched him back, and I thought I glimpsed real intelligence peering out at me from that face. The back of my neck tightened. Something about this meeting was all wrong. I stalled, chatting about inconsequential details. Why was Menken coming to me for answers? I was the newest member of his staff. Why not go to Pete, or Dave Smith? Or was he trying to find out what I knew for some other, more ominous reason? Was he concerned that I'd been spilling the beans to the police?

By and by the phone rang, and I was dismissed. Somewhat shaken, not to mention burdened by the load of lasagne that still sat, unmoving, in my stomach, I wandered back to my office and sat down. When Maddie came back from lunch, I was glad to see her. Of Maddie's grip on reality, I had no doubt.

As she settled back to coloring the map in front of her, she belched. "Love them Texas hot links," she declared.

"Do what?" I offered.

"Slant Hole."

"Huh?"

"That sounds more like you." She started humming.

Fritz walked in with some well logs for Maddie. "Hey, Fritz," I asked, "what's a slant hole?"

He looked arrows at Maddie. "You mean *the* Slant Hole. It's a dive over by Broadway. Texas barbecue beans and strippers. Ecch." He left.

I picked up one of the papers on my desk and pretended to read it. *Somehow,* I promised myself, *I'm not sure just exactly how, but I am going to get through this with my sanity.*

I couldn't find a position in that damned chair that was comfortable. After an hour or so, my resolution to hold still and occupy a swivel chair for a living once again began to sag, this time under the weight of simple boredom.

Days had passed, enough days that the homicide department of this big city ought to have been able to uncover the pattern of suicide in Scott's death, if it were there. It followed, therefore, that someone who had been in the building that night was involved in that death. Throwing my lot in with these people took on a new dimension: would my naïveté buy me a ticket for a sixteen-story lesson on corporate politics? Even Maddie looked like One of Them. With that paranoid thought, I could keep my bottom planted in my swivel chair no longer.

I headed out for the sixteenth floor, thwacking my hand on the metal handrail in the staircase to hear the sound echo against the dank cement, whistling in the dark to keep my courage up, as it were. *No harm in this,* I told myself. *If I find anything out, I'll just keep it to myself. It will be an exercise in curiosity, nothing more.* On sixteen, I hung out in the women's room for a while, on the off chance that someone might come in and start gossiping about the deaths, but when that didn't happen, I ventured farther down the hall, to The Window.

It was boarded up again, but this time it was also barricaded. It was festooned with yellow police tape, but more imposingly, there was a large folding table jammed across the access to it. I thought about the poor janitor, wrestling that table into place, cussing at the Fates and the Furies.

Without quite wanting to I moved closer to the window, and soon found myself leaning across the tape to touch the barricade. The wood felt cold and rough against my hand. For a flickering moment, I felt myself both there and in the lobby, with massive death on the sidewalk beyond, and I thought, *This is one way to leave.*

The building seemed to sway. I felt myself hurling through space, the barricade rotating upward to grab me.

"Lady!" the janitor screamed, as he grabbed me from behind, hauling me back into the depths of the hallway. "I thought you was falling! You okay, lady?"

I spun around in his grasp, and found myself close enough to smell the oil on his hair, close enough to see his pulse throb in his throat. His eyes were great dark disks in a sea of yellow, alarmed and deep with concern. "I cain't lose another," he said. "Please don't. I jus' cain't."

I tried to find my voice, but it was caught in my throat. What had happened? Had I fainted?

The janitor was trembling. He shifted his grasp from my person to great handfuls of my tweed jacket. "I'm sorry, I don't mean to handle you. You jus' settle down, okay?"

"Okay," I managed. "I don't know what happened. I just got dizzy. I was there that night, in the lobby; I've seen things falling ever since. I keep trying to fit into this job, and . . ." *Dear God, I'm babbling at a total stranger.*

He steered me ponderously over to the middle of the hallway and settled me on a leather-padded bench, all the while speaking softly, whispering to me as if I were a doll. "I know, I know. My sister Lizzie had a scare like that once. She saw a man die in a crash. He called to her, but she couldn't reach him. She couldn't sleep sound for days and months, kept seeing him again in her dreams."

"What did she do to get over it?"

"One day she upped and went out to the street where it happened. She took flowers and said the words you say for the dead. She had to honor his passing, she said. Everybody stopped and stared at her, and the po-lice tried to make her leave, said she was obstructing traffic, but she stayed and said her bit. She said it got better after that."

This wasn't what I wanted to hear.

I thanked the man and left, or should I say, he shepherded me to the elevator and stood guard until the doors closed and the car dropped me to the floor where I belonged.

But I wasn't done with the sixteenth floor yet. I returned to my desk for a while and tried to talk myself out of going back up there, but in the end reason lost out over compulsion, and I headed back upstairs. Via the elevator this time.

I looked both ways before getting off the car, not wanting to rob the janitor of what peace he had left. Then I hurried across the hallway into the main office of Love and Christiansen.

I was confronted with a wide mahogany reception desk, but no receptionist. So I kept going, down a short hall and around a corner, until I was confronted with a secretary.

That's putting it mildly. That's like calling the devil a little imp; this woman was to "secretary" what Mussolini was to "despot."

"What do you want?" she barked, narrowing already tiny eyes at me.

Well, I could have said something mild, like "Nothing," or diverted her and played on her sympathies with an innocent diversion, such as "I'm lost," but no, I always have to justify my existence. I said, "I'm looking for Simon." Hey, it's just the first name that popped into my head. The only time I've ever even known anyone who knew anyone by that name was the previous Monday, when Scott had answered the phone and scribbled down the caller's name. I figured Attila the Secretary would give me a scorching *There's no one here by that name* and send me packing.

What she said was, "He's out."

So then I had to say, "When will he be back?"

And she said, "Next week, maybe."

And I said, "Where is he?"

The answer was a growly "Whom shall I say was looking for him?" No more Ms. Nice Secretary.

So I got real wise and said, "Libby Hopkins." And left quickly, before she could refuel her flamethrower. I don't know why I told her Libby Hopkins, either; all the way back down to my office, I wished ardently I were someone else, like maybe someone who has the cool and refinement not to mix it up with asshole secretaries. Blabbing a real person's name had undoubtedly been a mistake. The possibility this Simon and Libby Hopkins knew each other was real, considering that Rachel and Topsy had known Scott, and Scott had known Gerald Luftweiller, who had worked for Love and Christiansen, and Scott had also known at least one dude named Simon.

The threads of connection around Denver were beginning to pull into a big ugly knot.

Trying not to give a damn about the world when the world isn't done with you has serious side effects. By the end of the afternoon, I had settled down somewhat, having perfected the fine art of looking like I was working on a file while scribbling a letter to Frank on a tablet next to it. I had thrown out three tries at a newsy letter, and stalled out in the middle of the fourth. There was certainly a lot to tell him, but I somehow couldn't find the right words. Frank had been friend, lover, and father confessor to me all summer, but now as I tried to decide what to say in the letter, he seemed too far away to hear me, and everything I wrote seemed obnoxiously flippant or embarrassingly self-obsessed. At four-thirty, I gave up on the try at correspondence and put the letter in a drawer. I told myself that as soon as I got home I'd take a nice hot shower with emphasis on the soap, and then give him a call.

At five o'clock sharp, Maddie rose from her chair, arched her back in a combined stretch and Richard Nixon victory pose, let out a howling yawn, and scratched her belly. I wondered whether her lime-green sheath was going to bear the strain. "Let's hear it for poet's day," she drawled, dragging her pocketbook out of a desk drawer.

"What's poet's day?" I asked.

"Stands for 'Piss on Everything, Tomorrow's Saturday,'" she replied, as she sauntered out the door.

I reached for my own gear, figuring I could share an elevator with her, then remembered how late I'd been that morning. *Best to occupy my chair for a full eight hours, whether there's anything to do or not.* I leaned back in my swivel chair, my arms dangling like they were made of lead. Before long, my eyes closed.

I'm not sure just how I became aware that Pete had come into the room. Perhaps my nose had become sensitized to the scent of expensive leather and subtle aftershave, or maybe my entire skin is an infrared heat sensor tuned to warm muscle under grey flannel. Anyway, I'm sure I didn't hear those loafers cross the carpet, but I knew he was there. When I opened my eyes, he was standing barely five feet away, his weight slung provocatively onto one leg, smiling a smile that ought to be outlawed.

"You look comfortable," he purred.

I crashed my chair back into an upright position, bouncing it a little on the casters. "Oh," I said. "It's you."

His smile faded. "What's wrong?" he asked.

"What do you mean?" I replied, trying the patented World's Worst Line for Evading Scrutiny.

Pete took a seat on the corner of my desk, swinging one of his fantastic, muscular legs very close to mine. "All the light's gone out of your eyes," he said, in a voice hushed with concern. He looked down at my near hand and shyly touched my smallest finger with his. "You look very much like you're angry with me."

All of my attention became intensely focused on the tiny area of my flesh that he was touching. "I'm just tired," I croaked.

Pete took my hand up in both of his. "I don't think that's all it is."

I looked away, withdrawing my hand. "That's not appropriate," I said, quite proud of myself for managing to say anything, even if it did sound priggishly judgmental.

"I don't understand," Pete said.

"You're married." I cringed at how petulant I sounded.

Pete's face lit with a cheerful smile. "Oh, is that all it is," he said, raising his left hand and examining his wedding ring. "I wonder why I don't take this thing off." He observed it a moment longer, a trace of pain now troubling the impossibly handsome sweep of his dark brows. His next words were barely audible: "It doesn't mean much anymore."

"It doesn't?" Why hadn't I noticed the ring before? Where had I been?

Pete sat back and folded his hands in his lap. "You're right.

You're a decent woman, a fine woman; you deserve a man who's free to treat you as you deserve. I can only hope you'll be around at such a time as I can offer you that. I'm sorry. It's just, well, that it's been so long already since Elizabeth left, that I've begun to think of myself as already, well, free to go on with my life."

I felt like a bully. *I overheard a stray comment in the women's room, and—* "I'm sorry," I whispered. "I jumped to conclusions."

He squeezed his eyes shut, forcing back emotion, and sub-consciously fiddled with his ring. "No, I'm the one who's sorry. My behavior must look awful to you. You must think I'm a—well, there are names for it."

"No," I said, and impulsively touched his hand, then pulled away again, fearful that *he* might think *me* too forward.

"Hey, Emily," he said, singing my name the way he did. He smiled his million-dollar smile again, its warmth pouring over me like warm chocolate. "Forgive a guy for getting his cart a little bit in front of his horse, okay?"

I grinned. "Sure." *Hey, can he help it if he oozes charm, good looks, and sexuality? Jesus, Em, he was born that way; give him a break.*

He smiled shyly. "What I came in here for was to see if you could join me for a drink after work. But maybe I should come back and ask you again—ah, later." He glanced pointedly at his wedding ring.

I sneaked a look at his thighs, where they rested against the edge of the desk. Little muscles tightened in my abdomen. I quickly raised my eyes higher in an attempt to stay out of trouble, but that wasn't any safer: the memory of the world of warmth underneath his suit coat was still too fresh. "I could use a drink," I said, tentatively, but quickly added, "You know, like between friends?"

"Friends it is." He gestured toward the door.

Well, I walked out of that office with my hips rolling like they'd just been lubed. The elevator ride was a pleasure. The lobby never looked so grand and spacious, and the air of Denver never tasted so sweet. Pete strode along beside me, chatting about the coming autumn, his long, catlike strides transforming the mundane sidewalk into a plaza for the gods. We headed down Seventeenth to Broadway and called in at Duffy's Bar.

It was strange: I've always tried to be moderate in drink, but after one beer, I quit worrying so much about who saw us. After two, I was amazed at what a wit I was. After three, I noticed we were eating Duffy's boiled dinner, and it tasted great. After that, I lost count. Before I knew it, we were walking around the Civic Center park, walking off Irish beer so Pete could drive me home.

Pete strolled along the narrow stonework around a dry fountain, putting one foot in front of the other like a tightrope walker, laughing at something I'd said. "You like the shape of the Heritage Center?" He gestured across the park at the wedge of architecture. "You don't think it's a takeoff ramp for visiting extraterrestrials? Okay, then how about that building they put the art museum in?"

"Looks like a computer punch card, doesn't it?" I answered. "But hey, who's this cowgirl to judge it?"

Pete laughed again. I liked the way his laughter sounded, slightly wild in the night air. "You're no cowgirl," he said.

"Born and bred in Chugwater, Wyoming. Raced the barrels with my Four-H team. Just moved here from the far-flung wilds of Meeteetse. What more could you want?"

"Then where'd you learn to dress like something out of the business section of *Women's Wear Daily?*"

I was just drunk enough on Pete and Guinness Stout that I said, "That's my grannie's doing. She lives in Boston."

"Blood breeds true. That's why I'm so attracted to you. Like the moth to the flame." He stopped walking and turned toward me, the streetlights playing around the planes of his face like a lover's hands.

"You're just saying that."

"No, it's true. I've never been able to resist an eastern blue blood, but you, Emily, you're fantastic. There's something about you those women never even see in their dreams."

I felt giddy. I struggled to bring the subject onto safe ground. "I'll bet your wife is special in her own way."

Pete laughed mirthlessly. "Sure. She's special. She can't even sleep unless all of her shoes are lined up perfectly in the bottom of her closet. She can't leave the house unless every dish is clean and in its place on the shelf. She can't—"

"Maybe I shouldn't be hearing this."

Pete nodded and fell silent.

There I was saying the right thing, but the Guinness Stout and my heart ran away with me, and I dreamt of ways I could make it up to him.

We walked back down Seventeenth Street and crossed into the parking garage beneath our building, where we descended two flights into its grey concrete depths, our footfalls echoing loudly in the abandoned night. High as I was, stray thoughts of the young rookie sealing off the exits from this same garage the night Scott died leaked into my happy pink haze. I was relieved when Pete unlocked the door of his Saab, letting me into the security of its fine upholstery and lavish appointments.

A little red light blinked on the dashboard. *Burglar alarm,* my brain informed my semicomatose self. *He'd better hurry, or the thing will go off.* But Pete strolled around the car at his leisure, even took time to fold the back seat up into place and fiddle with the latch that held it before he laid his coat across the seat and got in. "Isn't this sucker going to start to hoot?" I asked, pointing at the blinker.

"Hoot? You're an original, Emily. No, it's just a little blinking light, doing what it's supposed to do—look like a burglar alarm." He flashed me his smile and fired the ignition. The car moved smoothly up the ramps and out onto the street, accelerating down the lighted avenue like a bullet, the streetlights making lovely patterns on the wide, curved sweep of the windshield.

Lightning flashed in the western sky, the clear night giving way to black storm clouds. One massive thunderhead rose like a fist along the foothills, occluding the moonlight. The Saab rolled across the viaduct over the Platte River to the northwest side of Denver and climbed the bluff, the darkening night flowing past us like silk.

All too soon, the car slowed to a stop in front of Elyria's house. Pete left the engine idling.

"Thanks, Pete," I said.

"No, thank *you,* Emily. You're wonderful company."

"Um, want to come in for some coffee?"

Pete smiled a loaded smile. "No." He kissed me deftly on my nose. "I'm behaving myself, remember?"

I climbed out, suddenly awkward as I negotiated the curb. This was what I wanted, wasn't it, that I could just enjoy his company as—well, a friend? But now it seemed so silly. Even wasteful. I gave him one more look of invitation, as I reluctantly closed the door and stood back, but Pete just flashed the headlights and drove off into the night.

15

Alcohol and I have never been the best of friends. Now it had gotten its way with me once again, seducing me into utter foolishness and abandoning me to a siege of embarrassment and an early hangover. A querulous little voice in my head offered the opinion that a man like Pete could never really take an interest in me anyway, that he'd only been staving off the loneliness of impending divorce.

I got a beer out of the refrigerator in the vain hope that another hair of the dog would finish me off so I could pass out, if not sleep, and sat in the dark for a good half hour, unbearably lonesome and damned sorry for myself.

Through an open window I could hear the risings and fallings of a conversation being held on a porch near the corner. Ortega's family lived there, and everyone from Mama and Papa down to the smallest of the kids and their dog and half their close friends could be heard chatting and yapping and playing and shrieking until at least eleven P.M. any night of the week.

A car passed by on the street.

The cool breeze from the thunderstorm sighed in through the casement windows above the couch, carrying a distant rumbling of thunder and a mixture of stale city air and the dying perfume of Indian summer. This would be one of the last thunderstorms of the year. Soon, the mountain air that drained into Denver during the night would carry the first crisp breath of Colorado's short autumn. The aspen would already be showing gold on the higher slopes, and any morning now I would stumble out toward the bus stop and see a powdering of snow along the continental divide.

But for now, my neighbors still lived their evenings on the porch. Theirs was a pleasant hubbub, a background patter occasionally punctuated with a child's cry of rage or pain, followed by a hot string of Spanish if adult, or a falling chorus of wails if a child.

Another car approached. I peeked over the back of the couch and looked out, longing for the nerve to join the gathering. A police cruiser was just pulling up. Two men climbed out, one in uniform, the other not. I crouched low at the recognition of the plainclothesman, my own Sergeant Ortega. Both men kissed Mama and took seats on the porch, joining Papa in a cool *cerveza*.

I fought between the instinct to avoid this man and the desire to stroll down the sidewalk toward his gentle smile. Who knows, maybe the Ortegas would invite me onto the porch for a beer. Surely the sergeant wouldn't talk shop in his off-hours, with his family around.

No. I was on a nodding-hello basis with the family already, but I was just a *gringa,* some cracker who happened to live nearby. I imagined that "Hello" and "Nice day" was precisely as intimate as we could ever be.

The antique clock on the mantelpiece ticked disconsolately.

Another car passed by.

My beer went flat.

Elyria's dog yawned deeply in his spot by the fireplace, rose, and pattered out of the room in search of greater privacy.

I reached for my very ordinary *gringo* beer again, knowing it would taste sour. I took a swig and held it in my mouth, wincing, then spat it carefully back down inside the neck of the bottle. I considered turning on the TV, and immediately hated myself more. *What am I, a city bum already? No walks in the moonlight when I'm feeling shitty?*

The telephone in Bill's disused study began to loom in my consciousness, luring me. *I'm here and you know it, Em. You can be alone with me, get away from that hole in your chest. Just come to me and press my little buttons, and I'll get Frank on the line for you. He'll say, "There there," and, "Aw now Em honey," and all those other things you like to hear. So what if you left him back there in Wyoming? So what if he was kind of hurt to see you go? He'll understand, remember? He said so. He even said that if you stayed right now things would probably never work out between you, that you'd be off before spring came. Just dial me, you'll hear his voice. . . .*

But it was a Friday night. Frank would probably be out at the bar with his chums, if he wasn't at work. No point in calling. And how could I run to him for comfort when I felt such loneliness for another man?

16

I awoke Saturday morning with a fine case of cotton mouth, and spent what was left of the morning feeling exquisitely sorry for myself. I worked some of my self-pity out on another canine rodeo in the kitchen, then pumped two glasses of o.j. and a handful of B vitamins into my shattered stomach, and sulked in a hot bath for over an hour.

By one o'clock, I was enough recovered that I could focus my eyes on the rental ads in the *Rocky Mountain News*. If I was going to be the model oil company employee, I had to have a model oil company employee place to live. Which got me thinking about Scott Dinsmoore. He had spent his last morning on earth reading this same section of the classifieds. Scott's serene mood during the day could be interpreted as either the final peace of a man who's chosen to die, or of a man who had found a solution in living. Somehow, I couldn't feature a man on the brink of suicide perusing the house-to-rent section of the *Rocky Mountain News*. Maybe that was how Ortega had it figured, too: one doesn't simultaneously plan for life and death. What had been his living situation? I ran my eye down the page. Was it an individuality-for-the-masses cluster home in southeast Denver, or was it urban homestead Victorian chic on Capitol Hill?

I closed the paper in disgust, my hangover doubling back on me with a vengeance. Every single listing looked to me like an invitation to live in hell. The truth was, I wanted to live in a city like I wanted a hole drilled in my head with a rusty bit. To be fair, part of the problem was that I had never rented an apartment before; since leaving home I had lived in a series of dormitories and oil field trailers, and even in between times, I had stayed in the converted tack room of my Uncle Skinny's barn north of Casper. Oh, and then of course I'd just spent the summer with Frank, in his little house outside Meeteetse.

Frank. Shit, what was I going to do about Frank? He was a

quiet, very perceptive man; if I phoned him, would he detect my straying affections? Maybe a little later on I'd go get the letter I'd been writing to him, maybe even mail it.

The day wore on. It was another spectacular Colorado day, suitable for brisk walks in the foothills or at least hours lolling on the lawn, but all I could think of was my frustration over Pete Tutaraitis. I sat slumped at the kitchen table, wishing Elyria was home to talk some sense into me.

At two-thirty, the phone rang. When I answered it, Rachel Conant's contralto commanded the line, with her usual bare-bones conversation. "Em, can you come to brunch tomorrow? Libby's coming home, and she'd like to see you."

"Sure, why not," I said, matching her blasé tone. At times like this, Rachel Conant sounded like a stand-up comic doing an impression of someone like Rachel Conant.

"Eleven-thirty. We're on Washington Park, nine-eighty South Franklin, at Tennessee."

"Can I bring anything?" My manners crunched into gear as I scribbled the address on a supermarket receipt.

"Just yourself." The receiver clicked before I could give her my reflexively polite sign-off.

After indulging myself in a bit of virtuoso tooth-gnashing, I decided that exercise would improve my mood, such as a walk down to Sloan's Lake. I decided to take the pooch.

I regarded him with an attempt at friendliness. "So by the way, flea bag, what's your name?" I murmured, staring into his rheumy eyes.

Flea Bag moaned. He came alone willingly enough, if a little slowly, and we managed an hour's stroll among the brick bungalows. The dog stopped frequently to sniff bits of real estate with extreme suspicion. Fat men mowed their lawns. Several Flight-for-Life helicopters churned overhead on their way to and from St. Anthony's Hospital, and on one street, some kids were playing kickball. Normalcy incarnate. I'd say the whole tour was a howling success, if it weren't for the fact that at each new block I caught myself wondering if this one might be where Pete lived.

As we returned to Elyria's house, we passed the Ortega family, arrayed on the front porch of their bucolic brick Victorian. I nodded to them. Mrs. Ortega smiled broadly. Mr. Ortega bobbed his stout round head slightly and saluted me with a beer. Their dog barked at mine. The kids shrieked.

Back in the house, I found the message light blinking on

Elyria's answering machine. Through trial and error, I figured out the correct button to push to get the message to play back. Pete's voice warmed the speaker: "Hi, this is a message for Emily Hansen. I was just wondering if you were free to join a friend for a cup of coffee, but I'll see you on Monday. Ciao." A little electronic voice squawked the time the message had come in. I'd missed him by five minutes.

I bent right over onto the rug and started beating it with my fists. Then I pulled myself together enough to turn angst into action and pull out the phone book.

No Tutaraitis, Peter listed.

I tried Information. They had a Tutaraitis in Wheat Ridge, wrong first name, and a Peter in Boulder. I dialed it and heard a very pleasant announcement from another answering machine, but the male voice that answered certainly wasn't the Peter I knew.

Hell, I figured, *he has to have a phone.* I dimly remembered a confidential employee home phone list among the stack of papers good old Personnel had given me the day I signed on. Was I crazy enough to go in to work on a Saturday just to find out if my memory wasn't playing tricks?

Well, maybe.

Nah, said another part of me. *You have more cool than that. You have a perfectly good boyfriend in Wyoming, and he isn't even married to someone else. I mean, get serious: if you want a husband, why not get one of your own?* I sat there chuckling dryly at my own wit, until I remembered the letter to Frank that was moldering in my desk drawer.

Well, see? I gotta go mail that letter anyway.

Like hell.

No, really, it's no imposition; I wasn't doing anything, anyway.

Sucker.

Fine. But I'm going to the office.

After brief consideration of the bus lines, I grabbed a set of keys from the kitchen and headed for the garage. Hey, Elyria's note had said I should feel free to use Bill's truck if I needed to go for groceries or something. Why suffer the bus on a Saturday?

You're just afraid Mr. Wonderful won't wait around for you to return his call.

Shut up.

I couldn't get the truck started.

See? The Fates don't want you finding this guy.
Get lost.

There was a perfectly good bicycle in the garage, and the tires were even pretty well inflated. I wheeled it toward the street. The Ortegas waved. I waved back and aimed the bicycle downtown, a foolish grin spreading across my face.

Now I know why people don't ride their bikes to work in Denver. From Thirtieth I turned onto Speer Boulevard, where I had a near miss with a low-rider. Two different trucks swerved, horns blaring, as I crossed the long viaduct over the Platte River, Interstate 25, and the Union Pacific freight yards, and as I came down the other side, I almost lost the front wheel in a chuckhole. I cut onto Market Street as soon as I could, bouncing around over some patched-up pavement and old trolley tracks, then cut down the Sixteenth Street Mall, dodging pedestrians left and right. Once I got past the Tabor Center shopping extravaganza the foot traffic let up a little, but I had to run a slalom with the mall buses and their eardrum-shattering brakes all the way to Welton. As I bumped up over the curb at Seventeenth and wheeled the bike into the lobby of the Cattlemen's Exchange Building, the poisons from the previous night's alcoholic largess finally burst through my skin. I didn't have a lock for the bike, so I muscled it onto the elevator, punched twelve, and waited. The car trembled heavenward.

When the door opened at the twelfth floor, I found myself face-to-face with Peter Tutaraitis.

"Good afternoon, lady friend," he said, his smile widening into a grin.

I mentally took stock of my windblown, exhaust-shrouded hair, my worn blue jeans, and my faded flannel shirt soaked with sweat, and about sank to my knees in embarrassment. "Hi, Pete," I managed, in an asthmatic rasp.

"You're a sight for sore eyes," he said, impulsively taking my face in both of his hands and kissing the top of my head. "Better and better. I love a woman who can look classy all week, and then let her hair down on the weekends."

The elevator door tried to close against his shoulder and bounced back into its scabbards. I grabbed it to keep it from closing again, dropping the bicycle on Pete's feet. He laughed and took the bicycle from me, drawing it out into the hallway.

"So; can't get enough of dear old Blackfeet?" he asked.

"No, I just came down to pick up a letter I left here yesterday."

"Do you have a key?"

"A key?"

"Yes, the door's locked. No one's here."

"Oh," I said. "Right."

Pete produced his own key, and let me in through the back door, saying, "I'm glad I ran into you. I was just thinking about you. As a matter of fact, I called your house, but you were out."

"Oh, did you?"

"Are you in a hurry to get somewhere?"

"No, a cup of coffee would be great. I mean, how about a cup of coffee?"

"Like you were reading my mind."

Pete followed me into my office. I pretended I couldn't find the letter, but Pete pulled out the one desk drawer I avoided, and there lay the letter to Frank, right on top. "Is this it?" he said. "The one that starts out, 'Dear Frank'?"

"Right." Taking the letter from him as casually as I could, I crammed it into my back pocket and put a cheery smile on my face.

Pete returned my smile; a long, leisurely look, rich in appraisal.

I was suddenly uneasy. In the lapse between our words, the dead stillness of the building had crowded in. It was so quiet that I could hear my own breath whispering in and out. The usual rush and hum of the building was missing, the pulse and respiration of all systems shut down for the weekend. During the week, when the building had been full of bustling activity, it had been easier to forget that this was a place where death had occurred. Two deaths, of men who knew each other. Now that the offices were empty, death moved through them like a vapor.

I quit smiling.

17

Pete saw that look in my eyes and stepped toward me. "What is it?" he whispered. He grasped my shoulders.

I flinched, thinking, *Who is this guy really?*

He let go of me, but held his hands a few inches away, tipped his head closer. "Hey, what is it?" he repeated.

I squeezed my eyes shut. *Get a grip, Em.* When I opened my eyes again, Pete had straightened up and was stepping back, his mouth set in a line of pain. I was immediately anxious I'd offended him, then worried that I was repelling the one person in this office who was trying to be friendly. This sensitive, powerfully attractive . . . "I'm sorry," I said.

He stopped, put his hands in his pockets. "Someone had a hard week?"

I sighed. "A hard couple of weeks."

"Coffee," he said.

We locked the office and rode the elevator down to the street, where the long, golden light of late afternoon reached its fingers between the buildings. Pete wheeled the bike along, steering it by the seat with subtle, sure movements of his wrist. "I have an idea. Why not make this something more than coffee? Do you have anywhere you need to be? We could drive out to the foothills and catch the sunset."

"Sure."

"My car's over here; we can just throw your bicycle in back." He turned the corner at Welton Street and headed for the Saab, which was parked hallway down the block. As he reached the car, he paused by the back end, fished the keys out of his pocket, and started to unlock the trunk.

"Don't you need to fold the seats down from the inside?" I asked, peering in a side window of the sedan.

"No, this car's five years old. The catch isn't what it once was. The dog chewed it up. Watch." He hoisted the bike up and fed it straight into the trunk, knocking the seat forward

with the front tire. The bicycle fit in easily between the tail-
lights and the back of the front seat. "I've slept in this thing
before, car-camping," he added.

I tried to imagine all of Peter Tutaraitis laid out in that
space. He'd have to sleep diagonally. Then I remembered that
his wife would have been in there with him, and I suffered a
pang of jealousy, and found myself wondering how she could
dream of leaving such a man.

The next hours swept past in a sublime haze. We drove west
over the rise of suburbs that lies between Denver and the
foothills to the Alameda hogback, a great fin of upended rock
and dry chaparral that every geology student in the surrounding
five states has seen. It has footprints left by dinosaurs and rip-
ple marks formed by waters that flowed past tens of millions of
years ago. We parked the car and climbed a trail that ran along
the crest of the hogback through the mountain mahogany, gain-
ing a great view of the sun setting over the massive monoliths
of Red Rocks Park, then wandered into the tiny town of Morrison for buffalo steaks. The *cerveza* slid down smoothly. After
dinner we looked out over the lights of Denver for a while before climbing back into the Saab to return home.

As the car sped northward between the hogback and the
foothills and the time approached to say good-night, my anxiety that I'd offended him in any way at the office that afternoon came back. "Bad weeks drag, and good times end too
soon," I said.

Pete grinned. "Then let's take another little tour, shall we?"
He veered suddenly onto an entrance ramp for Interstate 70,
which led westward up Mount Vernon Canyon and into the
foothills, the route Elyria and I had taken to Georgetown. Had
that only been a week ago?

"Where exactly are we going?" I asked, as he turned right
onto a winding road that led northward, away from the highway.

"Have you ever seen the M?" he asked, mischief leaking out
of every pore.

"The M?"

"Yes, the M for Em. It's a big letter *M* on the side of Mount
Zion above Golden, above the School of Mines campus. You
can see it for miles. And it's lit up at night."

"I've only seen it by daytime, and from a distance. It's just
painted on the rocks, isn't it?"

"Whitewashed. Each rock is painted separately. They have
each freshman at Mines carry one up in the fall, the devils.

Miss Hansen, you're in for the thrill of a lifetime," he said, gearing down to take the turns even faster. "I've always wanted to do this."

"Do what?"

Pete just laughed. The twisting road crested the top of a wooded mesa and began to descend steeply. I caught glimpses of the lights of Denver. "This is where all the townies come to neck." He gestured to a row of cars parked in a narrow turnout, noses to the city lights. "Down there, you can see the Coors Brewery between North and South Table Mountain." He pointed to a bee's nest of lights and buildings between two pools of darkness.

Several long switchbacks down from the summit of Mount Zion, Pete parked the car on a stretch of shoulder barely wide enough to pull off the road. "Follow me," he ordered, heading for the high side of the road, where he disappeared into the darkness.

I looked up across the road, and finally saw it: an enormous white letter on the hillside, grotesquely foreshortened. As I scrambled up the path, I could see the whitewashed rocks, and hanging just above the rocks, arrayed on long strands of wire, were myriad little light bulbs, casting the chauvinistic initial of the School of Mines out into the night, that all its acolytes might feel their hearts pound proudly in their chests.

There was a ragged chain-link fence around the M. When I got to it, I saw that Pete had scaled it and was moving quickly down the line of lights, unscrewing them.

"What are you doing?" I asked.

"I'm sending School of Mines a message," he laughed. "The lights have never been out all night."

"Never?"

Pete's grin flashed. "There's a bunch of Neanderthals called the Blue Key Club who keep watch over the thing. They'll be up this hill in a flash. Come on, help me!"

I thought, *What the hell, Em, you only go around once,* and scaled the fence. Reaching the line of bulbs, I touched one gingerly. They were only twenty-five watts, barely warm to the touch. With a quarter turn, it was out. Then I noticed a tremendous litter of broken glass, testimony to less gentle techniques of dousing the M that had been used in the past.

I hurried down the far line of bulbs, scrabbling over the whitewashed stones, and met Pete in the middle. Grinning wildly with the thrill of the game, he threw an arm around me, tugged me close, and kissed me on the neck, in that tender, place by the corner of the jaw. He pulled just as quickly away, but the scent of his body clung to me like a narcotic.

As I followed him back down the slope through the mountain mahogany to his car, I felt I was capable of anything, a woman in charge of her fate.

The Blue Key Club, two Jeeps full of beefy engineering students, passed us in their mad charge to protect their honor when we were only two switchbacks down the mountain.

We hardly spoke as we drove back, taking the slow way, circling around behind the brewery and following Thirty-second Avenue all the way back through the suburbs.

"Surely you need a cup of coffee, to warm you up," I said, as Pete turned down the block toward Elyria's.

"Thanks, but it's late, and I wouldn't want to disturb your roommate."

I grinned. "She's out of town."

Pete agreed to come in for one quick cup of coffee, which he drank sitting in a wooden chair in the kitchen. The moment he finished his cup, he rose to go. At the door, he gave me a friendly smile and hugged me chastely.

I hugged him back, pulling him closer.

"Hey," he said, putting his hands on my shoulders, pushing me away to arm's length. "What's this?"

"I'm sorry." I wasn't sure why I said that, because I wasn't. What I was feeling was, well, aggressive. I can't remember what I was thinking.

"We agreed," he said, sliding his hands from my shoulders to my back in a slow massage.

"I'm sorry," I said again, smiling now.

"Don't do this to me," he said, his voice soft and thick. Pete drew me against his body, one hand searching through my hair for my face. After a moment, he kissed my throat, my ear, and then my lips, grasping my arms rhythmically like a giant cat purring over a treat.

Time passed, punctuated only by the moisture of his mouth and the hypnotic caress of his hands. Then he turned off the lights, and like someone speaking from a dream, he said, "Where's your bedroom?"

"Over there." I pointed. Night air touched my breasts. I realized my shirt was already open.

As Pete maneuvered me past the window toward my darkened room, streetlights played across his face. He was grinning.

18

I awoke in the darkness. Someone was moving around in the room. Where was I? What was happening?

Then I woke up far enough to remember that Pete was with me. I reached to the place next to me where I had left him through the night and found nothing. "Pete?"

"Over here." His voice came from the middle of the room.

"What are you doing?"

"Getting dressed."

"Why?" I peered at the lock. "It's only five o'clock. The sun isn't even up yet."

"I have to get home."

"Why? There's nobody there." I laughed, but it came out kind of squeaky, a telltale nervousness magnified by the darkness.

"Ah, no . . . but there's a neighbor coming over at eight, for breakfast. We're going to head up into the mountains for a drive, look for aspens changing color. It wouldn't look good if I wasn't there."

"That's not for three hours."

"I know, but I was awake anyway."

"Well, what? Were you going to leave without waking me?"

He sat down on the edge of the bed and kissed me, a quick smooch. "No, no; I was just about to wake you." He stood up again to tuck in his shirt.

"Pete?"

"Yes?"

"Is something wrong?"

"No, nothing's wrong. Well, listen, Em, things are a bit of a mess between me and Elizabeth. We haven't gotten along for years, to be honest, and there are a lot of hurt feelings. On both sides. I don't want it to get any worse." His voice held a mixture of irritation and sadness.

I felt a weird urge to apologize, even though I didn't think

I'd done anything wrong. I settled for saying something solicitous. "What went wrong?"

"What do you mean?"

"With your wife."

Pete didn't say anything, but I could hear his breath ease out
in a long, frustrated sigh.

I said, "I'm sorry, I guess it's none of my business."

"It's all right. I guess I don't really know what went wrong.
It's just, well, she can't seem to be happy here in Denver. It's
sad, because back when we first knew each other back east,
things were different. Well, maybe not perfect, but I thought
her unhappiness with me was because we weren't married yet.
I was pretty naive."

"What do you mean?"

"Oh, I thought she'd come to love me more." His voice
trailed off.

"She doesn't love you?"

His voice got very small. "I mean physically."

"What?"

"Listen, things may be bad between Elizabeth and me, but I
feel I owe it to her to maintain appearances until we get things
settled. It'll save trouble later on. Okay?"

I stared past him at the ceiling. It wasn't okay, but I didn't
know what I could say or do to make it any different. All I
knew was that I didn't want him to leave.

"Go back to sleep," he said, bending to kiss my eyes closed.

I heard his footsteps in the hallway, and the front door closing, and his car starting away from the curb. I lay awake,
watching through the gap in the curtains as the day arrived.

Coffee is the great cure. As the bitter brew woke me up, I
felt more sure of myself, and by the time I'd emptied the second cup on the back deck, the sun was growing warm on my
face and I was enjoying its red flush through my closed eyelids. On this suitably hot screen, I replayed scenes from the
night before: Em the masked bandit of Mount Zion, turning
out the lights; Em the wit; Em the bold lover; Pete the enig-
matic, sensual hunk.

I took a long bath with bubbles, admiring the shape of my
shell-pink feet at the far end of the tub, wondering how I had
lived with them all these years without noticing how lovely
they were. The thought of Pete's touch unleashed wonderful
hollow sensations in my solar plexus. It was like a certain

physical gravity had entered me, pulling me closer to the earthly pleasures of life. A stray thought of Frank flitted across my mind, but I pushed it aside. Frank was brooding and rough-edged, like weathered wood. Pete was dazzling and smooth.

It's amazing what good sex can do for one's sense of well-being. The day had a special glow, every drop of dew in the garden a precious gem. Even Elyria's dog seemed an old friend, hardly cowering as I approached him after the bath. He only spit his pill out once.

I was in the middle of dressing when I heard a knock at the door. Okay, the first thought through my head was *It's Pete*, but I managed to control myself on the way to the door, even taking time to walk around the coffee table instead of jumping over it.

It was Sergeant Ortega. "Hi, neighbor, I just dropped my mother off after church and thought I'd stop in, see if you have some coffee for the nice policeman."

I stiffened. Was this going to be more pressure for me to discuss Blackfeet's business?

Ortega's face fell. "I'm sorry, is this a bad time? You seemed uncomfortable being questioned at work, so I thought it might be better here." He waited, his head cocked to one side, eyeing me with polite curiosity, and, as time stretched without a reply, confusion.

Curiosity got the better of me. Besides, he was a neighbor. I stepped back and pointed the way to the kitchen. "Cream or sugar?"

"*Azúcar, pro favor.*"

"*Aquí está.*" I set the sugar bowl on the table, hoping my accent wasn't as atrocious as I feared.

"*¿Se habla castellaño?*"

I dredged my memory for a little more of my high school Spanish, intimidated by his elegant, rich pronunication. "Ah, *sí, pero solamente un poquito.*"

"*Qué linda, señorita; es muy bueno.*"

"*No, es muy malo.*"

"*Bueno.*" He made a grand gesture, appropriate for the bull ring.

"*Ustéd es loco, señor policía.*"

He laughed, patting his round knee. "That's very good."

"*No es verdad.*"

Ortega's whole body bounced with his quiet laughter.

"Is English your second language? You speak it with a trace of an accent."

"No, I learned both languages together, when I was *un niño*. The accent is that of the Mexicans of *el valle,* where we lived back then."

"*El valle?* Is that in Mexico?"

"No. The San Luis Valley, down by Alamosa."

"But you call yourself a Mexican, and not a Chicano or Latino?"

"*Sí*. We were Mexicans before Colorado was part of the United States; we are Mexicans now," he explained. He squared his shoulders with exaggerated dignity. "I am the proud Mexican." He winked, and smiled.

"Then what's a Latino?"

"A more general term, like Hispanic."

"And Chicano?"

"A more political person."

"Oh, I see." I was lying; his logic sounded pretty political to me. So I said, "A matter of, um, the *corazón.*"

His smile spread into a grin. "*Sí, del corazón,*" he said, patting his heart. Then tapped his head. "*Tú eres muy inteligente.*"

His switch from the formal to the familiar *you* wasn't lost on me. "You're a most charming liar, Sergeant Ortega. You must want information very badly."

He shrugged. "Well, okay. Yes, you're right; information, always information. Just a few more questions, so we can wrap things up." He opened his palms apologetically. "So sorry to interrupt your Sunday." He smiled merrily and added three spoonfuls of sugar to his coffee. "I would have come last evening, but you had company."

I felt the blood rush to my face. "Uh, yeah, a friend kind of dropped over."

Ortega's eyes danced.

Now I was irritated. It wasn't any of his damned business if a guy came to see me and didn't leave until late. Or was it? Had he seen who it was? Shit!

As if he'd read my mind, Ortega dropped his gaze. He tasted his coffee and added more sugar.

I'm not sure whether I was more worried that Pete's indiscretion might be uncovered or that Ortega might draw the wrong conclusion about two people connected with Blackfeet and Scott's death meeting on the sly. Without even trying to hide my irritation, I muttered, "So what did you want to ask me?"

Ortega bowed his head, making a detailed study of the inside of his coffee cup. I could almost see the little gears in his head working. He was here because he needed information from inside, and he was out. He was out not just because he was the cop threatening to invade the sanctity of oil company secrets, but because in that white Anglo-Saxon kingdom he lacked social connections, or perhaps just the right color skin. It was irony of the deepest kind that he would come to Em Hansen, rookie girl geologist from Chugwater, Wyoming, for entree anywhere. No one knew better than I how tough it was to get information out of that place. "What did you want to ask me?" I repeated, in a kinder tone.

Ortega's face brightened. "Okay, well, I'm trying to figure out a few things. Like, did Mr. Dinsmoore have chapped lips?"

"Chapped lips? I don't know." What kind of a question was that? Was that going to be the mode of death?

"Okay, and I'm still trying to track down this red notebook." As if to emphasize his statement, Ortega flipped down his own notebook.

"Wait, what about chapped lips?"

"It's nothing."

"But—"

Ortega bowed his head over his work and lifted one hand in a self-deprecating wave. "Really. I run down a lot of dead ends in this job."

"All right, what about the rental ads? Did you call any of the numbers he'd circled?"

"More dead ends. I'm trying to understand what Mr. Dinsmoore's notes about his conversation with this Simon fellow meant." He riffled through the pages, but I remembered the words as if I'd just read them: "LC—told Simon latest gas tests wet. Cycling?"

"I'm a geologist, not an engineer," I said, hoping to end his line of inquiry before it really got started.

"Geologists don't know these things?"

That nettled. I wanted to tell him that geologists know almost everything there is to know in the universe, but I said, "Well, you see, geologists are sort of more interested in the rock that the oil and gas is in than the oil and gas itself. That's how they do their bit, sort of like looking for a rabbit by looking for a likely place for a rabbit to make his home, rather than for the rabbit himself. Engineers take it from the opposite perspective; they're more interested in the oil and gas, and don't care much about the rock. Did you ask Dave Smith about this?"

"Yes, he said he didn't know what the note meant."

"That sounds like a load of road apples to me."

"Okay, let's see what a rock specialist *does* know, then. First, what does it mean when a gas is wet?"

He wasn't going to let up. I smiled in spite of myself. He reminded me of a small South American animal called a kinkajou. My fifth-grade teacher had one as a pet. It was so soft and furry that I was pleased when it curled up in my lap and I thought it was being sweet when it put its little mouth around one of the small bones of my hand and began to gnaw gently. What I didn't understand until the teacher hastened to pull it away was that it had tremendously strong jaw muscles, and was reputed to keep chewing until it heard bones crack.

Well, it couldn't hurt to explain something that was in every textbook. "The gist of it is that, um, the oil and gas in the reservoir—you know, way underground—are at a much higher temperature and pressure than up at the surface. So when you raise the stuff up to the surface, it can change phase."

"Phase?"

"Yeah, water is in the solid phase when it's ice, in the liquid phase when it's water, and in the gaseous phase when it's steam. See? So, hydrocarbons have the same sort of thing, only it's a little more complicated, because water is just water—you know, H_2O, always the same. Well, you see, hydrocarbons can be lots of things, the atoms arranged in chains, or rings, or—well, the point is we're talking about zillions of different possible molecules, as long as the basic ingredients are hydrogen and carbon atoms. So 'gas' can mean either the gas phase, or probably in this case he meant the short-chain hydrocarbons—like methane through butane."

"Like gas that comes out of the stove."

"Right. So if the hydrocarbon is in the gas phase at surface conditions, it's called a gas; if it's a liquid, it's called oil."

"And if it's a solid?"

"Tar. You drive around on it."

Ortega's eyes danced. "I didn't know I'd have a chemistry lesson today. But what I wanted to know is, what does it mean when a gas is 'wet'?"

"Oh. Well, it sort of means that when you draw it to the surface, some liquid condenses out because you've dropped the temperature and pressure."

"And some gasses are dry, meaning nothing condenses out."

"Right."

"Okay, what's the gas like at Lost Coyote?"

That question caught in my craw. Here I was lecturing a police detective on organic chemistry, and I hadn't had the brains to find out what kind of gas was coming out of the ground at Lost Coyote. I muttered, "I don't know."

"Okay, maybe you'll find out."

"Maybe."

"Thank you."

Mercifully, we were interrupted by another knock at the door. When I opened it, I found Ortega's partner on the doorstep. "Hi, remember me? Lieutenant Flint. I'm told my wandering partner is here." He smiled and kind of bent the lower half of his face around, showing some astonishingly long teeth, but although his eyes looked friendly enough, the balance of his face looked paralyzed. In general, he would have been better off to settle for looking glum and ugly, rather than jovial and warped.

"This way, Lieutenant. How do you take your coffee?"

"Oh, God. Is Ortega fraternizing with the civilians again? I take cream."

"Will milk do?" I muttered, leading him to the kitchen.

Flint cuffed Ortega on the arm and said, "Morning, boss, you dumb spic."

Ortega beamed a friendly welcome. "Flint, you ugly thing, *qué pasa?*"

"Nada mucho," Flint said, in the lousiest attempt at Spanish I've heard this side of Boston.

I busied myself at the stove. Flint sat down next to Ortega and the two spoke quietly, but I could still make out their words:

"So what you finding out, bro?"

"Miss Hansen here has been teaching me about hydrocarbons. It's very interesting."

"Hah? Who cares? Let's play a little good cop bad cop, get this case settled and the poor fellah buried, maybe even take the afternoon off. I'm itching for nine holes of golf, nice day like this."

"You'll play golf when I take up needlepoint, you old lounge lizard."

"Hah? Nah, I'm gonna take up bullfighting, show your lazy Mexican ass a few things. So what's the skinny? You over here telling the witness everything you know? You gonna get thrown off the force yet, you keep this up."

"Still wondering about this red notebook thing."

"Nnnh. This kid's straight, hah?"

"Miss Hansen? Like new snow, you *hijo del diablo*."

Flint's voice dropped really low for a moment, but I caught bits of it: "So what about this . . . Tutar . . . car . . . all night?"

"Okay, well, but that's . . . business. I just hope . . . doesn't get in trouble."

I went nuts trying to make out their words. It was obvious that not only had Ortega seen that I had a visitor, but he knew full well who that visitor was, and approximately when he left.

"You guys always work on Sundays, or is this treatment special for me?" I marched over to the table and set Flint's coffee down. Hard. Some of the brew slopped onto his lap, and after he flinched, he smiled admiringly.

Which totally blew my indignation. It's hard for me to stay mad at someone who approves of me.

Flint picked up his coffee, sucked at it noisily, and answered my question. "Nah, we don't work Sundays unless we got a case going. Then it's eighteen-hour days until we get it wrapped."

"You push this hard over a suicide?"

Flint and Ortega exchanged looks. Flint said, "We really can't talk about the case, ma'am. Ortega here has a big mouth. A real maverick. It gets him in lots of trouble. Right, *gordo?*"

Ortega rolled his eyes. "You were just about to tell me more about the gas at Lost Coyote, Miss Hansen."

"I don't know anything more about it. You can call me Em. Flint here can call me Miss Hansen."

Flint warped his face into an appreciative grimace of a smile.

"Okay, then," said Ortega, carefully entering notes in his little book. "You have any other ideas for us?"

"No," I said.

"Right," Flint said. "We best get on with it then, Carlos. Thanks for the coffee, Miss Hansen."

19

Rachel's house was a small brick Tudor, a little nicer than the bungalows that made up the bulk of the houses near Washington Park. I'd been told that Washington Park was the "in" place for the up-and-coming to live, and judging by the flashy duds on the joggers and bicyclists who huffed purposefully by, this was so.

After spraying half a can of ether into the carburetor to get it started, I hadn't had time to run Bill's truck through a car wash, so I parked it a block away from Rachel's house.

Rachel came to the door wearing elegant gabardine slacks and a sweater the color of oatmeal. She gestured me in with her drink. "Em; glad you could make it on such short notice. Libby's on the verandah. This way."

I crossed a hardwood floor onto a thick Persian rug, passing mahogany and cherrywood antiques the likes of which I hadn't seen this side of the Appalachians. On beyond the dining room, a pair of French doors stood wide, opening out onto a small garden full of flowers. As I crossed the threshold, I could see an arbor, heavy with clematis and flanked with a wild spray of late anemones. There, under the protective arch of the arbor, stood Libby Hopkins, as frail and beautiful as ever, her translucent alabaster skin flushed with the last dying heat of summer. As she saw me, she smiled, and came toward me with her arms extended for an embrace, the sun playing across the reddish lights in her crown of golden hair. She presented her greeting with great delicacy, like a butterfly lighting for one fragile moment on a tender flower. I smiled. The princess remembered me. Why had I never noticed her friendliness before?

"Emmy, I'm so glad you're here," she said. Her voice hadn't changed in the years since I'd seen her, either. It still held a strange, unexpected fullness, like a fruit that holds more flavor than its scent suggests.

"Hi, Libby. It's nice to see you."

We ate at a glass-topped table in the garden, dining on egg[s] Florentine, hot crusty bread and imported marmalade. The co[f]fee was strong and rich. It was a pleasant, easy meal, and fo[r] once I didn't even worry whether I was dropping an inordinat[e] amount of crumbs around my plate.

Rachel leaned back with a cigarette, abstractedly tipping th[e] ash onto the wreckage of the half-eaten meal on her Wedge[-]wood plate. She seemed lost in thought, presiding over the oc[-]casion with the patient disinterest of a runner jogging in place.

By contrast, Libby's attention seldom wandered. She ha[d] gazed straight at me throughout the meal. "Remember th[e] weekends you came to stay with me from school?" she wa[s] asking.

"Yes," I answered, partially lying. She had, in fact, only in[-]vited me once. Usually she took Rachel, or some other mem[-]ber of her tight coterie of friends. Even though I had presume[d] the invitation a prefunctory act of social obligation, set in mo[-]tion by the social machinery my grandmother oiled, I had en[-]joyed myself: Libby had arranged for me to bring my hors[e] and had stabled her next to hers in the barn. Her family's es[-]tate outside Boston sprawled across a hillside, its crouching ar[-]chitecture glowering down an immense lawn toward [a] wonderful lake. We had rowed around and around the lake— [I] had rowed; she was not as strong—and had then taken th[e] horses out riding through the surrounding woodlands.

"Remember that picnic we took to the big rock in th[e] woods?" she asked.

She really does remember, I thought, amazed. "Yes. You[r] cook made great ham sandwiches."

"Yes, and Popsicles for dessert, but they had half melted even though we wrapped them in towels next to a bag of ice. You showed me how to rig a saddlebag out of our rucksacks."

"Yes." I began to smile at the memory. "Yes, I remembe[r] that day. The leaves were turning." How odd, to feel nostalgi[c] for New England.

"Yes, they were," Libby echoed, "and they're turning now. They're beautiful this year." A hollow look passed across he[r] face, but she chased it away with her fragile smile. "I went u[p] into the mountains this morning, to see the aspens turning. Bu[t] they're not the same." Her eyes focused on me again, with [a] sudden haunting depth. "Then later that day, remember, we se[t] up bales of hay, and you showed me how to ride the barrels[?]

and later how to rope the fence post. You were always so clever, Em." Her smile was warm, her gaze intense.

I felt elevated, almost drunk, first by the satisfactions of the evening before, and now by finding some kind of acceptance at last among my schoolmates. The snubbing I'd received at work began to fade in importance, and bitter memories of being the girl who didn't fit in took on a sweeter quality, as if that were some other girl, who had learned the proscribed lesson and grown up wise and strong and forgiven.

In this sentimental glow, I tried on the notion that we were all mature now, that old slights and prejudices could be set aside. *On both sides,* I thought, realizing that I hadn't exactly broken my neck to please these people. Had that been my sin? *How odd, to find out Libby has always liked me. Why have I never noticed? Was she more shy than I realized, afraid to declare herself until now? Have I failed her somehow, never giving her the friendship she wanted?* I moved to meet her kindness. I said, "Then after dinner, we sat up telling stories. Remember that? We told scarier and scarier stories, and got more and more afraid to go to sleep, and it got later and later, and your dad came in and he told us more stories."

Rachel shifted suddenly in her chair, as if she had a cramp. She stared fixedly at something visible only to her, her jaw muscles bunched into a knot.

"Oh yes, the stories," said Libby. She took Rachel's hand, and held it to her cheek. "Remember Daddy's stories, Rachel?"

Rachel pulled her hand away. "Right. Let's move inside, shall we? We can have our sherbert where the sun won't strike it." Abruptly, she rose and headed for the kitchen.

Libby rose more slowly, picking her dishes up with great care, the action apparently absorbing every gram of her attention.

I was left alone in the garden, staring at the way crumbs stuck to the streaks of egg yolk on my plate, the smear and chaos coating the delicate design.

Over tea and sherbert, the conversation began anew. "I hear you're working at Blackfeet," Libby said. "How do you like it?"

"Fine," I replied. "How did you know where I work?"

Libby leaned against me and grasped my arm. She said, "Isn't it terrible what happened to Scott Dinsmoore?"

"Yes," I said, trying to get my bearings in this new turn in the conversation.

"Isn't it strange that Scott and Gerry should both die like that, so close together?" Libby continued. "Don't you think so, Rachel?"

Rachel didn't answer. At least not verbally; she did get up and pour herself a shot of bourbon. Libby followed her with her eyes.

I pounced on the topic. "I think it's strange, all right. Just how did they know each other?"

"At college," said Libby. "They were roommates for a year at Haverford, before Scott moved into the fraternity house. You know, when I was at Bryn Mawr."

The next town, I thought. At last, here was a chance to ask someone about Gerald Luftweiller. Someone who actually knew him. "Did you know him well? I mean Gerald. Did he study accounting at Haverford?"

"I don't know. And no. I only knew him through Scott. Scott and I dated a bit. Just out to a movie now and then."

Rachel began to pace.

"What was Gerald like?" I persisted.

"Nervous."

"What do you mean, nervous?"

"Well—" Libby began, but Rachel broke in.

"He wasn't very stable, Em." Her tone warned me to stop asking questions.

What's the connection? Is there a connection? I scanned all I knew about Gerald Luftweiller, which was precious little. My mind ricocheted around the events of the last few days, eventually climbing the stairs to the sixteenth floor from my office in the Cattlemen's Exchange Building, where it dithered over the broken window before heading into the offices of Love and Christiansen.

And remembered Simon, the mysterious phone caller, who maybe worked at Love and Christiansen. "Do you guys know Simon, too?" I asked, hoping that Libby did not. If she did, things were going to get dicey when Simon picked up his messages from his secretary.

"Oh my God, Simon," Rachel muttered, and poured herself another drink.

"Do you mean Simon Bunting?" asked Libby.

"Ah—the Simon at Love and Christiansen."

"That's him."

I almost spat out my tea. "What does Simon do for Love and Christiansen?"

"He's an engineer," Libby answered. "He majored in engineering, just like Scott. I think they were even fraternity brothers. They roomed together senior year, then Simon came out here and took a master's at Colorado School of Mines."

"And Gerald Luftweiller?"

Libby smiled coyly, as if I'd asked her a slightly naughty question. "Gerry was a year behind them at Haverford. He tried to pledge their fraternity, but he wasn't chosen."

For some reason, Rachel again dropped the headsman's axe on the conversation. "Let's talk about something else," she snarled, the bourbon making her even more direct than usual.

Libby cast a quick, measuring glance her way and rose to her feet. "I hadn't noticed the time," she said sweetly. "I must run along. Rachel, thank you for a lovely meal, dear." She gave her a tiny kiss on the cheek. "Emmy, we must get together again, now that I know you're here. How can I reach you?"

"I'm staying with—"

"Oh, but of course, I can phone you at work. How silly of me. I look forward." She wrapped her slender arms around my neck and squeezed, surprising me again with the warmth of her farewell. Grabbing her pocketbook, she headed quickly out the door. I moved to follow, offering hurried thanks, but Rachel cut me off, gripping my arm at the biceps. "Watch out," she said, glaring at me.

I recoiled. "Watch out for what?"

"Just watch it, Em," she said, the fury disappearing as quickly as it had appeared. Her eyes sank back toward the bottle of bourbon. I was dismissed.

I again tried to thank her, but when she didn't respond, I closed the door behind myself and headed down the block to Bill's truck.

I was just firing up its hefty V-8 engine when a car pulled up next to me. It was a blue Saab, and my heart quickened as I thought for a moment that it might be Pete. The window slid smoothly down into the door, eliminating the glare that divided me from a view of the driver. It was Libby.

"How about lunch some day this week?" she caroled. "I wanted to invite you in there, but Rachel was getting into such an ugly mood."

"What got her going?"

"I don't know. Rachel's my closest friend, but I can't say I understand her. Now, about lunch . . ."

"Sure."

"Wonderful. Tuesday?"

"Sure."

"I'll come get you at your office."

"You don't need to do that. I can meet you somewhere. My office is way up on the twelfth floor, and it costs a mint to park—"

She smiled. "I know exactly where it is, and besides—"

"Libby, how is it you know where I'm working? I don't remember telling you, or Rachel, for that matter."

"My husband told me. He works at Blackfeet, too. I can just zip into the garage and park the car"—she wiggled the monthly pass ticket that hung from the rearview mirror—"and leave it there while we eat. It's where I always park when I come downtown on a weekday. See you then."

The window slid back up into place and the Saab pulled away. As it rolled past, I saw that its back seat was folded down. A bright branch of yellow aspen leaves lay in the back, where my bicycle had been.

Libby. Elizabeth. Libby; of course, a nickname for Elizabeth. So many of us were letting go of girlhood nicknames, now that we were grown. Elizabeth Tutaraitis. No, Elizabeth Hopkins; why take a surname one couldn't spell, especially in this day and age?

A pair of earnest joggers panted past the truck, a miscellaneous flash of fluorescent spandex lodging somewhere in my memory. Stunned, I sat staring through the windshield at nothing, as the great truck engine mindlessly idled, pumping blue exhaust into the rarified Denver air.

20

I considered packing up and heading home to the ranch. Even my mother seemed tame after what I had run into in those first two weeks in Denver. Winter was coming; surely Dad needed help with the cattle. Hey, he was getting older, right? Didn't he need me more than ever? Perhaps Mother wouldn't even ask why the little geologist was showing up so soon, calling up without warning from the bus stop in Cheyenne with my damned suitcases full of fancy suits.

"Get a grip on yourself," I muttered aloud, as I muscled the big old truck into Elyria's driveway. "You can't quit after only two weeks. So what if—"

If what? If it takes you twelve years to figure out Libby likes you, and now you find you've just slept with her husband?

I hurried out of the truck and stumbled through the house, into the living room, where I flopped onto the living room couch and squeezed my eyes shut. I couldn't get it together to cry it out, and if I had, I wasn't sure what I would have cried about, as the selection of humiliations seemed limitless. My mind trotted out one unkind image after another: me, laughing in business clothing; me in the committee room, pretending to be a geologist; me at lunch with Pete, making an ass of myself, sucking up Udon noodles like a sow, not even smart enough to check his ring finger to see if he's married. *How could he lie to me like that? She hadn't left him; she was there, waiting for him at home.*

Or did he know that? Didn't Rachel say Libby had just come back? Yes, that must be it.

I switched on the message playback on the answering machine, hoping it was Pete with some wild explanation of events, but another voice broke the silence of the room, deep and rough and uncertain: "Um—hi, Em. Ah, this is Frank. Yeah, I guess you know that. I'm ah—not used to these answering things. Give me a call, okay?"

Frank, oh no. . . . I tried to comfort myself that at least I still had good, kind, dependable, moody old Frank. But my body wanted Pete. I felt too guilty to even think of calling Frank back. As I sat there trying to figure out what to do about him, the phone rang again. With a sigh, I picked it up.

It was dear old Grannie phoning from Boston.

"Emily, have you gotten together with your classmates as I suggested?"

Yeah, and with their husbands. "Yes, Grandmother, I have."

"With Rachel Conant, and the Warren girl?"

At least I had this one frail accomplishment to report, but my tone sounded dead even to me. "Yeah, and I just saw Rachel again. She had me to brunch with Libby Hopkins."

"The Hopkins girl? How lovely. She's in Denver? Why, she just came to tea on Friday. Heavens, that was only two days ago. You'll remember her grandmother, Anne Kilbourne; she's one of my oldest friends. Libby is her only grandchild. Anne usually comes on Wednesday, but Libby wasn't available." As my grandmother's voice took on a harsh note of complaint, I quit listening. What had she said? They had tea on Friday? *Then Libby only came back last night. Maybe Pete didn't know she was coming, didn't expect her to return.* I said, "Really? Friday? The day before yesterday?"

"Yes, Emily; I'm not senile. In my day, it was two days by train to Denver, and the track was uneven west of Chicago." My grandmother had no use for the West, other than as a compass direction to disregard. She spoke of it very seldom, as if my mother's elopement to Wyoming was caught in the emotional amber of the railroad age.

"It's just a four-hour flight now, Grandmother," I said, struggling to keep my voice level. "And from the airport, it's barely two hours' drive north to Chugwater," I added, daring to remind her that she had never visited us on the ranch.

After a pause, my grandmother's voice came back over the line, placing the subject firmly back where she wanted it. "Libby seemed so terribly interested in hearing all about what you were doing."

If Libby only knew. "How nice."

"Yes, such a pleasant girl. You'd do well to cultivate her friendship, you know. She's very well connected. I always thought her father beneath Anne Kilbourne's family, but perhaps he has some redeeming qualities after all; he set those children up quite well. It all but broke Anne's heart to have

Libby gone so far away, but the dear girl does get back to visit quite often."

Had Libby's "desertion" been one of her frequent visits to see her grandmother? "How nice," I muttered.

"Really, Emily, you're such a sullen girl. Now, the reason for my call: I hear that Barbara Dinsmoore's nephew Scott died this week. You might have known him at school. He was living out west somewhere. Do send her a note, won't you? It's important to make the right gesture. It will help her in her grief."

"Sure," I said. "But it wasn't just out here somewhere. He was living right here, in Denver. He was working at Blackfeet, with me."

My grandmother's voice dropped in volume, its martial fire diminishing in a hush of discomfort. "Oh, my poor dear, I didn't know."

"Right."

There was silence on the other end of the line. I waited a moment, listening to my breath on the receiver, then told her that I had to get off the phone.

"Good-bye, Emily," she said. For the first time in my knowledge of her, she sounded old and frail.

I took the bicycle west along Thirty-second Avenue, riding high up a rise to a place where I could see the mountains of the Front Range and the clouds above them, and finally had my cry.

Monday morning, the dog and I were both so disconsolate that I almost ate his pill for him. Late for the bus again, I staggered in to work under the derisive gaze of the receptionist and went straight for the coffee room. I then retreated to my office and pretended to read the Lost Coyote well files for the better part of an hour, at which time the entire office headed down Broadway for Scott's memorial service.

I dawdled behind the crowd, putting off my next meeting with Pete as long as I could. I was most of a block behind him, trailing along with the secretaries in spike heels, when I realized that Pete was making this very easy for me. He never glanced around. My heart weighted my chest like a rock.

St. Andrew's Episcopal was a somber grey stone affair with the usual stained-glass saints rolling their humble eyes heavenward. After several minutes of fairly nice organ music, the priest made his entrance. He couldn't have been much past thirty, judging by his full head of limp brown hair and flawless skin, but his jaw was locked in pompous irritability, and he moved up the aisle as rigidly as a man of ninety. When he reached the altar and began to speak, his voice swelled and swooped weirdly out of synchronization with his words, and it was obvious from what he chose to say that he had never met Scott.

As the hymns and testimonies rumbled on, I scanned through the dim atmosphere of the church, trying to place all the mourners. Libby sat with Rachel and Topsy on the right side of the aisle, serenely heading the group of social acquaintances.

J. C. Menken and Dave Smith sat at the front of the Blackfeet group, looking noble. They had established their importance by arriving at the last minute, sliding up to the curb in Menken's Mercedes-Benz instead of walking with the rest of us. Smith was as unreadable as ever, but nonetheless clearly commanded the surviving engineers, who huddled in a silent knot right behind him. The rest of Blackfeet's personnel sat in clots along the left side of the aisle.

Clots. My mind moved spasmodically to the image of that strange something—Scottie—dropping past the glass in the Cattlemen's Exchange Building. The scene appeared in my mind's eye like a small dim window flickering open in a velvet darkness. I rubbed my hand over my eyes, trying to squeeze that window shut, but it flicked open again and again.

When I opened my eyes, I was staring at the back of Pete's neck. He had seated himself on the left side of the aisle with the Blackfeet crew, next to Maddie. He leaned toward her and whispered something. She rotated her head toward him and screwed her nose up like he stank, and chewed her gum.

My attention drifted to a fellow who sat immediately behind the last of the Blackfeet engineers, crammed up against the aisle as if he wasn't sure whether he was a friend or a colleague, his broad shoulders looming high above the back of the pew. He had a turret-shaped head crowned with thick, closely cropped blond curls. Had I seen him somewhere before? There was something familiar about him. No, I figured, second-guessing myself, he's just a type. I must have seen at last five dozen guys just like him at prep school.

But something about him kept catching my eye: each time he turned profile to glance at my old classmates, I found myself watching him. *Preppius americanus var. boyjockus,* I mused. *Common name, pinhead locker room stud. Thinks he's God's gift; a dime a dozen.* In my mind's eye, I rigged him up in lacrosse gear with vicious thick and heavy gloves, tiny pig eyes peering out through the wire face cage of the helmet.

The service began to wind toward its merciful end. At the first moment that could remotely be construed as polite, I made my move toward the door and the bright air of outdoors where I could breathe and make a run for my office, but as I passed through the vestibule, I spied two familiar forms ahead of me in the doorway.

Lieutenant Flint creased the lower half of his face in his hi-there-fellow-space-traveler grin as he moved calmly toward a new post outside the entrance to the church. He selected a position from which, I presumed, he could breathe down each mourner's neck. Sergeant Ortega moved more quickly, positioning himself farther out on the sidewalk where he could observe the gathering with strategic ease. When he saw me, he bowed gravely from the waist.

I decided to stick around, but moved over to an inconspicuous position at one side of the entrance where I wouldn't have to cross paths with either Pete or Libby.

Abruptly, the mourners disgorged from the church, but upon reaching the sidewalk, they milled about in confusion. They had no central mourner to file past, no script indicating how to behave next.

I watched as the tall blond jock type tried to figure out what to do with himself, and the longer I watched him, the more certain I was that I'd seen him before. Suddenly, he leaned forward and grabbed the arm of the person next to him to mutter something I couldn't hear.

Bingo. I'd seen that gesture before. Recently. This was the guy who had buttonholed Pete on the sidewalk the day I had lunch with Rachel and Topsy. The day after Scott died. Who was he?

As I pondered that, mourners continued to ooze from the church. As they idled on the sidewalk, I could have sworn I saw a chain reaction of pregnant glances, precipitated as Libby alighted on the sidewalk, flanked by Rachel and Topsy. The turret-headed blond man straightened up and stared nastily at Libby, who averted her eyes sadly toward Rachel. Rachel scorched the guy with a single, telegraphic glare. The guy wheeled on Pete, who was just wandering out with his hands in his pockets. Pete gave him a *Who, me?* kind of shrug and

glanced at Fred Crick. Crick stared helplessly at Smith. Smith
fixed his stare hard on Pete, who gave him the same amount of
notice he would if he were waiting for a bus in a crowd of
strangers. Then the receptionist joined the scene. She tripped
daintily as she crossed the threshold of the church and froze
her delicate face into a poisonous glare, which she applied to
Pete, Libby, Rachel, and me in turn.

As I was trying to sort out this sequence of nonverbal com-
munications, Menken strode out into the sun and squinted,
thrust a hand inside his suit jacket for his sunglasses, and oc-
cupied himself with applying them to his face. All eyes turned
to him, waiting for him to climb into his Mercedes, so they
could politely leave. Ortega and Flint nodded genteelly to each
mourner in turn. The other members of the office wandered
around, muttering things that sounded appropriate while they
waited for Menken to make a move.

The tension finally got the better of me. The whole revolting
mess, and every person involved with it, had my stomach
churning. I moved to the edge of the crowd and turned away.

And spotted one more person who was casting pregnant
stares upon the multitude. There by the end of the building, in
all his wild sartorial splendor, stood the strange man the police
had spirited out of the parking garage the night of Scottie's
death. He was huddled up against the stone as if for warmth,
taking in the spectacle like it was some of his own brand of
street theater. What was his name? Archie Arch, that was what
Ortega had called him. I turned, caught Ortega's eyes, and
tipped my head toward Archie. Ortega lowered his eyelids
slowly and raised them again, an unmistakable signal that he
had the guy well fixed on his radar screen.

The crowd milled, more and more ill at ease, but still no one
broke loose and started the flow back north to the office. It
seemed they were waiting for some signal from Menken, who
stood smiling in the midst of the miasma, apparently thriving
on the high energy of emotional chaos. The muscles at the
back of my neck tightened. I was just contemplating hurling a
parking meter into the throng when Topsy broke the tension
for me: releasing her grip on Libby, she threw herself at the
man with the turret-shaped head and the Aryan curls, hugged
him to her squashy bosom, and bellowed, "Oh, Simon, what's
it like to lose your best friend in the whole world?"

21

So this obstruction is Simon Bunting, eh? I thought, as I squeezed past well-clothed elbows. *I want to talk to you, Bubba.* I was two strides from the wrestling match between Simon and Topsy when a hand closed on my elbow. Firmly. I spun around, and was surprised to find that the strong grip belonged to J. C. Menken. He drew me backward, extracting me from the crowd. He said, "Emily, let me give you a ride."

At the curb, Dave Smith was waiting for Menken to unlock the car door for him. At the sight of me, his gaze turned hard as stone. Menken opened the door to the Mercedes and helped me in. Smith waited, expecting Menken to at least unlock a back door for him, but Menken climbed into the driver's seat, pressed a button to open the sunroof, gunned the motor, and pulled away from the curb. I felt Smith's eyes boring into me just as if he were pressing at my skull with a thumb.

Menken spoke in a confidential tone: "I'm sure this is very difficult for you, coming to work for us, and then losing one of your colleagues so suddenly. You've hardly had a chance to get used to us, and here you are in the midst of our grief."

Menken sounded positively lucid. It gave me the crawly sensation an antelope must experience when a coyote shifts a little closer to it, approaching from downwind. "Thank you, sir," I mumbled.

"Who were all those people in the church? You seemed to know some of them."

"Friends of Scott's from school."

"Tell me about them," he said.

"I don't really know them," I lied. The last thing I wanted was to be Menken's ambassador to this mare's nest of intertwined relationships.

The Mercedes boomed into the parking garage, its heavy motor echoing off the overhead concrete until Menken closed

the sunroof. He pulled smoothly into a space right next to the
door on the main level. No subbasement for this man.

I suffered two more minutes of his prying as the elevator swallowed us and raised us to the twelfth floor, but as soon as we hit
Blackfeet's lobby, Irma Triff mercifully cut off the conversation
with a pile of pink While You Were Out phone message slips.

I ducked into the women's room and took a roost, hoping to
evade detection until everyone was back at their desks and settled down.

Wrong strategy. A few minutes later, the receptionist came
in. I watched her delicate ankles under the divider as she
pointed her little toes toward the neighboring porcelain god,
genuflected, and offered up her breakfast. As she retreated to
the sink and rinsed her mouth, the outside door opened again
and in they came, the whole raucous Greek chorus of gossiping girl engineers and geologists.

". . . see Menken move on Hansen?"

"Yeah, like wow. You think she's his new toy?"

Peals of laughter. "Maybe that's how she got the job."

I pulled my feet up onto the seat, but it was too late: I heard
a swat and more laughter, as one of them lowered her voice
and said, "What if that's her in that stall?" The door groaned
open and their giggles moved into the hall.

I counted to sixty and stormed back to my office. *So that's
what they think, huh? They think the little twit without the
master's degree is such a retard she has to fuck for a living,
huh? I'll show them a thing or two. Watch this.* Plopping into
my chair, I gave Maddie a nasty look and grabbed a stack of
well logs.

Maddie popped her eyes at me and stuck a finger into her
cheek. "Something y'all et?" she drawled.

"Yeah: shit." I flipped open the first fan-folded log. The
long squiggly line on the graph paper held no music for me,
but by God, I was going to stare at it until it sang a full octave.

"Sure, sweetums," I heard Maddie say, as I screwed my
mind to the log, "but was it *good* shit?"

The first log meant nothing to me. In exasperation, I folded
it back up and arranged the logs on top of my desk and stared
at them, daring them to spill the beans about the field. The
swine just lay there, each little fan-folded stack baring only its
header, which primly listed well name, location, and other sta-
tistics of no earth-shattering importance. I contemplated
threatening them with a match.

But wait, one was subtly different. I smiled at my old trick of noticing the one that didn't quite conform to pattern: the information on its header was filled in by hand, in contrast to the sterile sans-serif typeface the others presented to the world. Scrawled across the top of the header were the words *field print*.

I pounced. Field prints I understood: they were the preliminary copies of the logs printed right in the logging trailer in the field. I flipped it open, and found nirvana: some marvelous logging engineer had marked the tops and bottoms of all the rock formations from surface down through the sandstone I had been trying to recognize. With this information, I at last had a handle with which to open the door to understanding Lost Coyote Field.

About then, Fritz tossed the morning report onto my desk. It slid across my logs and into my lap, scattering paper and pencils onto the floor. I sat up for a moment and blinked.

Maddie smiled at him and made kissy lips.

All the morning report had to say about Lost Coyote Field was that the rig was drilling merrily away, engineer or no. I made a note of the progress in the well file. The I jittered for about five minutes, wondering what I was going to do with the well logs now that I had the Rosetta Stone. It was like pulling a book off the shelf and opening it without knowing how to read: knowing which wiggle was the "pay" interval was great, but to make sense of the correlation, I still had to know something about the geometry of the sandstone. I needed a conceptual model to start with, a template to compare with what I saw on the logs.

That was where the papers I'd been reading were supposed to come in. I opened the one that showed a map of the geography of Wyoming as it hypothetically appeared ninety million years ago, and dove in.

I mean literally. Eastern Wyoming was under water at the time. The middle of the continent had warped downward during that epoch, inundating the Great Plains with a shallow sea. Seas have waves. Waves move sand along the shoreline, forming beaches. Beach sand makes highly permeable sandstones, which make wonderful petroleum reservoirs if they happen to wind up buried under, say, a shale or a limestone, and a few thousand feet of other sediments.

"Maddie," I said, "this sandstone at Lost Coyote. You think it's beach sand?"

"Naw, I think that far west you're in the fluvial facies."

That brought me up short. Maddie had just spoken genuine geologese, cluing me in that this sandstone had been deposited by the river that flowed from the highlands to the sea, not by the waves that swept along the shore. The beach sands would be farther east.

And then I could see it: the log showed me thick lenses of sandstone laid down in the changeable channels of a river, encased in shales deposited as part of the adjacent floodplain. Sandstone, shale, sandstone, shale. Channel, bank, channel, bank. It was like opening my eyes and really seeing for the first time.

In my excitement, I forgot to be blasé. "Maddie! This is great! Show me how to correlate this stuff."

Maddie hopped up from her chair and came over to my desk. "The only trick's in figuring out where one channel disappears laterally and another begins, because these fluvial sands is somewhat erratic, geometrically speaking, kind of like lace. Look: the sandstone signature in these two wells—this big blocky-looking hummer—match up pretty well. That's your gravy boat." She fished through the stack of logs for the next well to the west. "Here it is in the next hole." She traced the curve of the log signature with her finger. "See? It's got a nose on it like Jimmy Durante, real distinctive." The curve swung to the right, then the left. "Then over here it's getting thinner, just like you'd expect at the edge of the channel."

Maddie then showed me how to slide the logs up and down to make a correlation, using idiosyncrasies in the shale signatures above and below to confirm the match in the sandstones. "Y'all got it. You're a natural," she declared, punching me in the shoulder. She went back to her desk and sat down. "One hell of a field. You're looking at clean sand forty feet thick, permeable as hell and chock-full of oil and gas. It's a barnburner." Pulling a new stick of gum out of the lap drawer of her desk, she mugged at me briefly and went back to work.

Using Maddie's techniques, I tacked the well logs up on the wall, where I could see them better. Then I rearranged them this way and that, stepping back to check my work. Suddenly I saw something very interesting. The biggest river channel sandstone in the field, the one that was producing most of the gas, was really thick right in the middle of the field, and then in the next well to the west it was a bit thinner but just as good a producer, then there was the well that was drilling, and then—

Then the edge of the field.

Or was it the edge?

I glanced back at the map. There was another well I could patch in to the correlation, a bit north of my line of correlation, but close enough. Where was the log for that one?

I dug through the remaining logs. It wasn't there. I looked for its well file. Ditto.

The fifty-million-dollar question was, how far did the sandstone go? Did it peter out between the existing well and our new well? The wells farther north and south were okay, but no barn-burners, as Maddie said. Had the existing wells already defined the edge of the field? Or was the sandstone as thick to the west? We'd want to find out, right? And the way to find out was to drill a new well, right? If we hit the sandstone in the new well, it was likely to be the best producer in the field.

So why the debate about drilling the new well?

And where the hell was that log?

I left my work spread out on my desk and headed for the elevator.

The vault madam was in residence. I gave her a big smile. "When I came down here Friday, did you give me everything you had for Lost Coyote?" I asked.

She coughed and nodded her head.

"Could you double-check?"

Her face pursed up like she was trying to swap her mouth for her nose.

"Please?" I smiled as sweetly as I knew how, loading on the charm with a trowel.

She lurched off of her stool and shuffled slowly toward the back of the file room. While she searched, I riffled back through her sign-out book again, this time reading the column that listed what was signed out. Nothing. *Nada.* I was the only one other than Scott who had checked anything out from Lost Coyote in months.

The woman returned, shaking her head. I thanked her profusely, and headed upstairs. As the elevator yanked me upward through the bowels of the building, I wracked my memory for the second time, trying to remember the color of the tab on the file Pete had been carrying. *Well, even it if was orange, it could be any field in Wyoming, right? Right, but then why did he have a Wyoming file at all, if he was California?* I wondered if I had the nerve to go ask him.

It occurred to me that Scott might have had the files. I tried to remember if there were any logs on his desk when I was looking for the red notebook. *Maybe it was the well he'd been testing,* I thought, as I got out of the elevator and hurried down the hall. *Maybe he just forgot to sign it out.* The hallway seemed to have grown in length, dangerously long, and I wanted to duck into Scott's office before anyone saw me. I broke into a run, and grabbed the door frame as I banked the curve into his office. There was someone sitting behind Scott's desk: my old pal Sergeant Ortega.

"I'm the bad penny, huh?" he said, smiling merrily. I had evidently interrupted him while he was going through the lap drawer with a pair of tweezers.

I started to back out of the room. Ortega bowed his head sadly and looked at his hands. "I don't want to get you in trouble," he said, in his soft song of a voice.

I stopped. What was he looking for?

He gestured at the open drawer. "Just grasping for straws," he explained. "You never know what you're going to find."

I stepped back into the room, dodging to one side of the doorway where I couldn't be seen from the hall, and craned my neck, trying to get a look inside the drawer.

Ortega straightened up in Scott's chair and grinned at me. He was clearly enjoying himself. This was one detective who would chase a dead man's ghost forever if he had to, just to learn the cause of death. I was beginning to find his one-pointed focus almost soothing, as simple as the appeal of drawing close to a warm, well-tended hearth on a cold night.

"What were you looking for this time?" he asked, his round brown face now beaming.

"I was looking for a well log," I said, drawing closer to the desk. "And the well file that went with it."

Ortega shook his head. "I don't think it's here. What do they look like?"

I tried to explain, gesturing with my hands as to size, and describing the manila file with its orange tab.

"No, definitely no file with an orange tab, and no log. Why do you want them?"

I was just trying to decide whether it was okay to tell him, when I heard a loud clearing of throat from behind me.

I spun around. And found Dave Smith, an inch and a half away.

22

Smith's eyes were narrow, opaque, but his voice was smooth. "Say, Em, could you come to my office for just a moment?" he asked. He rotated toward Ortega. "Sorry to interrupt, Sergeant, but I must insist that company business come first."

Ortega smiled affably. My stomach contracting into a knot, I turned and followed Smith down the hall, marveling once again at the lack of animation in his carriage. Once we were inside his office, Smith closed the door and indicated a seat for me across the desk from him. He sat down and gazed steadily at me.

"What did you want to see me about, sir?" I asked, unconsciously slipping into prep school manners.

Smith continued his unblinking stare, a cobra frightening its prey into paralysis. I waited for him to speak. And waited. As the seconds ticked past with no reply, it became clearer and clearer that this was a conscious attempt to intimidate me. And a successful one. When every last muscle in my body had stiffened, he finally said, "You're new here, Em, and I'm concerned that no one has spent enough time orienting you to company policies." The words were solicitous, but the tone was icy. "Has anyone explained to you our policy toward proprietary information? Hmm?"

No one needed to, damn it.

"It's vitally important that we keep company matters within the company."

"Yes, I know that," I snapped.

He continued as if I hadn't said anything. "We must maintain Blackfeet's edge over the competition. Y'see, Em, a casual comment here or there could cause us considerable damage if overheard by the wrong party. Even mentioning your work to someone else in this company, say, over lunch down the street; why, it could be overheard by a competitor."

His eyes had not left mine since we'd sat down. I tried to return his stare, wondering what there was in the presence of the police that worried him so. Certainly not just the idea that a freshman geologist might be indiscreet with proprietary information?

"Take Lost Coyote Field, as an example. You may think, why, this is a development project, what's the danger? Well, Em, the wells are on public record, but company policy regarding their operation and our interpretation of the geology of the field are not."

He paused for emphasis.

"Now, Em, we understand that you want to come up to speed as a geologist, being new in from mudlogging"—he paused again, rubbing this in—"and of course, you want to know the field. But you also want to keep an eye toward maximizing your efficiency. This is really a very simple field, fully contained stratigraphically, and it's given us no real problems. One of our best producers, as a matter of fact. The engineering staff have it well in hand." He turned a great flat palm upward on his desk top as he delivered his final blow. "So you'll spend no further time on it at present."

"But—"

"But what, Em?"

But there's nothing else for me to do around here. And what the hell do you mean, the engineers have it well in hand? Engineers don't know stratigraphy. And if it's such a simple little field, why do you care who knows it?

He hadn't blinked or looked away from me since he'd sat down. I tried to stare back at him in defiance, but could not. I began to squirm in my chair. *What a filthy trick,* I thought furiously. *Don't his eyes dry out?*

"Good," he said, his tone now fully glacial. "You're a smart girl; I knew you'd understand. I've had Fritz collect the files for Lost Coyote from your office."

I was wasting time thinking, *I'm not a girl, you sorry piece of shit, I am a full-grown and very angry woman,* when it hit me: this monster had just taken my work away from me, had stolen it right off my desk. "You what?" I shouted. I stared straight into his nasty eyes. "Listen, I was in the middle of—"

"The files will stay in the vault until this investigation is closed, Miss Hansen." His voice darkened to a low rumble as he delivered his final words: "Let this stand as a warning to you. That is all." He flicked his fingertips at me, imbedding his threat with the insult of dismissal.

I stood, suddenly aware of what little armor business clothes afford the flesh. I backed toward the door. His words had done their damage: I had no idea what the company policy was on these things, and his tactics had rocked me hard enough that I was already scrutinizing myself for error. I turned and left his office.

I headed straight for Fred Crick's office. I would demand my right to do my job. His door was closed. I knocked; no answer. The geology secretary advised me that Crick would be gone until the middle of next week.

"Where is he?" I asked.

"Tulsa."

"Can I reach him there?"

"Well, he's at a conference. Is it urgent?" She eyed me nervously.

Couldn't these people see that I was just a normal honest person trying to make a living? Or was honesty not normal in the oil business? All at once I realized that I wasn't even sure what I was going to say or ask if I had found Fred Crick, considering his management style. Or lack of. "No, I guess it can wait."

Deflated, I dragged myself down the hall to my office.

But when I got there and saw empty space where my only decent work had been, rage swelled within me all over again. I spun on my heel and stared at Maddie. "Is this really standard operating procedure, to take someone's work away just like that?" I demanded, pointing at the wall.

"Do what, honey?"

I could have smacked her. "This business of taking my work down without asking me is *do what*. This business of telling me to work on a field and then keeping information from me is *do what*. This business of telling me that my opinion doesn't count for shit, that the engineers can 'do' the geology for me is goddamn *do what*. Honey."

"Don't look at me, sweetie pea." She widened her eyes like she didn't know what I was talking about. "I jus' works here, massuh. I be a good geol'gis', massuh; I don't make no trouble."

"Oh come on, McNutt, engineers are just number crunchers. The data have to get in a straight line and salute before those guys get the picture. They can't do geology; maybe they can spot crude oil five falls out of ten when they find it in a stock tank, but they don't know sandstone from Shinola. Shit. They couldn't find their asses with both hands and a road map." It was quite a speech. It impressed even me.

Maddie draped herself across her desk top and batted her eyelashes at me. "Is that so?"

I blew. "Great. So where the fuck were you when they were taking my work down? Get serious, Maddie."

Maddie straightened up very slowly, flipping her long-suffering eraser up and down in one hand.

I lasted a whole ten seconds in *that* staring match, too.

I sat down, completely out of steam. Confrontation isn't my long suit, and Maddie wasn't even the person I needed to confront. In a very small voice, I asked, "What's going on here, Maddie?"

Maddie folded her arms tightly across her chest and stared out the window for a moment. In a soft little drawl, she said, "A girl needs to watch her ass around this man's oil patch, honey pie."

"But Maddie, they took my only assignment away from me. If they don't want me to do the work, then why did they hire me?"

"Got me, buck-o."

"I was starting to get somewhere this morning. It was important."

Maddie shrugged.

"Crick's out of the office. Should I go to Menken?"

"Aw, c'mon, Emmy, don't do that. Y'all might interrupt one of his real estate deals."

"His what?"

She tossed up her hands. "He's on the phone most of the time, wheeling and dealing in real estate." Her voice trailed off. She leaned back and closed her eyes in meditation.

"Real estate?" I asked.

I watched her a while, fascinated at this new person emerging from within the bouncy, bombproof exterior. By and by she sat up, blinked her eyes, and yawned, as if she were just waking up from a heavy sleep. "Menken's on company business for state occasions like hirings and firings and committee meetings only," she said, her tone crisply matter-of-fact.

"Then maybe I should call a committee meeting."

"See? Now, that's exactly what I mean. Where's that gonna getcha, supergirl?" She laughed dryly, shaking her head. "Em, honey, y'all's got it wrong. Y'all think a committee meeting's a place where Menken and the boys listens to folks and makes decisions. Y'all been living out there in the oil fields with the boys so long that you think you're one of the boys. Worse yet, you think they think like you think, all straightforward and reasonable like. Wake up, honey bun. The fact of life is, they do most of their serious business in the Gents."

"In the what?"

"The latrines. They aims their whizzers at the porcelain and talks turkey."

"Shit," I said.

Maddie smiled. "No, mostly just shakin' the dew off the lily, standing there straight up for ease of comparing lengths." She held her hands up about three inches apart and pondered this image a moment, snapping her gum thoughtfully. "They pro'ly save the full squat for corporate mergers. Hey, look at the bright side, sweet peach, at least you got a job!" With that benediction, she hunkered down over her desk and went back to work, whistling a little Hank Williams riff.

I stared at the top of her head, wishing things were as clear to me, or that I could manage life as easily as she.

My eyes sagged shut with a fatigue that was painful.

In the darkness behind my eyelids, I saw Scott flailing past me in his last instant of life, but this time there were threads connected to his hands and feet, like a ghastly marionette. The image played again and again, demanding that I put him to rest in the cold, damp body of the earth.

In panic I opened my eyes. The room seemed stark, too brightly lit. All at once, I could see the price of playing it safe to keep this job, and that price was entirely too dear. Where in hell had I gotten the idea I could cooperate with a system that fostered violent death?

I couldn't. And by God, I wouldn't.

A strange calm settled over me. I knew that Maddie, in her dependable way, would rise from her desk shortly after five, toss down her eraser, scratch her stomach, and head for home.

I waited quietly, my hand resting palms-upward in my lap. When she had left, I pulled the phone book off the bookshelf, looked up the number I needed, and dialed.

A brisk, martial voice answered: "Denver Police."

"Homicide," I said. "Sergeant Ortega, please."

23

Ortega presented himself at Elyria's at eight P.M. sharp. He smiled kindly as he stepped through the front door, and nodded hopefully toward the kitchen.

"Sure," I said. "Coffee's just the thing. Or would you prefer something stronger?"

Ortega sighed. "Coffee. I'm on du-ty," he sang. He passed through the living room and stepped politely over the dog, who was doing his impression of a corpse in the doorway to the kitchen. Ortega sat down at the round wooden table by the stove and pulled out his battered notebook.

I appreciated his getting right down to business. It gave me room to be just as direct, and not waste mental energy on some attempt at social niceties. I put the kettle on to boil and sat down across from him. "So, Sergeant, this is murder, not suicide, right?"

Ortega nodded.

"Will you tell me how you know?"

He smiled wanly. "Okay. Okay, if you'll tell me how *you* know."

I studied Ortega carefully, trying to decide what I could tell him. I was no longer a child, who could look at a problem as if it were all black and white: Scottie might be dead, but everyone else at Blackfeet was still alive and trying to make a living in an increasingly difficult world. Who was I to open up company business, risking putting even one of them out of work? No, I'd keep quiet about the workings of Lost Coyote Field until I truly understood them, and make my best judgment from there. "Listen, I'm in a bad position. There are things that have me wondering, but I don't even know if they have anything to do with Scottie's death."

Ortega smiled. "Try me."

"No, they wouldn't mean anything to you, anyway. They're technical matters. I know you can subpoena me, or whatever it is you do, but that still won't get you anywhere, because I don't understand these things myself, and anyone else at Blackfeet will just tell you I'm imagining things, or too new at my job. But I will promise you this: I'm working as fast as I can, and when I do understand them, I'll tell you everything that has a bearing on Scott's death."

Ortega considered this. "That's fair. But at least tell me in a general way why you think it's murder."

"Because there are too many connections between Scott's death and everyone who knew him."

Ortega nodded.

I hung my head, staring at my hands. "I hate this. There are people involved in this that I know from a long time ago, and from back east, and others I've just met here. Somehow, they all know each other, and they're all connected one way or another to my work. It's like a maze that keeps bringing me back to the same point. I didn't want to be mixed up in this." I stopped, afraid that Ortega might think I was whining, but when I looked up, he was listening intently, his pencil put away, his hands folded on the table in front of him. There was nothing indifferent or impersonal in the look in his eyes. Sergeant Ortega probably wasn't more than eight or ten years older than I, but he had in his serene gaze the wisdom of someone who had walked this earth for ages. "There's just too many ways the paths cross near Scottie's death," I concluded quickly, wondering if I were making any sense at all.

"Yes. Our man was at the center of everything."

"So that's why you think it's murder too, and not suicide?"

Ortega shook his head. "No. Most murders, they're simpler than this. The murderer stands out like a scar, catching your notice like the pain that caused it. But this one, the pain of the killing is obscured. Everyone around it is angry, defensive, covering the pain." He made a fluttering gesture with his hands, like bats chasing about in the dark, and stared blankly at the table top. "I can't get to this one."

The kettle screamed, and I got up to make the coffee. Ortega was being more philosophical than informative, again deflecting my question. I tried a different tack. "Okay, I thought about it a lot this afternoon, and I can count at least five people who might have a motive to kill Scott, but none of their motives seem quite strong enough. Perhaps you'd say no one has quite enough pain, or is quite angry enough to have done this."

I shuddered at the thought of Dave Smith's coldness. "Unless we think of the people who might be doing it for sheer profit."

Ortega smiled sadly. "People seldom kill for money. More often they kill for the power they think comes with it."

"Power? Okay. Dave Smith wants power. And Menken has power and probably doesn't want to lose it." Was Smith setting Menken up for a fall? Perhaps. Certainly, money was the common denominator among all these people who were connected with the murder. Blackfeet was in business to find oil, but it takes money—investment capital—to find that oil. Without that capital and cash flow, Menken would fall from power. If Smith could grasp control of the money, he would take the power from him, and eliminate Fred Crick while he was at it. As financial manager, Jon Hathaway was frantic about money and probably didn't care exactly where it came from. Pete, of course, stood to gain directly through overriding royalties on all oil produced from Lost Coyote. Good old Pete.

As I set the coffee to drip through the grounds into the pot on the stove, I ran down my mental list of suspects. Who else had been in the building that night? The receptionist? I didn't know enough about her to know how she might stand to gain from Scott's death. Simon Bunting: had he been there? His interest in Lost Coyote Field would be at a professional level, rather than financial, or would it? And was the suicide of Love and Christiansen's accountant connected to all of this?

Ortega sat quietly, saying nothing further. I did the same, hoping the weight of silence might persuade him to talk. I'd met my part in the bargain, now it was his turn.

The coffee finished dripping. I poured Ortega a cup but let it sit conspicuously on the counter.

Ortega smiled at me and picked up his pencil. "I'll just catch up on my notes," he said.

That did it. I slapped the countertop, hard, surprising even myself. "Are you going to tell me or not?"

Ortega stared at the table in front of him, his cheeks turning a deep mahogany red. "I'm sorry. If I tell you any more, it would involve you—"

"I'm already involved."

"You can still get out. You're young. You'll heal."

Heal? I see falling bodies on the backs of my eyelids, and I'll heal? "Listen, Sergeant, if you won't let me work *with* you, I'll work *without* you."

Ortega's dark eyes went coal black. He leaned across the

table and tapped it with one short finger. "And maybe get yourself hurt. *You* listen to *me:* someone rigged this murder so well that no one in a building full of people saw it done. My job is not just solving murders; I'm supposed to *keep* people from getting killed."

"Fine. You've said your piece."

Ortega squeezed his eyes shut. He balled his hands into fists and muttered something I couldn't understand in Spanish. I believe he would have spat if his culture had not forbade such gestures in front of women. Opening his eyes and looking at his hands, he said, "There are things I can tell you directly, and things I cannot. It's a matter of evidence, particular things I have to keep quiet about. Then, if you or anyone else were to confess, I could say, 'How did you do it?' and you'd say how, and then I'd know if you did it or not by what you knew."

So we were *both* concealing proprietary information. At least that puts us on even ground.

"Ask me something else," he offered.

"Did you find a witness who saw someone leaving the parking garage that night?"

Ortega opened his eyes in surprise. "No. Why do you ask?"

"Before you got there, a couple of cops were talking about possible routes people could have taken out of the building. There was one route out of the parking garage that wasn't covered, and then the question of the dock door."

"We got it covered. They both let out onto Glenarm. The doorman at the Fairmont had a good view down there the whole time. He remembers, because all the traffic started going funny on Seventeenth, and he came out to the corner to find out why."

"Oh." That meant it was one of the people in the lobby that night. Or did it? "Did you and your men find anyone upstairs when you searched the building?"

"Just a couple janitors, on the eighth floor." He shook his head. "They didn't do it."

"And Archie was the only one in the garage?"

"Yes."

"And the guy who takes the money in the parking garage was clean?"

"Okay, yes; he's disabled, gets around on crutches. And his machine records the time of each transaction. There wasn't time for him to make it to the sixteenth floor and back, even if he could walk at a normal rate. We timed it."

Then it was true: the killer was someone who'd been standing in that lobby. I looked away, surprised to find how much I'd hoped it wasn't one of the people I worked with. Especially Pete. I sighed in exasperation. Was *that* the real issue here, to prove to myself that I hadn't slept with a murderer? Was I that vain?

I said, "Let me ask my question another way: why did you have to consider suicide, and not just accident and murder?"

Ortega dug his spoon ponderously into the sugar bowl. One heaping spoonful went into that half cup of coffee. Two. Three. He stared into the cup and stirred, a man transfixed by a demon. "Because it is good form to consider every possibility, and because the pattern of Mr. Dinsmoore's behavior was, as we say, consistent with suicide."

"But he was circling ads for houses to rent."

"He could have borrowed the paper from somebody else, already marked."

"He seemed so happy and serene that last day."

"Okay, yes, but gloomy and agitated just before. This is the pattern of a man chased by a thousand devils, who is despairing, and finally makes his peace. Unfortunately for such people, they only see one way to grasp their peace. Very common in suicides."

Menken's words floated up: *These people, they can't seem to think up a better option than killing themselves*. Was he right? "No, the whole picture doesn't fit. Someone as humorless as Scottie wouldn't choose to publicly end his life wearing something as, well, laughable as tartan pants. No, your forensics lab must have given you physical evidence that confirmed that Scott was murdered. Let me guess: you found plywood splinters in the back of his jacket, proving he was pushed."

Ortega closed his eyes and whispered, "*Hijo de Dios*. I will never make lieutenant." Opening his eyes again, he said: "No, a pocketknife was used to cut through the duct tape that was holding the plywood in place over the window on the sixteenth floor. The plywood was neatly set aside." He pantomimed the removal of the barrier.

"You can't find the knife?"

"Oh, we have the knife, all right, that's how we know a knife was used: it has the adhesive on it from the duct tape. The knife was in the deceased's pocket. But the fingerprints on the knife were wrong."

I leaned forward, thinking, *At last he's telling me how he knows*. "They were someone else's fingerprints?"

"Oh, no, they were his, but the grip was wrong." He demonstrated on his pencil. "To hold the grip right for cutting, you'd do this." He wrapped his fingers around the pencil in a good grip, then shifted it to an awkward, loose grip. "This wouldn't work at all." He pressed down on the table top with the pencil, and it slid out of his hand. "Besides"—and here he smiled—"our boy's a lefty. The prints were from his right." He shook his head, smiling at the joke. "These foolish murderers. They always screw up."

24

After Sergeant Ortega left, I sat up late outlining my ideas about who might have murdered Scott, and why. *For the solution to this little puzzle to make sense,* I reasoned, *there must be some connection to Lost Coyote Field. It follows from there that there's a connection to Hat Rock Field and Gerald Luftweiller, and from him to my old schoolmates, and from them . . .*

There my logic bogged down. I needed some way to sort out the pieces that fit from the extraneous ones that didn't.

Think like a geologist, Em, my critical conscience said, helpful for once. *Remember what your geology professor used to say? That the simpler explanation for a complex pattern was usually the correct one? Why not just look for the obvious stuff, and add in the flourishes only if they prove to be part of the whole?*

That seemed to make sense, so I went with it, outlining things on a piece of yellow legal paper in Bill's study. The dog wandered in and napped on the area rug, perhaps companionably. Or perhaps, that was just his spot. I wrote:

> Fact: Scott dies of a fall from 16th floor window.
> Fact: Persons present in building at time include

Here I trailed off, because the first person who popped into my mind was, of course, Pete Tutaraitis.

My mind tightened up into a knot. For the umpteenth time that day, I flailed myself with, *How could you do that, Em?*

In penance, I wrote PETER TUTARAITIS in letters about an inch high. Then I added several other names: Menken, Dave Smith, Crick. Moving to the right, I added a second column, entitled MOTIVE.

Well, for Pete I wasn't sure what to write under MOTIVE. His marriage could be part of another puzzle, not this one. I finally settled for writing "Financial interest in oil field," and stared at that for a while, trying to figure out how it might be a motive for murder. Could Scott have known something that would hurt Pete's interest in the field? The production rates were high. If someone was going to monkey with them to rip someone off, it would make more sense to underreport them and sell the overage on the black market without paying royalties. And in that case, Pete would lose out rather than gain, because his profits came from an overriding royalty, paid out of gross profits. And finally, if Pete were doing something illegal, it would be more to his interest if the drilling moved forward without publicity, so why kill someone and draw attention to the field?

And all of this presumed that there was indeed something nonkosher about this field. Which brought it back to my desk. What the hell was going on at Lost Coyote?

I went on to Menken, the next name on the list. His possible motivation didn't seem any clearer, but it was true that Scott had pulled a full court press on him shortly before his death. Had they really discussed a raise or promotion? If so, did that spell blackmail? Menken might be callous enough to commit murder, or perhaps just enough abstracted from the normal ebb and flow of human emotion. But I had been dismissing him as a lightweight, too involved in his manicured fingernails and real estate deals to get excited enough to kill anyone. And he hadn't seemed shrewd enough. From everything I'd seen so far, Smith was driving Menken like a car, steering the committee meetings and Menken's interaction with the police as if Menken were a halfwit. But then, there was Menken's split-second evaluation of the motivation for suicide, which had been right on the money. Was he really that dim, or did he just let people think he was?

I moved along to Dave Smith, who was so anxious to keep Lost Coyote Field's mystery a mystery that he'd taken my work away from me. Why did I always think of him by both names, instead of as just Smith? Menken was Menken, why wasn't Smith Smith? Was it because Smith was such a common name? *No, it's because it's such an opaque name. It's like camouflage; it disguises him as ordinary. And "Dave" isn't any more distinctive: I need both names just to keep track of him in my mind.* For Smith's possible motives, I put down "Power, Kingdom Building. Lack of Morality."

I looked back at my list. *Oh, yeah, Fred Crick, my phantom boss.* He was a complete mystery to me. It was clear that he was in competition with Dave Smith, although their jurisdictions didn't really overlap. Crick was in charge of geology, and Smith was engineering. Was Smith trying to run Crick clear out of the company? And if so, how? I sighed. I was just going to have to get onto the grapevine and swing.

Who else was there? The receptionist with the open-toed shoes and the weak stomach had been present that night, glaring at me. It was hard imagining someone who couldn't even keep her breakfast down committing violent murder, but I wrote "receptionist" on the list anyway.

I leaned back in Bill's swivel chair, trying to sort through this maze of inconclusive information. The squeak the chair made as it gave way on its springs awakened the dog, who looked at me indignantly and then rearranged himself with his knobby old spine toward me.

Well, I sure couldn't come up with a motive for the receptionist. Who else was there? Jon Hathaway. Irma Triff. Were they involved? I wrote their names down just in case. Maddie? No; probably down at the Slant Hole, frying her innards with hot links. At least I wasn't sharing an office with a murderess. Or was I? The murderer hadn't necessarily appeared in the lobby. *Naw, Maddie left hours earlier.*

Inconclusive.

But surely not Maddie . . .

Next, I tried to list what I could eliminate as being coincidental. I wanted fervently to remove my classmates from the picture, not because I felt any great loyalty to them, but because the thought that the roots of murder might reach back to those horrible prep school days turned my stomach. I'd spent the ten years since graduation trying to disassociate myself from these people, and now they were back with a vengeance. *Vengeance, now there's a motive . . .*

I gave up and went to bed, but my mind wouldn't rest. I lay rigid late into the night, my mind reaching into the darkness to divine where coincidence stopped and murder began.

I'll see Libby tomorrow for lunch; maybe she'll tell me more without Rachel there to silence her. Yes, I shall ask the princess for the boon of information, I decided, as my mind finally descended into an uneasy sleep.

As the first ripples of dreamscape bent the logic of my thoughts, Libby swam past me in robes laced with silver threads, her golden hair woven rich with ribbons and precious stones. I stared up at her from the bottom of the moat below her castle, watching her elegance unfold above me, now banners uncurling in the wind above the castle walls.

25

Tuesday began with the humble sound of Elyria's cat hacking up hair balls on the foot of my bed. I opened one eye and stared at her. "Save it for your boyfriends, fuzz wad," I growled, jumping out of bed. The radio alarm blared a few minutes later, but I silenced the news, figuring I had enough to contend with in my personal corner of the world.

I showered briskly, ironed a shirt, and buffed my shoes, singing a Hank Williams tune the while, a precontest ritual reminiscent of my barrel-racing days. By the time the kettle screamed on the stove I had fully armored myself in tweed, had given the dog his pill, and was pulling the raw materials for a proper breakfast out of the fridge. *Em Hansen, champion investigator and peerless professional of the western world, eats a wholesome breakfast. Eschewing Pop-Tarts in favor of a more balanced menu, our heroine—*

The phone rang. It was Elyria.

"I'll be home tonight," she said, with a sigh.

"I'll be glad to see you," I said, with feeling. *I'll have your horse saddled,* compañera. *We have miles to ride.* I could think of no one better than Elyria to bounce ideas off of as I worked on this case.

I caught the 7:35 bus downtown. I said good-morning to drooling Howie and watched a blind man seated across from us read *Playboy* in braille as I made a mental list of people I'd need to see that day and questions I wanted to ask. I'd pump Maddie, and there was of course Libby, and Topsy and Rachel for that matter. And who was that who phoned Topsy to spread the news of Scott's death? Marcie Jacobson. I remembered her from prep school. She wasn't a bad egg, but a gossip of the first water. And Simon Bunting: I'd take another stab at finding him.

I added Menken to the list: perhaps he was good for another round of cuisine de lasagne, with a what's-your-act chaser.

Smith? *Save your breath.*

Crick? *Hard to interview a disappearing act.*

Hathaway? *That would be coy: you've never even been introduced, and you're going to drop in and casually ask him a few questions about a murder?*

Tutaraitis?

Tutaraitis. My heart sank, as a bit of longing slipped past my defenses. I squeezed my eyes shut, trying not to think about him, but my desire for him was not a thing of the mind alone. *Maybe Libby was the one who was untruthful, and Pete had really thought she wasn't coming back. Besides, he said he had to keep up appearances, right? Maybe—*

"Hurt?"

The voice came from right next to my ear. It was Howie, his ever-cheerful face soft with worry. I smiled at him and shook my head, then realized what had prompted his question: I was clutching my stomach so hard that I was bent forward. I must have looked like I was on my way to the hospital with an attack of appendicitis.

Howie tipped his torso side to side, all concerned.

"Yes, hurt," I replied, admitting it to myself as well.

Howie lifted a hand and patted me on the shoulder: pat, pat, pat. I almost bawled.

The bus pulled into the Market Street station, and I switched for the shuttle that ran down the Sixteenth Street Mall. After three slow blocks, impatience levitated me out of the shuttle. I slapped the buzzer, descended to the curb, and marched down the granite flagstones, outstripping the arrival of the shuttle by five minutes or more. By God, I had fire in the belly to get to work at last.

One block up from Sixteenth Street and around the corner stood the Cattlemen's Exchange Building, jutting from the earth into a cobalt-blue sky. As I approached its base, where the steel and glass sheathing gripped the sidewalk, the reflection of a red car passing in the street flashed past the corner of my eye like a splash of blood. I stopped and closed my eyes, struggling to dispel the image. *I need to get more sleep,* I told myself firmly. *That's all it is; fatigue.*

I hesitated, summoning strength of will. I leaned my head back and searched sixteen floors above me for the one chink in the building's reflective armor. The boarded window was a dull blip impossibly far overhead, in a mirror of the sky.

The sky was so beautiful. On a clear day like this, it was the same sky which slid on over my prairie. With the comfort of this thought, I drew myself up and went inside.

Then everything ground to a halt. Maddie wasn't there. Crick wasn't there. Menken was on an important conference call. And as I said, I was too much of a wimp to march into Dave Smith's office under any circumstances, let alone on some trumped-up pretense designed to get him to talk. I sat in my office, uncertain whether to chance a trip to the coffee room. Could the engineers and geologists who congregated there smell the subtle scent of traitor over the thin chemical reek of paint and carpeting? *Probably not. Suck it up, Em, you're getting paranoid, not to mention a touch grandiose. The assholes probably don't even know you exist.*

Thanks for the vote of confidence.

Think nothing of it.

In frustration, I scrawled a note that said "I need to talk to you. Please contact me as soon as you return," signed it, folded it in three, and carried it down the hall to Fred Crick's desk. I set his coffee cup on top of it, not so much to hold it down in the event of high wind as to hide it from the view of anyone who looked into Crick's office through the glass panel by the door. I managed to get in and out without being seen.

After that, I got out the phone book and dialed the number for Love and Christiansen. A hushed and confidential-sounding voice informed me that Simon Bunting was still out, could she take a message?

"Do you know when he'll be back? It's important."

"No, I don't. I expected him back on Thursday. I believe he might be ill."

Ill? Scott had been murdered the day before that—Wednesday—and I'd just seen him up and walking around at the memorial service Monday, not twenty-four hours ago. AWOL, more likely. Well, maybe if he was a close friend of Scott's, he was just taking time off to grieve.

"Do you have his home number?" I asked.

"Oh, no, I can't give you that," the voice said, scandalized. "That's strictly against policy."

"Thanks anyway." I pressed down the button on the phone before she could ask my name again, and pawed back to the B's in the phone book. *Bunting, Bunting, Bunting . . . 'bye baby bunting, pappy's gone a-hunting . . .* I found a Simon Bunting on South Gilpin Street and dialed. If memory served,

Gilpin Street was near Washington Park, right near Rachel's house.

A recorded message clicked on after the second ring. The voice was Scott's. "You have reached the home of Simon Bunting and Scott Dinsmoore. No one can take your call just now, but—" *Blah blah, blah . . . What? They were housemates here in Denver? Nobody told me that.* Quickly, I checked the number for Dinsmoore, Scott. Same number.

I was still sitting there with my mouth hanging open when the message beep attempted to shatter my eardrum. I listened to dead air for a moment, unable to figure out what to say to an answering machine. Coming from rural Wyoming rig life, I wasn't exactly used to the goddamned things.

The machine shut off. It was voice-actuated, and I wasn't making any voice. That meant I had to dial the number and listen to the beyond-the-grave voice of Scott Dinsmoore all over again, but when the squeal came this time, I was a little more prepared. "Ah, er . . . this is Em Hansen, calling from Blackfeet Oil Company. I'd like to talk to, ah . . . Simon Bunting. Please call me at . . . ah . . ." I dug one of my business cards out of a drawer and read off the phone number, threw in Elyria's number for good measure, and hung up.

After that little shock, I felt the need to get up and walk around a bit. I made a cursory attempt at checking the logs and files for Lost Coyote back out of the vault, but when I told the old mastodon with the juicy cough what I wanted, she waved her hand no between hacks and tottered back to her desk. "*Damn* Dave Smith," I muttered to myself, as I headed back for the elevator.

Back in my office, I drank too much coffee and spun vivid fantasies about how to get around Dave Smith. Making a mint in the stock market so I could buy the company and fire him might take too long, and a letter bomb seemed a bit coarse. I decided instead to phone Wanda McCandless, who subcontracted as a files researcher at the Wyoming State Oil and Gas Commission in Casper. It might take a few days, but Wanda could get me duplicate copies of the well logs and miscellaneous reports. I'd used her services once before, when I was still a mudlogger.

Just then, Maddie arrived. She had on the dress with the big polka dots again, and this time had added an enormous bow in the hair to match. I didn't dare phone Wanda with Maddie in earshot.

Instead, I tried to pump Maddie, but she couldn't talk; she was getting something ready for an early-afternoon committee meeting. Maybe that was the occasion for the bow in her hair.

I lounged at my desk, trying to figure out how I could get a call through to Wanda. Call from Scott's office? Too noticeable. Leave the office and call her from a pay phone? No, she had a beeper system, and frequently had to return the calls later, ringing through from the pay phone in the lobby of the Oil and Gas Commission. It might be a while before she could call back.

It was an hour before Maddie's bladder filled up, even though I got her an extra cup of coffee. She proved in fact to be the Amoco Cadiz supertanker among coffee drinkers, but at long last she got up and wandered down the hall toward the women's room.

I dove for the phone, dialed information for Wyoming, and got through to Wanda. It was nice to hear a Wyoming accent. I said, "This is Em Hansen, calling from Denver. I need some information for Lost Coyote Field."

Wanda quoted her hourly rate and charge per photocopy. She was, as I remembered, wonderfully cheap for the bounty of information she could provide. "What do you need?" she wanted to know.

"The pay sections of the logs, the production reports, basic filings, and any maps. How long will this take?"

"Well, not so long as all that. I'd normally charge you for a rush job, but to be truthful, I don't have anything else going on just now. I can probably even get this in the mail this evening, or maybe tomorrow. This is Tuesday? You'll have it Friday or so, maybe Saturday if you take your mail on the weekend."

"Any way to get it faster?"

"FedEx, but that would cost ten or fifteen dollars extra."

"Go for it."

"Who did you say you worked for?"

"I didn't say. I'm, ah.—independent."

"Well, Miss Hansen, I only offer that service to my established customers, because of the financial risk," she said, trailing off suggestively. It was clear that I was sounding too fly-by-night for her tastes.

"We did business once before, last April."

"Can't see as I remember," she said, her voice icing up. "I'd just have to have something in advance, and I don't take credit cards. They charge me a percentage."

My mind went into high gear, tossing out strategies such as wiring her the money, or FedEx-ing a check. All seemed logistically nightmarish. In desperation, I wailed, "I grew up in Chugwater."

Her voice thawed. "Well, why didn't you say so. I have an aunt in Horse Creek. Do you know Thelma McCandless?"

"Thelma McCandless! I knew that name sounded familiar," I lied heartily.

"What's your address in Denver?"

I gave her Elyria's address on West Thirtieth, smiling. Wyoming had its own little version of the old school tie, or the old girl network, at least.

"One other thing," Wanda said. "You know, don't you, that a lot of the records filed here have a way of disappearing?"

"Meaning?"

"Oh, those boys do like to walk in here with their attaché cases and they do just forget to put the files they copy back into the cabinets and not into their attachés. There's a lot missing for some fields."

"Accidents do happen," I sighed, and rang off.

I got myself another cup of coffee and swilled it down. When the phone rang at eleven, the caffeine had me so wired that I jumped. It was Libby. In my excitement over reaching Wanda, I'd forgotten about our lunch.

"Hi," she said. "I've made reservations for noon at Little Pepina's. Do you like Sicilian food?"

"*Perfect.*" *Sure, Em; red sauce on top of a stomach full of coffee; just the ticket.*

"Listen, Pete took the Saab today. I have the Volvo, which doesn't have a parking tag for your garage, so wait for me by the entrance to the Fairmont, okay? I'd pick you up in front of your building, but I'll be coming from the art museum, and the streets are so complicated with all those one-ways."

"I'll be there."

At five past twelve, Libby arrived in a green round-nosed Volvo, circa 1965. So very New England, to buy quality and run it until the last lug nut spins off into the great highway in the sky. She reached over and unlocked my side, and I lowered myself into the seat, demurely doing it just as my grandmother had taught me: sit first, swivel, then bring both feet in together, rather than lurch in one leg at a time, as I automatically would have done in any other circumstances. Libby always did raise the level of the game.

Little Pepina's was across the Platte River from downtown, snuggled into a small Italian neighborhood along the west bank. Humble as the neighborhood appeared, the restaurant was quiet and genteel, with a spacious feeling and deep linen tablecloths.

The waiter's eyes went soft with devotion the instant he spotted Libby. He fawned over her, hurrying past other people's upraised index fingers to rush her order to the kitchen, and hovering by her side to refill her water glass each time she took the tiniest sip. I wondered how she did it. *Perhaps she doesn't really exist. Perhaps she's just a holographic projection on the pleasure center of the brain,* I mused.

I wrapped my tongue around a succulent bit of veal while Libby dawdled over her *pasta e fagioli* and picked at a green salad. We played Do You Remember So-and-So and So-and-So-Else for a while, but as soon as I found a favorable opening I asked her how long she had known Scott.

"Since seventh grade. He was always there, sweet little Scottie with his freckles and his blushes." She went on to tell me some tender stories about his humorless attention, standing by like the most unlikely knight attending the lady fair. "I was glad to see him again when he came out here to work. We were really very dear friends." She stared mournfully at the tablecloth. "What's being done to find out who killed him?" she asked.

I stopped with a forkful of veal halfway to my mouth. Maybe Libby had a way of being disarming, but I wasn't ready for anything as direct as that. "The police haven't ruled on it yet," I said carefully. "Why do you suppose it's murder?"

Libby laid down her fork, placing it carefully across the right side of her plate, aligned with her knife. She closed her eyes and sat very straight and still. I was afraid she might cry. "The police don't know Scottie," she said, in a very small voice. "He would never kill himself."

The waiter appeared from nowhere to whisk her plate from the table, and as he bent far enough to see her expression, he cringed slightly, in anguish to find her unhappy. He shot me a look that said *How dare you upset her?*

I rewarded him with my best *Suck pasta* look. "I agree," I said. "I don't think he killed himself, either."

Libby opened her eyes. I had expected to see sadness, even

tears in them, but what I saw instead was the light of desperation. "Isn't anybody doing anything about this? It's not right.
Whoever killed him should be put away. Forever."

Perversely I asked, "Was he sad when he lost you to Pete?"
I was beginning to get like Cousin Lester again, just rubbing
my nose in my own irritants.

Libby looked startled. Then she collected herself, shook her
head and smiled with pursed lips, indicating that I was being
rather rude.

"So how did you meet Pete?" I persisted stubbornly. I suppose I was hoping to get a similar reaction, or even a direct
confidence that they were splitting up. And when.

"I think it was at a dance." She shrugged her shoulders, as if
the exact occasion of their first meeting had not really stayed
in her memory. A little hard to believe, but then, Pete had said
that she hadn't loved him—how did he put it?—physically.
Perhaps she was for some reason immune or oblivious to sexual heat. *What a waste,* I thought bitterly.

Libby shifted a leaf of escarole to another position on her
plate. The light from the tall windows bounced diffusely off
the white tablecloth, illuminating her face like one of Fra An-
gelico's angels. "Pete studied geology at City College. Isn't it
funny that you're both geologists," she said.

"Why funny?" It piqued my curiosity that she would offer
the information that he had attended some school less socially
elite than the Ivy League. And what kind of a geology department did City College have? Did they run field trips via sub-
way to study building stones of Manhattan?

"You and Pete are so different, from such opposite ends of
the universe, but yet you work at the same task. He's a city
boy, you know, from New Jersey; Newark to be exact. There's
quite a large Lithuanian community there."

Lithuanian. That explained the fantastic Baltic angles to his
face. Sigh.

"Of course, his mother is Polish. He's really quite—er, ex-
otic. Have you met him?" Her gaze lifted from her plate and
held me, her pale eyes trained on me like the twin lenses of an
antique view camera about to freeze my image for posterity.

My stomach began to tremble. Why was she telling me this?
Why would she choose to tell me those few particular things
about Pete that anyone from her social set would normally
take pains to obscure? He had not gone to the right school. He
was not from the right town. He was not of preferred lineage. I

thought of saying something self-righteously defensive, but then it hit me: perhaps she *knows*. Perhaps this was how ladies tell other ladies that the game is not in season. I watched her from the corner of my eye as I took my last bite of veal, trying to divine from the tilt of her head if she was aware that she was looking at her rival, or if I was just being paranoid. "Hasn't he done well," I commented, in as even a tone as I could manage.

"Oh, yes, hasn't he," Libby said, as she called for the check.

On the drive back from lunch, I tried repeatedly to take control of our conversation, but Libby seemed lost in a trance. When a truck suddenly pulled out from the curb, she didn't react to swerve away, and I was grabbing for the Volvo's wheel by the time the truck driver found his brakes.

It was a relief to return to the office, where I could count on Maddie to notice everything larger than a dust mote and leave me with no doubt about anything that crossed her mind, however draped in Texan idiom it might be. I found her sitting at her desk with her feet up on an open drawer, eating a chocolate-nut bar and reading a fat paperback. She grinned, munching happily away.

"Committee over?" I asked.

"Yessiree Bob, and I sold my prospect." She waved her candy bar and book in the air. "I's celebrating!"

"Congratulations. Nice work."

"Do what? Aw, it warn't nothing. I just threatened to take a bullwhip to 'em if they all didn't go along with it. Makes 'em shit their britches every time."

As I said, one always knows what's what with Maddie.

I cleared my throat. "Maddie," I began, launching straight into what was on *my* mind, "you seem to have a handle on what makes the world turn here at Blackfeet. Tell me more about the power struggles. Where's your money, on Dave Smith or Fred Crick?"

"Smith, damn his viperous eyes."

"Why so?"

"Well, something's got to give, is all. This kennel's shrinking just like everybody else's, what with the recession and the oil slump and all, so's they got too many alpha pooches hanging about."

"You mean management's top-heavy." I was getting pretty good at translating from Maddie-ese into English.

"Yes ma'am. You ask me, someone's going to get his balls chomped off any minute, and I'll bet it's Crick as winds up the soprano. Poor fucker hasn't got the moves. A good geologist, but no kind of politician."

"So you think Smith is going to cull him from the herd?"

"Like I said."

"Well, what if there was something funny about one of the oil fields? Who would stand to lose?"

Maddie looked up with a nasty y'all's-figgering-it-out-ain't-ya glint in her eyes. "Smith, if you're talking about Lost Coyote." The twangy cadence and jargon to her voice had suddenly disappeared.

"How do you figure?" I asked, likewise lowering my voice.

Maddie put down her book and came over to lean on my desk so she could whisper. "Hell, I don't know," she said, studiously consuming another mouthful of chocolate. "Crick's been fighting development of that field right along, kicking and screaming that we're drilling faster than the new wells can be properly tested. Why? You find something out 'at's going to embarrass someone?"

"Maybe."

Maddie smacked her lips thoughtfully over the candy and straightened up. "I don't know, Em. This ain't my cup of tea. I tell ya, those boys play kind of rough." She raised her eyes overhead, then dropped them rapidly to the floor, letting out a long whistle that culminated in a splattering sound.

Maddie left early.

The walls of my office took on a menace, as if the hostility I felt all around was pressing them slowly toward me. I wanted out of that building. I became unavoidably aware of the distance my soft, fragile body hung above the street, saved from fatal descent only by the temporary cooperation of man-made materials.

I decided to pay a call on Rachel Conant.

I knew Rachel worked for the governor, but there wasn't any listing in the phone book for "Rachel at the Governor's Office," and I couldn't figure out which of the numbers listed under the state pages in the government section applied. I decided to take a walk over to the capitol and see what I could see.

The capitol was only a few blocks away. On the way, I was panhandled once and informed of the sexual fantasies of total strangers twice. When a guy with a three-days' growth of beard sidled up to me as I waited for a Walk light at Colfax Avenue, I almost slugged him; as it turned out, he was merely lost, some rangy student looking for the art museum. I mutely pointed across the Civic Center and crossed against traffic, not slackening my pace again until I was climbing the wide stone steps that lead to the main entrance of the Capitol Building.

The Capitol Building is a classical sweep of grey stone surmounted by a guilded dome. It has all the features that impress a child on a school visit: echoing rotunda, immense raked chambers for the houses of government, and a terrific view of the mountains. After ten or fifteen minutes of searching directory boards and asking around, I was shown through a labyrinth of offices and anterooms into a room that must have been on the other side of the wall from where I'd started.

It was pretty nice. It had a high ceiling and monumental amounts of fine wood paneling. Rachel sat behind a heavy mahogany desk. I had caught her off guard, her lap full of half-sorted correspondence. She stared at me with her customary frankness.

"Hi," I said.

"Hi," she said quietly.

"Um, I just wanted to pay you a visit." I pointed toward Seventeenth Street. "I just work over there a few blocks. I was kind of taking a break, and—"

"Could you lower your voice, please? The governor's right through that door." She pointed toward an innermost chamber.

"Oh."

Some glint of shrewd curiosity lit Rachel's eyes. She held up a finger. "Hold on just a moment. I'll finish these and take a break." Bowing her head back over the letters, she pointed at a chair for me to sit on.

An older woman in one of those suits that never goes out of style because it was never in stalked into the room on heels so spindly that I wondered if her Achilles tendon might be permanently shortened. She chirped, "Rachel, dear, what's left on the docket for today?"

Rachel glanced at a page on her desk. "Police awards at three-thirty, Cub Scout Pack Twenty-three at three thirty-five, Save the Planet Week at three-forty, then that bicycle race promotion at three forty-five. Looks like we'll be done early today. Can you handle these without me, Louise? I have a visitor." She gestured toward me. "Em Hansen, from school."

Louise shined a well-oiled smile on me. "How nice to meet you, Miss Hansen. Certainly, Rachel."

A tall young man in a suit came in and lifted one hand imperiously toward Rachel and Louise. "The boys in blue are here, ladies," he said, in a nasal tone. "Heads up."

A dozen or more policemen shuffled quietly in, their hats in their hands, their hair slicked down, and their shoes polished to a high gloss. Louise extended one arm toward the inner chamber door. "Just wait here until the signal."

Rachel put down a letter and pushed a button on her desk. After a moment, the inner chamber door was opened from inside by another young man, revealing a much larger wood-paneled room with a much larger desk, behind which sat a man with an even larger smile occupying the lower half of his face. He was dwarfed by the enormous flags that hung beside his desk; a Colorado tricolor on one side, and a drape of stars and stripes on the other. The policemen shuffled meekly into the governor's office and the door swung shut. The outer door swung open again, and a group of cub scouts trooped in, accompanied by some very pure-looking scoutmasters, their clear blue eyes registering nothing more than the rapture of the moment.

Rachel put the last of the letters down and rose to her feet. "Come on," she whispered, "before one of these little monsters puts a finger up his nose."

I followed her out into the rotunda. We crossed the echoing stone floor and climbed into a slow-moving elevator that labored asthmatically skyward and put us out several levels up near a doorway that opened to a balcony overlooking the Civic Center. Rachel walked directly over to the thick stone railing and leaned on it. "God, I hate the Boy Scouts," she said.

"I think they were cub scouts," I offered.

"Cub scouts, boy scouts, they're all the same."

"I take it this job bores you."

Rachel rubbed her sinuses with one hand. "To tears," she said.

"What was that bit with the groups? Is it Meet the Governor Day, or something?"

"Every day is Meet the Governor Day. They run them through like that at five-minute intervals most afternoons. One benevolent society after another, all getting their picture taken with The Man for politics and glory. They queue them up like that, staging them through the outer office, then my office, then into the governor's chamber, then out a door that flushes them right back into the rotunda. The adults are okay; they're all so cowed that they're going to meet someone important that they don't say much. Just stand there and jitter; I've gotten used to it. But the kids, they're awful. You can't get a kid to hold still for five minutes like that, and by the time they get into my office, they've already been on a bus for who knows how long and then caged up in the outer office. They're animals. They get into everything. And today I have such cramps."

This was a view of Rachel I'd never seen. I always thought everything was done for her, and that all the advantages landed in her lap. It never occurred to me that she knew a moment's discomfort, let alone enduring menstrual cramps and ricocheting cub scouts while trying to pick through someone else's mail. "I'm sorry to have interrupted."

"I welcome the interruption."

Rachel? Welcome me? I'd come here to pry information from a hostile subject, and now that subject was turning the tables, making it a social event. That wouldn't do. Being treated with kindness by Libby made my job hard enough; what if I found out Rachel was a human being, too?

I looked out over the murk of Denver's atmosphere toward the mountains, trying to get my bearings. I felt like someone waking from a coma after ten years of oblivion, trying to grasp all at once how much the world had changed. I was definitely going to have to rethink a few things. And yet, something in my internal gyroscopes kept telling me I was still nobody from nowhere. That was a message that used to come from outside; I remember hearing it. Was it only coming from inside now? I felt moved to make a gesture, to do my part in closing the gap between us. I said, "Do you want some aspirin?" I started to rummage through my purse, although I knew there was nothing in there but a tube of lip balm, a key to Elyria's house, and my wallet. I wouldn't have even owned the purse if my grandmother hadn't bought it to go with the suit.

"No, I'm half gone on Motrin already." She looked at me out of the corner of her eye, the set of her lips finally betraying distrust. "So what did you want, anyway?"

Good question. What *was* I going to ask her? *Listen up, Rachel, I'm investigating the murder of Scott Dinsmoore, and you're on my list?* Fat chance. That would win a terse command to go to hell; Rachel hadn't changed *that* much. Worse yet, if she were somehow involved in his death, we were too damned close to a very long drop.

I looked back over my shoulder to gauge my exit, should I need to make a quick one. "I'm trying to find out more about Scott," I said bluntly. "The police keep hanging around. It's got me wondering, so I thought I'd ask."

Rachel's eyes turned opaque. "Ask what?"

Another good question "Well, you know . . . ," I said, buying time.

Rachel sighed with exasperation. "I hear you had lunch with Libby today. Is that what's on your mind?"

I said, "Kind of." *Sure, let's see where that takes us.* "Well, I don't know, she seemed to be in kind of a weird mood. Distracted, kind of." A weak little part of my brain wanted to ask, *Is Libby upset with me for some reason?* but was afraid the answer might be yes. Rachel was no dummy; knowing her orientation on the universe, it would take no hints at all for her to guess how I'd spent Saturday night.

Rachel's eyes suddenly turned to ice. "I'm not in the mood, Em. Come to the point."

This wasn't going well. What was so offensive about my questions? "I didn't know I was hitting a sore point."

"This isn't a sore point," Rachel said, her eyes narrowing further. She turned abruptly and started past me to the exit, her body stiff with repressed emotion.

I followed her into the echoing upper story of the rotunda, keeping well away from the railing. "I'm sorry, Rachel, I was just trying to understand. I mean, my God, what are you all doing out here? It just seems so strange that you'd all wind up in the same town." I followed her onto the elevator. What was eating her? What nerve had I struck?

Rachel studied me in calculating appraisal, then smiled dryly. As the car descended toward the main floor, she spoke in a formal tone, as if to a total stranger, perhaps a reporter from the society page of the *Rocky Mountain News*; so polite and formal that there had to be some irony imbedded in it: "My husband and I came first, two years after college. He has a good job, the transfer was a promotion, and the skiing is better here than in the East. My father got me this job. It's boring, but I really can't complain, and it helps us have money for extras. Topsy found her way out here a year or so later. Libby and her husband"—her voice faltered for some reason over this reference to Pete—"came out two years ago. Libby does not like it here. She visits her family back east regularly. Scott came out about two years ago, too, and yes, he probably followed her here. Gerald probably followed Scott, knowing him, or perhaps it was Simon he had in mind. What else would you like to know?"

I returned Rachel's calculating look, no longer bothering to pretend this was an idle social visit, and silently vowed to turn this particular wildcat over to the talents of Sergeant Ortega and Lieutenant Flint. I knew that overpolite tone of voice she was using: it meant I *was* out, wasting my time.

As I trudged slowly down the steps that descended the slope in front of the Capitol Building, I wondered how many times at school I'd heard that kind of recitation. It was the fine art of hiding a deadly secret behind a pretty veneer of truth.

26

Elyria met me at the door as I stumbled in from the bus stop that evening. "I see that you're in deep with this murder investigation," she said.

"How did you know?"

"You're walking straighter, for one. And you left notes all over Bill's desk which made great reading. And Carlos called to say he will be here in fifteen minutes to take us out to Chubby's and debrief you."

"Carlos?"

"Sergeant Ortega to you, no doubt. He's serious about his professionalism, or at least he defines it."

Somehow the obvious fact that Sergeant Ortega had a first name startled me. I liked the private, mannerly little world we had been constructing, and I didn't want it to change. "Yes," I said doubtfully, "Sergeant Ortega to me."

I went into my bedroom and skinned out of my suit. As I hung it up, I smoothed it carefully, making sure it wouldn't crease as it hung against the other clothes in the closet. There was something stuck to the seat of the skirt. I looked closer. It was a thick hair, about four inches long.

"Elyria," I called. "Come look at this."

I was wiggling into my jeans as she came in the door. "Well, you look more normal to me now. Is that what I was supposed to see?"

"No." I picked the hair up off the top of the dresser, where I had carefully laid it. "This. Does it look familiar?"

"It looks like a red hair." She was definitely in a droll mood.

"But what kind of a red hair?"

"This is a game, right? Where do I start? Animal, vegetable, mineral?"

"Animal. It's important."

Elyria sobered up and scrutinized the hair, holding it up to the light. "It looks like it came from an Irish setter."

"It came off the seat of my skirt."

She studied me, waiting for me to fill her in on the significance of this earth-shattering bit of information, but before I could speak, the doorbell sounded. Elyria hurried toward the door, carrying the hair. I heard her open the bolt. "Carlos," I heard her say, as I hurried to tuck in my shirt, "do come in. Em was just teasing me with dog hairs."

There was a pause, and then Ortega's voice, triumphant: "You see? I tell her we've got dog hairs in the victim's car, and she finds me another. Em! Where did you get this?"

I hurried out into the living room, expecting to be greeted by Ortega's jubilant smile, focused on me and me only. Wrong. He was smiling at Elyria, basking in her lovely presence as one might take in the *Pietà*—humbly, peacefully, engrossed in spiritual experience. He glanced at me and winked.

On the way to dinner, I gave him an innocuous sampling of my day; about the source of the dog hair, and my chat with Rachel. I didn't tell him that I had ordered the well logs from Casper. That was my department.

"Okay, this is really good," Ortega said, turning the unmarked car north onto Federal Boulevard. "I'll see what Flint and I can do with this Simon guy, and you can leave Miss Conant to us. What's her voice like?"

"Her voice?"

"Is it high-pitched? Like a little girl?"

"No, I'd say an alto. Why?"

Ortega didn't answer. I thought about this, as we wound through the brick neighborhood toward Federal Boulevard. Ortega asked his questions casually, as if he were just making small talk.

I had promised myself that the next time I heard that tone in his voice, I'd pin him to the wall, and find out what essential bit of information he was hiding in plain sight. "Why?" I repeated.

Ortega's face lit up, but he didn't say anything.

Elyria took in his expression and said, "I know this grin, Em. Whatever it is, you'll never get it out of him now."

"Maybe he just wants to handle the women himself," I said.

Ortega blushed, but grinned even wider and said, "We'll send the dog hair to the lab, see if it matches the ones we found in Mr. Dinsmoore's vehicle."

"And that's another one," I said, starting to smile in spite of my attempts to display exasperation. "You didn't tell me Scott was roommates with Simon Bunting."

Ortega beamed at me in approval. "I didn't know it mattered, until now. His office kept telling us he was out of town. We thought it was very interesting that we couldn't find this Mr. Bunting, but we'll look harder now."

As Ortega drove, I took in the sights of northwest Denver—old commercial buildings and a mixture of two-story Victorian houses and one-story bungalows. He turned right on Thirty-eighth and headed downhill toward one of the viaducts that spanned the railroad yards and the Platte River Valley. The neighborhood grew darker and poorer. At Lipan Street, he dodged in behind a low building with crumbling stucco and parked the car. "All out for Chubby's, home of the best burrito in Denver," he said, leading the way around to the front of the building.

I heard the squeal of tires before I saw the car. It was an old Chevy, chopped and riding low to the pavement. The driver had swerved, and was accelerating straight toward Sergeant Ortega.

Ortega threw himself away from us, selflessly using his body as a decoy. I saw his round eyes widen, and as time telescoped, he seemed to drift away from us as if floating on a river of air.

The Chevy bounced against the curb with a horrific clashing of metal. I heard the driver shout: *"Chingaso!* You hurt my car, man! Next time I kill you!" With a hand held high in insult from the driver's side window the Chevy careened up Thirty-eighth Street and disappeared over the rise.

As Ortega regained his footing and brushed himself off, I saw Elyria's eyes flare with rage. "The stupid *pendejo*," she said, teeth bared, "he could have hurt someone."

Ortega blushed deeply at Elyria's language, a rich rose-red beneath his brown skin.

I tried to recover my wits. "That man threatened to kill you!" I said, trying to steady my voice.

Ortega shook his head with frustration. "Hipolito's a problem" was all he'd say.

I looked pleadingly at Elyria. What kind of a place was this I had come to live in?

"Welcome to the *barrio*," she said haughtily. "Home of great burritos and even greater *machismo*."

"Just a little occupational hazard," Ortega said. "They get

offended when they think you break away from the culture. Something about my job. I don't know."

Elyria stormed ahead into Chubby's and slammed the door.

Ortega watched her go, smiling in admiration. "*She* says *we* have tempers," he said, a chuckle arising from his belly.

Chubby's turned out to be a claustrophobic hole in the wall with a small order window and two minute Formica tables. Ortega leaned through the window and ordered, joking in his musical Spanish with the cook and a teenaged girl who was delivering fresh tortillas from the factory up the street.

When we got our burritos, we sat in the car, savoring their fragrant, spicy fillings. I felt something strange in my chest, perhaps just my heart growing larger. It was a relief to sit in a plain sedan having a simple dinner with two people who were treating me with uncomplicated regard. I realized that for the first time since leaving Wyoming, I was happy; not excited and overwhelmed, as I had been with Pete, but quietly and comfortably happy.

The feeling lasted until we had returned to Elyria's and had a cup of hot chocolate, which Sergeant Ortega cooked up on Elyria's stove from a stash of Mexican Imbaburra he kept in his car. Before he left, he turned to me. "We can't find Archie Arch. You remember him?"

"Yeah. He's the street person you hauled out of the parking garage the night of the murder."

"Right."

"He was on the sidewalk yesterday morning after the memorial service, too, wasn't he?"

"Right. You seen him since then?"

"No. Why do you ask?"

Ortega shrugged.

Here we go again. I prepared myself to pry information out of Ortega. Or barring that, to get as many stray clues as I could from him. "Is he homeless?"

"Okay, you could say Archie is homeless, because he doesn't have a home. But Archie is different: he doesn't want a home."

I found this hard to imagine. In Denver, temperatures get down to twenty below most winters, and the mercury drops close to freezing even during summer nights. "How does he survive? I mean, why would anyone choose to live on the streets?"

"Oh, Archie's different. He's an artist."

"What kind of an artist?"

"A poet. He performs on the street. Performance art, I think they call it." Ortega smiled at some inside joke and shook his head. "He told me once that having a regular home would upset his 'creative process.' On the street, he gets inspired. We wanted to talk to him after the memorial service, but he, um— went away before we could get through that crowd."

"You think he knows something?"

Ortega smiled his *Who, me?* smile. "I have to wonder why he came to the service."

"How could I find him if you and the whole Denver Police Department can't?"

Ortega's smile grew very broad as he rose to go. "You have your ways, Em. I know this about you. Besides, the last place we know he's been staying was the parking garage in your building. We found him in level B, sleeping on an I-beam."

The phone started to ring as Elyria walked Ortega to the door. "I'll get it," I said, scheming to leave him alone with her for a moment.

"Maybe that's Frank," Elyria said. "I forgot to tell you. He called just before you got home. He'd like you to call him, Em. He's worried."

I ran back to the kitchen. The thought of speaking with Frank brought mixed feelings of relief and guilt. *Well, I can tell him I at least wrote him a letter,* I reasoned. *Maybe that would make it okay that I haven't called.*

But when I picked it up and spoke to it, I didn't find Frank's voice on the other end of the line.

It was Pete.

27

"Emily," he crooned through the earpiece. "How are you?"

I wasn't at all sure. What was I supposed to say to him?

"Emily? Well, hey, I'm heading out to walk my dog. There's a great ice cream store over on Gaylord, about five blocks east of Washington Park; I was wondering if you wanted to join me."

"Well . . ."

"I thought we could talk."

Yes, I wanted to tell him a few things, but the thought of meeting clandestinely now filled me with shame. "No," I said, "I can't. Can't make it, sorry."

"Hey, lady. Is there something wrong?"

I stared into the mouthpiece of the telephone.

"Emily?" He sounded worried.

My heart had turned into a hundred-pound weight.

"Well, maybe next time," he said, sounding hurt. He said good-bye and hung up.

I stood holding the phone for a while, mouth gaping, then hung it up and walked numbly into the living room.

Elyria and Sergeant Ortega were still talking on the front stoop. "Who was it?" she asked.

"Pete Tutaraitis," I answered, the words tumbling out as if someone else was talking. "Just wanted to know if I could help him walk his dog."

"His dog?" said Sergeant Ortega. "Where was he going?"

"Some ice cream shop on Gaylord," I mumbled. I looked at the floor in confusion.

He nodded and politely took his leave.

"Okay, out with it," Elyria demanded, after she closed the door behind him. "You look like your best friend just died."

I couldn't tell her. There was no way to explain.

Elyria's eyes grew dark. "Let me guess," she said quietly. "Pete seduced you."

I started to cry; big, burning tears of humiliation. "No, it's worse than that! I seduced him!"

Elyria came and put an arm around me. "Listen here, friend. It's not so bad."

"Yes it is. I let myself believe—but he's married. And to Libby Hopkins. She never did anything to harm me, and here I've gone and slept with her husband." The tears coursed from my eyes, and my lips began to swell as blood rushed to my face. In a moment, my nose would run. How I hated to cry when anyone could see me. "I was such a stupid shit!"

Elyria steered me to the couch and sat me down. "Shh, shh. Now really, Em, was he honest with you? Did he tell you he was married?"

"Yes. He said she'd left him. He said he wanted to wait."

"Em, dear, don't be so damned hard on yourself. *He* broke a vow, not you. And I do know he's a handsome man, who is well acquainted with the effect he has on women. In retrospect, you made a mistake. But you've learned from it, eh?"

"Yes." I wasn't convinced.

"Of course you have. This is called growing up. Come now, chin up."

I couldn't look Elyria in the eye. There were things I hadn't told her. Like that Pete was the man I'd always dreamed of, back in those long, sad days in prep school, and that the dream was not yet dead.

Perhaps a more grievous omission, I hadn't told her that Pete might have stolen critical data from Lost Coyote Field. And that his response had seemed insincere, even giddy, when the police told him that a close colleague had just suffered a violent death. And that he was right now walking a dog that I would bet any money had long, red hair, identical to the hair unaccountably found in a car that belonged to that dead colleague, who for some reason hated Pete.

If you ever hear me claim to be a wise woman, fully in control of her faculties, lock me up. I thanked Elyria for her sympathy and told her I was going for a drive to calm down.

"Give my regards to Pete," she said, as she handed me the keys to Bill's truck.

I never could hide a damned thing from her.

I pulled the truck over by the unlit sidewalk a half block short of the ice cream shop, suddenly uncertain what I was going to say when I saw Pete. Now that I was here, I hesitated, unready to climb out of the shadows that filled the cab of the truck. I decided to wait outside and talk to him in private.

A dog was chained to a signpost at the curb, waiting in the bright light that spilled from the shop's windows. His long, russet Irish setter hair fell in elegant waves down his back.

Five minutes passed. Pete stepped out of the store, licking a long plastic spoon. Pausing in the door frame, he lowered the spoon into the tall cup he held in the other hand, retrieving another dollop of chocolate. It disappeared slowly between his lips.

I sank back against my seat, trying to collect my thoughts.

The driver's side door of a car parked two lengths in front of me opened, and a woman stepped out. I was immediately glad I'd waited: Rachel's aristocratic stride was unmistakably familiar. She strode around the back of her car and stopped in the shadows at the edge of the sidewalk, a slim, square-shouldered figure in wool jacket and corduroy slacks.

Pete turned toward her and smiled. It wasn't a hey-hi-there smile, or an I-didn't-expect-to-see-you, but a slow, sensual *ahhhh*. His spine and pelvis moving with the slow rhythms of a cat, Pete strolled toward her, and as he advanced, Rachel receded from him, drawing him down the sidewalk toward my truck.

I oozed into the heaviest shadow in the cab of the truck and held my breath, my jaws clamped tightly. I cursed the fact that the side window of the truck was open, fearful that they might hear my breath. I didn't dare slide the rest of the way down below the dashboard of the truck, for fear I'd draw their notice. In a last, irrational effort not to be seen, I closed my eyes.

I heard Pete's warm voice. "Rachel," he purred. "Thanks for coming."

The truck let out a ping as its sheet metal began to cool. My eyes snapped open. I tensed, fearful that they would turn and see me in the shadows. They were so close to me that even in the darkness I could see the soft curve of Rachel's throat against the crisp open collar of her shirt. "Listen, Pete," she hissed, "George will be home soon. This isn't the time."

Pete moved on her, backing her up against the truck. "Rachel, my sweet, you seem agitated. Whatever could be the problem?"

Rachel leaned back against the fender of the truck and arched her neck, tipping her head away from him. Her voice was low and thick with anger. "Cut it out, Pete. We have business to look after, and you know it."

Pete's voice was deep, sassing: "What business?"

"The police haven't closed the book on Scottie yet. You said they'd call it suicide and that would be an end to it. Well, they haven't, and now Em Hansen's coming around asking her stupid little questions. You have to watch out for her, Pete; she's not the ignorant little hick she appears."

Pete pressed his hips against hers. The truck trembled with the movement. He ran his spoon between his lips again, as if to absorb every last molecule of sweetness, then turned it toward Rachel, waving it close in front of her eyes. "What's your worry, little Rachel?" he teased. "You think I can't handle her?"

"Stop it."

With a barely audible growl, he lowered the spoon down between the starched wings of her collar, probing deeper and deeper.

Rachel moaned softly, whispered, "Please, Pete, it's got to end."

Pete's eyes darkened. "You know I can't stay with Libby without you," he murmured. He pulled the spoon out of her blouse. He kissed her neck, set the cup on the hood of the truck. His arms slid around her.

She whispered, "Things are different now, and you know it."

The truck swayed.

I slid the rest of the way down onto the seat. I no longer feared that they would notice me. I wanted only to become tiny, and fly away.

An engine coughed into activity behind me. It whined and caught, and headlights suddenly erased the night.

The motion at the front of my truck stopped. I heard Pete laugh.

The car that had started pulled away from the curb and rolled past the truck. A horn sounded briefly, and then a familiar voice joined the night sounds of Denver.

"Is that your dog, Mr. Tutaraitis?" said Sergeant Ortega.

Rachel's steps receded quickly down the sidewalk. She opened her car door and slammed it, gunned the motor, and squealed away from the curb. The next I heard Pete's voice, it was near the dog: "Yes, Detective, he's mine."

"Get in, I'll give you a ride."

"That's okay, I can walk."

Ortega's tone became firmer. "Do me the honor, sir."

I heard the door on the right side of the sergeant's car open and close before the sound of its engine melted into the night.

I lay on my back on the seat, tears painting my cheeks with warmth, uncertain which was more painful: the loss of hope, or the sweetness of knowing that a man named Ortega held me in such regard that he would blow a stakeout to spare my feelings.

28

Wednesday morning, long before the alarm went off, I was jolted from twisting dreams by the telephone. Elyria appeared at my doorway, eyes almost closed with sleep. "It's for you. Wouldn't say who it is."

The house was cold. I moved along the walls to the phone in the kitchen, groping in the predawn darkness. Fumbling with the mouthpiece, I croaked, "Hello?"

A baby-doll woman's voice came onto the line, childish and high. "Is this Em Hansen?"

"Yeah. Who's this?"

"You called for Simon. What did you want?"

"Who *is* this?" I demanded. Whoever she was, she was someone with access to Simon's answering machine, someone perhaps who could come and go from his house at will.

The voice took on a nasty edge. "A friend." It was a phony voice, as if a woman with a normal voice was speaking in a falsetto.

"Don't give me that shit. Anybody gets me out of bed at this hour is no friend of mine."

"Simon knows why Scottie died."

"And why's that?"

Silence

I waited. I was waking up fast, and had plenty of questions for this person, but I figured that if I didn't say anything, someone twisted enough to phone in the middle of the night might get nervous or impatient enough to just spit it out, instead of playing games.

The line went dead. Dial tone.

"Who was it?" Elyria asked, now swathed in a silk dressing gown and slippers.

I sat down on a kitchen chair and pulled my knees up under my flannel nightgown, feeling like a little girl. "A real sick-o, jerking my chain about Scott. Should I call the sergeant?"

"Let him sleep."

"What time is it?"

"I don't know. We had a power outage during the night." The digital clock on the microwave oven was flashing "RESET." She disappeared for a moment and reappeared with a wristwatch. "Four fifty-three. Lovely manners your caller has."

"Right. I'm wide awake now." Too many years on drill rigs, having to come awake on a moment's notice to deal with some emergency. Only I never learned the skill that's supposed to go with it, the one where you go back to sleep on a moment's notice, too.

Elyria yawned, running a hand through her glossy hair. How I longed to be more like her; graceful and lovely even when completely disheveled. Some bit of early-morning wisdom wandered into my head: *You get to be like whomever you'd like.*

Elyria smiled and said, "Let's go out to breakfast."

By five-thirty, I was showered, dressed, and ready to leave. Elyria was still in the shower, luxuriating in steam and hot water, singing a Bulgarian love song her mother taught her. Its eerily beautiful minor keys and microtones reverberated off the bathroom tile and laced through the house.

I sat in the darkness of the living room, unable to avoid thinking about the clandestine meeting I had witnessed the night before. Slightly delirious with lost sleep, my mind alternated between fond delusions that I had dreamt what I had seen and heard outside the ice cream shop, and self-hating certainty that it had been quite real. The implications of the meeting were inescapable. Aside from the unwelcome knowledge that they were (a) intimate, and (b) given to discussing me as some hick bloodhound who asked stupid questions, Rachel and Pete were deeply involved with Scott's death. My job was getting uglier by the minute.

I itched for something to do, some action to take. It was too early to phone anyone here in Denver. But aha! It was after eight on the East Coast. I picked up the phone and called Virginia Information, in hopes of a number for Marcie Jacobson, the classmate who had known of Scott's death almost as soon as I had.

No luck. I didn't even know what town she lived in.

With some misgivings, I phoned my grandmother to see if she had a lead on Marcie. Her housekeeper answered, and got the old barracuda on the line. My grandmother's voice had an odd lift of excitement to it. "Good morning, Emily. To what do I owe the honor of this call?" Unless I deceive myself, she was truly pleased to hear from me.

I'm not heartless. I made small talk for a while, even told her how many compliments I was getting on the clothes she had bought me. I let her steer the conversation for a while.

"Have you been getting together with your classmates?" she asked.

"Yes, Grandmother."

"How lovely. You know how pleased I am."

Inspiration struck. "Yes, but I'm worried about them, Grandmother. This business of Scott Dinsmoore dying. Everyone's terribly upset."

"How sad, dear."

I weighed my next words carefully. I knew that anything I said would hit the Brahmin broadcast system, so I had to decide what news I wanted out there. "Yes, it's shocking. The police—"

"Police!" my grandmother cried. "This doesn't involve the police, does it?" Involvement with the police: a fate worse than taxes.

Grannie hadn't heard. This meant that the old girl network was saving face: Scott's family was imposing a news blackout, horrified at implications of which they had to be aware. "Grammie," I said, unconsciously using my childhood pet name for her, "can you help? Please understand, I know the police detectives personally. One lives right here in my neighborhood," I added, knowing that my grandmother would conjure the image of a gentleman police detective living in a fine neighborhood before she would imagine her granddaughter living on the edge of the *barrio*. For good measure, I threw in, "They're *friends* of mine and Elyria's. You'd like Elyria *so* much." *That should cover the confidentiality problem,* I thought. *Personal alliances buy generations-long group silences in New England.* I began to feel bad at how thoroughly I was misleading the old dame; for once, I didn't feel she deserved it. "I need your help," I repeated, not lying.

"Certainly, dear. You know you may rely on me."

"Thank you."

"Now, Emily, just what is going on there?"

In the end, I told her only that there was some uncertainty about how Scott died, and—here I led her astray again, maybe—that it was of utmost importance to me to prove that my old friends from school had no connection whatsoever to the "situation," as I called it.

I never did get around to asking her for Marcie Jacobson's whereabouts. It wasn't necessary. I knew that by lunchtime, my grandmother would have her entire generation canvassed, and would be starting on the next.

Breakfast was sausage and eggs, a comforting old favorite, but daylight was a greater tonic, diluting my sense of humiliation and loss with the ordinary details of life. As my mind focused more fully, new directions of inquiry opened within it.

I headed in to work on the bus, steeling myself for another day of reconnaissance in the glass-and-steel jungle. I looked down at my hands where they lay, so soft and vulnerable, in my lap. I imagined my fine tweeds soaked in blood, my grandmother's horror at my demise, her hope that the family genes would be passed to yet one more generation shattered. *I need more sleep*, I told myself, as I shambled to my feet and gingerly descended from the shuttle at Welton Street. *My imagination's running away with me.*

In the twelfth-floor lobby, the receptionist flared her delicate nostrils at the sight of me. Irma Triff lowered her mascara-heavy eyelashes in clear contempt. And to add continuing insult to this injury, Pete looked past me as if I were a stranger as he strolled by me in the hall with his hands in his grey flannel pockets.

I huddled at my desk, warming my hands around my coffee cup, wishing Maddie would appear. I glanced at my watch. Eight exactly. It was only because I'd been awakened so early that I had arrived before her. That was it, I was just tired—no, exhausted.

An engineer—what was her name: Angie?—walked past in the hallway, staring in at me as if I were some ugly, contemptible bottom-feeding fish in a public aquarium. I cast an eye about my desk top for something to train my attention on. Thanks to Dave Smith, there was nothing there. With hands that were beginning to tremble, I pulled open a drawer on my desk to get out a pad of paper, then yanked open the lap drawer in search of a pen.

I was greeted by a piece of white paper, folded in three, addressed in my own handwriting. It was the note I had left on Fred Crick's desk.

The eggs and sausage I had consumed with such pleasure started to rise from my stomach. I forced my breathing deep into my abdomen and counted to ten. When I was certain my stomach had stabilized, I picked up two pens and used them to carefully unfold the paper. It was my note, all right: "I need to talk to you. Please contact me as soon as you return." But something had been added. One line of type—Courier 12, just like nineteen out of twenty office electronic typewriters: "Good girls mind their own business."

I picked up the phone and made an inside call. After two rings, the receptionist picked up the line. "Yes?" Her voice was brisk, icy.

"Is Fred Crick back from Tulsa yet?"

"No."

I waited. When no further sound came over the line, I placed the receiver back in its cradle. I closed my eyes.

"Stomach cancer?"

I jumped at the sound of Maddie's voice, and realized that I'd been clutching my stomach. Maddie looked genuinely concerned. I said, "It's nothing," before I even thought, and tried to push the drawer closed.

Maddie was too fast for me. She had her hand on the drawer before it was halfway shut. The note was still open. "What's this?" Before I could stop her, she flipped the note over, and saw to whom it was addressed. "Uh-oh, so that's what's going on. You got your tit in the wringer now, sister."

"Says who!"

Maddie shook her head at me, a long, leisurely message that I wasn't fooling any babe from Texas. "It's on the wind in the coffee room. I heard those jackals yammering about your inappropriate behavior as I came down the hall just now. From the sound of it, I thought you'd gone to bed with Menken, or something. But this is worse. I take it you left Freddie a little note, and someone short-stopped it."

"Who?"

Maddie looked at me like I was nuts. "Who knows? We're not talking about a spat you have going with some bully at the school yard. Whoever did this knows better than to show his face."

"But you said they were talking about it—"

"I said they were talking about *you*. They probably don't know about your note. From the looks of it, whoever put this here started a little whispering campaign against you to make sure no one'd talk to you."

"Then who—"

"Take your pick. Keep in mind that these folks are trained observers, who make their living analyzing the data that get set before them. They just *look* like morons. It ain't escaped their notice that you got your little puppy fangs sunk into a bone they hold dear."

I squinted at her. "But do you at least have an *idea* who did this, Maddie?"

Maddie glanced at the doorway. No one was there. In a whisper, she said, "Smith. The jerk's been sending his goons out bad-mouthing you." Without waiting for a reply, she moved quickly to her desk, picked up her eraser, and lowered her head in concentration.

At lunchtime, I descended to the street and left the building, stretching my legs out into long, fast strides, hurrying to get as far from the building as I could. I moved over to the mall and beat out a tattoo on the granite pavers, threading my way through meandering pairs of midday shoppers with baby strollers and white-collar workers who promenaded aimlessly, sunning themselves in the midday glare. By the time I reached Larimer Street, I felt better, and as I slowed my pace on the Fifteenth Street viaduct, Dave Smith had shrunk in my mind from a monster to the more manageable size of a petty bully who had to rely on whispering campaigns and other cheap forms of intimidation. I stopped and leaned on the bridge rail, staring into the murky waters of the Platte. Protruding from the thin flow I saw broken bricks, a mutilated shopping cart, somebody's shoe. Farther down its course, an old man walked his pit bull along an elegant, winding path, some civic leader's bid at urban renewal. I filled my lungs with the stale air that hung in the valley and stared back toward Blackfeet, my feet moving much more slowly.

At Larimer, I headed northeast back to Sixteenth, and at Lawrence, I pumped up my courage for Seventeenth Street.

A block or so down Seventeenth, I spotted Maddie. She was moving casually along the sidewalk in her fuchsia dress, her black curls bouncing and shining in the sun, her muscular hips swaying with the pleasure of her stride. She carried her shoulders proudly, her neck as straight as any queen's. Heads swiveled with interest as she passed.

I lengthened my own stride to catch up with her. I was about in hailing distance when the damnedest thing happened. Around the corner came a troupe of what? Dancers, I guess. They were dancing, at least; sort of shuffling along in a stamping rhythm, shaking rattles and beating skin drums. It was a bit hard to focus my attention on that detail, you see, because these, ah—dancers were almost naked, except for the fact that their skins were completely covered.

Let me start over. Around the corner came half a dozen men clothed in loincloths and mud, with large earthen pots covering their heads. Some were fat and some were skinny, and they were completely brown from their necks to their bare toes, as if they were spawned of the same clay that formed their jug heads. These heads were mute and imposing, ornamented only with vacuous dark holes in the eye positions, small semicircular slots by their ears, and tubular spouts for mouths. They wore necklaces and anklets of crude beads, and feathers strung on gut. Best yet, their leader wore a fedora atop his jug, and marched along in the tight-assed swagger of an eighteenth-century fop, carrying an attaché case, an umbrella, and a rolled-up newspaper.

Maddie stopped perhaps fifteen feet from the dancers, grinning.

The lead mud man's troubadours gathered around him. He set down his attaché. He opened the paper. He read, howling through his tubular mouth hole into the gathering crowd: "Wah, wah, wah, wah! Angry Woman Bites Dog! Beauty Queen Transvestite Hog! Middle East Detests the West, whaddawegonna DO?"

"RAH!" shouted the mud man chorus, taking a short hop toward the crowd. Men in tailored suits stepped back nervously, forcing smiles to show that they hadn't really been startled. Women stared. Maddie grinned and puffed out her chest, holding her ground.

The mud man with the fedora turned the page and read on: "Woo, woo, woo, woo! Cancer Caused by Carrot Sticks! White House Sale on Dirty Tricks! Hollywood Is Turning Tricks! Haddiwegetso SCREWED?"

"HAH!" shouted the chorus, charging into the crowd, which immediately scattered.

Except for Maddie.

Maddie stepped right toward the chief, swung a hand around in a wide arc that ended with a loud smack on the chief's left buttock. The chief dropped his paper and pranced with delight, then stopped and wrestled open his attaché case. He fished something out and dropped it into Maddie's hand. She clutched his offering to her ample bosom and stood on tiptoes to kiss him on the jug. He shimmied in ecstasy, then aimed his mouth tube at her ear and whispered something, tipped his hat to an older woman who seemed frozen to the sidewalk in catatonic shock, and strolled out of sight back around the corner.

Maddie resumed her progress down the sidewalk as if it were all in an afternoon's stroll.

"Friend of yours?" I shouted, jogging to catch up.

She looked over her shoulder and smiled. "Old Archie? Shit, yes; he's a pistol. Don't make 'em like that back in Texas."

Archie. Of course. Street performer. Poetry. That had been Archie Arch under all that mud.

I spun around. No sign of Archie or any of his henchmen; the whole scene might not ever have happened. I sprinted back to the corner, but Archie had once again melted into the stone and concrete of Denver.

Maddie was waiting for me where I left her. "Ain'ch y'll never seen a mud man before?" she drawled, savoring the juiciness of her chewing gum.

"You know Archie?" I asked, trying to sound cool. *I was so close!*

"Sure. Don't everybody?"

We started walking again. "I mean, know him personally."

"Well, I ain't certain *anybody* knows Archie *personal* like. He's a little unusual, as you might have noticed. Why you so interested?" she asked, cocking her head to one side. There was no toying with Maddie McNutt.

I tried to divert her with another question, kind of like diverting the Mississippi with a spatula. "What did he give you back there, anyway?"

Maddie opened her hand, revealing a square plastic packet with an unmistakable circular shape bumping up inside it, "SAFE SEX," it said, in crudely applied ink. He'd given her a condom.

"Guess ol' Archie's trying to perform a public service," she said, breaking into a maniacal cackle. "*Ain't* he a pistol. *So* thoughtful." She trained her canny eyes on me. "But y'all were about to explain your interest in the man, now weren't you?"

"Me?" I looked all about. "Hey, I just don't see that kind of stuff every day. Why, back in Chugwater—"

Maddie tipped her head back and laughed. "Y'll 'bout as subtle as a pig with wings. What is this, some more of this detective work I hadn't noticed? Y'all Em ace superstar go-it-alone don't need no help off no-body Hansen? Your problem, honey bun, is ya'll's gotta figger out who yer friends is."

I sighed. "I want to meet Archie," I muttered.

"Well why didn't y'll say so?" she shouted. "Just stick with me, slick. I'm meeting his ass later on, after these stiffs go home to their TV dinners. Whoo-ee!"

29

A block short of Blackfeet, Maddie suddenly remembered an errand she had to run. I couldn't blame her if she didn't want to be seen walking into the building with me. Her absence left me walking into the belly of that building solo, without a buddy to watch my back. My neck and shoulders tightened into a cramp, and my feet grew strangely heavy. *Keep moving. This is silly.* I pushed open the heavy doors, pressed myself into the cool air of the street-level lobby. *See? So far, so good.*

Two husky overgrown bully-boy engineers from Blackfeet hurried past me, the sound of their heavy footfalls swallowed by the carpeting. I slowed my stride, hoping I wouldn't be noticed. They reached the elevator and pressed the button to call the car, then turned and watched me, their mouths moving with words they kept too quiet for me to hear. As the elevator doors opened, one of them braced them with his hand to hold it for me, his rude stare belying the chivalry of his gesture.

No way. I wasn't getting on that car. I cut to the left, heading into the staircase. Inside, I sucked concrete-flavored air in great lungfuls, gripping the handrail.

Come on, Em. You got what, three hours sleep? You skipped lunch. You're getting paranoid. Where do you get the idea anyone around here even gives a shit what you know? That overgrown sandlot hero probably got stiffed by his girlfriend at lunch or something. You think everything's about you? I sat down on the cold step and hung my head, trying to control a deep, slow trembling that had invaded my bones, but no amount of self-scolding could control it. I needed rest. I needed a place to exist, to be welcome, to not be Other.

Twenty minutes later, I was still sitting there. My nerves had quieted, but it was occurring to me by degrees that I was going to have to leave the staircase eventually. I couldn't live there, like Archie Arch sleeping on a girder in the parking garage. I stood up, my legs aching with fatigue. Taking a deep breath, I pushed open the fire door and stepped back out into the lobby.

No one was there.

I approached the elevator call buttons, disgusted at my cowardice. What did I think was waiting for me up there, a last cigarette and a firing squad? *You're as mad as Archie.*

As I stood there screwing up the courage to walk back into the fray, the red down light dinged on over the doors, and the sheaves slid open. An elderly businessman was standing inside, holding the doors open for me with one arthritic hand. "Going down?" he rasped.

"Why not?" I got onto the dreaded elevator and journeyed downward with him. He got off at basement level A. I stayed on to the bottom, to basement level B.

The elevator door hissed open, letting in stale air. As I stepped out of the car, the hair stood up on the back of my neck. It was a crawly feeling, as if someone, or perhaps some*thing*, was watching me. *Psst, hey Em*, the sensation said. *Over here.*

For a moment, I considered heading back upstairs, but the car had already left again, and here, at least, no one was staring at me like I was the lowest form of life.

It didn't take long to figure out where Archie had been hiding, or living if you prefer. The only I-beam I could find that was exposed was not far from the elevator bank. It formed a lintel over the steel fire door that opened into the inner staircase. On first glance, there was no sign of Archie's habitation, so I pushed at the fire door to see if he had left any clues in the stairwell. The door swung open stiffly at first, but then swung loose all at once and banged against a hip-level steel post that jutted out of the floor to one side of the door to prevent the door from hitting people on the outside when it was opened from the inside. Smudged concrete walls greeted me on the other side of the door.

Back out in the garage, I tried to figure out how Archie had gotten up onto the I-beam. I could barely reach the bottom fin of the beam at full stretch, and I didn't remember Archie as a very tall man. After a few minutes' study, I saw how he had done it.

I hitched up my skirt. Reaching again for the bottom of the beam with my hands, I put one foot up on the steel doorstop and lurched upward. Once balanced on the top of the post, I could get my other foot on the doorknob, and pull myself up to a good view of the accommodations on top of the beam. It formed a shelf about two feet deep and maybe six feet long, with excess head space of a spare twelve inches. Not the Brown Palace exactly, but definitely out of the weather, and guaranteed to please any ascetic. Scribbled all along the back wall of the alcove were verses, metered out in a squirrelly little hand in blurry felt-tip pen. I strained my eyes in the gloom, but couldn't quite read what the odd man had written.

My feet started to ache from the pressure of their precarious points of balance. My calf muscles trembled. In a moment, my feet would slip; it was either up or down, and no amount of squinting was going to bring those words any closer. Pulling with all my strength, I hauled myself up on the lintel, scrambling to catch traction on the cold, dirty steel. A button on my jacket caught on the edge of the beam, nearly pitching me off into an awkward fall, but as my skirt worked its way up my thigh, I finally gained enough skin-to-steel friction to haul myself onto the beam.

I rolled onto my back, and pushed my skirt back down toward my knees. The concrete above my face was cloyingly close. In that claustrophobic space, I feared at first that the building might let down its weight and crush me, but as I lay there, I suddenly experienced a feeling that Archie must have felt, as he lay there through the long night hours, wrapped in darkness. Privacy. Absolute unmolested removal from all that was going on around me.

As my eyes adjusted to the shadow, I could just make out a verse directly above my face:

> The ardent monk of darkness dwells
> Within a steel and concrete hell
> To earn his keep he watches while
> The goblins dance in city style
> With life and death the same to them
> His penance lasts at others whim.

Not much for punctuation, but it evoked an image. I contemplated it a while, savoring the strange perspective it evoked. Farther down toward my stomach, I found something a little lighter:

> jungle cat
> same as that

likes to chat
wears no hat
drives drives
runs along
mating song

A work in progress? There was another that was probably a
tone poem, as it just seemed a string of nonsense words that
sounded nice together, then another that looked like the dress
rehearsal for the Mud Man Stomp I'd heard at noon. That was
pretty much it, other than a few groups of four vertical
scratches crossed by a fifth, as if he'd been counting the days
in a prison cell. At least the guy had a sense of humor.

I was just surveying possible routes back down when I
heard someone coming down the staircase. I pressed myself
farther into the shadow, certain that this was no place to be
discovered. *If I have to, I can lead with my feet, and kick like
hell.*

The door swung open.

Once again, when I was least ready to deal with him, it was
Pete.

I forced my lungs to take very shallow, quiet breaths so he
wouldn't hear me.

He crossed the space between the door and the first line of
parked cars. Halfway across that short distance, he stopped,
tensing as if at an unexpected sound. Had he sensed my presence? I held my breath and didn't move, praying that he
wouldn't look up into the shadow and see me. Unsatisfied, he
turned slowly, peering left and right, but mercifully he did not
think to look near the ceiling. Still frowning, he fished his car
keys out of one pocket and moved between the cars. He
moved quickly to the old green Volvo and unlocked the door,
and curved his indecently handsome body into the seat.

As I looked down on the Volvo, the crawly feeling that had
plagued me since I first entered the garage returned, intensi-
fied. *What is it?* I asked myself, as the Volvo's engine fired.
The car rolled backward out of the space and stopped. Pete
rolled down the window and looked around the garage.

Once again, he didn't see me. I closed my eyes, listening to
the rhythmic sounds of the Volvo as Pete pulled away and
wound it up through its gears, gunning the car up the concrete

ramp toward the street. "He's not worth it," I whispered. "I made a mistake, and I learned from it."

My mind interrupted. *There's something really important here*, it insisted. *Pay attention.* I breathed deeply and fought to slow my pulse, so that the knowledge could rise to the surface. What was trying to get through to me? Had Archie watched Pete from this ledge? No, Archie had been flushed from the garage before Pete drove me home. Perhaps some other evening, Archie had watched. I lay a while longer on the beam, bathed in foul air and the echoes of Archie's strange existence, trying to peer through time and space. *How interesting, to lie cocooned in the taproot of this building.* I felt like an insect about to hatch, confused and vulnerable after painful metamorphosis. I wondered idly if my insect's brain was really large enough to deal with what was happening. At length, I decided I was losing my mind.

I managed to get down off the beam without ripping my clothes, but they were destined for the cleaner's. With a sigh, I surveyed lines of soot that ran all down my jacket, and I found that the skirt was a different color than it had been an hour before. I took the jacket off and brushed it, shaking my head at little Em who *still* couldn't keep herself clean. *Never fear, Mother, you need not scold me anymore. I've taken over the job.* I whacked at my skirt next, carefully using the back of my hand, and then dusted my shoes with my cuff. After straightening my skirt and making a rudimentary attempt at tucking in my blouse, I turned and headed through the fire door, resolving to hike the fourteen stories up to my office in penance.

As the door closed behind me, I turned and peeked through the small pane of wire-reinforced glass that was set in the door, trying once again to dispel the uneasy sense that something was watching me. With a twinge, I realized that Pete had felt it, too; that it hadn't necessarily been me he had sensed. The thought put me briefly inside his skin, an unwelcome intimacy of shared experience, a primal *us* united against the unseen foe.

I leaned my forehead against the cool glass. It was a perfect view back toward the parking space where the Volvo had been parked. "Fuck you, Pete," I muttered.

And then my eyes came to rest on a faint bit of scrawling just below the glass. It was Archie's handwriting again, but this time carefully inscribed in pencil, so as to be almost invisible. It was not his own verse, though, but part of an old nursery rhyme. What it said was: "Ashes, Ashes, All Fall Down."

30

It was a long trudge up fourteen flights of stairs. With every step, my resolve strengthened. I was going to crack this case. I was going to find out which of Archie's "goblins" had pushed Scott from that window. And I was going to free more than one "monk" from a steel-and-concrete hell, damn it.

As I staggered out of the fire door onto the twelfth floor, I turned immediately toward the women's room. There I cleaned myself up as best I could. Then I skulked to Menken's office, waiting for him to return from what proved to be a very long lunch. It was time to hold the old boy's feet to the fire, find out what he really knew about Lost Coyote Field.

Irma Triff was soon sick of me. "He's a very busy man," she growled. "I'll let him know you want to see him, but the likelihood that he can fit you in this afternoon is nil."

Maddie overheard this last, as she strolled by on her way in from the elevator. I could hear her whistling "The Yellow Rose of Texas" as she gyrated down the hallway, and when I followed her into our office a half minute later, she was just hanging up the phone. She grinned at me, a kind of Campbell's-soup-kid-with-tits provocation number. I wondered what she'd been up to.

At four-fifteen, we were sitting around working off a little angst shooting rubber bands at each other when our phone rang. Maddie picked it up. "McNutt," she drawled into the mouthpiece. "Un-*huh*, un-*huh*." She even drawled her uh-huh's. Putting down the receiver, she turned to me. "Menken's back, but he's got company—someone who came off the elevator with him. Simca says give him ten minutes and charge."

"Simca?"

"The receptionist. She's got a name, baby cakes. Y'all seemed to want to visit with Menken, so I told her to call me when his nibs dragged his butt back from wherever. Old Irma can be a mite unhelpful, when she's a mind to."

"Thanks."

"Think nothing of it."

I clocked ten minutes and started down the hall. As I closed the distance, Irma drew a bead on me from her lair by her master's door. I looked at her and she looked at me, our eyes locked in nonverbal communication:

—*Yes, I'm coming to your desk.*

—*Oh, you are, are you?*

—*Yes, and you're going to ring through to your boss.*

—*Oh, I am, am I?*

—*Yes, you are; and yes, he will see me.*

Irma visibly braced herself against my advance. She was just arranging her mouth for the formality of asking me what I wanted when Menken's door swung open and Simon Bunting backed out into the hall. I couldn't see his face, but his wide shoulders and turret-shaped head were now engraved in my memory, unmistakable from any angle. He closed the door with deliberate care.

I swerved toward Simon, changing plans. I could corner him. Easy pickings. *And what in hell's name is Scott's ex-roommate doing in Menken's office, if he isn't showing up in his own?*

Reading my intent like a billboard, Irma yanked her phone off its cradle and punched a button. "Miss Hansen is here to see you, Mr. Menken," she croaked, her eyes betraying ever so subtle a shine of anxiety.

Simon turned around. The expression on his dull face was an unself-conscious mixture of disgust and pleasure, as if he were showing off a painful rash on his private parts and enjoying the horror it stimulated in others.

I tried to lengthen my stride, but the cut of my skirt was too narrow.

Irma quickly recradled the phone. "Mr. Menken will see you now," she barked.

Simon glanced at me. No interest; to him, I was just another face in the multitude. I wanted to leap at him.

Simon moved across the reception area toward the elevator with the peculiar speed of the long-legged. Discarding any attempt to look casual about what I was doing, I hiked up one side of my skirt for an all-out dash. I had narrowed the distance between us to less than ten feet when Menken's door opened.

"Why Emily! Come in!" Menken called.

I stopped, my gears jammed.

The elevator door opened and swallowed Simon.

As I looked back toward Menken's door, my eyes swept past the receptionist, Simca, who recoiled from me as if I were threatening her with a handful of shit. Why? My train of thought careened down a sidetrack, squealing, *Jesus, lady, what's biting you?*

Irma's already arid face tightened further, as if to repress a smile.

Avoiding her gaze, I turned on one high heel, lost my balance on its unfamiliar foundation, and stumbled. Catching myself just short of a full-length fall, I followed Menken into his office. What had started out as a storming of the Bastille had degenerated into the ragtag shuffle of the prisoner of war.

"Emily, sit down, sit down!" he said, in a slightly diminished variant of his usual good cheer.

I sat, preparing my questions.

Oblivious to my silence, Menken chatted along with his usual garrulous drivel, yammering about a *Wall Street Journal* article he'd just read. He paced up and down in front of the big windows that looked out over Seventeenth Street, his hands clasped behind his back and his eyes on the carpet. Stopping abruptly, he stared down at the street, rocking back and forth on his heels. As he ran low on pearls of wisdom, he turned to me. "So, Emily: how are you liking Blackfeet, now that you've been here a while?"

"Uh, fine, sir." I thought, *What just happened in here? If he squeezes his buttocks any tighter together, they'll squeak.*

"Lovely fall weather we're having," he said. "I like the autumn best of any season, here in Colorado."

He's talking about the weather? This is serious.

"Back in Connecticut, where I grew up, autumn was a longer season, full of different colors, but here, it's short and brisk. Colorado really comes to the point, don't you think?"

I searched his words for a second meaning. *Fall? Comes to the point?*

"Certainly, sir." *Yes, come to the point. Why was Simon here? Get a grip, Em; you're in here to hold this mutant's feet to the fire, not exchange pleasantries.* I cleared my throat, trying to think up some catchy phrase or manipulative question to get him to talk about what he and Simon had just discussed.

Menken stopped rocking, but continued to stare out the window, his eyes glazed with preoccupation. Just as I decided he must have gone into catatonic shock, he said, "Please don't call me 'sir.'" His tone surprised me: it was soft, and rather sad.

"Okay, ah, Mr. Menken."

He turned toward me and smiled weakly. "Please call me J.C. What a day it's been, Emily."

"A day, sir? I mean, ah—J.C.?" The name caught on my tongue like dry cracker crumbs.

He shook his head distractedly. At least he didn't ask something like, "Why did you come to see me?"

"A day, J.C.?" I asked again, more forcibly this time.

"Yes. What do you make of a woman who sounds like a little girl who calls me up in the middle of the night to tell me she knows why one of my employees has died?"

I felt like the room had just been jerked sideways a foot. Menken had heard from the baby-doll voice too, the mystery midnight caller who was so intent on stirring the pot. I opened my mouth to make some reply, but Menken threw me another curve. He said: "Emily, let's go for a drive."

I said, "Let me get my coat," and hurried down the hall. If Menken wanted to drop bombs like that one and pretend he was just being chatty, that was fine. *Hey, he can spill his guts in semaphores, if he wants. He wants to go for a drive during business hours, we go for a drive. He's the boss.*

Back in our office, Maddie was just starting to straighten her desk up for the night. "Small change of plans," I said. "Duty calls. When and where are you meeting Archie?"

Maddie cocked an eyebrow at me. "Duty, huh?"

"Yeah, duty. So where can I find you?"

"I'm having dinner at the Slant Hole with Billy Bob and Bubba, a couple of those cretinous stereotypes from Texas y'all hear about. Join us there any time until around eight." Maddie smiled slyly. "I'll leave from there to meet Archie," she added not answering my question.

I squinched up my face. "Jus' *love* that Texas barbecue," I drawled.

"Put hair on your chest," she sang, as I hurried out the door.

Halfway down the hall, I dodged into Scott's empty office to phone Elyria. She wasn't home, so I left a message on her answering machine saying that I was going driving with Menken to find out what Simon Bunting had been doing in his office, and to watch out for a low-flying grey Mercedes.

Menken was waiting by Irma Triff's desk with his attaché

case in hand, giving her a few final instructions for the day. "Ah, there you are," he said. "Time's a-wasting. We don't want to get stuck in rush hour traffic."

We strode toward the lobby. I locked eyes with the receptionist as I passed her desk, perversely documenting the increments by which she was indicating that she despised me. This time, her expression was almost unreadable, but the air around her perfect coif fairly crackled with repressed emotion. I glared at her, squaring my shoulders in challenge: *Yes, I'm leaving with Menken, Simca. Stuff that up your grapevine, why don't you? Menken's toy, my ass: this is surveillance, and you all are in a peck of trouble.*

The elevator took its time coming to Menken's summons. I tapped my foot impatiently, praying that it would arrive before any of my dear colleagues saw us, or worse, joined us for the ride down. I might be tough enough to stare down the receptionist, but now put to the test, I didn't want to deal with any more crap from the engineers and geologists.

When I heard the muted *ding* and saw the light go on over the elevator doors, I realized that I hadn't been breathing. The doors opened. Menken and I stepped into the car. I started a lunge for the Close Door button, but Menken blocked me. "No, no, my dear, let me get it," he said, as he slowly picked out the button for the main level of the parking garage.

I clenched my teeth. *Come on, two seconds, one . . .*

Maddie rounded the corner from the hallway and whooped.

Menken smiled and caught the doors just as they started to close. "Ah, Maddie. Always willing to hold the door for a lovely lady from the Lone Star State."

Maddie's eyes widened and began to dance as she saw me with the boss. Worse yet, she took so much time wriggling into her coat as she crossed the lobby that another geologist came into view, and then an accountant, and then Pete.

Pete.

If I'd clamped my teeth together any tighter, my molars would have cracked.

Everyone loaded onto the elevator car, assuming the position; hands folded in front, eyes forward. Maddie leaned back against the back wall of the car, humming a tune.

Pete positioned himself right next to me and looked to the front of the car.

I stared at my feet, waiting miserably for everyone to call

out their floors to the accountant, who was now closest to the buttons.

Maddie's tune bounced around inside my head like a drunken bumblebee. It was strangely familiar, out of context yet right on the edge of memory. I concentrated on it, the better to ignore Pete's presence.

As the car plummeted, Maddie's tune came into register. Of course it had been hard to place: it was Gilbert and Sullivan with a Texas drawl. But which operetta? When the refrain circled by for the second time, I placed it: *Ruddigore, or the Witch's Curse* act two, the ghost scene: "For duty, duty must be done, this rule applies to everyone. . . ."

"Maddie," I said, "I didn't know you were so cultured."

She grinned. "Honey pie, I'm as cultured as a pearl." The car stopped at the Seventeenth Street level. "Knockers up, toots," she added with a stage wink, and strolled out into the lobby.

I burst into a graceless fit of laughter. Pete stepped out of the car. He stopped just outside the car and hesitated, staring at me, his face completely blank. Still grinning uncontrollably, I reached across Menken and punched the Close Door button.

Pete stood frozen in the lobby, still staring at me. As the door closed between us, I had for that one shining moment the pleasure of knowing just how the Cheshire cat must have felt as he disappeared, leaving nothing behind but his grin.

Menken's big grey Mercedes rolled out of the parking structure onto Welton Street. I glanced at him. His mind was anywhere but on his driving. I wondered if I was going to have to grab the steering wheel, as I had with Libby. "Where to?" I asked, trying to sound casual.

Menken's lips crimped into a smug smile. "There's a little something I want to show you."

"What kind of something?"

"Now Emily, you must restrain that curiosity of yours."

"How many guesses do I get?" As the car paused for a few seconds at the traffic light at Colfax Avenue, I wondered if I might be better served to get out. I gripped the door handle, trying to decide. *Maybe this is one of those bits I can leave to Sergeant Ortega. Except he wouldn't necessarily tell me what he found out.*

Menken looked at me abstractly, as an entomologist might study an interesting species. He shook his head. "Really,

Emily, I thought you were more adventuresome than this. I'm just taking you to see a horse. It's a wonderful quarter horse, a chestnut mare. I was pleased to acquire such a fine—"

Was I just his next round of applause? I exhaled slowly, wondering if this trip was going to be a waste of time. I interrupted Menken's self-congratulatory dissertation with a hopeful conversation opener: "Say, who was that guy in your office before I came in?"

"Let's not talk about the office," he said, abruptly. "After a long day, I like to relax."

I glanced at the clock on the dash. It was almost five. I had to be back by eight. Seeing Archie was *certainly* important. As Menken blathered away about equine blood lines, I memorized the route the Mercedes was traveling, in case my boss forgot which planet he was on and I needed to find my own way home. We flowed south with one-way traffic on Broadway, and then turned west on Eighth, spinning around Denver General Hospital and picking up the ramp for Highway 6 at the big interchange with Interstate 25. The big car rode smoothly, promoting the eery sensation that it wasn't moving at all, that we were holding still and the scenery outside was flowing past us like a movie. We started to rise up the western ramp of the Denver Basin, rising above the smog, gliding past the bedroom sprawl of Lakewood and Green Mountain. There we broke from suburb to exurb, the scenery now dominated by the ramparts of the massive hogbacks and foothills rising from short-grass prairie. Menken took the exit for Interstate 70, sliced through the massive Morrison Formation hogback, and headed up Mount Vernon Canyon into the foothills. I began to despair of making it back to Denver before Easter.

Then a few miles up Mount Vernon Canyon, we turned off onto a two-lane road. Déj vu took hold of me. Were we going to unscrew the damned light bulbs again? In broad daylight?

Menken was now talking about the sugar beet crop in southeast Wyoming, throwing in terms like "gross" and "tare," which I supposed were intended to make him sound like an insider.

The road crossed a bridge to the south side of the Interstate and stretched onward, cresting a rise and winding through the Ponderosa pine forest. Familiar territory dropped away, vanishing from the rearview mirror.

I slouched down in my seat. I had always thought I'd leave

this life shot out of the hard leather of a saddle, not bored to death in the soft leather of Mercedes upholstery.

A mile down the road, the view opened to a made-for-TV housing development for the wealthy, a weird congregation of overstuffed cedar-sided Mineshack Modern luxury homes improbably tossed into what had once been a beautiful meadow. Sweeping decks sprouted hot tubs, and pristine driveways branched from meandering blacktops toward three- and four-car garages. I could see no people on the lawns or patios, and the roads were devoid of any traffic except for the car we were in. Where had the occupants gone? I wondered whether even Menken truly lived there, or if he just dissolved on crossing the threshold, to be created anew each morning as he reemerged.

Menken pulled into a driveway in front of a particularly expansive house equipped with the cedar-shake version of flying buttresses reminiscent of a medieval fortress. He squared off on the right-hand bay of a three-car garage and pressed the button for the automatic opener. We rolled in, coming to dock on a cold grey expanse of concrete. There was almost nothing else in the garage; no bicycles, no lawn mower, none of the usual flotsam of habitation.

I stepped out of the Mercedes and looked around. There was an oil stain on the floor of the next bay. It had to be someone's parking space, and if so, that someone clearly wasn't home. His wife's car? Had Menken brought me up here in her absence, in hope of a little tryst? I imagined Menken calling his mate to say, *Take your time coming home, dear, I have a little business to look after anyway.*

Menken opened a door and disappeared through it. I followed at a distance, checking the side door to the garage in case I had to make an unorthodox exit.

The inside of the house was as disturbingly vacant as the outside. The decor was tastefully done, as far as it went, but it only increased my impression that no one was home. We passed down a long hallway. One archway opened onto a vast living room, regally fitted with empty wooden-legged sofas and chairs on a vast Persian carpet, but there were no magazines on the coffee table, no collectibles, no trace of hobbies or human interests anywhere in sight.

Dining room, same. No flowers in the designer vase on the dining table. No crumbs, no cheerful little rings from wet glasses.

Kitchen. As pristine as the rest, except—well, something was scrawled on the refrigerator door. Something brazen, wild colorful strokes of complaint and bile.

As Menken continued down the hall to the front entrance to hang up his coat, I dodged into the kitchen, made certain that the door onto the back patio opened easily, and moved closer to the refrigerator to read the inscription. It was written in neon orange crayon in a crude, childish, angry hand, difficult to read. I could make out the second word: *Mommy's*—

"Get out! Get out, get out, get *out!*"

I spun around to see what went with the high-pitched screams, bracing myself in case it was armed. A teenaged girl, as rangy as a half-starved antelope, careened toward me, colliding with solid objects and banging every surface with her hands. Her straight dark hair hung in wild ropes about her face. I caught a glimpse of dark, feverish eyes beneath the locks, and a raw wound of a mouth pulled down at the corners.

I braced myself to fend off the intruder, maybe grab flailing wrists and wrestle her to the floor, but she was all ruckus and no fight: she halted two strides from me, hissing at me through bared teeth.

"Celia!" bellowed Menken. "Be nice to our guest!" He hurried into the room and took the pocket-sized hurricane by the shoulders, pulling her gently but firmly back against his chest. Speaking quietly in her ear, he said, "Now, Cecelia, this is Miss Hansen, a geologist from my company. I would appreciate it if you would show her some manners."

"Hello," Cecelia moaned, her strangled voice now a despairing monotone. Rolling her eyes back in her head. She passively held out a hand to be shaken.

I played my part, taking hold of Cecelia's limp little hand and moving it up and down in something approximating a handshake. Now that she wasn't jumping up and down and taking up space with her lungs, it was clear that she wasn't even fully grown. Maybe a tall eleven, or at best twelve. It was hard to gauge the face through the hair, but I didn't see any curves from the shoulders down.

"Now, Cecelia," Menken said, speaking to her in even, measured tones, "Miss Hansen has come all the way up here to see Velvet."

Velvet? The damned horse's name is Velvet? Don't you folks have any pride, you can't think up a more original name than Velvet? I forced a smile. "Oh, yes. I like horses, Cecelia."

Cecelia sulked.

Menken beamed at me. "Velvet is an outstanding horse. She's out of Stellar Pleasure by Handy's Grand Charger."

I'd heard of Grand Charger. Not bad.

Cecelia stuck out her lower lip.

"Miss Hansen is from Wyoming. She's quite a barrel racer."

Cecelia swept one tight little paw across her face to clear the tangle of hair from her vision and gawked at me. "Barrels?"

"Sure," I said. I smiled, knowing the feeling: at her age, the women who rode the barrels were goddesses to me, standing proud in their western-cut shirts and Triple-X beaver hats with the feather bands. How I had longed to fill their Levi's.

"Oh, Miss Hansen, *would* you look at Velvet? She's just the prettiest horse ever. I could go get her right now."

"Sure." Cecelia's eyes shone with worship. I was surprised to find my own were growing moist.

Cecelia scampered out of the room and down the hall, shouting, "It'll be just a minute! I have to ride my bike over to the ranch where I keep her, and then I have to catch her!" The door into the garage slammed shut.

I turned and studied Menken. He was smiling an almost indecently self-satisfied smile, his eyes shining but unfocused. His emotional state seemed weirdly off-center. Had he really brought me all the way up here just to see this horse? He seemed bent on distracting himself from something outside of the room, something he pushed repeatedly out of his awareness, only to find it crowding back in on him again and again.

His eyes focused briefly on me. "How about a drink while we wait? It will take her more than a minute to get her horse; half an hour, more likely. I'm afraid Velvet is a spirited horse, who prefers her freedom." He moved close and placed a hand against the small of my back to guide me toward a doorway.

I stiffened and drew away, awkwardly trying to contradict any fantasy of sexual attraction he might be entertaining. At a distance, I followed him into a second living room, this one sunken and sumptuously fitted with soft, low leather couches and inviting recliners, but still oddly devoid of any sense of warmth. I strategically chose a narrow ottoman and sat down.

Menken took his place at a built-in bar. "What'll you have?"

"Gin and tonic." It was the only mixed drink name I could think of.

Menken stooped to get some ice out of the midget refrigerator behind the bar. "Damn, no ice," he announced.

I saw my chance to take another pass at the graffiti. "I'll get some from the kitchen," I said, and jogged out of the room before he could stop me.

The scrawling turned out to be a limerick. A pretty good one, at that:

> *Oh, Mommy's up in Aspen snorting coke*
> *She left Friday with a friendly looking dope*
> *Dear old Dad's in the Jacuzzi*
> *With his brand new buddy Suzie*
> *Trying to see if they can make the bourbon float.*

Menken's hand shot past me, gripping a sponge. "I apologize for Cecelia again," he said, rubbing with manic vigor at the words on the door. "She has a rather overactive imagination. My wife has gone to—er, attend a workshop in Aspen. Cecelia has it in her head that Miriam's not coming back." He laughed woodenly. "Cecelia's a headstrong girl: this is the third time she's put this up here since Saturday. I see she's come up with something a little harder to erase this time." He manufactured a smile that showed a lot of teeth. "I like a strong will in my women."

"She's a natural poet," I prattled, trying to say something nice.

"No, the rhyme is off. See this? Coke, dope, float. They don't rhyme." He scrubbed even harder, his jaws gnashing with the force of this last-ditch effort at erasing reality.

"Well, okay, but Jacuzzi, Suzie is pretty good. Damned good for a twelve-year-old."

"Cecelia is a late-blooming fourteen," said Menken, huffily.

Suddenly a drink sounded awfully good. I yanked open the freezer door, grabbed the ice tray, and herded him back into the other room.

As he mixed my drink, Menken went a little heavy on the gin. He went even heavier on his bourbon, pouring it neat into a highball glass. Something was bothering him, all right. I took one whiff of my drink, set it down untouched by the foot of the ottoman, and began calculating how long it would take to call a taxi to Menken's and then ride in it to the Slant Hole.

Menken's drink disappeared at an astonishing clip. He paced up and back on the deep carpet, gassing away about the horse, the great deal he'd gotten on her, and so forth.

I'd heard enough of the wilderness of Menken's existence to

last me a long time. Figuring he'd had enough bourbon to get chatty, I interrupted: "So, what did Simon Bunting want?"

Menken stopped in mid-stride. "Who?"

"Simon Bunting. The guy who was in your office just ahead of me."

Menken sank down into a immense grey leather couch and looked at me as if I were hallucinating. "That gentleman's name was George Taylor."

I felt my mouth sag open. Had Simon lied to Menken, or was Menken quite a liar, himself? "Well, what did he want?"

Menken leaned forward and put down his drink. "Really, Em, I'm not in the business of explaining my schedule to my employees."

"Ah, yeah, um, I'm sorry, sir. Just making small talk."

Menken observed me for a moment, the tips of his fingers laid neatly together in polite menace. "Is this Em Hansen the private investigator from whom I am at last hearing?"

I didn't answer.

"Good," he said. "If you have no guile, at least keep your silence. That's important."

My pulse raced.

Menken rose from the couch. "I'm glad to know you're *helping*, Miss Hansen," he said, beginning to pace. "I *trust* I can count on your discretion, although I perceive you to be a very *independent* young lady."

"Helping with what, sir?" *Shit, of all the weirdos in the world, I have to go to work for someone whose thinking gets clearer when he drinks.*

"You were supposed to report to me, not try to run this as a lone wolf."

"Run what, sir?"

"Run what? This investigation. Really, Emily, you insult my intelligence. Why do you think I hired you?"

"Um, to replace Bill Kretzmer, sir?"

"My dear Emily, these are hard times. Jobs are at a premium. I could have replaced Bill with any number of geologists who are far more experienced than you."

I itched to kick Menken's overtightened buttocks right up between his supercilious ears. *Fuck with my self-esteem, will you?* I thought, surprised to find that for the first time in my life I had enough self-esteem to be fucked with. *With which to be fucked,* I told myself, with the full dignity of my educational background.

Menken's tone suddenly became more solicitous. "You, Emily"—he smiled joyously, holding his hands outstretched toward me like a politician welcoming the crowd—"you have a God-given talent. When you figured out how, and er, why Bill Kretzmer died, I *had* to have you working for me." His eyes flashed with the fever of possession, and he lunged toward me. For one fleeting moment, I feared he was going to grab me or worse yet, kneel before me, but he stopped, a hand quivering in air to either side of my head. His face darkened abruptly. Was he going to box my ears? Or strangle me while his daughter was gone? "I had hoped you would simply report to me as a matter of course, but now I see you have a little ego problem around your independence." He straightened up and stared at me, eyes boring into my skull.

This was not what was supposed to be happening. I was supposed to be pumping this brain-dead executive for semivital information, but instead he was taking charge of the conversation, turning the tables on me. It reminded me of the one time I tried to ride my horse circus style, standing up, and had found myself with a very long walk home.

The only thing to do was to play along. I gave him a contrite smile. "I'm sorry, sir. I guess I'm used to working alone."

Menken's face went through another one of its rapid changes. He beamed approval at me. "That's better. Now, report." He cheerfully poured himself another drink.

Report? "Ah, sure, sure; well, I'm a little confused about the way things are at Blackfeet." For rank improvisation, it was pretty good.

Menken sighed. "Yes! Things have been more than a little odd at Blackfeet for quite some time. There's been a mood around the place, you see. Competition. Competition is good, but this is beyond what's healthy for the company."

Huh? Now where are we? Are we even discussing the same problem? "You mean the competition between Smith and Crick," I suggested.

"Precisely!"

Well what do you expect, when you tie two cats' tails together and throw them over a clothesline? I had trouble keeping sarcasm out of my voice. "Why do you suppose they have trouble getting along?"

"I don't know." Now the bourbon was certainly hitting him. That kind of candor couldn't be natural. Or was this another smoke screen?

"Has there been any suggestion that Blackfeet might have to downsize, and that one of them might have to go?"

"Well, Emily, Blackfeet is top-heavy. They're both good men, so I've set them the challenge of proving which is the better manager. To the victor belong the spoils, that's the real world. Healthy competition. It keeps them sharp."

So Maddie was right: someone was about to get castrated. I wondered what there was in the male code of honor that made it easier for them to fight to the death than consider an above-board review of the situation. "Do you suppose there might be a connection between that and what Scott wanted to talk to you about two days before he died?"

He looked at me quizzically. "You mean when he came in asking for a promotion? I fail to understand what that has to do with—"

"What were his exact words?"

"What do you mean?"

"How did he ask for the promotion?"

Menken looked confused. "I think he said, 'I must consider my future with the company.'"

"Are you sure he wasn't talking about the future *of* the company, not his future *with* the company?"

Menken considered this. "Perhaps."

I wanted to smack him. "What else did he say?"

"He said we had to stop drilling at Lost Coyote." Menken smiled happily. "Maybe you're right. That would make more sense that way. Yes, Scott *was* on the nay-saying side of that issue, wasn't he?"

"How did the conversation end?"

"I had to take a telephone call. An important real estate connection. You know, Denver's prices are depressed just now, and—"

"So you dismissed him."

"Yes. I told him to take the next day off. The poor boy seemed on edge; I thought a rest might do him good. He was a very tense young man, Emily."

I couldn't believe what I was hearing. Here, this man claimed to be enlisting my help in finding out what ailed his company, but when Scott Dinsmoore had come to him and offered to make him a present of the answer, Menken claimed to have sent him home. I began to think he was telling me the truth. No one could invent such stupidity. Or could he? I was going to have to ponder this at length.

I heard the doorbell sound, echoing off the terrazzo floor in the distant entrance foyer, followed by the dull thuds of someone pounding on the heavy front door.

"Who can that be?" Menken said, rearranging his face into an expression of mystification. "No one ever drops in on us here." He headed across the sea of carpet and disappeared into the foyer, conversation still spilling from his lips as he disappeared around the corner: "Now, back in Connecticut, dropping by was *de rigueur*, but this is Colorado—" I heard the dead bolts click and the door groan on its hinges, then Menken's voice again, this time bright with joy: "Elyria!"

31

I dashed after him. What the hell was Elyria doing there? She hovered anxiously just outside the open door, one hand gripping her shoulder bag with uncharacteristic tension.

"Em, there you are," she said breathlessly. "I'm so glad I figured out where you were."

Menken's complexion had flushed pinker than I'd ever seen it. "Elyria! This is an unprecedented pleasure. Do come in."

It didn't take a clairvoyant to see that Menken had a major crush on Elyria. He all but rolled onto his back and showed her his belly.

Elyria smiled politely, but stayed firmly on the doorstep. "How kind of you, J.C. I'm sorry, but I can't stay; I've just come to fetch Em."

"Why?" I blurted.

Her smile setting up like concrete around her perfect teeth, Elyria flared her eyes at me as if to say, *Don't ask questions.* "Happy news, Em: your Aunt Gertrude called, from Kansas City. She and her husband are going to be at the airport between flights in"—she glanced at her watch—"forty minutes. They'll only have an hour and a quarter between planes, but she wants *so much* to see you. Isn't that *wonderful?*"

I started to say, *I don't have an Aunt Gertrude*, but caught myself in time. If something had Elyria Kretzmer on edge, it was not to be trifled with, and unless I missed my guess, that something was Menken. Jumping into action, I pushed past him onto the front walk. "Gee, I'm sorry I can't finish my drink," I said.

Menken frowned. "But Cecelia is coming with the horse."

Cecelia. I tensed, trying to figure out how to ask Elyria in code if we could stay that long. "How long does it take to get to the airport?" I asked, glancing at my watch. It was already six.

Then I heard hoofbeats behind me. I turned. Cecelia came loping across the meadow in the golden light of early evening, mounted bareback on a breathtaking quarter horse. She held the reins in relaxed hands and leaned back, working her own small mass into the power of the horse's back. I could feel in my own spine the intense pleasure of each rhythmic stride. Grinning, she charged straight at us, only reining in her mount at the last moment, all but skidding the horse onto the doorstoop.

I beamed up at her. In the instant it had taken Cecelia to cross the meadow, she had carried me back through time, to an age when my horse and I ruled the prairie west of Chugwater. I reached forward and embraced Velvet's glossy neck and filled my nostrils with her vital horse perfume. "Beautiful," I said. The universe seemed to shift, to click quietly back into a registration that made more sense. What was I doing here, matching wits with the likes of Menken, when a saner world existed?

Elyria's tone grew more urgent. "That is a wonderful horse, Em, but we *really must go.*"

I looked up at Cecelia with apology in my eyes.

Cecelia smiled forgiveness. "You can come back and ride her any time," she offered.

"I'd love to Cecelia," I said. "How long have you been riding?"

"All my life." Pride swelled her narrow chest. "Or at least, since I was four."

"Em—" Elyria urged.

I ignored her. My Aunt Gertrude, whoever the hell she was, was going to have to wait a moment longer. "Did you break her yourself?"

Elyria became insistent, her voice now frantic. "Em, I *promised* your aunt."

Cecelia wiggled up closer to the horse's neck and leaned close to my ear. Whispering, she said, "Why don't you come back some time when these guys aren't here?"

I gave her the wink, nodded, and followed Elyria to her car, but Menken was harder to shake off. "Listen, are you sure you have to rush off like this? I could call the airlines, make sure the flight is on time. They're frequently late."

"So sorry," Elyria said, and pulled away so fast that I had to twist my neck back to yell, "Thanks for the drink," through the open windows. As we sped down the street, I said, "What the hell was that all about?"

Elyria didn't answer. She was busy extracting a two-way radio in a black leather case from her handbag. She flicked a switch and held it to her mouth. "Got her," she said into the receiver.

A familiar voice squawked out of the speaker. "Okay, good. She okay?"

"Fine."

"We're just over the hill."

As our car crested a short rise, I spotted an antenna, and then a car beneath it, idling in the twilight with its headlights on. For such a bland-looking car, it was beginning to be terribly familiar, and even more familiar was the Mutt and Jeff team in the front seat: Ortega and Flint.

As Elyria pulled over next to the unmarked police car, Ortega climbed out of the left-hand side. I could hear the static and gargling of a bigger radio unit on their dashboard. Flint picked up a hand microphone and mumbled into it.

Ortega leaned on my windowsill. "Emily Hansen," he said. "You scared me, you know?"

I squinted in disbelief. "How do you figure, Sergeant?"

He straightened up and backed away from the car, sighing with exasperation. "Did you tell her, Elyria?"

"No."

I looked over at Elyria. She sat drumming her fingers on the steering wheel.

"Okay. So what in hell's name is going on?" I demanded. "You've got my attention, so spare me the theatrics."

Elyria didn't mince words. "They just found Simon Bunting, Em. It's not good."

"Found Simon? Not good? What do you mean, *found* Simon Bunting?" Had a *third* person found his way out that window?

Elyria's eyes narrowed. "The police didn't find him, Emily, but ambulance crews do make a habit of phoning the police when they find men in business suits who've been skinned alive from involuntarily exiting automobiles at high speed." She pointed at Flint. "Floyd recognized the name. Carlos called our house, to warn you, and I'd just found your message saying you were on Simon's trail. I think we can be forgiven for being a little worried under the circumstances," she added, her voice dripping with sarcasm.

"So you guys came out here to get me?"

"Obviously," she said, glaring at me. "What were we supposed to do? Give you a call and suggest you take the bus?"

I turned to Ortega and Flint. "Simon Bunting was thrown out of a car?"

Flint said, "Standard dump job," and moved to answer the summons of his car phone.

Sergeant Ortega spoke. "He's alive, but unconscious. Someone found him in the middle of the street, down on Wyncoop by Union Station."

My mind raced back through my brief hour with Menken. Had I been in danger? Had I missed something, misjudged the situation? Shaken, I looked at my watch. "I saw Simon at four-thirty, coming out of Menken's office—"

Ortega nodded. "That pegs the time."

"What time? When did you find him? You might have the wrong guy."

"Five-o-five," Ortega said. "That gives him over twenty minutes to cover ten blocks. Easy by car or shuttle bus, even walking."

"You covered a lot more territory than that in twenty minutes," Elyria gestured at the surrounding houses. "You're just lucky this little duchy has a private security force," she said. "The man on duty is a retired police officer, a friend of Carlos's. Carlos gave him a call. He'd seen the Mercedes come in."

I was starting to get angry. "But if I was with Menken, then Menken wasn't out rolling people out of cars below Market Street, was he?"

"We didn't know that, did we, Miss Private Detective? For all we knew, Menken rolled this Simon fellow out on Wyncoop and was planning on littering the Interstate with *you*."

I blew. "Damn it, Elyria, climb off. Whoever pushed Scottie did it at night, without a single witness. Half the office saw me leave with Menken, and in broad daylight. You get scared, that's your business. I don't need you bullying me—"

"Bullying you?" Elyria's voice soared. "You'd rather people *didn't* care about you?"

"I left you a message, damn it!"

Ortega broke in, his hands dancing with agitation. "Please. Maybe we need to get in the cars and go."

Flint hung up his car phone and rejoined the festivities. He grinned, uncovering a rack of teeth that screamed for orthodontia. "Bunting's still in dreamland, but station says we got a witness on the dump job. So Em, Menken with you the whole time?"

"Yeah, didn't even take a pee break. That lets him off the hook, right?" I asked.

Flint shook his head. "Naw. A stiff like him would hire the job done. If Menken put a contract on Bunting, you're his alibi."

Uh-oh . . .

Ortega's face sagged with worry. "Em, I have a bad feeling about this. This case, it's taking unexpected turns. Whoever killed Mr. Dinsmoore planned it carefully; the work of a technician. This throwing Simon Bunting out of a car was sloppy; the work of a bully."

"So?"

"We may have a second killer at work."

"Yeah," said Flint. "The dump job was done by two guys in a late-model sedan, possibly a rental. Witness said one had dark hair and a mustache." Flint rolled his eyes skyward. "Dark hair and mustache. Lessee; could have been that fellah Tutaraitis."

Instead of racing out to the airport to meet the mythical Aunt Gertrude, we convoyed down to Elyria's house and ripped into a bag of taco chips. Elyria cracked open a bottle of ale, but the fuzz brothers were on duty and I was feeling more jittery than a beer would tend to help.

Elyria was still indulging herself in a little righteous glowering, but seemed on the way toward forgiving me. She pushed an unopened letter with my name on it across the table to me. It was from Frank. She looked a question at me. Still a little sore at her for getting so huffy with me, I stuffed it into my suit jacket pocket and ignored her.

Ortega was debriefing Flint, who had just called the station again. "Is Crick back from Tulsa yet?"

Flint nodded. "Freddie clocked in on the five-fifteen. Sandy has him staked out. She says he looks like hell. He's home with the wife and kiddies, getting shitfaced drunk."

"Then his ploy didn't work," Elyria said.

"What ploy?" I asked.

She turned a palm upward. "The oil patch is a small town, Em. One of my clients called me about him this afternoon, to get my opinion of his ability to handle a truly big project. He was trying to land Blackfeet a working interest in my client's project in the Anadarko Basin." She looked a plea at Sergeant Ortega. "You won't have to make that public, will you?"

So this was Crick's bet against extinction. Crick smelled a rat at Lost Coyote Field, and that was why he'd advised

Menken to wait on drilling. The sweat was rolling. All Smith had to do to look good was push the well through and let Crick look like a gutless worrier. So Crick was in Tulsa, looking to strengthen his position by bringing a fat new property to Blackfeet. "And what did you tell your client?" I asked.

Elyria closed her eyes. "I recommended he wait." She opened her eyes and looked at me apologetically. "Em, I know it's your boss and your company that loses out, but this is my job. If I start compromising my judgment to serve special interests, I may as well start looking for other work."

Flint turned to me. "Okay, Em, spill."

"Spill what?"

"Spill what!" Flint sassed.

Ortega moved in as Jane to Flint's Tarzan. "Okay, he just wants to know if *you* learned anything today." He smiled encouragement, his soft eyes shyly averted.

Elyria settled for giving me a schoolmarm glare, and took another swig of her beer.

I stalled, stuffing a handful of chips into my mouth and processing them noisily into a mash. It was a major coup to have arranged a meeting with Archie, but after their reaction to my sortie with Menken, maybe it wasn't safe to tell them I had another appointment. "Okay," I said, "here's how it is. Simon Bunting was still a no-show at work today; no one knew where he was or when he was coming back. Then he shows up at Menken's office, only Menken says he identified himself as George—um, ah, Taylor, I think it was."

Flint spoke. "Fred Taylor's a city reporter with the *Denver Post*. You sure that wasn't him?"

"Not unless he's Simon Bunting's twin brother. Besides, you said Bunting was seen. You got an observer watching the lobby, or something?" I asked facetiously.

"Yeah, your receptionist, Simca."

"What!"

"We showed her a snap of Bunting and asked her to give us a jingle if she saw him. Of course, you don't need to pass that around."

I remembered the little surveillance task Simca had performed for Maddie, so this fit, but at the same time didn't. Why would she inform on her company? There was something unsettling—or at least, unsettled—about Simca.

"You were saying," Flint prompted.

"So, I'm closing in on Menken's office because I'm going

to pump him, and his secretary's on guard, doesn't want me to see Menken, like something's up. I try to get to Simon, but the secretary suddenly goose-walks me into Menken's office. Menken's weirder than ever, real preoccupied, and then he says he wants to go for a ride."

"Okay, so that's how you got to Menken's," Ortega said.

"Yeah. He says we're going to see his daughter's horse. And the daughter looks like she's just climbed down out of a tree, and she's beside herself that her mother's disappeared and there's a strange woman in the house, and I'm not the first, judging by a weird limerick she's scrawled on the refrigerator door." I quoted the verse.

"Let's fix her up with Archie," Flint said.

"Yeah, Archie doesn't like punctuation, either—" I stopped, afraid I'd opened a topic that was better kept closed. "What time is it?" I asked, trying to sound like I was simply tired and out of things to report.

Elyria lifted her wrist. "Seven-fifteen."

I stood up. "Listen, are we done? I've got a dinner date."

"Siddown," Flint rumbled. "I ain't done with you yet."

Ortega leaned back in his chair and sighed. His eyes filled with pain, and he rubbed the side of his head to soothe himself. "Please, Em, I'd feel better if you stayed home."

Elyria took a dainty swig of her ale and smiled at me with a you're-going-out-over-my-dead-body glint in her eye.

"I'll be with Maddie McNutt. She can handle a whole motorcycle chainsaw gang on angel dust."

"Of course," said Flint. "And she knows kung fu and karate. Siddown."

Ortega was as usual more subtle, and shrewd: "Perhaps we jump to conclusions, Em. Is there something special about this dinner?"

All right, so much for keeping it to myself. "I saw Archie today."

Ortega's head jerked forward an inch.

"He was dancing in the street, all done up in mud, with a clay head."

"Archie's a mud man?" Ortega smiled. The idea clearly charmed him. "Of course. Those guys are sly. You get to talk to him?"

"No, but . . ."

Flint wrinkled his ugly nose as if he smelled something bad. "Little asshole knows something, or he's scared we think he

does. Probably knows something. We'll catch up with him
sooner or later."

Ortega smiled. "I think Em will catch up with him sooner. Is
Archie a friend of Ms. McNutt's?"

Elyria jumped in. "Em, you leave this to Carlos and Floyd."

I addressed myself directly to Ortega: "I don't think Archie
will talk to you. He might talk to me."

"Good idea," Flint said, pulling a microcassette recorder out
of his pocket. "You just tape the whole works for us." Without
asking, he pulled open my jacket and slipped the recorder into
my inside pocket, then started feeding a wire down the inside
of my sleeve. It was a ticklish project, but he was so quick I
didn't even have time to move. "You flick it on like this, and
make sure you keep the mike on this wire in line of sight.
Under a table doesn't work so good."

"Isn't it against the law to record a conversation without
someone knowing it?" I asked.

"Nah, just can't use it in court. Much."

Ortega spoke. "I don't know, Floyd, I'm not sure about this.
Maybe this can wait."

Elyria rose to her feet, a sure sign she was angry. "You're
damned straight it can wait. Em, you—"

"Elyria, I can make my own decisions! Excuse me a moment," I said to Ortega, and headed out of the room.

Flint bellowed, "Where d'you think *you're* going, sister?"

I spun around and hooked a thumb over my shoulder toward
the bathroom. "Three guesses. The first two don't count, and
the third one's none of your business."

Once escaped to the sanctity of the porcelain palace, I lowered the lid on the toilet to make a seat and sat down to think.
The fact was, I *was* nervous setting out into the wilds of a city
night, even with Maddie. If Ortega was right, I now needed to
watch my back for not one, but two killers. I hadn't forgotten
the warning I'd found in my desk. I needed to redouble safety
precautions, but the truth was I didn't know what that re-
quired. I couldn't approach Archie with a police escort, left
alone Elyria scowling over my shoulder.

But it wasn't just that. There was something even closer to
the skin that was far more worrisome: did I really not belong
here? Could I just not take the pressure of the real world?

What I needed was a good night's sleep, then I could sort
things out clearly. How had life gotten so unclear, so quickly?

Maybe it's time to give up. If I were in Wyoming, I'd sleep next to Frank tonight, warm, secure . . .

I pulled Frank's letter out of my pocket and opened it, smiling with abstract affection at the telltale smudges left on the envelope from his laborer's hands. His message was short, sweet, and to the point.

Dear Em,
Seems we've missed connections a lot lately. I'm no fool, you're taking life head on like you always do, and I'm behind you not ahead. Well I miss you fiercely, but never mind, only a fool tries to bottle the wind. Give a call or write when you want, but I've got to go on with my life too.

> Always,
> Frank

The letters blurred on the page. *Frank gone from my life? That couldn't be.* I reread his note, trying to force another meaning from his words, but even as I did so, I knew deep within myself that this was right and just. Worse yet, it was the direction my life needed to be flowing.

I replaced the paper in its envelope with the delicacy due a religious relic and held it a while. Then I slipped it into my pocket and left the bathroom.

Instead of crossing the hallway back into the kitchen, I passed quietly into the darkened living room, opened the front door, and slid out into the street. As if sent by the powers that move the planets in their orbits, the Number 32 was just nearing the bus stop as I reached that avenue. At my command, the driver braked the empty mammoth to a stop and opened its doors. I climbed in, showed my pass, and seated myself for the ride downtown to meet Archie.

32

The Slant Hole was toward the steamy end of the saloon spectrum. I tugged open a heavy wooden door with a handle made out of a pipe wrench, and wandered in. Inside, a clientele of rowdy young businesspeople sat lounging at café tables, as a muscular young woman wearing not much more than spike heels and her best smile gyrated on the bar.

I stopped and turned toward the bar for a moment to take in the performance. Hell, they don't have these things in Chugwater, and girls with her talents didn't frequent the schools Grannie sent me to. She held her hands behind her neck and writhed like a snake, grinning with the visceral pleasure of the movement. After two good bumps and a grind, she raised her hands over her head, and I realized she was holding a forty- or fifty-pound dumbbell. As ascending cigarette smoke spiraled around her, she pumped that dumbbell up and down, eyeing a challenge to the men. One howled like a coyote, and she stepped lightly onto his table, the better to show him just what he was up against.

I heard a familiar voice behind me. "Hey, Emmy! Over here!"

Turning, I saw Maddie McNutt, ensconced between two matching mesomorphs straight out of the football cretins' hall of fame. As I approached the table, they lurched onto their feet, unable to move gracefully in the tiny space between the fixed seats of the booth and their table.

I pulled up a chair and examined the remains of a gargantuan feed of hot links and beans.

"This here's Duane," Maddie said, planting a finger in the middle of one man's chest, "and this one's Donny. They's brothers. Identical twins. Ain't that cute?"

It sure was. They even had matching freckles and crew cuts. But it was the matching muscles that struck me the most. I looked into their dim little eyes to see if anyone was home.

Duane pulled back nervously and pursed his lips, but Donny smiled happily, like a puppy hoping for a treat. "Glad to meetcha," I said, offering my hand to be shaken. Donny dragged the cuff of his suit coat through the beans to grab my hand. I took pity on Duane and withdrew my hand after Donny was done crushing it.

"I about gave you up," said Maddie. "So tell me, how was y'all's little drive with big Josie?"

"It's Josie now?"

"Josiah Carberry Menken, ace entrepreneur of the western world. *El jefe*, to us."

"Amen, sister."

A deafening cheer from the end of the room drowned our conversation. We turned in time to see a woman dressed up as a carrot arrive at a long table full of upwardly mobile professionals. *Hoot! Shriek!* The yuppies clapped and broke into a debauched chorus of "Happy Birthday to You" as the humiliated, cringing birthday boy leaned onto his elbows, covering his face with his hands. Carrot Woman postured and strutted in her enormous orange tuber, bending occasionally to whap him on the head with her plume of greens as she delivered one hideous vegetable pun after another. "Lettuce entertain you!" she screamed over the din. "Orange you liking my jokes?"

The man collapsed the rest of the way onto the table, burying his head in his arms.

"Well then, maybe you'll like Fifi better!" she screamed, and with a theatrical windup, swung her right index finger into a button on the side of a boom box she was carrying. The raucous strains of "The Stripper" moaned out of the box at top volume. The back door into the room swung open. A gorgeous woman dressed in a black sequined dress strolled in and started taking it off.

An ear-splitting whistle from close range shattered my eardrums. Maddie was halfway out of her seat with excitement. "Give him hell, sister!" she hollered. "Give him hell!"

Men whistled; women roared and waved their arms in glee, clapping to the raucous beat. The lady in black danced her way out of her dress, her slip, her hose, her shoes, and her bra, spun around, and stood flexing each buttock in alternating splendor to the beat of the song. The object of this honor clasped his head in his hands and looked on in rapturous horror.

Duane eyed me suspiciously throughout the performance. It was like being watched by a great paranoid gibbon that couldn't decide whether to run or attack. The more he watched me instead of the stripper, the more certain I was that old Duane was a can short of a six-pack. I began to wonder if it would do any harm to just let Ortega know where I was. "Is Archie meeting us here?" I asked Maddie, figuring I'd slip away and find a phone.

"Nah, at another joint. Just keep your shirt on."

"Oh. What's the name of the place?"

"I forget." Maddie gave me a stage wink, then looked left and right at the muscle brothers to give me a hint of some kind.

The look on Duane's face suggested that he'd settled on attacking.

I got to my feet. "I think it's almost time to go. Where to?"

Maddie wiggled past Donny and dragged me toward the door. "Shut your mouth, honey, we got to ditch the dwarfs," she said, her face so close to mine that the smell of hot links nearly dropped me. "We take these hulks where we're going and they'll start a fight."

The dingdong twins paid the bill and hurried after us. With elaborate chivalry, they showed us out onto the street and into a Thunderbird parked by the curb, tossed the parking ticket that adorned the windshield into the gutter, bent their muscle-bound bodies into the seats beside us, and pulled away from the curb. I realized I had yet to hear either one of them say a word, but perhaps that wasn't their purpose in life. I was not comforted to wind up in the back seat with Duane, who continued to watch me out of the corner of his eye.

The Thunderbird wound through the Gordian knot of one-way streets toward the parking garage at the Cattlemen's Exchange Building. Maddie leaned over the back of her seat to talk to me. She patted Donny on the head. "Donny here's a smart rat. He knows how to find his way through this maze. Right, Donny? Where's the cheese, Bubba?" She wrapped her arms around his neck and soaked his ear with a kiss, just as he pulled into the parking garage.

Two levels down, Donny pulled the Thunderbird up next to a bright red El Camino. "Y'all sure you don't want us to come along, Maddie?" he drawled pettishly.

Maddie stroked his crew cut tenderly. "Naw, thanks for the concern, Billy Bob. A pal of mine will look after us, anything happens."

Duane collected his wits long enough to open my door and

show me to the El Camino like a muscle-bound Texas-style Galahad. He sulked and waited as Maddie and I settled ourselves in her car and got it rolling. On Donny's signal, the two jumped into their Thunderbird and pulled away behind us, flagrantly following us. Maddie roared up the ramps and out onto the street, where she led them a merry chase around corners and through alleys. "Shee-it," she drawled. "Those boys was clamped onto my leg like they could hump it all night!"

"So where *are* we going?" I demanded.

"Honey pie," Maddie hollered, slapping the steering wheel, "we-all's getting our buns down to the Chapultepec, the best little jazz bar north of Austin. Prepare y'allself for a religious experience." Maddie wheeled the El Camino all over downtown Denver trying to lose them, from Broadway to Coors Field, and from the Convention Center to Sakura Square. Finally, at Twenty-first and Market Streets, in what looked to me like the darkest corner of the city, she glanced in the rearview mirror one last time, said, "Well, fuck 'em," and pulled over to the curb behind a string of old cars.

Maddie jumped out of the El Camino and hollered, "Do I look like I need a couple guard dogs? You boys go on home, or you seen the last of Maddie McNutt!"

The Thunderbird squealed away in a haze of burning rubber.

I looked around, suddenly sad to see our matched bodyguards leave. "What jazz bar?" I squealed. "All I see is warehouses." I could hear jubilant voices, but no music. Maddie started moving, cussing cheerfully about Donny's fantasy life as she made a beeline for the only illuminated doorway in sight. Light spilled onto the sidewalk, and neon glowed into the settling darkness, calling from windows framed with glass brick that Coors and Michelob were available on the premises. Above the corner entrance the neon proclaimed CANTINA in yellow, over a glowing green cactus, and in red: BAR. CAFE. On the Twenty-second Street side, a curving arrow glowed EAT.

As we reached the doorway, a crash of fresh salsa music erupted from the building and washed out onto the street. A mountainous Moor with a diamond stud earring appeared and flashed a smile at Maddie, revealing a gold tooth that reflected the neon in an oily array. "Maddie, my flower," he boomed, bending for a hug.

"Cosmo!" Maddie shouted over the din. "How's it hanging?"

"Wash your mouth, Miss Maddie."

"Aw, Cosmo, y'all's just no fun anymore, since you got religion."

Cosmo grinned. "Jesus loves you, Maddie," he crooned, grabbing an enormous handful of a drunk who had been trying to squeeze in the doorway and ejecting him smoothly back onto the street. "Git lost, Tommy," he added sweetly.

"Who's playing tonight?" Maddie hollered over the din. "Sounds good."

"Freddie Garcia. First set just started."

Maddie stared past Cosmo into the narrow, crowded room. Customers packed three-deep out from the bar, their faces warmed by low lights reflected in the back-bar mirrors as they hoisted their beers through the smoky soup of city-bar air. "There's our seat," she said.

"Where?" I couldn't see past the first twenty sardine-packed bodies. I saw Hispanics, blue-collar whites, and leather-elbow-patch tweed-o's in even proportions. There were few women in the crush, high heels planted wide as they knocked back Corona longnecks. I couldn't see the walls, let alone a pay phone from which to call Ortega. I hesitated, trying to decide if it was really necessary to call him. Elyria would answer the phone, and I certainly didn't want to hear what she had to say to me now.

"Cosmo, honey, this here's my buddy Em," Maddie shouted, heading on in.

Cosmo took me in through enormous doe eyes. "It looks rough, but it ain't so bad," he said.

"Got a pen?" I asked.

Cosmo produced an ancient ballpoint with no cap.

I pulled out a five-dollar bill and scribbled Elyria's number on it. "Can you make a phone call for me?" I asked, pressing the greenback into his colossal hand.

Cosmo nodded soberly.

"Great. Just tell the woman who answers where I am. She's a worrier."

Cosmo took my hand and raised it to his lips for a kiss, then passed me into the Cantina.

Inside, I swam through air sultry with smoke and human moisture. It was standing room only, and I immediately found myself tweed to denim with staggering revelers. Tensing against this unaccustomed closeness, I reached inside my jacket and switched on the microcassette recorder, then checked the position of the microphone against the inside of my wrist. It had hitched up in the time since Flint had positioned it, so I eased a little more wire out of the pocket and down my sleeve.

I had lost Maddie. Through an archway, I glimpsed a second room, where rotund Chicanos sneered at lounging superannuated preppies as their *compadre* made a run of a pool table. The *anglos* had lined up quarters rested along the bumpers, mute challenge to the man's prowess.

Maddie reappeared and dragged me through the crowd by my sleeve, squirming past stomachs and elbows toward the band. There was barely space for the width of three packed bodies between the bar stools and the booths. In some places I was tempted to climb to shoulder level and swim. Here and there, I caught glimpses of the band: saxophone, bass, guitar, and drums crammed into a space the size of Elyria's kitchen table. They jostled against each other as they played, protected only by a thin plywood barrier from the boisterous crowd. A couple danced the world's tightest jitterbug on a stretch of floor the size of a dinner plate.

Maddie's hand tugged me to the right and I followed it, making friends with a six-foot-six bearded monolith wearing a very humid sweater. A button on his chest declared, "I Tecate My Body." As I wiggled past him, Maddie yanked two men out of their seats at a nearby booth. "Have some manners," she caroled. "They's ladies present!"

Me, she summarily heaved into the seat.

I found myself nose to nose with Archie Arch, mud man, poet, and foremost street citizen of the universe. I carefully laid my left hand on the table top, aiming the microcassette recorder's microphone directly at Archie, and lifted the other in greeting. "Pleased to meet you," I hollered. "I been hoping to make your acquaintance."

If I thought the formal approach was the best, I was wrong. Archie kept his arms at his sides and instead oozed toward me like a cat, rubbing against my left side with everything from his chin to his brisket. "Mmmmmmm," he purred. Saints be praised he was recently bathed and his hair was combed, even styled. He reeked only of patchouli oil.

The band finished a number. Archie pushed harder, rubbing his eyeteeth against me, marking territory or something. Maddie squashed me even harder against him as she reached across to tousle his hair. "Quit messing with Emmy, she ain't from these parts."

Archie rubbed harder yet. I felt a tingling in my toes.

Maddie chattered on. "Archie, honey, thanks for the rubber. Let's go break it in sometime."

Archie looked down at his chest and smiled and narrowed his eyes. His likeness to a cat was complete: his was the kind of meditative self-satisfaction I've seen on the faces of cats as they purr in the laundry basket, kneading the ripest shirt in the place. I wanted to believe that this was more of his street theater, but wasn't sure that anyone could fake it that well. Archie now began to preen his cheeks with the edges of his hands.

Maddie yanked at Archie's lapel. "Say, what you got on there, under that coat?"

He was wearing a jet-black trench coat, and his earlobes were festooned with earrings, but other than a twisted length of bailing wire around his neck, he appeared to have on nothing else, or at least nothing above the waist, which was all I could see above the table. "I couldn't decide what to wear," he crowed, pleasure crumpling his face into a tearful grin. "So I didn't wear *anything*."

"Hot damn!" cheered Maddie, stuffing a hand down his coat. Archie writhed wildly.

"Emmy here's been dying to meet you. I think she wants to ask you something."

My cue. I opened my mouth. With a rousing bleat on the saxophone, the band started playing again, drowning out the conversation. I shouted, "I saw your performance this afternoon on Seventeenth Street. I was very impressed."

"O-o-ooh, thank you," Archie sang, dancing around in his seat.

"You lived on the street long?" I hollered. I felt like a reporter trying to coax an intimate interview in the middle of a typhoon.

Archie started nibbling on my shoulder.

I tightened up like a raisin. "Will you read some of your poetry to me sometime?"

He was starting to suck. With mounting anxiety, I wondered how long until the moisture made it through to my skin, and to the wire that hung down my sleeve. The threat of electrical shock levitated me half out of my seat. In desperation, I shouted, "Your poetry in the parking garage. I understand."

Archie let go of my shoulder. His eyes closed. His mouth

and forehead relaxed, revealing the fine planes of a once hand-some face. His lips moved. He spoke in a rhythmic chant, his words half swallowed by the din of the band: "... *hark* the lady *dark* she doesn't *see* but rides for *free*."

"That's beautiful, Archie," I shouted over the tumult. "I don't remember that from the garage. Is that new?"

The band crashed louder. Archie sang: "Deep cocoon [drum roll] *tomb*, arises *when*, he seeks his [blast]." Archie popped his eyes open and stared at me wildly. "I see you *here* your soul so *dear* [honk] wish you *well* [bash boop] *hell*." He smiled, his eyes suddenly as clear and unself-conscious as a baby's.

My pulse was racing. Was he talking about Pete and me in the parking garage? He couldn't have; the police had moved him by then. "Tell me again, Archie," I said.

His eyelids drooped. His lips moved. I couldn't hear. I leaned close to him, contorting my arm and my spine to get the microphone closer to his lips. The microphone slipped out and dangled six inches beneath his nose.

Archie's eyes snapped open and focused in alarm on the microphone. "Aaaaaah!" he screamed. "Nobody records Archie!" He rose out of his seat and started to climb over the table, making a beeline over the back of the booth toward the door. I lunged for his ankle, and was just closing my hand around it in triumph when Maddie crashed hard against my opposite shoulder, wrestling playfully with the enormous man with the Tecate button. Panicking, I screamed, "Help!"

I have to say, Ortega and Flint handled the collaring of Archie with remarkable sensitivity, although it wouldn't have worked if someone two booths down hadn't pushed him off his table and into the throng. Flint materialized from the doorway and grabbed Archie's arm firmly. Archie spun around and bit him. Flint yowled but didn't lose his grip. He handcuffed himself to Archie, threw his coat over the juncture so it wouldn't show, shifted the whole arrangement into a position that seemed to motivate the poet to move, and mumbled something friendly in his ear. Ortega appeared next, playing Moses parting the waters as we hustled Archie through the crowd and out the door.

On the sidewalk, Ortega turned to me. A deep blush suffused his cheeks. "Thanks for calling," he said, with a little bow.

I couldn't think of a reply. "Well . . ."

"You're a natural." Ortega absentmindedly cuffed Flint, who was doing a strange jig to restrain Archie, who was now doing an impression of a python. "Soon as I can get rid of Flint here, why don't you join the force and be my partner."

I found myself bowing, too, so that I wouldn't have to meet his eyes.

Maddie's voice rose over the chaos of the throng. She burst past Cosmo like a linebacker, shouting with indignation. "Hey! Assholes! I wanted to help, but don't go treating my buddy like a criminal! He ain't hurt nobody!" She ran up alongside Flint and kicked him in the shins. Hard.

Flint crumpled over his injured shin with a dreamlike smile. "Sorry, ma'am," he said, regarding her with genuine admiration.

"Here, gimme that key" Maddie snarled, thrusting a hand deep into Flint's pants pocket. Flint's eyes rolled heavenward in ecstasy. When Maddie's hand reappeared, it held the keys. Bustling around in front of them, she dumped Flint's coat onto the sidewalk and opened the lock, but instead of freeing Archie entirely, she freed Flint's wrist only, and locked the loose bracelet back over her own. Lastly, she dropped Flint's keys down her *décolletage*. "There," she said, beaming with satisfaction. "If Bubba here's done something wrong, then he oughta pay, but if he ain't, he's got Maddie McNutt to protect him."

33

After Flint waved off two prowl cars and Duane and Donny, who had apparently circled around the block and lingered, we loaded into the unmarked car, Flint trailing behind in Maddie's El Camino. Maddie insisted that she'd phone a lawyer and make certain Archie wouldn't talk if Ortega and Flint "ran us in," so after some discussion we wound up at Elyria's drinking coffee and beer.

Archie wouldn't talk anyway. He vacillated between deep swoons in Elyria's direction and histrionic collapses into Maddie's lap.

Ortega offered to take the proceedings out onto the couch on his mother's porch, in case Archie's problem was claustrophobia, but Archie just curled up in the fetal position and sucked his free thumb, a neat trick in a kitchen chair. In the end, Maddie decreed that she would bed him down on the fold-out couch in Elyria's basement rec room, suggesting that a good night's sleep might improve his sociability.

Flint phoned the station to report his position and give instructions to be passed on to officers who were staking out suspects. Then he and Ortega and I settled in the kitchen.

"I want to know more about that carrot," Flint said, as I finished.

"Straighten up, Floyd, we're all tired," Ortega groaned.

Flint plowed ahead. "Okay, whadda we got? Menken has an alibi for the dump job, but either he lied about their meeting or Bunting is doing a little detective work of his own. I called Denver General, and Bunting's still dreaming, so we won't know for a while, yet. They say he'll live. We got no tabs on any of the other Blackfeet hopefuls for that hour yet except for Crick, who was on his way back from Tulsa."

"Hopefuls?" I said.

"Suspects."

I sighed. "Who's still on the list?"

"Smith."

"Didn't see him all day today."

"Hathaway."

"God knows."

For the next on the list, Flint simply pointed toward the basement.

"No," said Ortega.

I said, "You don't really suspect *her*, do you?"

Flint presented his variant on the human smile. "Nah, just wishful thinking. I like my women mean. Tutaraitis," he slipped in, watching me out of the corner of his eye.

Ortega pursed his lips in a soundless whistle and examined the table top.

I gritted my teeth. "He rode the elevator down with me and Menken. He got off at the street. That's all I know, other than that he left the building at about two P.M. in an old green Volvo. So, sometimes between two and four-something he came back."

Ortega and Flint exchanged a look. "Out renting a car?" Flint said.

Ortega shrugged.

"Walking that red mutt of his again, maybe," Flint suggested.

I sagged back in my chair. "So how do you think the dog's hair got into Scott's car?" I asked. "I can't believe Pete got into the car with him. They weren't exactly friends."

Ortega shrugged his shoulders. "This I don't know. We checked around. The neighbor was looking after the dog while Mr. Tutaraitis was in California and Missus Tutaraitis"—it took me a moment to realize he was talking about Libby— "was away visiting her relatives. The neighbor came to feed the dog twice a day. He was kept in the backyard, behind a six-foot fence. The neighbor got to taking him for walks during the day, even after Mr. Tutaraitis came back. Then one day, he comes to get the dog, but it's gone. The next day, he's back. The day he went missing was the day Mr. Dinsmoore died."

I put my mind to this puzzle-within-a-puzzle, but couldn't come up with a logical explanation. Scott had been in the office that day, but perhaps not all day. Had he been playing hooky, taking the dog for a ride in his car for some reason? Was this some act of defiance, to make friends with one's rival's dog?

Elyria emerged from the basement, where she had been heaping quilts on top of Maddie and Archie. She passed through the kitchen into the living room, and I heard her play back the answering machine messages before she returned. "Your grandmother phoned while you were out giving people heart attacks, Em," she announced, taking a seat at the table.

I glanced at my watch. Ten-thirty. In Massachusetts it would be past midnight, and my grandmother always went to bed by ten. Way too late to return the call. What had she discovered? I made a mental note to set the alarm for six and ring her.

A soft knocking sound at the back door. Elyria started to rise, but Ortega gestured for her to sit, and went to the door himself. He stood to one side of the glass panel and switched on the outside light. The knocking was repeated. Ortega swept the ruffly white curtain aside and looked out at an angle. His face tightened in a frown. "I can't see anyone," he said. The knocking came again.

With utmost care, the sergeant rotated the key in the lock, turned the knob, and drew the door open. Outside was a screened door that was solid wood from the doorknob down. We saw nothing. Then a little voice said, *"Buenas noches, Carlos. Tengo este para la señorita."*

Sergeant Ortega's face lit with delight. He swung the screened door wide, revealing a tiny moppet with a face even rounder than his. He lifted the boy into his arms and kissed him. One little arm swung wide, displaying a Federal Express envelope.

I jumped up and took the envelope from the tiny hand. *"Muchas gracias,"* I said. Wanda McCandless had come through!

"You're welcome," said the boy.

Ortega returned to the door. "Mama," he called out into the dark, "come in here."

Another face appeared at the screened door, a lovely face, grown heavy with age and childbearing, but the dancing eyes were the same as Ortega's, taking in every detail of the scene.

Ortega gestured to her, coaxing her to step inside. The woman silently held her position. Elyria hastened to the door to open it for her. *"Entra, señora, por favor. Me da gusto."*

Mrs. Ortega stepped into the kitchen with a regal modesty and followed Elyria to the stove to be served a cup of tea. The two women took seats at the far side of the table and fell into quiet conversation on the subject of the arrival of the envelope: the driver had come, and no one was home. Julio—a middle-sized brother—had been mowing Elyria's lawn, and he signed for it, but had brought it back to the Ortegas' and had not told anyone it was there. Esperanza—number-two daughter—had found it only after we had come home and left again. Mrs. Ortega had been watching for us ever since, because she knew it must be important, but the evening had grown cold, and she had moved in off the porch. Julio was supposed to have watched for us from their living room as he watched TV and she started the beans for tomorrow, but he had fallen asleep. It had been left for tiny Salvador to notice that we were home. *Qué lástima,* and she hoped there was no harm done.

Elyria assured her that we had been completely busy until then, *No te preocupes.*

While this conversation wound softly along, both women kept their eyes riveted on the envelope. Sergeant Ortega sat down at the table, lifted Salvador onto his lap and gave him a sip of his beer. At me he smiled. "Well, Em. What's in the envelope? Or are you trying to make me crazy?"

I smiled apologetically. "I hope I can tell you in a minute," I said, and headed downstairs into Bill's study.

Once in private, I ripped the envelope open and spread its contents on the table. Good old Wanda: she had photocopied the important sections of almost all of the logs for both Lost Coyote and Hat Rock Fields, and had even found some production curves and a couple of lease maps. One of the maps I hadn't seen before. I looked closely at the half section where the RACO number two was located, the well that was now drilling. Down at the lower edge of that lease was the name of the lease holder. "Conant," it said. I looked at the other leases. Over half of them said "Conant." With a shock, I realized what RACO stood for. "Jesus, it's been staring me in the face," I muttered aloud, the memory of Pete and Rachel's meeting at the ice cream shop gnawing its way into my consciousness. RACO was an abbreviation for "Rachel Conant."

I worked furiously, lining up the logs and slipping them up and down, trying to reconstruct the correlations I had made on my office wall. I tried to string together one long cross section that ran from the east edge of Lost Coyote clear across to the west edge of Hat Rock, to see where Lost Coyote's sandstone pinched out and Hat Rock's began. I rummaged through Wanda's packet, looking for the logs for the RACO number four, the one I feared had been "checked out" by Pete. She had included a note:

RACO #4 log also missing from O&G Commission files. I called the field office of the logging company, to see if they had another copy. They said master copy long since sent to Denver c/o geologist responsible for the field. They didn't keep the computer tapes. I called around to a few of my friends and found a copy made before log went missing. Xerox enclosed, sorry different scale.

Now I laid the missing log in place where it belonged, between the Hat Rock cross section and the one from Lost Coyote, just east of the gap that the new well, the one we were now drilling, would fill.

The log signatures for the two fields at first looked dissimilar because of the differing scales, but as I slid the log from the easternmost Hat Rock well up next to that off-scale, westernmost one from Lost Coyote, I saw something frightening.

Hat Rock Field had a nice, big, thick sandstone with a signature just like the one for the RACO number four, the log that Peter Tutaraitis had taken such pains to make disappear. I looked back and forth between the map and the cross section, my stomach sinking. I could see no pinch-out between the fields. Hat Rock and Lost Coyote were like Siamese twins, sharing one main artery from which the precious crude flowed. For just a moment, I put my face down on the desk top. It seemed fitting to have a moment of silence for the demise of Blackfeet Oil Company, and the job I had just done too well.

After a moment, I noticed that I was not alone. I turned. Elyria was standing in the doorway, quietly waiting. She was leaning her head against the door frame as if it weighed heavily. The irritation she'd been showing me all evening was gone. "How bad is it?" she asked, her voice full of sympathy. I suppose she'd stood there like that many times before, watching Bill work, and had learned to read success or failure from the tension in his spine.

"It's bad."

She nodded, but stayed where she was, not demanding an

explanation. She was there as a friend, not a competitor in the cutthroat world of the oil patch.

"I'd like to wake Maddie," I said. "I think I need a little help with this."

Elyria said, "Maddie is awake. When I left her, she was reading." She nodded toward the door into the rec room. "You know the way."

I rolled up the cross sections and maps and gestured for Elyria to follow. Maddie was sitting up against the back of the fold-out couch reading a copy of the *New Yorker* magazine, her legs stretched out on the unfolded mattress, wearing some of the snazziest underwear I'd ever seen: peacock-blue elastic lace bra and panties with hot pink trim, cut down to there and up to here. Her fuchsia dress was arranged neatly on a hanger by the door.

Archie, still handcuffed to her wrist, lay snoring under a fine old quilt, his head on her thigh. Maddie said, "Y'all might watch he doesn't get patchouli oil all over your pillows, 'Lyria. I'm holding this greased-up pompadour of his off of them for now, but when I pass out he might roll over. Y'all got a towel, or something?"

While Elyria fetched a towel from the laundry, I showed Maddie what I'd found, and told her about the cryptic message Scott had written in his disappearing red notebook.

"Hot spit!" she said. "Will you look at that! We's stealing their gas."

"That's what I was afraid of. So that explains Scottie's note about wet gas tests. When L and C reinjects the gas here, it's dry, meaning it's all short-chain hydrocarbons. When they pump the gas out here, it's picked up some liquids, the longer chains, right?"

"Right."

"So that's what they mean by 'cycling.'"

Maddie nodded. "Yep, I reckon so; in here and out there, in here and out there. If our boys knew it was happening, it's grand larceny."

"Well, before we order up the arrest warrants, let's make double sure. The sandstones correlate stratigraphically between the two fields, but can you show me how to see if they correlate structurally? I mean, there could be a fault that's sealed off communication, or a syncline that makes the sandstone dip down in between."

"I'd bet my firstborn there isn't, baby cakes. Love and

Christiansen is reinjecting the gas they produce to store it until prices go back up. Our gas production from Lost Coyote has always been above expectation. It's clear as day. Look at that there; that well in Hat Rock is an injector."

"How do you know?"

"Some slob marked it right there on the log. See? I-N-J—"

"Got you. So how do I make sure there's no dip or fault between the fields?"

"Easy. You see here on the log headers?" She pointed to a box below the well name. "Here's the surface elevation on this line. Then you go down here to your datum mark, the one you hung the correlation on, and you subtract that depth from the surface elevation."

I did so, working the cross section from left to right. Each number was essentially the same. There was no sag.

Maddie smiled. "There you have it. We're sucking up everything L and C pumps into the ground."

Elyria chose that moment to return with the towel. "That's not good," she said. "Let me guess: Crick knows, or at least suspects. Smith doesn't care. Hathaway probably doesn't want to know. Menken either knows or he should."

In my mind, I picked up where Elyria left off. Unless Pete was all salesman and no geologist, he knew. Simon clearly knew, but for some reason apparently hadn't told his boss. And Rachel, who owned the mineral rights for the new well, had gone to Pete when I came sniffing around for information.

The three of us women exchanged looks, each knowing the implications of our discovery: more faithful to his profession than to his job, Scott Dinsmoore had been poised to blow the whistle. Now he was dead. Simon had picked up where Scott left off, and had been pushed from a car at high speed.

Elyria spelled out the potential damage to Blackfeet: "If it can be demonstrated that Blackfeet knowingly lied about the situation using telephone, fax, or such, then they've violated the federal RICO laws—Racketeering in Corrupt Organizations. That would make them liable for triple damages. Depending on how long the theft has gone on, that could be considerable. But the real damage will be in loss of investors. An independent oil company like Blackfeet does not exist without its investors."

I said, "Scott's desk diary would document the whole thing, every phone call, every fax, at least the ones he made."

Maddie shrugged her shoulders, a kind of what-the-hell gesture. "*Adiós* Blackfeet."

Archie snored.

But Scottie wouldn't have been recording phone calls other than his own. "I think the fat lady hasn't sung yet. A, we don't know who's going to jail. B, given who stays, it ain't over 'til it's over. I think a lot rides on Menken, providing he's just a thief and not a murderer."

Elyria said, "But as soon as Carlos and Floyd find out who did it, that person will be arraigned, and there will be pretrial hearings, and a trial. Everything will come out."

"Then we'll have to arrange a confession."

Maddie grinned. "Sure, buck-o, I want to see that." But as Elyria's smile bloomed less derisive, she asked, "What do you got in mind?"

I laughed dryly. "Oh, something along the lines of the committee meeting from hell."

34

Elyria and I returned to the kitchen. Lieutenant Flint was on the phone, checking in with the nerve center at the police station. Mrs. Ortega had taken Salvador onto her lap. The sergeant was still sitting at the table, his hands folded across his stomach. He appeared to be asleep.

I explained what Maddie and I had discovered, and Elyria filled in the financial implications, asking for their discretion.

Ortega opened one eye. "Okay, this helps. It tells why some of these guys acted the way they acted, like who had a stake in covering this thing up or making it uncovered." He let out an ironical snort. "But it doesn't eliminate any suspects."

"Don't you have *anything* that points at one of these guys more than the others?" I asked.

Ortega smiled, as if at a private joke. "Well, okay; we have one little thing, as soon as the report comes from the lab. A possible tissue culture; you know, DNA. But we have to narrow it down; there are too many people to test for a match who have a motive. We can't go taking a sample from each of them. It's against the law."

"What tissue?"

Flint answered. "There was stuff underneath Dinsmoore's fingernails that wasn't his, that sort of stuff."

I thought of the dismal scene of the detectives placing plastic bags over Scottie's delicate hands. "What *kind* of tissue was under his fingernails?"

Flint shrugged. Ortega stared at the ceiling.

"Damn you, I give you Archie on a platter, and you won't tell me—"

Ortega put his hands over his head to ward off my fury. "There wasn't any tissue under his fingernails, only pigment and fibers."

"What pigment? What fibers?"

"We don't have all the stuff back from the lab—"

"And what damned tissue samples?"

Ortega waved his hands around nervously. "I told you there were some things I couldn't tell you."

"I'm trusting *you* with *my* job."

Ortega sighed. "Okay, we found what looks like it belongs to someone else."

"Where?"

Ortega bowed his head in embarrassment. "In his mouth."

Sergeant Ortega once again feigned sleep. I let him be. I wanted a moment to myself, to try to piece together what I knew, and try to figure out where the remaining holes in my knowledge gaped widest.

Flint droned away on the phone, giving instructions in a nasal monotone. At length he stood up, stretched, and gave me his worst smile. "Everything's buttoned down for the night. I got men on each of them to make sure nobody takes a walk. The hospital says Sleeping Beauty is feeling better, but still snoozing. I made a date to kiss him at six. Beans here is a flakeout, and I could use some zees myself."

Mrs. Ortega reached out and jiggled her son's wrist. *"Despiértetse, Carlos, vamos a dormir."*

Ortega opened one eye.

She put Salvador on his feet and staggered to her own, then tugged at Ortega's arm. *"Vámonos."*

"Come wake me when you need me," Ortega said, following his mother to the door.

Halfway out the door, Mrs. Ortega turned and made a face at Flint. *"¿Y tú, Señor Flint?"*

Flint grinned. "Nah, I'll just join the party downstairs."

"¡Hijo de Dios!" she spat, and disappeared into the darkness.

I tried to sleep, but my eyes kept opening, only to stare at the odd patterns of light and darkness that played across the ceiling as cars passed in the street. Would I have a job left the day after tomorrow? And if I did, would it be any place I could, in good conscience, work?

I rewound a copy of the tape of Archie's poetry and listened several times to the fragmentary thread of his vision, looking for the elusive bit of meaning I felt must be there. Archie might be crazy, but he wasn't stupid. Besides, he was an artist, and artists deal in the expression of truths. I figured that as a geologist, I had honed much of the same intuitive processes that Archie might be using.

I let the rhythms of his speech sink into my subconscious, hoping that I would grasp understanding as I awoke. But waking meant that first I must find sleep.

Midnight passed in silence, and soon twelve-thirty, and then one. I lay alert and rigid in the embrace of quilts which five nights earlier had been a landscape of pleasure as Pete Tutaraitis taught me things about my own flesh I'd never known. I tried to force him from my mind.

I grew so tired that my mind began to slip. I saw myself falling toward the street, but I never struck the sidewalk. I fell through a dark place where right and wrong were not opposites, but just different, both wonderful, both frightening. In desperation, I imagined myself climbing to the sixteenth floor and stepping willingly from the wreckage of that window. I sailed down, plummeting, falling toward the earth. *If I can see myself die, I can rest.*

But still the drop would not end.

Who killed Scott Dinsmoore? I rubbed my eyes, willing them to see through the shadows to the moment of the crime, to limn its pattern, perceive its dance. I tried to align all the evidence together and comb it like hair, so I could see the one strand out of place.

I ran my proposed committee meeting like a movie on the backs of my twitching eyelids, testing scenarios. Vague notions formed and dissolved as I searched for a nerve that, once pressed, would so irritate Scott's murderer that he would step into the open. What would I do once I had everyone together in the committee room?

And everyone still included Pete. No matter what resolution the morning might bring, Pete would lose. When the word of Blackfeet's theft of gas from Hat Rock Field came to light, he would be exposed as a murderer, a thief, or at best a royalty holder in a bankrupt oil field.

The clock hummed faintly on the dresser, filling the room with the intimate hollowness of night. I teetered between a shameful pleasure in the thought of getting even with Pete and a self-contempt so complete I feared I'd never trust myself again. Until I'd witnessed Pete's meeting with Rachel, I had been able to delude myself that he had loved me, however premature his pursuit. I told myself that the look I'd seen in his eyes had been a lie, but as I tried to pry him from my heart finally and absolutely, he melted and re-formed, caressing me like silk. In that moment I realized the price I was paying for seeing Pete as loving and kind: to assign him goodness, I was taking onto myself all badness, and seeing myself as a freak who ruined all she touched.

35

Flint shook me awake at five-thirty. "Rise and shine, Sherlock," he said. "We got a date with a fall guy."

"Huh?" It was such a shock to see Flint's face at that hour that I couldn't make sense out of what he had said.

"Crybaby Bunting," he said.

"Huh?"

"Time to turn up the heat. Sleeping Beauty is awake, but he ain't talking, except to whine that the nurses aren't giving him enough drugs. It seems the members of my profession ain't up to his level of conversation. Maybe he'll warble for you."

I stumbled out of bed and began to pull a pair of jeans on under my nightgown. "How long will this take?"

"Couple hours."

"I won't be talking to him for two hours, will I?"

"I gotta grill you afterward. I'll spring for breakfast, even."

"I've got a better idea. I'll get into my business rig. Let's mooch breakfast off of Menken."

"Whuffor?"

I gave him a screw-you grin. "I'm going to turn up the heat."

I dove through the shower and got dressed. Flint had a police cruiser waiting outside when I was done, with a uniformed cop at the wheel. And Archie Arch locked up in the back seat.

"How the hell you get him in there?" I gasped. "Where's Maddie?"

Flint's face stretched into an ugly yawn. "Maddie sleeps kind of heavy. I keep a copy of the key in my wallet, for when I run into a comedian. It wasn't easy getting Archie out of the bed without waking her, but it's amazing what you can do with enough duct tape." His face fell. "I only hope she forgives me. They don't make 'em like that back in Jersey."

Simon Bunting did not look good. His legs were broken. His face was black and blue, and shone with a strong-smelling ointment smeared on to treat the road rash he'd taken on the left side.

I eased myself into the chair by his bed and held Flint's microcassette recorder below the edge of the bed where Simon couldn't see it. When I was ready to be noticed, I made one of those throat-clearing noises.

Simon opened his eyes halfway and squinted at me, trying to place me through the delirium of concussion. "Who . . . the hell are—?" He flared his nostrils as if I carried some unpleasant odor. "How the fuck . . . you get in here?" He started to rise from the mattress, but crumpled with pain.

"Take it easy," I said. "I'm Em Hansen. I worked with Scottie."

"Oh. Yeah. The new girl."

Woman, damn you. "Do you know who did this to you?"

Warily, he said, "Who sent you? Menken?"

"No. I'm trying to help you. Whoever did this to you might try again."

Simon tried to shift on the mattress, but grunted in pain. "You won't go to the police?"

"No," I lied. *They'll come to me.* "I was trying to help Scott. I can help you."

"Why?"

"I knew Libby and Rachel at school. I need to know what's going on."

Simon regarded me at length through his little pig eyes. "It was some asshole spicks in a Buick."

So the dark hair and the mustache didn't belong to Pete? I felt relieved, in spite of myself. "Did you know them?"

"Fuck."

"You must suspect someone."

"Go to hell."

I would have been glad to leave. Unpleasant as I found his attitude, he was in terrible pain, and I wished nothing more than to leave him in peace. But I needed to know everything I could if the committee meeting was going to have the desired effect. I started peppering him with the questions Flint and I had rehearsed in the car, trying to spit them out and get them over with. One hit pay dirt: "Who's your friend with the baby-doll voice?"

"Wouldn't I like to know," Simon said, eyeing me with deepening suspicion. "How'd you know about the bitch on the phone?"

"Then you've only heard her voice on the phone?"

"Yeah. Bitch calls me all hours of the day and night, saying she knows who killed Scott. Who the fuck she working for—Menken?" He spoke the name like the word tasted bad in his mouth.

"Maybe she was Scott's girlfriend."

"Scott didn't have a girlfriend. He was too busy carrying a torch."

"This woman with the little voice was able to monitor your messages. I left you a message and she called me back. Is there a remote access code on your answering machine?"

"Damn it to hell. All you have to do is punch a couple numbers and it plays the messages back. Cheap machine."

"What numbers?"

"I'm not telling *you!*"

"Would Scott have told anyone the code?"

"Why don't you the fuck leave?" His eyes clouded, and he looked like a drunk who was passing out.

I tried to shock him back awake. "Did you kill Scott?"

Simon's bandaged hands flew up to his nose. "Go to hell!"

"Then why have you been hiding?"

No answer, to that question or the next half dozen. He was too busy struggling to control his pain.

I stared at him in frustration. How many years had I suffered at the hands of such self-serving privileged punks as he, and now when I had my chance to harass one that was pinned down and helpless, he had me pitying him. In a much smaller voice, I said, "What about Gerald Luftweiller?"

"Oh, what *about* Gerald Luftweiller," he spat. "He should have kept his nose in Accounting if he couldn't stand the heat."

Oh really? The cash flow numbers do spring from the production numbers, fellah. "So Gerald knew about the gas storage imbalance, did he?"

"Oh, yeah, and he comes waving the map in my face, tells me I have to tell Christiansen, like that's the right thing to do. What the hell does he know what's right and wrong, is he God or something? How was I supposed to know he was going to jump?"

"What did you do?"

Simon's arm dropped away and his eyes shot open in anger. "What did I *do?* I told him something I should have told him years ago: I told him to get out of my sight or I'd squeeze his nuts to pulp. Listen, you try having some skinny little nothing follow you around all those years. 'Simon, you're so wonderful. Simon, you're so smart.' People start thinking you're a fag." Simon gingerly laid an arm across his face. "Little fucker thought he was an engineer or something. I told him stay out of my business. Then he gets all Christian on me, wants me to go to church and fucking *pray* with him. Says am I on the take or something? I'm goddamn *glad* he's dead."

Now I knew what had killed Gerald Luftweiller. The thought that his idol might have larcenous feet of clay must have driven him to the edge. Simon's outburst had pushed him over it. "Well, why *didn't* you tell your boss?"

"Why? Are you brain-dead? Scott would have been out of a job! I was giving him time to straighten things out."

The old school tie, the gentlemen's solution. "Couldn't you have stepped forward after Scott was dead?"

"Are you nuts? What am I doing in this bed? Treating a hangnail?"

"But you went to Menken's office."

"I figured I'd stir things up a little."

"Did you tell him you were a reporter?"

"How'd you know?"

Had Menken bought that? Or did he already know who Simon was? "Menken might have seen you at Scott's memorial service."

For the first time, Simon looked sad, rather than just angry. "I figured it was worth the risk." He was beginning to fade again, his eyes closing with the double pain of a broken body and a lost companion.

I turned off the microcassette recorder and left the room, handing the tiny gadget off to Flint as I passed him and the uniformed policeman who was guarding Simon outside the door. As Flint moved out of earshot to listen to the tape, I leaned against the wall in the cold white hallway. I had carried Gerald Luftweiller in my heart all the long days since I had arrived at Blackfeet, but now I saw that he hadn't been altogether real to me. My mind had done its job of rationalization after all, demoting him to a mere character in a newspaper, a small fly caught in life's web. Now, in all his frailty, he was real; another fool who harbored grand illusions, like myself.

I telephoned my grandmother from a pay booth on the ground floor of Denver General Hospital. "Oh Emily, there you are," she said, her voice tense with worry. "I was about to try you again. I have something important to tell you."

"What, Grammie?" I was leaning against the wall next to the phone, rubbing my forehead to dispel a thick mixture of fatigue and sadness.

"My dear, this is very complicated. I'm afraid it involves money."

At this, I smiled. Money was slightly indecent to her; it was as if she'd had to say the word *sex* in public. "But it's something you think I'd better know," I prompted, using a tone I hoped carried the correct amount of respect.

"Yes, dear. It involves an oil field in your company's portfolio."

I found myself grinning. She was speaking as if I was properly idle rich, nominally employed and drawing my living from investments. "Let me guess; are we talking about Lost Coyote Field?"

"Yes. Oh dear, are you involved with it, Emily?"

"Yes, I'm the geologist assigned to that field," I said, unexpectedly proud.

"Oh dear. Yes, well then perhaps you know that the mineral interests belong to the Hopkins girl, and her husband, and to Rachel Conant's family." Tone of voice suitable for announcement of End of World. The idea of becoming financially involved with friends must seem to her like going ahead and having that sex in a public place.

"Well, I just found out about the Conants, and yes, I know that, ah—Libby's husband has what's called an overriding royalty. Why?"

My grandmother paused. She was going against her own grain to tell me these things. Her voice became more organized, defaulting to an almost marital air. "Emily, what I have to tell you is not pleasant."

"I think I can handle it. Please continue."

"Yes of course, dear. You remind me of myself." Leaving me no time to reply to this break from form, she hurried into her grim announcement: "Emily, Libby's family does not approve of her choice in a husband. The truth is that they set her up out there in Denver so that he wouldn't be seen with them."

"You mean Libby's in exile?"

"Well, in a manner of speaking yes. She and her—ah, husband have the income from this ah, oil property, but their interest is contingent on maintaining their residence in the West."

Another piece of the puzzle fell miserably into place. Hadn't my grandmother said Libby's father had looked after her? "Um, Grammie, do you mean that Mr. Hopkins bought the interests?" Had Pete done *none* of the work?

"Yes, I suppose. However such business is done. He made an arrangement with George Conant, your classmate Rachel's father. Mr. Conant is a senator, and I suppose he thought it best that someone else handle his business interests while he serves in office."

Yes, it can avoid a little something called a conflict of interest. "So Libby's husband found a job here at Blackfeet, and Mr. Hopkins arranged for Blackfeet to drill the Conants' lease?"

"I rather think it was the other way around; that your company was promised the lease if they hired Libby's husband."

"The Hopkinses *bought* Pete a job?"

"In my day, we called this a remittance arrangement. She may visit her family, but she may not bring him home. I could not discover why. I know this sounds terribly bigoted, but there you have it. Perhaps he's a perfectly nice young man, perhaps he is not. Either way, it is not a good situation, and you might prefer not to get involved. I am sorry to have pressed you to do so."

My heart sagged. *A bit late, Grammie.* For a moment I wished that she had known and warned me earlier, but such a warning would probably have only sparked rebellion in me, and I might have gotten even more involved. I wished equally that I could blame her for extorting my parents into sending me to school with these people in the first place. But then I thought beyond my own unhappiness to the pain that Libby must feel, strung between a husband who betrayed her and a family that insisted on keeping her a child.

I stood in the broad, antiseptic hallway, watching through a plate glass window as the sun rose over Denver. I stretched the phone wire toward the glass and bathed my face in the lemon-colored light that two hours before, and two thousand miles to the east, had touched my grandmother's face. Her ancient visage appeared in my mind, lined with worry, and for the first time it occurred to me how very much she must have wished certain things for my mother and me, however inappropriate we may have found them.

I rolled down the window of the police cruiser to catch the fresh mountain air, washing away the hospital stink and the smut of the city. I could still smell cigarette smoke from the Chapultepec Cantina in my hair.

By the end of the day, my career as a geologist would probably be over, either through my own impolitic behavior, or because Blackfeet Oil would be no more. I smiled wryly; it was right and fitting that I should ride to my career's execution with a police escort.

Flint sat between me and the patrolman who was driving, talking on the car phone. Ortega sat behind the cage in the back seat, keeping Archie company over the coffee and sopapillas Mrs. Ortega had sent along. His eyes were swollen with lack of sleep.

I turned in my seat and looked at Archie. "Can you talk to me now, friend?" I asked.

Archie rolled his eyes up into his forehead, as if trying to hide from me. As I continued to stare, he squirmed around and looked out the back window, laying his elbows along the back of the seat.

I tried to imagine what there was about life on the streets, or in a parking garage, for heaven's sake, that appealed to this strange little man. I mentally peered over his shoulder, trying to see what he had seen from his nest on the I-beam. For a penitent monk, he was oddly voyeuristic, like a monkey chattering on a branch while the predators walked by on the jungle floor.

I grabbed a piece of paper and a pen off the driver's clipboard and wrote, "I'll have you out of this cage soon," folded it up, and handed it to Ortega. "Stick that in Archie's pocket," I said.

Archie snatched the note, read it, and squinched his face up like he was trying to pull his features in through his nostrils.

Ortega patted Archie's shoulder and offered him a cup of coffee. He spoke to him with kindness. "Okay, this is how we got to do this, Archie. We got to flush out this murderer. We can get close, but we got to have proof, and a confession would be nice. I think a little pressure will work." Divide and conquer. Ortega's approach to things was always deceptively simple. It misled people, lulling them into thinking that there was no harm in telling the nice policeman the most damning information, because he looked like he'd never catch up enough to put two and two together, and even if he did, someone as unimposing couldn't possibly do anything rash, like arresting anybody.

I smiled. "You want pressure? I'm going to ask Menken to call a committee meeting," I said.

"Ahh, that will be perfect. You go in there and show them what you showed me." He smiled happily.

Flint dragged a hand down his face. "Is that why you got us driving up there? Hey, we got a car phone right here. You call him and I'll pull over for breakfast."

"No," I said, "I need to see his reaction to finding police at the door."

Ortega's smile spread into a grin. He patted his knee, and said, "Now it's Em's turn to keep us in the dark."

I bowed my head and buried my face in my hands. "So Sergeant," I asked, "you've gotten calls from someone with a little bitty voice?"

He smiled, nodding. "Two calls, if you mean a woman who sounds like a little girl."

"How'd you know it was a woman? It could have been a man speaking in a falsetto."

"You know, it just sounded that way."

I agreed. "What did she want?"

"She wanted to make sure I was doing my job."

"So answer me this: what's the connection between a woman with a voice like a little girl who wants to know if you're doing your job, and the job we're talking about here?"

Ortega raised his shoulders slightly. "I don't know. All she said was, 'Don't forget about Scottie.'"

"And you said?"

"I'm not forgetting."

"And she said?"

"She hung up."

The car phone rang. Flint grabbed it from its cradle and listened, then twisted around to face Ortega. "Yes!" he shouted. He kissed the palm of his hand and patted his cheek with it. "The stone man comes through!" He spoke into the mouthpiece. "Shake them down and cut an arrest warrant as soon as you find out who hired them." He hung up.

"Yes?" Ortega asked.

"The car they pitched Bunting from has been traced. Arrests to follow."

"How'd you figure that one?"

"My mama was a travel agent 'til her emphysema got too bad," said Flint. "She taught me the moves with the car reservation computers. I put a man on it hours ago, while you slobs were in dreamland."

"Very nice," Ortega said.

"There's something I've been meaning to ask you fellows," I said. "You're a team, right? But Lieutenant Flint, you rank him, right? Yet you seem to wait for your cues from him. Is this part of your act?"

Flint racked his face with a smile. "I got talent, but Ortega's the brains of the outfit."

The uniformed officer who was driving nodded his head.

"Get lost, Floyd," Ortega whispered, from the back seat. He was done eating, and his eyes were closed again. He leaned back into the seat with his arms crossed in front of his round stomach, just a little brown man with a pleasant face.

Flint pressed his point. "No, it's true. I asked to be assigned with him. He'd have made lieutenant long ago, if he weren't such a maverick. Ain't that right, Beans."

"I am the proud Mexican," said Ortega. "I dance to a different mariachi."

"He keeps getting passed over for promotion. Every time it's the same thing: he's gone and done things his way again, yakking it up with the civilians. Ya dumb spick. Hey, give me one of them sofa pillows, bro." He stuck his fingers through the wire cage, reaching for one of Mrs. Ortega's pastries. "You et enough already. You're fat. Couldn't drown you in the river, it'd cost me too much in cement to weigh you down."

Menken did a fine job of covering his surprise at seeing us on his doorstep at half past seven. "Come in," he said affably, stepping politely aside in his bathrobe. He led the way to the kitchen, where Cecelia sat glowering over a bowl of cereal. At the sight of me, her face lit up. There was still no sign of any Mrs. Menken.

"So, Officers, what can I do for you this fine morning?"

The detectives deferred to me.

"I want you to call a committee meeting, for nine o'clock this morning," I began.

Menken bobbed his head respectfully and took a sip of juice. "That can be done, but I would of course like to know why." He seemed to be enjoying this, just as he had seemed to thrive on the hostility of that first committee meeting and on the tension of the memorial service.

"I believe I can demonstrate that we are producing gas from Lost Coyote Field that is being injected at Hat Rock Field, next door." I laid out the cross section on his breakfast table.

Menken put his orange juice down and stared at the cross section. I watched for any sign of subterfuge in his face, but for once, it was simply blank. Was this the face of a murderer? I looked at Cecelia, who had put down her spoon to listen. No, Menken was way out there in the thin air, but he loved his daughter. He would never chance having the police into his kitchen if they might arrest him in front of her.

"Did Scott mention any of this to you that time he came to your office?" I asked mildly. There was nothing to be gained by getting rough.

Menken blinked his eyes, once. "No. As I say, we were interrupted." His face assumed a certain pensiveness. "I take it you think that there is some complicity involved with this."

"Yes, and I hoped you might know how to deal with the political problems this poses," I said, making an understatement worthy of a Yankee. I figured the bottom line was in fact the bottom line: Menken had to be shrewd to have gotten to where he was, and a lot of people's jobs rested on his ability to stay there.

Menken glanced at me. He didn't let much slip, just a quick view of his mental machinery shifting into gear. "And you think a committee meeting might bring a few things to light."

"Exactly."

He gave the table a little pat, just as he had done that day in the committee room. "Done," he said. "The phone is there, and I have all the numbers in my case. If anyone questions why you are calling them instead of me, just put me on the line."

That's my boy, Menken, delegate responsibility. You're good at it. Perhaps too good.

I phoned from the hallway. Smith, Crick, and Hathaway were easy to reach, and surprisingly cooperative. When the boss man says jump, you jump, I guess.

I paused over Pete's number, then gritted my teeth and dialed. My heart caught in my throat when Libby answered the phone.

She sounded happy to hear from me. "Oh, good morning, Em. Pete's out for a jog with the dog, but he'll be back soon." I imagined some fat cop who had drawn the assignment of staking him out done up in spandex tights, trying to keep up with Pete's morning workout. "Can I give him a message?"

"Yes, um, I'm trying to get the word out that Menken has called a committee meeting, for nine o'clock."

"Oh, I'll tell him," she said. "Can we have lunch again soon?"

"Sure," I said, wishing the future could hold such quiet things for us.

After I hung up the phone, I turned to Flint. "After Pete leaves for the office today, send someone around to get Libby. Tell her the meeting is about Lost Coyote Field, and that as a royalty interest holder, she needs to be there. Get her to bring Rachel Conant. And can you get a search warrant for Pete's house?"

"Yeah."

"While she's out, take a look. You might find Scott's red notebook there."

Flint looked jubilant as he picked up the phone to dial.

Suddenly, I wasn't certain I could go through with my plan. Who was I, to rip at other people's lives? Was I so pure that I could mete out justice? I hurried outside, and looked up at the pines along the ridge, trying to believe I was doing the right thing.

A moment later, I heard Ortega's soft voice behind me: "Nice morning. Air's real clean here."

"Yeah." I willed him to go back into the house, but he stayed.

"Flint's about got a fix on who hired the attempt on Simon Bunting."

I sighed. I was not going to be allowed to quit, no matter how much I wobbled. "Who?"

"He thinks it's Smith. The description matches."

I got one of those feelings like I'd just shopped frantically all day for a new dress and shown up at the right house, only to find out the party had been last week. In part I was relieved, but I felt embarrassed to find that mostly I was let down. "So that's our man?" It didn't seem to fit.

"Maybe."

"And maybe not?"

"I don't know. We have enough for an arrest warrant for conspiracy to kill Simon Bunting, but not enough to get him or anyone else for killing Mr. Dinsmoore. Maybe when the DNA tests come back from the lab."

"DNA?"

"Yes, from the tissue samples. And the pigment and fibers."

Pigment and fibers under Scott's fingernails. I imagined him clawing madly for something to hold on to—paint, fabric, or carpeting—as he was thrust backward out of the window. But then, why would he have let someone back him up to that window? Nothing fit. I tried to remember if anyone had unusual marks on him that night in the lobby, as the police questioned everyone. Did anyone have scratches on their face?

In the same conversational tone, Ortega asked, "You get hold of everyone?"

"Yes."

"This is hard for you, eh?"

I couldn't answer.

His voice quieted with shyness. "Maybe it's time to get mad."

"I *am* angry!" I spun around, ready to take it out on Ortega, but when I looked into his eyes, I hung my head.

"See?" he said softly. "You're always angry at yourself. How you going to see what's in front of you, if you look at your feet all the time?"

That tore it. I looked up at him, my eyes narrowed. "Back off," I said. "I'm bound to help you find out who killed Scott, but how I feel about it is a private matter."

Ortega smiled. "That's better. *Ojos calientes.* You look at me through those eyes, and what do you see?"

"I see someone who sticks his nose in other people's business."

Ortega's face lit with pleasure. "Perfect! Your illusion is burst. Now you really see me." Still smiling, he turned and headed for the cruiser.

36

The sun burnished the side of the capitol dome as we drove back into Denver. As the police cruiser plowed through traffic, I stared at the busloads of commuters chugging up Lincoln Street, wheeled tin cans full of blank-faced people who had the luxury of going to jobs that posed no challenge to their integrity. Well, I had some integrity at stake today, and I intended to leave with it intact. In an hour, I would no longer be Em Hansen, the hayseed in a suit, I would be Em Hansen, the one who ended the game. So be it.

By prior agreement, the cruiser pulled into the central police station behind the courthouse, and I walked the remaining four blocks to Seventeenth Street.

The reflective glass sheath that covered the Cattlemen's Exchange Building burned harshly in the morning light. I paused before the entrance, informing the building that I had business on its twelfth floor. It opened its mouth and let me in.

I stopped by my office to fill the time remaining before the committee meeting. Maddie was there, bright-eyed and bushy-tailed, her curvaceous little body squeezed into a demure shade of taupe that Elyria had found for her in her closet. Maddie didn't look quite right, and it wasn't just the fit.

"Are you mad at Lieutenant Flint?" I asked.

"Hell no. He was just doing his job. I admire that in a man. Besides, he's kind of cute."

I gagged.

Maddie grinned.

"Thanks for the help last night."

"Best time I've ever had with my shoes on."

"I mean the correlations."

"That was fun, too. So what's on the docket for today?"

"Committee meeting, two minutes," I said, imitating the re-

doubtable Fritz. "I've invited Ortega and Flint to join the festivities. There'll be some changes made around here."

As I passed her desk, Maddie howled and slapped me a high
five, stuffed a fresh piece of gum in her mouth, picked up her
eraser, and got down to her day's work.

This time, as I walked into the committee room and closed
the door, all eyes were on me. The thick wall coverings ab-
sorbed all incidental sounds of breathing, of pencils tapping, of
blood pulsing quickly through veins. I heard my own pulse
loudly in my ears. Someone had set the lights down low, and
my tired mind asked me if night had just fallen.

I glanced around the room. On one side of the table sat
Sergeant Ortega and a woman I had never seen before. On the
other side sat Fred Crick, Pete Tutaraitis, Jon Hathaway and
Dave Smith, all in a row like schoolboys waiting for a lecture.
Their faces were blank, except for Hathaway's, which was
florid with agitation.

I couldn't look at Pete, no matter what Sergeant Ortega had
said.

I felt only a deep, disquieting fatigue. I had survived since
noon the day before on a diet of coffee, corn chips, sopapillas,
and beer, and had slept little for days. My eyelids burned with
the lack of rest, and one tiny muscle in my upper lip was beginning to twitch.

Menken spoke. "Gentlemen, ladies, we are here to discuss a
problem that involves Lost Coyote Field, and quite possibly its
neighbor Hat Rock Field, to the west." He paused, to let his
statement sink in. He stood very straight, with his hands
tightly gripping a pointer, but for the first time in my acquaintance with him, I knew what he was feeling: beneath his
cheery, chivalrous exterior, he was deeply, dangerously angry.

Menken continued. "You all know Ms. Christiansen, president of Love and Christiansen. She has kindly accepted my invitation to join us today." He gestured to the woman. She was
short and boxy, and was upholstered in a suit unworthy of an
overstuffed chair. A disorganized fringe of straight, black hair
shot with white stuck out in several directions around her
ruddy, angry face, and her dark blue eyes twitched from one
man's face to the next. It was clear that she already knew what
was afoot. I had to hand it to Menken; he had clearly done
some executive footwork since breakfast.

The door opened, and Lieutenant Flint entered. Instead of

closing the door, he turned and held it open. All eyes shifted to the doorway.

In walked Libby, trembling like a small nervous bird, clinging to the elbow of Rachel Conant. Rachel stepped toward the table and pulled out a chair for her, then stood behind it like an imperial guard. Once behind Libby's line of sight, Rachel shot fierce looks of warning left and right.

Pete rose halfway out of his seat, but at a signal from Flint, quickly sat down again. "Libby," Pete said, in a stage whisper, "what are you doing here? This is a committee meeting."

I shook my head. *Yeah, and the OK Corral was an ice cream social.*

Libby leaned across the table toward her husband, reaching for his hand. When he pointedly kept his in his lap, she dropped her hands to the hem of her sweater and worked it like a seamstress gone mad. "Pete," she said aloud, "they searched the house. They took books and papers out of your study. They took the keys to the cars, and dirty glasses from the sink. What's going on?"

My stomach began to churn. I had to fight an urge to take Libby under my arm and shepherd her out of the room.

Menken stared at Libby and began to pace, perhaps angry at being upstaged. He marched up and down the committee room, his stride lengthening as he once again began to speak: "This morning, I was advised by the *newest* member of our staff"—he paused again, to drive home the point that none of my seniors had had the brains to come to him—"that it is entirely possible that our fields are in communication, and that gas injected into Hat Rock is being produced from Lost Coyote. Ms. Christiansen confirms from preliminary review of their records that they have been experiencing dramatically less than predicted reservoir pressures." He stopped, and pointed at my cross sections. "These sections, gentlemen, *these ones here*"—he slammed his hand onto the table so hard I heard the paper tear—"were made from *data available in a public place!* We have better copies in our vault; now, don't we, Mr. Smith?" Menken loomed over the table, his eyes trained on Dave Smith, who from all outward appearances was calmly examining the cross sections.

Smith turned a flaccid palm upward. "Now, J.C., if you have a question about our company policy—"

"Mr. Smith, you will address me as Mr. Menken!"

Smith sat quietly, examining the papers.

Hathaway lost what was left of his composure all at once. He grasped his balding head with his hands and wailed, "Jesus God, what are we going to do? This will ruin us! We're barely making costs as it is! And I turned down another job for this. I should have never come to Denver. How will I support my family?" He collapsed onto the table and started to weep.

Scratch Hathaway from the list. I stared at Crick. He looked like hell. The dark circles under his eyes sagged like rucksacks, and his eyes were rimmed red with fatigue. But when he spoke, his voice was calm as death. "Well, Dave, here we are. And it looks like you've really done it this time. You've really showed them how to manage a field, haven't you? Did you push your boy out that window, too?"

Smith spun toward Fred Crick. "Crick, you fool, it wasn't me. It was him!" He thrust out a hand, his index finger all but gouging into Pete's face.

All eyes focused on Pete.

Pete's mouth stiffened with rage. He sprung from his chair and backed toward the door, shouting, "You blood-sucking bastards, you aren't going to hang this one on me! You're all alike. You think you can stick it to the kid from the projects, but this time it's not going to work. I have an interest in that field, and I'm going to keep it. I'm fucking going to retire on it, and you can kiss *my* ass for a change!" He spat as he shouted, great globules of saliva spraying out over his chin.

My eyes opened wide, and I looked at him, really looked. In that one, brief moment, Pete's polished demeanor had disintegrated into an ugly mask. Or was I seeing him without his mask for the first time?

I glanced at Libby. She sat quietly erect, just as I remember her sitting in English class at school, hands folded in her lap, legs crossed at the ankles, gaze deflected to her hands. Rachel gripped her shoulders, staring unflinchingly at Pete.

Pete reached the door and extended one hand for the knob. With one last poisonous look, he threw the door wide.

Two uniformed officers filled the doorway, blocking his escape.

This is your cue, Flint; come on!

Flint yawned. "Thank you, Mr. Menken. We got what we needed."

Ortega spoke quietly from his chair. "The warrants in order, Floyd?"

"Yes." With great flair, he whipped out two papers. "David

James Smith, you are under arrest for conspiracy to murder Simon Bunting. Next time have your hit men rent their car a little farther from downtown."

Smith rose abruptly to his feet but said nothing. His hands hung limply at his sides. As Flint slid the warrant down the table at him, the room was so quiet I could hear the paper spin.

"Peter Tutaraitis." Flint held up another paper. "You're coming with us, too. I think you got something to tell us." He raised a hand as if to present a benediction. "Gentlemen, you have the right to remain silent . . ."

37

They put Pete in a small room on the second floor of the police station, and told him they wanted to ask a few questions. Flint sat Pete down in a plastic chair under a clock. I stood hidden in the shadows of the next room, next to a technician who was preparing a video camera, watching.

Flint's voice crackled through a speaker. "See that mirror?" he said. "That's one-way glass. I'm going to ask you a few questions, and there's a camera on the other side of that glass that's going to record everything you say and do. Do not get out of the chair; I wouldn't like that. See that clock? The camera sees that, too, so's we can prove we didn't monkey with the tape."

Pete looked toward the mirror with eyes as dark as pitch. Unfocused, they bored into me, seething with hatred.

"He has a police record back in New Jersey," Sergeant Ortega said quietly, from behind me. "Juvenile stuff. I wanted to warn you. Flint's going to use it."

I looked around. He had posted himself in the darkest corner of the room, in a chair as uncomforting as Pete's. He stared at nothing in particular, the fatigue of round-the-clock effort dragging at his face.

I looked back through the glass. Flint fiddled with his notebook and pen, stalling. "Now, Mr. Tutaraitis, you know what you're in here for, don't you?"

Pete did not reply.

The door into our room from the hallway opened. In stepped Libby Hopkins, her angelic blond hair backlit by the lights from the corridor. Behind her was Rachel, ferocious and frowning, a brooding lady-in-waiting relentlessly carrying the train of the frail princess's robe.

"Hello, Libby," I whispered, fighting a weird urge to drop a curtsy. Old training dies hard.

She squeezed my hand. It was warm and soft, like a child's.

Holding herself erect and composed, she moved up to the one-way glass and stopped, her arms folded across her breasts as if she were clutching an infant.

Sergeant Ortega got up and came to a tangle of cables near the video camera. "Excuse me," he said. "I just got to turn on this tape recorder." He pressed a switch and then spoke into a microphone. "Okay," he said. His voice looped back through the speakers from the other room, squealing slightly with feedback.

Flint looked at Pete. "Okay, we searched your house while you were in that committee meeting this morning. We had a warrant. You know about those things, don't you?" He pointed at a row of neatly marked plastic Ziploc bags and a large, bulging manila envelope.

Pete hooked the toes of his oxblood loafers around the metal legs of the chair and tipped it back against the wall, leaning his head against the cold plaster. His eyes slid insolently toward Flint. He said nothing.

"We got your record from New Jersey," Flint continued. "I'm from Jersey myself, Pete. This is quite a little story we got here . . . lessee, breaking and entering, possession of an illegal firearm . . ."

Pete continued to stare.

"So Pete, we kept you in mind while we nosed around this murder, here. Looky here!" Flint tapped his finger on a Ziploc bag that encased a very familiar red notebook.

Rachel stepped toward the glass.

I was barely breathing. I looked at Libby. Her golden hair glowed in the soft light that came through the one-way glass. Her face was growing agitated, but her voice was icy calm and light, almost childlike: "When the police came this morning after Pete left for the meeting, I thought there must be some mistake. But then they showed me the warrant, and of course I had to let them search . . ." Her voice trailed off. She began to lick her lips with her perfect tongue.

Flint's voice droned on. "You knew what Dinsmoore had on you would ruin you. If he got to Menken with that information about Lost Coyote, you'd be out on the street. The field would be worthless, after Love and Christiansen was done with you. You couldn't face living on your own again, could you, pretty boy?"

I wished Flint would stop. Could stop.

Rachel moved toward Libby, trying to take her from the room.

Libby put out a hand to stop her. "No, I must watch this."

Rachel began to pace. I watched her for a moment, weighing her behavior.

Libby licked her lips again. The motion of her lips and tongue were erotic, and her chest heaved as she fought to contain herself. With deep revulsion, I realized she was enjoying this.

I removed the thin black tube from my pocket and raised it into her peripheral vision. "Would you like some of my lip balm," I asked, "or do you use a prescription brand? Your lips will get dry in this climate, you keep licking them like that."

She didn't respond. Ortega stepped forward. He gently relieved her of her pocketbook and slipped it into another Ziploc bag.

I said, "You kissed Scott good-bye, didn't you, Libby? You left lip balm on him, and saliva in his mouth." Someone else's tissue in Scott's mouth: saliva was full of squamous cells from the inside of the cheeks.

Libby turned toward me, her eyes glassy. "Yes," she whispered, through paper-dry lips.

Rachel spun around and faced her.

Ortega spoke from behind Libby. "Isn't that a strange thing to do, to kiss a man you're about to kill?"

Her chest kept heaving. "It was the kind thing to do. He loved me."

Rachel slapped her. "Goddamn it, Libby, shut up! They're taping this side, too!"

To Ortega, I said, "Bring Archie in now, please."

Ortega opened the door and collected Archie from an officer in the hall. He shuffled into the room and squinted, quickly adjusting his eyes to the darkness. When he saw Libby, he smiled and cringed, a serf bowing before a queen he feared.

"Cocoon?" I said.

He nodded. "Cocoon."

Ortega knocked on the one-way glass. Flint pulled a dark wig out of the manila folder.

Libby's eyes locked on the wig, and she smiled, a sweet, private smile, like a sweetheart recalling her lover's touch.

"How did you lure Scott up to that hallway, Libby? Did you promise you'd leave Pete? Was that why Scott was looking for a house, so you could live with him?" I could picture her in that hallway, disguised in that wig, her hands demurely gloved. She had Scott's pocketknife ready, having perhaps taken it from his house during the afternoon, while he worked. She slit the tape while she waited for him, and as she kissed him one last time, she pressed the knife clumsily into his hand, making certain his prints would be on it. "Did you have him move the plywood away from the window for you?" I asked.

Her voice was growing higher, more childlike. "No. I moved it before he came. You always thought me frail." She smiled coyly, proud of this small thing.

"And then you pushed him?"

Her smile grew wide, and her head began to rock, side to side. Her voice rose the rest of the way up into the sickly sweet baby-doll singsong I had heard in that morning phone call. "It was so easy. I stepped toward the hole, as if it were I who wanted to die, and he came close to catch me. He was always afraid of heights; so brave. Little Scottie. I kissed him, then I let him go." With childlike movements of her hands, she gestured toward a shattered window, a hole that lived serenely in her mind.

Rachel leaned against the glass, staring sightlessly into the other room, her body burdened with unwept tears.

Archie began to sway and chant. "We must *hark* the lady *dark* she smiles at *me* and rides for *free* in deep co*coon* a car trunk *tomb* of mustached *man* with busy *hands*."

"That's right, Archie," I said. "These goblins will stop dancing, now." I turned back to Libby. "Well planned. Your only risk was being recognized in that black wig, as you went down the stairs to the garage and climbed into the trunk of the Saab." I envisioned her running down the sixteen flights of stairs, her feet carrying her down into the earth to basement level B, where she pushed open the heavy fire door below Archie's shadowy perch. I closed my eyes, knowing then that as Pete had driven me home that night, she had been there behind the seat, listening to my every foolish word and sigh. She had only to stay there until Pete shut the engine off for the last time that night, safely parked in the shadows of their driveway. "The catches were broken on the seat back, so it was easy for you to climb out through the passenger compartment, right? Then all you had to do was walk to a pay phone in Washington Park, and call a taxi to take you back to the airport."

"Yes," she said. "I paid cash for the plane ticket. Scott was so sweet: he even left his car for me at the airport, so I wouldn't have to take a cab. I drove all around. I even took Pete's dog for a ride. It was fun. I was only gone from Mum and Daddy's for fourteen hours." She giggled. "And they think Denver is so far away."

I shook my head. Her alibi cemented, Libby had only to sit back and wait for the police to drag her deceitful husband off to prison in her stead. "Did you really think it would work, Libby?" I asked. "Did you think we would get rid of Pete for you, so you could go home?"

She stared coyly at the floor, her body swaying from head to foot like a four-year-old's. "It almost worked," she said, now completely gone into the baby-doll identity. "But it did work, didn't it? They'll fire him now, and he'll have to give up all those other girls. They'll take away his money when they find what happened to that gas. Scottie knew. He told Gerry, and Gerry asked me what to do. I said he had to tell. I kept phoning him and phoning him, but all he did was kill himself. I told Scottie he had to tell them and he tried to tell, but they wouldn't listen. So I *made* them listen."

38

I drove Rachel home in the Saab. She had not wanted to leave; in fact, she fought furiously to stay with Libby, but in the end, there was nothing more she could do. She had arranged for a lawyer, and had stayed by Libby's side until he came, trying resolutely but unsuccessfully to force her into silence. Even after the lawyer had arrived, Rachel had paced frantically at the thought of the press reaching Libby before she could be "put away somewhere." She had come away only when I telephoned Libby's father. He had asked to speak with Rachel. With that she had tensed, and headed suddenly toward the door.

Rachel was quiet during the ride home, exhausted from her vigilance. She leaned her head against the far window, gripping the shoulder restraint in one white hand. Once inside her house, a little of her old fire returned as she poured herself the first in a quick succession of drinks. "Well, thank you, Em, I guess," she said bitterly. Thinking better of her sarcasm, she grudgingly added, "Well, maybe it was that police detective who nailed her."

"No, Rachel. You can thank me for that. But when this whole mess started, the last person I thought I was looking for was Libby. Did you know?"

Rachel was silent except for the sound her ice made as she tipped the heavy leaded glass to her lips.

"Right," I said, "it would be foolish of you to answer me if you did know. It would make you an accessory after the fact."

Rachel shook her head slowly, her eyes glazed in a thousand-yard stare focused somewhere beyond my left shoulder.

"Have you seen Libby like that before?" I asked.

Rachel pondered my question. "I used to think it was an act, like she was kidding." Suddenly Rachel's eyes focused on me. "But it wasn't Libby's fault, Em. You understand? It was that son of a bitch!"

"Pete?"

"No," she shouted.

I was confused. Who was she talking about? I sat quietly, waiting to hear what she might add.

Rachel downed another drink. After a while, her face contorted into a sardonic smile. "We always envied you, Em. Libby and I. You always had that damned horse. A true friend, who would never leave you. You always seemed as if you always knew just what you wanted."

"All I wanted was to be on that horse and in Wyoming," I replied.

"Just as I said. We were too busy hiding to think that far ahead." She drained her glass again and poured another, this time without the ice.

I sighed. I knew this act. I'd seen my mother play the part half the evenings of my childhood: talk in bitter riddles until you're drunk enough, then tell the truth as cruelly as possible. But watching Rachel play the part was different. The script had new words, frighteningly revised for a more mature viewing audience.

Rachel observed me from beneath eyelids heavy with vodka. "Libby used to say, 'I'd like to be like Em Hansen. I'd just ride away on my horse, and that would be an end to it.'"

"And end to what, Rachel?"

She ignored the question.

I steeled myself to wait for the alcohol to loosen her tongue a little further. Staring at the cut-glass decanter with a deep and abiding hatred, I reminded myself bitterly that mine was a passive role, a waiting role; it was the alcohol that was directing the play.

I filled the time with lesser questions. "When did you all meet Peter?"

Rachel moved in her chair as if I had awakened her from a nap. "Junior year. I met him first."

"Just like with Scottie."

"Just like with Scottie. I'd go out and find them, and she'd sit back and watch." Rachel spoke with no rancor. This was recitation, a numb retelling of ritual. "Then if there was one she wanted, she just smiled, and over he'd come."

"Didn't you get angry?"

Rachel looked at me as if I were some kind of idiot, and I wasn't sure whether I was supposed to conclude that of course she had been angry, or that anger had not, for some reason, been indicated.

I began to press her. "So, Libby and Pete dated right from junior year?"

Rachel shook her head irritably, the drink making her head wobble. "No. It was on again off again, right from the start. She'd reel him in, then throw him back. In between times, he'd find someone else."

"You?"

"Yes, me as often as anyone else. Why not. He was one hell of a lover."

Past tense, already. Poor old Pete has finally been thrown back for the last time. "Yes," I agreed aloud, surprising myself with my candor. Perhaps it was finally time for an end to all this hiding.

Rachel looked up. Her tone was flippant. "You poor kid." She took another gulp of her drink. "It really wasn't anything personal."

"What wasn't?"

"The way they ran their relationship."

"How did they run their relationship?"

"By proxy. She never wanted his heat." She looked at me closely, one of those you-know-what-I-mean looks. When I nodded, she continued: "So she always went away when he got too hot. It was always, 'I'm visiting Grandma,' or, 'I need a week at the shore,' but he knew, and I knew. So he'd go out and find someone to cool him off. Then it got to where he was taunting her with it. God knows, maybe it started the other way around." She leaned forward and grabbed for the decanter. I watched it rise from the table and spill liquid into her glass as if it were moving her hand, rather than the reverse.

"If this started that far back, why did they get married?"

Rachel thought for a moment. "I don't have an answer for that one." She waved a hand irritably.

I nodded. "So somewhere along the line, she had enough."

"She had enough before she ever met him."

I had also had enough. The sight of Rachel in my mother's pose was making me sick: she seemed perverted by some trick of memory, lost in my mother's flesh, like a little girl in lipstick and high-heeled shoes. Impatiently I said, "Rachel, I wish you'd get to the point."

Panic took hold of Rachel's face. "You spent the weekend with her once. Don't you remember?"

"Her mother was always drunk," I said, all attempts at politeness disintegrating. "Was that it?" Even as I said it, it didn't feel like enough. After all, I had survived such horrors without killing anyone, why couldn't she?

"Yes, but that was nothing?"

"Nothing, Rachel? How can you say that?" I wanted to shake her. Didn't she know how much it hurt to watch one's mother slowly drown?

Rachel returned my stare with poison in her eyes. "Sure. Her mother was a drunk, like me. But it was her father, Em, her *father*, for Christ's sake. Why do you think the old bag drank in the first place?"

"Why, what do you mean? He was sober. He'd tell us a bedtime story, for crap's sake, about the brave little girl who lived in the woods." I prattled on, my voice outrunning my brain. "It was a funny story, in a nasty sort of way. The little girl always had a friend who protected her from the wolf."

Rachel shook her head. "Emmy, Emmy, Emmy. How did you grow up so innocent?"

The heavy longing in her voice forced me to look at her. For a moment, her eyes were clear and lucid, and I saw into the depths of her pain, to the horror of young girls huddling together in their nightgowns to hold the storyteller at bay.

I began to tremble. Had Libby pushed Rachel at *him*, too? I stood up, unable to stay seated with such an image.

"Yes, why don't you go now, Em," Rachel said quietly. She raised her glass in a toast. A sporting, half-numb smile dressed her lips, and she said, "Go ride your horse, Em."

I looked down on Rachel's soft dark hair, and at the well-formed hands that clutched the drink, wishing I could take away even a drop of her agony. "You always stuck by her, Rachel," I said, meaning it to be a compliment. "How did you do it, if she was using you like that?"

Rachel stared up at me, her eyes dull and opaque. "Of course I did," she said. "She was my friend."

39

I drove the Saab downtown and left it in Pete's space in the parking garage. It was a spooky experience, driving it in there myself, but in some way it felt right, rather like retracing my steps in order to erase them. I considered backing down Seventeenth Street and right up the Interstate to Wyoming, to see if I could erase everything that had happened since I arrived, but I knew that bodies couldn't fly up from the sidewalk and reenter high windows.

I rode the elevator up to the twelfth floor, intending to leave the keys with Simca, but she wasn't there. Neither was Irma Triff, or Menken, for that matter. In fact, the office was almost empty. It was kind of a letdown. The rats, it seemed, had left the sinking ship. With great relief, I found that Maddie was there, holding forth in our office as if nothing had happened.

"Whatcha know?" she hollered, when she saw me. "Y'all sure shook things up in here, dincha? We got the word which little bird it was you finally chased out of the bush."

I tried to smile. "No one was more surprised than me. Where is everybody?"

"Aw, who knows? Menken and big Irma is upstairs doing damage control with Battlestar Christiansen. Everybody else kind of figures it's a holiday, I guess."

"Did Pete come back here from the police station?" I asked. "I've got his, er, car keys." Talking with Maddie was like a tonic. I could feel myself coming back to life.

Maddie let out a hoot. "Hell no. Menken sent Fritz—Fritz, for Chrissake, down there to invite him to take all the leave that was coming to him, sick or vacation. Word down in Bookkeeping has it there's some loophole in his contract, that if the wife and him are kaput, he's out his royalties and they revert to her. Yeah boy, it's been quite a morning. Irma's been on the phone getting a lawyer for Smith. What a howl. Them old boys really know how to play the game, don't they?"

"What do you mean?"

Maddie kicked off her shoes and arranged her feet on her desk, rotating her shapely ankles. "Feature it! Smith porking Irma Triff, and I didn't even notice. I must be losing my touch. But then, you don't notice the growth of tomato hornworms, either, until *wham*, your whole plant's been et."

"You can't be serious. Irma and Dave Smith?" I was back in the groove, chasing the next thread in the great unraveling. Leave it to Maddie to make life seem like it was worth living.

Maddie fairly shimmied with prurient delight. "I shit thee not: Dave Smith and Irma Triff, fun couple of the year. Why, if I'd known he was such a Don Juan, I'd—"

"Maddie, how did you find all this out?"

"Oh hey, the last hour or so, this place has been the bestest little gossip mill this side of the Pecos."

I slammed my hand on the wall. "Damn it! You'd think someone could have spoken up sooner. It would have saved me one hell of a lot of trouble."

"Naw, cool your jets, Em, nobody knew. I just heard ten minutes ago from Menken, when he came in here to chat."

"Menken? Came in here?"

"Sure. He was looking for you, but yours truly was here. It was fun. The old dog ain't usually that forthright about things, but I guess he was a mite excited."

Good old J.C. I guess when an actor wants to rehearse his lines, he needs an audience. "Well, okay, but how did he find out about Irma and Smith?"

"Well, he didn't. I got that part from Simca. She couldn't help overhearing Irma; the old bat was almost shouting into her phone. Anyways, she's telling this lawyer that this Simon fellah was riding around like the Lone Ranger, putting the heat to Smith. So Smith was using Irma to filter out who got in to see Menken."

"But Simon did get in, and so did Scottie."

"Yeah, but Irma knows Menken real well. She waits until folks are wound up so tight they aren't hardly making sense. She knows if people come at him all excited, he just rationalizes everything they say into nothing."

As always, Maddie had the world figured. Menken's ability to demote full-scale nuclear war to a fender-bender was second to none.

Maddie opened another stick of gum in celebration. "Yup, a five-star morning for this place, let me tell you."

I about had to close my gaping mouth with my hands. "But

what about your job, Maddie? Aren't you mad at me? This could sink the company."

Maddie stared down at the maps on her desk top. "What's this I see? Looks like work to me."

"Work nothing, what if the front door's locked tomorrow and you can't get *to* your desk?"

"So that's *your* fault? Get real, Em, *you* didn't swipe anybody's gas. And I'll be all right. God's got a warm spot for girls from Texas."

I suppose she was right; the collective guilt of the universe did not rest on my shoulders alone.

I had one more question for her, as long as she was feeling garrulous. "Maddie, tell me something about Simca. She seems to hate the sight of me. What's that all about?"

Maddie worked her mouth around her gum as if she were trying to make a decision.

"Is it something personal?"

Maddie looked pained. "Naw. I mean, oh hell, I guess you're going to know soon enough, as soon as she files suit."

"What suit?"

Maddie got up and came over and made a fuss out of sitting me down in my chair. "Simca's pregnant, Em," she said. "It seems old Petey-poo's the daddy, and Simca's going to need a little help supporting the poor little screamer. With the mess Pete's in now, she's probably going to have to drag his ass through the courts to get nickel one."

Well, I sure hadn't figured that one. Here poor lovely Simca, coming in to work each day, losing her breakfast with, well, it was morning sickness, right? And watching the man who had helped her get that way strut by with the next object of his so-called affections. It meant only one thing: that Pete was capable of true cruelty.

Maddie stood by like an army triage nurse, all but taking my pulse. When I looked up at her, she shrugged her shoulders as if to say, *So what? Y'all had a good time, didn't you?*

I winced.

"Aw, don't y'all worry your little head over this, Em. People just acts a little stupid sometimes around members of the opposite sex. They think, I'm tough, I can get the better of this situation, I can go to bed with this so-and-so without half caring. But this Pete here's a little more like a drug. Guys like him make y'all crazy for a spell, but relax: he'll wash out of your system in a week or so. Maybe y'all get a headache and don't feel so good for a while, but sleep is good for that."

I touched the button to summon the elevator, idly experimenting with how much contact it took to set off the heat sensors. My house key didn't do it, but my fingertip did, with just the barest of contact.

When the car arrived at the twelfth floor and the doors opened, Menken and his—or was it Dave Smith's?—executive secretary stepped out. I smiled politely and moved to step past them into the car, but Menken grabbed me by the arm and hastened me into his office. Irma Triff made fish eyes at me but kept out of my way, for once.

"Emily, my dear," Menken said, closing the door on Irma, "I can't thank you enough. I realize this problem with Hat Rock Field looks bad for Blackfeet, but because you brought it to my attention before Love and Christiansen discovered it, we need only compensate them for their loss. We won't pay damages." He gestured me toward a seat.

I sat. I wasn't certain I could believe my ears. "But Christiansen looked mad as hops," I said.

Menken arranged himself in his great overstuffed swivel chair and smiled expansively. "Nicole's a reasonable woman, Emily. I've arranged quite a nice agreement with her, in fact: we pay out over three years, with interest. We will also unitize production of the two fields into one—after all, they are only one field, as you so cleverly discovered—and Blackfeet will produce it."

"Blackfeet?" I couldn't believe it. He had just transformed being caught with his hand in the cookie jar into a paid demonstration of gourmet food handling. "Why isn't Love and Christiansen producing?"

Menken's face filled with such smugness I feared it might explode. "Well, Emily, it seems that L and C have been having a bit of a cash flow crisis, and could barely afford to keep operating. Hardly the position from which to expand into the production of a large field. We, on the other hand, have a very sharp geologist already hard at work on the field, and a much stronger financial base. Perhaps certain members of our staff did not come off unscathed, but, well—I offered them a deal. They keep the interest on the principal we owe them to affordable rates, and we take over operations of the combined field. Of course, we'll take a proportionate share of the expanded profit base."

I stared at him, my mouth agape. "So our position has improved."

Menken puckered his lips with smug glee. "Yes, in a word. Now, Emily, I'll be counting on you. I'm afraid Misters Smith and Tutaraitis won't be with us for the foreseeable future, and might possibly find themselves other situations—that's of course not for public consumption. I know I can count on your discretion, my dear. I am asking quite a lot of you, but I am abundantly confident in your abilities." Menken rose. Our interview was over.

"Well, I'm glad everything came out all right, sir."

"Really, there was nothing to worry about. Take the rest of the day off. I'll expect you in here bright and early tomorrow, fully rested. We have a lot to do," he said, as he flushed me out the door.

As I crossed the outer office, I felt Irma's eyes burning into me. I turned toward her in a leisurely manner and fixed her with a look that said, *He may be fooled, but I'm not.* I stared her down until she looked away first, then I turned and sauntered toward the elevator, taking my time to inspect all that artwork in the fancy gilt frames.

The elevator door opened instantly at my touch. I stepped into the car, turned, and as the doors closed, stared regally back across the lobby toward my new domain.

I walked over to Daddy Bruce's and got takeout barbecue and potato salad, and caught a bus home. As we licked the delicious sauce from the ribs over the kitchen table, I told Elyria about Menken's coup with Love and Christiansen.

Elyria said, "He's not out of the woods yet, Em. Just wait until the news hits the street; his investors are going to want to know how this happened."

"Think I'll still have a job tomorrow morning?"

Elyria shrugged. "Things don't happen *that* fast."

At least I hadn't rented an apartment yet. "Think I can stay here a while longer?"

She smiled. "I was rather hoping you would. Life's more interesting with you around."

I stuck out my hand to be shaken. "Deal. I'll have to thank Menken for finding me a fine roommate." Elyria winked.

"Elyria, how does Menken stay so optimistic about everything? I mean, he doesn't even seem to know his wife has deserted him."

"It's congenital, dear; he's a venture capitalist. He knows his wife has left him. He's just waiting for it to be old news. After it's lost its shock value, he'll acknowledge it as if he'd never denied it. Perhaps he'll just begin speaking of her in the past tense one day."

Arranging my milk glass between us for protection, I said, "I think he likes you, Elyria."

Elyria straightened her spine and closed her eyes in consummate disgust.

Late that afternoon, Sergeant Ortega tapped at the kitchen door. Flint followed him into the living room. I offered them seats, but Flint stood fidgeting.

Ortega came and sat down beside me on the couch. He smiled shyly, his quiet nature picking up where his professional persona was leaving off. "Flint here wants Maddie's phone number," he said.

I rolled my eyes. "I'm sure he knows how to find Blackfeet in the telephone book. And I'm sure she's there. And I'm sure she'd be glad to hear from him."

Flint raced for the kitchen phone. As he carried on in the kitchen, I told Ortega what I learned from Rachel as she drank herself numb. Ortega listened intently, the tips of his short, thick fingers gently touching.

When I was done with my story, I sat watching him out of the corner of my eye. I suppose he felt as I did that there was something to be settled between us; he had, after all, just jailed a person I had known a very long time.

I touched his arm. "Okay. Did you know it was Libby all along?"

"No," he answered, patting his fingertips together like genteel pattycakes. "You never really know until they open their mouth and say, 'I did it.' Even then, sometimes, you don't know." He shook his head and smiled, as if it was some big joke on him. "You're the one who brought her out."

I rubbed my aching eyes, trying to forget that I had been the one to pull off her mask. The enormity of her crime weighed on me, as if by catching her I had taken on her guilt. "The way you handled her as you arrested her, it's like you understood her." I was immediately sorry I'd said it that way; it couldn't have sounded quite right.

Ortega's lips curled into a smile again, but this time with little mirth. "Okay. Maybe you're right, I understood her. You

see, I am a Mexican, descended from *los aztecas,* but also from
the Spanish. I have the proud blood of *los indios,* but also the
vain blood of those who conquered them. You understand?"

"No."

"I'm talking about the stresses in the heart." He tapped his
chest, hard. "I search for the piece that doesn't fit. Your friend
looks happy, but everything about her is sad. She has no
power. In order to survive, to be the princess, she has to cooperate with terrible things. It made her very angry. It shamed
her. It was a hurt so deep . . ." He trailed off, his silence more
eloquent than words. "Sometimes a princess is just a slave in
pretty clothes."

I tried to look on Libby with his compassion, but at that moment, all I found inside myself was my own anger and pain.

Ortega ran his soft brown hand across his dark hair. He was
opening his heart to me—no, opening my eyes, so I could see
that his heart had never been closed; but there was something
in the enormity of his compassion that made me fight him. I
said, "Libby killed a man. How can you care about her? And
we didn't spare her; she's going to pay one way or the other,
either in jail or locked away in some asylum. Either you save
her or you punish her. You can't do both."

Ortega squeezed his eyes closed. "It's not my job to punish
her. The people decide this, or the judge."

"But *we* put her in front of the judge."

"Em, everyone has anger, everyone has pain. But everybody
gets a choice what they do with it. This Libby is in pain. But
it's not right for her to give it to someone else. And so it's also
not right for me to leave her alone with this pain."

"I don't understand."

"It would not be respectful. It is my job to bring her pain to
light, so she can hope to make amends, and heal."

His words held such tenderness that all the fight drained
right out of me. "Does it work? Do they heal?"

"Sometimes." At last Ortega looked at me and smiled sadly.
"Besides, they must want us to catch them, the way they come
to us with their clues."

That was how it ended, except that the next morning, I had
to get up and start work for real.

The morning air was cold, full of the high lenticular clouds
that form in series when a layer of moist air ripples off the
mountain front, as the moisture turns to ice crystals wherever

it rises above the freezing level. As I dressed, I chose a thick Harris tweed for the warmth, and wondered how long it would be before winter's breath sent dry snow swirling like ghosts down frozen streets.

Elyria was singing in the shower again. As I made the coffee, my eyes took in each particular of the layout of the kitchen. This was going to be home for a while. How long, I didn't know, but for now, home it was.

I took my coffee to the kitchen table and laid out a piece of paper and a pen. When the coffee had begun to warm me, I wrote:

Dear Frank,
    You were right and kind to let me go. I feel like I'm on a long trip somewhere, and I have no right to ask you to wait. I don't even know if this is the kind of travel that brings me back home when I'm done. I'm excited. I miss you terribly. I'll always love you.
    There's more to say, but I don't understand it yet myself. I do hope you're a patient man.

                                                            Em.

I had the letter addressed and stamped and safely tucked into my pocketbook, and was offering the dog his pill when the doorbell rang. It was Pete. He stood on the front steps with his weight slung provocatively onto one leg, his eyes gleaming with his best come-hither, his face decorated with the most beguiling smile I'd seen on him yet.

I felt the tug. "What do you want, Pete?" I asked. "I'm getting ready for work." I tried to keep the tone of my voice matter-of-fact, but my throat tightened.

Pete shifted his weight to the other leg. "Can I come in? Hey, are you awake?" His smile faded. "Emily?" he said, trying to sing my name again, but the gold in his voice had turned to tin.

Embarrassed, I dropped my gaze to his shoes.

Pete brought his weight up evenly onto both feet. "Listen, ah, Em. Okay, I'll cut to the chase. I wanted you to know that it's settled now between Elizabeth and me. We discussed it yesterday afternoon, and we'll be divorced. Quite soon." He labored to keep his smile propped up, eyeing me carefully, as if watching for cues. "Perhaps you think that crass, that we settled it on such an occasion as that."

No, I think you got dumped. What Libby couldn't tell you,

her parents' lawyers could. I stared at him, appalled to think
he thought me this stupid, this slow to learn. Growing anger
cleared my vision. "I know about Simca, Pete. And Rachel.
Leave me out of your game."

Pete's eyes popped open. He *had* thought me that stupid.

The hostility I felt was so strong and sudden that something
snapped open and began to uncoil inside of me. It was an odd
sensation, an almost frightening sense of growing cavernous
inside.

I looked around the neighborhood, taking in each common-
place detail as if awakened from sleep. I felt calm and detached, at last in balance.

And yet I was far from elated. From this calmness came a
thought that was no comfort: *I'll see more clearly now, but
won't like everything I see.* "Good-bye, Pete," I whispered. "I
wish you well."

Pete grabbed my hand.

"No," I said, trying to pull my hand away. Pete held on to it,
squeezing it now in desperate entreaty.

I stood straight and looked deep inside him from the center
of everything I knew.

Pete's jaw dropped, and he let go of my hand. For a moment, he peered in through my eyes as if they were a window.
Then, with a smile that insinuated that he spoke as one preda-
tor to another, he said, "You're amazing, Em. You change so
fast, like quicksilver. It thrills me."

"You're right, Pete, I am something special. So special it
won't work. Nice try."

Pete shifted his weight to the other foot and tried a how-can-
you-hurt-me-so look. When I didn't budge, he left. He didn't
say good-bye, or you must be mistaken; he just strolled down
the walk, got into his car, and drove away. I suppose he knew
better than to waste energy on someone he could no longer
reach through her estrogen.

I took a giddy breath and exhaled. Disoriented, I looked
down at my fine clothes and my strong, soft hands. I liked
what I saw. And I noticed for the first time that the suit I was
wearing had been fitted to me, not me to it.

It was time to go to work. I closed the door and started
down the walk, soon lengthening my stride with the joy that
rang through me.

Author's Note

In 1973, the OPEC cartel placed limits on oil production, pushing the price of crude oil sky high. I remember long lines at the gasoline pump. As American oil companies went into a hiring frenzy to boost production capabilities, American women demanded a fair share of the new jobs. Thus, as a side effect of OPEC's action (and one I am certain the Arab oil barons did not intend), I went to work in the oil patch.

The U.S. Geological Survey hired me into the fledgling Branch of Oil and Gas Resources, headquartered in Denver. The experience was great, but the pay was minimal. I remember crowding into car pools with other Survey geologists to share gas and parking fees so we could afford an occasional luncheon meeting downtown at the Rocky Mountain Association of Geologists. We'd sit at the banquet tables in our JC Penney double knits peeking sideways at the oil company geologists, who lolled back in their expensive suits gorging on expense account freebies. Seven years and a master's degree later, I left the USGS and went to work with the fat cats at Amoco.

I had no previous experience in the business world, having come from a long line of prep school teachers. When I telephoned my parents to report the starting salary Amoco was offering, the phone line became so silent for a moment that I thought the connection had been broken. Finally, my father's voice returned to the line, appalled and restrained, saying, "Well, dear, I suppose there's nothing sinful about making a decent living."

I reported to work at Amoco in the fall of 1980. I didn't own a suit, so I lifted one of my grandmother's fine old Peck and Peck tweeds out of mothballs, a suit so old that it had come back into style. As I strode down Seventeenth Street toward the Amoco Building that first morning, I was terrified. Here I was going to work for a giant, inhuman corporation. My four years of prep school Latin kept flashing the root word *corpus* across my brain. *Corpus* meant "body"; didn't that suggest a monster with no head? Academics are not necessarily sane people.

My mood was not improved when one of my new colleagues informed me that the week before, a man had hurled himself through a plate glass window on the fourteenth floor of the building next door. During my first week at work there were two look-alike suicides, one from the Brown Palace Hotel Annex, and another farther down Seventeenth Street. I rubbed my burning sinuses and wondered what in hell I was doing there.

In sum, I was deeply intimidated by my new situation, but I figured the best defense was to pretend I knew what I was doing.

To add to my angst, some of my co-workers treated me very oddly. One fellow from Alabama wouldn't speak to me. I thought at first that he didn't like women, but then found that he was pleasantly conversational with every other woman on our floor. My feelings were hurt, but being a Yankee, I suffered in silence. Months of silence passed between us before fate seated him next to me at a lunch that was being held in a private dining room at the Brown Palace Hotel. When the waiter set finger bowls before us, the fellow from Alabama finally spoke to me, sneering, "What are *those*, Andrews? *You* ought to know." Came the dawn. Realizing at last that he had presumed in me the New England silver-spoon preppie snobbery that often comes packed in suits like my grandmother's, I hoisted the bowl to my lips and drained it in two gulps. "Pretty good," I said. He smiled. The fellow sitting to his left belched and wiped his mouth with his necktie, the party moved into high gear, and I began to entertain the hope that I might survive the oil patch.

I survived it and enjoyed it, often purely amazed at what sorts of nonsense a bunch of young people with more money than sense, myself included, could think up for entertainment. I really did see a woman tell carrot jokes in a now-defunct joint called the Slant Hole, for instance, so I hope I can be forgiven for including a few such anachronistic touches, truth being stranger than fiction.

Oil prices began to slide in 1982. I outsurfed the waves of layoffs until the spring of 1986, when OPEC's hold on oil prices finally collapsed. There was a certain symmetry in this: having been put to work by Arab solidarity, I was put back out of work by Arab squabbles. From such conundrums are great stories grown, but that particular conundrum wasn't at the center of this one.

What is at the center, for better or for worse, is the passion of my co-workers. I learned from them among other things that corporations may be monsters, but good or bad they are far from inhuman: they're run by capitalists, and the Latin root for that word is *caput,* which means "head."

I have a little more to say about my grandmother's suit, and my grandmother. I have a perverse sense of humor, in the way I draw from life to create characters, often turning black into white and vice versa. My grandmother was a lively, stylish woman with a big smile who called me Sally and baked extraordinary deep-dish blueberry pies. When it came to suits, she bought quality, and I remember her showing me why her Chanel suit was worth designer prices. Planting her feet, she extended her arms straight out and crossed them at the elbows. The jacket stayed put, without riding up or limiting her range of motion. She said, "Coco Chanel knew what she was doing when she cut this cloth. A woman deserves to be comfortable every bit as much as a man. Remember that, Sally: Don't ever buy a suit in which you cannot move freely."

The constrictions I found in the oil business were not in my suit of clothes, but in trying to figure out who I was amidst the heady seductions of money, power, glamour, and special privilege offered in lieu of dignity and self-esteem. Under such stress, despair was never far away, but before I was done in Denver and Denver was done with me, I had begun to understand my grandmother's words.